Writers Praise
The Cost of Living

Roberge is the bard of the rough road, singer of the long haul, both lyrical and ferociously realistic. A new Roberge novel is always cause for celebration and *The Cost of Living* is his best yet.   —Janet Fitch, bestselling author of *White Oleander* (Oprah's Book Club selection)

Roberge is among a handful of contemporary novelists who can elicit truly profound empathy from a reader. *The Cost of Living* shows him at his best.
   —Craig Clevenger, author of *The Contortionist's Handbook*

Roberge is a great writer whose work should be more widely known.   —Stephen Elliott, founder of The Rumpus

Like a great alt-country tune, *The Cost of Living* is a rhythmic, jangling ride through addiction, lost loves, and busted hands. Roberge possesses a rare and irresistible voice: arresting, sincere, wounded, and cautionary. Nobody's done a better job showing the dark side of the rock-and-roll dream. Narrator Bud Barrett belongs on the top shelf of literature's big-hearted lowlifes, alongside Bukowski's Henry Chinaski and Denis Johnson's Fuckhead.
   —Tyler McMahon, author of *How the Mistakes Were Made*

Musicians Praise
The Cost of Living

Sometimes, if the "cost of living" doesn't kill you, there's hope that you just may live long enough for it to make you stronger. In this novel of rock 'n' roll and the vicious cycle of addiction, recovery, and relapse, Roberge nails the soul-sucking twenty-three hours of the day it takes to get to that *one* hour onstage with the band you love and hate for the same reasons. This darkly funny and surprisingly hopeful, empathic novel is so good I read it twice.

—Billy Pitman, guitar player for Jimmie Vaughan

Roberge's words bring it all back to life for me—the sounds, the sights, the smells, and the tastes. And it's not always a pretty ride. I like that Roberge never takes the easy way out. Real bad things happen to real likeable people, and while I would never wish that on anyone I know, it sure makes for a good read.

—Steve Wynn, The Dream Syndicate

THE
COST
OF
LIVING

THE
COST
OF
LIVING

Rob Roberge

OTHER VOICES BOOKS

OTHER VOICES BOOKS.
An imprint of Dzanc Books.
3629 N. Hoyne
Chicago, Il 60618
www.ovbooks.org
OVBooks@gmail.com

The following chapters appeared previously (in sometimes radically different forms):
"Money and the Getting of Money" in *Sensitive Skin*
"The Indifference of Heaven" (as "Border Radio") in *Santi: Lives of the Saints*
(Black Arrow) and in *Working Backwards From the Worst Moment of My Life* (Red Hen)
"Broken" in The Nervous Breakdown
"Interstate" in *Washington Square Review*
"Diverters" in *Orange County Noir* (Akashic Books)
"The Four Queens" (as "Stooge") in *Black Clock*

Book design by Steven Seighman
Cover photos by Nancy Racina Landin

ISBN: 978-1938604294

First edition: April 2013

10 9 8 7 6 5 4 3 2 1

For François Camoin

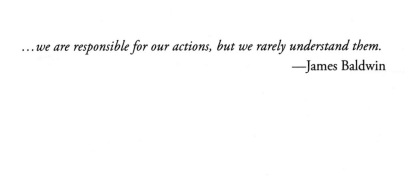

...we are responsible for our actions, but we rarely understand them.

—James Baldwin

YOU CAN'T PUT YOUR ARMS AROUND A MEMORY

(June 2011)

DECEMBER 30, 1983

Police search waters for missing woman. MIDDLETOWN—
Police and firefighters in several towns are looking for a missing
Middletown resident, whose car was found running on Route
3 by the Putnam Bridge early Tuesday morning. Sarah Barrett,
42, of Middletown, was last seen by a friend around 7:30 am on
Tuesday. A state police trooper found her car in the northbound
lane of Route 3 just north of the bridge around 8:20 am, state
police said.

MAY 12, 1984

The body of Sarah Barrett, 42, of Middletown, was found in the
Connecticut River Saturday morning in the waters off the Deep
River landing area. Deep River and Middletown Fire Depart-
ments responded to recover the body around 10:30 am, after re-
ceiving a 9-1-1 call from a fisherman alerting them to the discov-
ery. Barrett had been missing since December, after her car was
found running near the Putnam Bridge in Glastonbury.

The night before my father would beg me to kill him, I sat alone in a hotel room across the street from his hospital, rereading old newspaper articles about my mother's suicide. I had six months clean for the second time in my life. The first time stuck for six years. But that seemed impossible to do again. My skin itched and my body crackled and I had no idea how I'd get through the next five minutes, let alone the night, or the rest of my fucking life without being loaded. I was freezing and the room wasn't cold. I went into the bathroom and turned on the heat lamp, which came on along with a fan, and I paced for a minute. I sat on the toilet, fully clothed with the seat down and counted the square-inch white tiles on the floor three times while breathing deeply. I listened closely to the fan's small jetlike idle to block any thoughts that might come. I tried counting the tiles on the walls but couldn't concentrate. I looked back down at the floor. I let my sight blur, and the moldy grout started to form a pattern that looked like floating chicken wire.

I needed sleep. Without it, I was apt to fly into a manic episode my brain stabilizers and antidepressants and sleeping pills could never reach. I was allowed to travel with a few benzos, which frightened me, but I needed them for anxiety attacks. They couldn't really tame a manic swing, anyway. If I was lucky enough to skip a psychotic episode, there would still be the inevitable depressive suicidal down—and I'd fought through enough of those over the years to be exhausted at the thought.

The meds had been more or less working. For the first time in my life, they'd found a combination that seemed to keep me steady and fucked less with my weight or sex drive than the other pills. Though I didn't really have much use for a sex drive unless Olivia took me back. She'd never divorced me, but she probably would have if I'd had my own insurance for rehab and the meds. But still, I told myself far too often for it to be healthy: if she hadn't divorced me, maybe that was a sign there was still a chance we could be together again.

I closed my eyes and tried to breathe with my head between my legs and I felt the heat lamp on the back of my neck.

Ten minutes later I was dripping sweat. The floor tiles came up a different number every time. I'd counted two hundred forty-two, two hundred thirty-eight, and two hundred and forty-four tiles as my sweat dripped and pooled on the ones closest to the toilet. I had to stay in there and count until I had hit the same number twice. Two counts later, I came up with two thirty-eight, and I could leave the bathroom and try to find a temperature that worked.

I wanted to call Olivia but was worried she wouldn't want to talk to me in this state. There was no way I could tell her I wanted to get high. She made it clear she'd seen and heard enough about that in her life. I scrolled through my contacts and looked at Ray's number. Ray was the guy the label sent out on tour with me to make sure I stayed clean. Part of the contract. It was embarrassing, but, with a track record like mine, I couldn't blame them for a minute. My ex-sponsor—when he was still my sponsor—told me I shouldn't have been planning a tour, but I said I had to make a living. He told me I had to stay clean and *that* was my full-time job until I heard differently. I wouldn't budge and he recommended Ray, who'd been, as my ex-sponsor dismissively called it, an "addict's babysitter" for a bunch of actors and musicians. Ray had turned out to be more help than the sponsor, though. He knew what touring was like. He knew what playing bars every night meant. I was surprised that I ended up liking a guy who was supposed to tell me what to do and to keep me in line.

I turned out the light and focused on my breathing.

My right hand ached. It was tight, and premature arthritis swelled the joints and the repaired tendons. I'd flown out of LAX early that morning, and the humidity of Connecticut made it feel like I had cut glass in every knuckle.

A car's headlights cut through the drapes and made the room bright for a while and then the light went out and I heard the car door open and close. There was the click of a woman's shoes on the asphalt.

My room faced the parking lot. They'd asked me which side I wanted. Like the hospital was ocean view or something.

The surgery scar on the back of my hand ran a deeper red color in the humid air. Looking at it, I thought about Olivia and thought about my relapse and quickly tried to stop thinking about either of them.

I'd left the heat lamp and fan on. The fan whirred and heat-coil light bled into the room through the open bathroom door. I closed my eyes and saw the ghosts of orange light for a while before it faded.

My mother left twice. First when I was thirteen, after my father killed that man, and again when she jumped off the bridge. If she ever explained her reasons for leaving me with him, he never told me, or showed me any letters. For years I was convinced she was sending me letters and that my father kept them away from me or burned them. I had no idea at the time if she ever really tried to get word to me, but I'd created a world in my mind where she overflowed with regret for leaving me and kept trying to get me back.

By the time I was staying at the hotel across from his hospital, I'd only talked to my father twice in twenty years, and he hadn't said much more than that my mother had gone crazy and that was that. That I'd started to believe his version near the end didn't matter for the first forty-five years of my life—when I believed what I wanted to believe. That she was the saint and he was the monster. That simple belief shaped so many years.

Things I remembered:

I remembered her working the night shift at the emergency room at St. Jude's Hospital, where I'd been born. We didn't have money for a sitter, she told me, explaining why she brought me to work. I've always been dug in and too stubborn to forgive my father for much of anything, but I've never blamed my mother for having me sit, night after night, in a room where people were wheeled in with gunshots or knife wounds, or had been beaten so badly their families couldn't have recognized their faces. Where I saw a construction worker with two feet of rebar that went in his mouth and came out the back of his neck and he was awake and conscious and when he tried to speak, I saw shattered teeth and blood fill his mouth the way water does when you dig a hole at the shore. When he tried to speak, he gurgled, and I heard what teeth he had left clatter against the rebar. At one point, his head sagged toward his chest and blood poured all over his orange reflector vest.

I remembered the woman who held a dead child she wouldn't let go of even after the police were called and stood over her dumbly for hours.

But back then, and in my memories, it became time with her and time away from him, which made it, no matter what surrounded the situation, part of the good times of my childhood. Or at least what seemed like, if not good times, safer times.

I remembered the man who'd been torn nearly in half in a car accident, his guts open, his intestines out of his body and snaking over his chest. Later that night, word came back to my mother at the desk that the man from the car accident was brain-dead. They were waiting for his family while my mother explained to me there were machines that could keep a person alive.

I asked, "Is he dead?"

"He's brain-dead, honey."

"What's brain-dead?"

"He's alive, but his brain doesn't think anymore."

What could a brain do if it didn't think anymore? I thought about Mike the Headless Chicken. In the late 1940s, some farm family was cutting a chicken's head off for dinner, but the chicken lived. It lived for seven years and got named Mike the Headless

Chicken, and the family made a small fortune charging people a nickel at county fairs and traveling sideshows to see Mike run around without his head. They fed it with an eyedropper. He died eventually when food got stuck in his feeding hole. I'd read about it in an encyclopedia.

I said, "Will he join the circus?"

"Who?" my mother said.

"The brain-dead man. Will he go to the state fair?"

She smiled sadly. "Sweetie, where do you get your ideas?" She hugged me tightly, and I hugged her and felt the stiff and mildly abrasive fabric of her uniform that smelled like soap when I huddled my face against her. "He'll live at the hospital." She released me. "For a while."

"What then?"

She didn't answer. One of the few sharp images I've been able to keep of her while she was alive is a snapshot of that moment. She hugged me again, her uniform so stiff and rough it felt like construction paper, and didn't let go for a long time.

I wondered what she thought, unable to tell me about death. What do you tell a five-year-old kid? She held me close and tight enough that the world felt safe, even with all the blood and the brain-dead man and everything else in that emergency room. I couldn't let go of those moments of her protecting me.

A woman protecting me, always, I've taken to mean love.

I'd forgiven her the fact that I should never have been in that hospital at that age. That she never should have allowed that. That I shouldn't have seen what I saw, and that it was her fault that I did. Instead, I cherished that moment of her holding me. And I tried to find that moment, again and again and again in so many women's arms over the years.

I called Ray and told him I wanted to get high. That I was thinking of killing myself, which—without warning—I was. That I was scared.

"All you're allowed to be is scared," he said.

I heard the whirl of his big aquarium and figured he was standing close to it. "Feeding the fish?"

"You call to talk about my fish? Talk about something that fucking matters."

I looked around the room. "How many hotel rooms you think you've been in, Ray?"

"What?"

"In your life," I said. I listened to the fan and went to the window and pulled the heavier curtains over the light gauzy ones that let in light from the parking lot. The room got darker. Large moths careened into the light outside my door. I was amazed they could live through even one blow that hard, let alone repeated ones until they finally destroyed themselves, smashing madly against the light and glass.

Ray said, "Who cares?"

"I've been in maybe a thousand." I thought about the years with the band when we played nearly three hundred dates a year. We had three years with over two hundred and seventy days on the road. Around two hundred and fifty shows. Before that, there were the years when we stayed on strangers' floors. "Maybe more."

"You want a fucking medal?"

I said, very calmly like I was ordering a coffee, "I'm really thinking of killing myself, Ray." I was actually thinking of doing it once my father died of his cancer. Whether he died in a day, or the week or two the doctors gave him at the outside. Once my parents were both gone, it seemed like I could just close the door on this whole fucked-up family if I still felt like this. But if I told Ray I was waiting to do it, he might have grabbed the next flight, so I made it seem like I was thinking of it right away. I needed to talk it out, whether I was going to wait a week or not. Or—I had to admit the possibility—I might not be able to go through with it.

He didn't say anything for a long time. Maybe forty-five seconds—an uncomfortably long pause on the phone. I listened to the fan in my background and the trickle of the aquarium in his.

He said, "You're in a bad place, Bud."

I laughed. "Isn't that kind of the definition of suicidal?"

"I'm talking a *literal* bad place," he said. "You're back home. Your father's dying."

"I'm reading old newspapers about my mother's suicide," I told him.

"Jesus," he said. "Triggerville."

"I know Triggerville pretty well," I said. "I grew up here. It's home." I paused. "Maybe I'm more comfortable here."

"Listen to you."

"What?"

"Feeling sorry for yourself. Asking for me to confirm your childish feelings, and I won't do that. I'm here for a lot of things, but that's not one of them." Ray could say words and make it sound like he'd spat them at your feet. He had killed his wife in a car accident eleven years before when he was driving drunk. He'd had to give the go-ahead to take her off the machines from his own hospital bed, where he stayed until he was well enough to go to prison for manslaughter. If he'd left her on life support, his lawyer said the charges would have been reduced to very little time away— maybe none with a deal. He knew about feeling sorry for himself, about what it was like to punish yourself for years.

He said, "You know what? You *are* more comfortable there."

I needed a cigarette and walked out of my room. The air was so thick and muggy it felt like I was breathing through a warm towel. "Thanks for all the help, Ray."

"You want to kill yourself, call some fucking fan that'll bring you dope just to say they got high with you. Don't call me."

I didn't say anything.

Ray said, "You still have a few fans. Go find one that wants to say he got you high."

I felt numb. Like my insides were a block of ice. More bugs thunked against the light. I lit a cigarette. I didn't have my key card with me and I left the door open a crack and several huge moths got into the room. Their shadows swirled around on the ceiling and I heard them banging into the walls in my room.

I thought about hanging up. "Look, I don't want to get angry."

Ray sounded kind for the first time. "Killing yourself, whether you're getting loaded or fucking hanging yourself in your thousandth hotel room closet—destroying yourself in front of people who love you is an act of anger. And cowardice. You've got a wife. You've got real friends. And you know what it does to people. If you're not guilty of that, make your case."

"I'm not in front of anybody I love."

"You always are."

I watched the smoke drift as I blew it out—gray in the dark and then slightly blue when it passed the light. "Maybe it's just in my fucking genes." A lot of stats backed me up.

"Your mother was crazy," he said. "You're not."

I felt the way you feel when you're a kid and the world gets to be too much—too swollen with emotion to keep it inside. I tried not to sound like I was close to crying, which was stupid, because Ray was one of the few people who wouldn't have cared. Who would have cared enough not to care. "I'm not trying to be . . . I don't know if I can live clean," I said. "I've tried. Really tried. It hasn't worked."

"Look, I love you. But you wouldn't be the first junkie or drunk I loved who went out and died. I had to make peace years ago that my life was going to be littered with people who couldn't stay clean and who didn't make it. What do you want me to say?" His voice sounded like a resigned shrug would look. "I'd miss you. I'll say nice things about you along with how pissed I am at you at your funeral. I can't make up your mind for you. You're afraid to change. You'd rather live your self-fulfilling prophecy of being a loser."

I leaned on the wall and smoked. My left arm grew stiff from holding the phone, and my right hand didn't work well enough to hold the cigarette between my index and middle fingers. I could just barely hold a guitar pick with that hand. I had to jab the cigarette between the middle and ring fingers junkie-style, the way I had for years because you couldn't drop it while you nodded out and burn whatever place you were in down to the ground. My hands were mangled. Every fingernail bitten bloody and malformed. My mother told me I started biting my nails when I got teeth. I was worried before I knew there was a word for it. "I *am* a loser—don't you get it?"

"I get plenty."

Whenever I was pissed at Ray, I forced myself to think again about him waking up in the hospital and hearing about his wife, dead but not dead yet because of him—with her somewhere in the same building but gone already. People had died around me most of my life. I'd hurt other people. But I hadn't killed anyone. Ray had been worse places than me. I stopped myself before I said anything stupid or hurtful. I watched my cigarette and thought, *Another thing I do that destroys me.* Inch by inch instead of mile by mile, but intentionally fucking myself just the same.

It felt like some storm inside seemed to have passed, at least for that moment. A fist had let loose a grip and opened up—had gone from clenched around my heart and lungs, to relaxed.

Ray seemed to sense it. "How's your father?"

"He's dying. All I know is what I told you this morning."

"But nothing went wrong when you talked to him?"

"I got here after visiting hours," I said. "There hasn't been a chance for something to go wrong yet."

There was a pause. Muffled noise came from a TV close to my room. Like most things I could barely hear, things at a distance hurt my ears and gave me blinding headaches.

Ray said, "You going to kill yourself tonight?"

I thought about it. "No."

"You going to get loaded?"

"I want to."

"That's not what I asked."

I tossed my cigarette into the parking lot and lit another. When I closed my Zippo, it clicked with cold metal authority. An ambulance siren swelled closer and closer until it turned across the street, into the emergency room.

"No," I said. "Not tonight."

"Good. Call me tomorrow," Ray said and hung up.

After St. Jude's and the emergency room, she worked at Fairfield Hills Mental Hospital—where I later learned she became a patient when she went crazy. I was six and with her at work after school when I took a pill off the floor of the pharmacy and OD'd for the first time. I'd crawled around on the cool tiles and the pill looked like a piece of candy. I felt that dreamy floating-out-of-my-body feeling for the first time and felt my brain lift like a state fair balloon and wondered why life couldn't always be like that and thought that maybe this was what it would be like to be kept alive by machines and brain-dead and maybe it was much easier than people thought. The next thing I knew I was in the hospital and they were flushing me with charcoal, and my mother cried and my father stood there, and I couldn't understand why everyone was so upset. That first overdose was the first time in my life I felt true peace.

And then there was the man my father killed. And then she was gone.

In my forties—when I was still clean—I allowed myself to see that she was crazy and nothing could have been done. But I found that out too late, and by then I'd learned there are few things worse in this world than learning something crucial about someone you loved too late for it to matter. Too late for you to do anything about it.

I found my key card so I could lock my guitar in the room. I smoked and walked around the building and saw across the city street the hospital where my father was dying. Some of the rooms flickered with blue TV light. Some still had their cold fluorescents on. I wondered which was his room. I wondered if he could sleep. I wondered what kind of person I was that part of me wanted him to be asleep and part of me wanted him to be awake and in pain for however many hours he had left.

The traffic light changed from green to red. The little white pedestrian lit up and told people when they could walk. Then the countdown numbers came—along with the beeps for the blind— one every second. Every beep a reminder of the treacherous sweep of the second hand. Of the seconds of pain I had just wished on my father. The lights changed again. I stood there for ten more cycles of Red, Yellow, Green. No one was out at this time of night, and the lights just did what they did whether anyone needed them or not.

It struck me that if my father lived as long as the doctors said he might, I could be here on my birthday—just two weeks away. I stood and smoked a cigarette and looked at the hospital where I'd been born, just shy of forty-five years earlier.

One night, alone in our house with my mother, I'd seen a spider with a body as big and dark as a black olive and I ran to see her.

"Are you scared?" she said.

I nodded.

"Most spiders aren't even deadly," she told me. "Things that scare us aren't that bad, most of the time." She licked her thumb and wiped something off my cheek. "What you're afraid of almost never happens." She held me with both of her straight arms on my shoulders and looked intensely into my eyes. "OK?"

I nodded again.

"You know what the most deadly insect on earth is?" she said.

"No."

"The mosquito," she said. "It's killed more people than any other bug. And people think they're harmless."

She pulled me closer.

"The smallest things, the ones nobody else notices, baby. That's what you need to be afraid of."

Before the suicide I expected her to come back and rescue me. When I asked my father about her, all he'd say was "your mother's gone" in a tone that made it clear that his answer was the end of the conversation.

I thought I must have done something that drove her away. Even years later, guessing and hoping it had to be because of my father, because of something I didn't know, I wondered why she left. How she could leave a kid. Before her suicide, I always thought someday I'd get the chance to ask her why.

The police, then the papers, said there was no note. Only her car, still running, on the side of the bridge. For too many years, I lived in her past and not my present. I woke up, sweating and hearing that car idling, smelling its exhaust in the cold morning air, even though I wasn't there. She'd crossed the road and jumped on the opposite side of where she'd parked. The driver's side door was open and her purse and wallet sat on the passenger seat.

I learned quickly not to romanticize her death. I did at first. I imagined her free, weightless, flying and empty of sorrow for a moment—and maybe empty of it forever after that. Like the overdose, but lasting until time would stop. Afterward, I read and read and read about bridge suicides. The impact is like being hit by a car. The water might as well be cement—the body hits the water and stops, and the organ tree keeps going and rips itself away from all the connective tissue that keeps us together.

The children of suicides are five times more likely to kill themselves than the rest of the world. Later, in one of the rehabs that didn't take—while they tried to find some combination of meds that would keep me from psychotic episodes—there was some doctor telling me that junkies are fourteen times more likely to kill themselves than their peers.

At four in the morning, I left the hotel. There was no way I could sleep. I walked ten city blocks to a Dunkin' Donuts and bought a coffee that spilled so hot it seemed like melting plastic on my fingers. I poured a third of it out and walked back to the hotel, smoking.

The sun wasn't up yet, but I smelled the salt in the air from Long Island Sound. At six thirty, I heard the Amtrak to New York City, and I remembered getting drunk under the railroad bridge with Tony when we were in our first band in high school. They had a maintenance level ten feet beneath the train level and you could drink wine and, as long as they weren't up on their ladders doing repairs, lie on the old wood supports and smell the tar in the railroad ties, mixed with cooler salty air from the water and listen to the seagulls and be wasted and feel the train coming from ten or fifteen miles away. First, a small vibration, maybe when it pulled out of Stamford. And then it would grow, and I would close my eyes and feel the heat and light of the summer sun and the train would get closer and louder and closer and louder until the noise swept everything else away and you prayed that it was a New York express so the noise would stay that loud for five full minutes because the train wouldn't stop like it would if it were a local.

I finished my coffee and lit a cigarette and went back to the hotel and waited for the sun to come up.

A life of questions. What brought her there to that place, that she was so out of options and without hope that any day would ever be different again? Always wondering how she felt. How different was her moment from my crossing of that line over the years? A loneliness that swelled so hard that it must have pushed against her skin from the inside, that she must have had a pain no words would ever reach. And could I have done something, anything, before she left? Could I have changed the course of events that brought her to that moment, that collection of seconds, when she stood and decided, finally, to fall toward the river, cold air in her hair and face, the wind pining back and fluttering her dress in that moment before impact?

And later, when I did attempt suicide, and even later after what I hoped was the last relapse, where I'd get close again to ending it all, when that same loneliness swallowed the world, I wondered: was I trying, in some sort of desperation, to get close to her, or trying, just as desperately, to get away?

MONEY AND THE GETTING OF MONEY

(December 2010)

I hadn't seen much of Johnny Mo after we'd had the trouble in Las Vegas with that guy Mike. After Mike's crazy father shattered my ankle with a .22 in the drug deal with Johnny Mo and Mike. It's not like there were bad feelings between the two of us, but maybe we'd fallen out of touch because of the bad luck of our last deal. Maybe we thought the next time would be worse—and in some ways, we were right to think that.

I ended up healing down in Long Beach with my friend Amber who worked as a dominatrix out of a house in LA and kept us in money while I was all but worthless, sleeping all day on her couch, taking more than half her drugs, which consisted mostly of the Percodans and Xanax she kept us in steadily enough for neither of us to get dopesick more than a few times in those months.

Amber's ex-girlfriend taught extreme sex education classes and got offered a high paying job in San Francisco and asked Amber to clean up and move back in with her, which left me without a place. I couldn't pay the rent in Long Beach. And without an apartment it was time to make some choices. I was still in love with Olivia, even though she'd kicked me out.

I entered a thirty-day residential rehab program.

I made it fifteen days before I called Johnny Mo to get me the hell out of there.

I'd turned forty-four. Since I was eighteen, I'd spent most of that time fucked up. That last full stint in rehab after my last possession arrest worked, and I thought I'd left my past in the past. I'd stayed clean for six years. Rebuilt my life. Got married and got back playing music and started a recording studio that was making decent money and good records for a few years. And then when I was on tour a couple years ago, I tore a tendon in my picking hand. Re-tore it, actually, as it's one that's been damaged a lot over the years of shameful abuse and neglect. Even before this injury, I had trouble closing a fist on my right hand, having dealt with broken bones along with the fraying tendon. For two shows, I played with the pinky duct-taped to the ring finger so I could hold a pick. The pain became too much. I went to an emergency room and got some Vicodin, thinking I'd grown up and could take them responsibly. The doctor gave me a hundred and twenty pills. The pills lasted three and a half days, and I was off and running.

And here I was, a couple of years later, broke, unemployed, with a shattered ankle that had escalated my opiate addiction, and separated from Olivia, who couldn't take what I'd become. She'd never seen me using. We'd met and married while I was sober. While I was working hard to be ethical and good and honest. She was a beautiful person and I'd chosen drugs over our life together and I hated myself for it. She kicked me out of the house we'd bought and the life we'd made together.

Her last words to me before I left were, "I love you too much to sit around and watch while you kill yourself."

Before the rehab I'd just left, I wasn't even really getting high anymore. I was, on a good day, getting just enough drugs to not feel sick. I hated myself with the intensity of a hurricane. It's one thing to be young and stupid and think you're only hurting yourself and whose business is what you do with your life anyway? It's another thing when you've gotten clean, faced up to your actions and their repercussions on other people, made amends and become a decent person, and then regressed into the beast you used to be. How much longer could I live like I lived? How many more people who loved me could I keep letting down?

My next overdose could be my last, and I wasn't sure I was too scared by that anymore.

The day Johnny Mo picked me up when I walked out of rehab it was pouring rain.

He wore a leather jacket against the wet and cold, or what passes for cold in a Southern California winter. He had Plasticsoul's *Peacock Swagger* on, which sounded like a great marriage between the Beatles and Badfinger, and it lightened my mood a little right off.

"So what's the plan?" he said.

"I just left rehab. I was hoping to get high." I said it, not even sure if it was totally true. Of course I *wanted* to get high. But the price was becoming enormous and devastating. I was just over a week removed from the end of full-blown dopesickness. The first three days of cleaning out are a pain and suffering you can't believe are happening. And the suffering gets wrapped in awareness that you did this to yourself. That you've been doing it to yourself for years. Every cramp, every sandpaper-hot rusty pained blink of your aching eyes, every stream and eruption of puke and piss and shit you can't control escaping from your clenched, hurt body, every nerve ending going off like a trillion simultaneous electric shocks, every second of begging for sleep and not getting it. Through all of that, you sit there, rolling on the floor, despising yourself and swearing you'll never, never, *never* go through this again, no matter what.

And here I was, ten days removed from getting the poison out of my body, feeling not really terrible at all at that point, save some massive cravings to feel really good again, and thinking, *Damn I'd love to get high.* Love to feel warm and numb. Love to shut off the never-ending waves of anxiety and dread and fear and noise and voices that flooded through my brain. I felt like a failure, too, so why not just accept that I was a fuck-up? But I knew, too, always, where using ended. It ended up with me lost, desperate, pleading to whatever force in the universe could possibly listen to please let this agony end.

"I've got about five eighty-milligram Oxys left," Johnny Mo said.

I laughed to myself when he said "about five." A pill junkie might not know what day it is. What month or even year it is. They don't know who's the number one pop singer or the newest famous reality TV star or their senator or whatever else passes for important news and information to most people. But they know, to the grain and spec, how many pills they have left once the number starts to get low. If you have six, you know it. If you have a hundred and eighty, you might not know how many you have left, but get under twenty and you know. The dumbest junkie I've ever met could do the quickest math imaginable about how much they had left and how long it could and would last. We can shift metric to standard in our heads and we can tally up the numbers of pills in our pockets faster than a room full of MIT grads with calculators.

"*About* five?" I said.

He smiled. "I have eight. You can have one, if you want. But just one. I don't know where the next are coming from." He lit a cigarette. "If we can make some money in the desert, I know a guy with some morphine. Then we're set."

And this, a single pill, while generous, was the sharpest of double-edged swords. One eighty-milligram would have me floating pretty well for about four to six hours, maybe a little more if there was any Xanax or Valium or Klonopin or any other benzo we could find to stretch the high. And then what?

It's always better to say no to a limited supply. But then, eventually, everything is a limited supply.

"I'll take it," I said. "And thanks."

"You sure?" Johnny Mo said, and it sounded like maybe he was worried for me or maybe it was he just didn't want to put a dent in his dwindling number of pills.

I looked at him and he gave me the little round blue pill with the "80" marked on it. I could chew it, but that would take about ten minutes to get in my system, plus it dulled the high a little bit. I reached in the backseat where Johnny Mo had a bunch of empty pill bottles. I ground the pill into the bottom of the bottle with the end of a Bic pen. Once the powder was fine enough, I took the top end off the pen, licked it and tasted the beautiful residue of the OxyContin, then poked the ink tube out so the barrel of the pen could act as a straw. Forty milligrams, half the pill, would probably get me going just fine to start, with my body clean. It wouldn't be the worst idea to save some for later. I snorted all eighty, hoping for a better high.

"New sober date," Johnny Mo said, smiling.

I didn't smile back and said, "Maybe someday."

We didn't say anything for a while and I started picking at this infected abscess on my left forearm with a 22-gauge piercing needle—one of many gauges Amber kept around the house for needle play. They took all of the ones I had at rehab intake, but this one was left from a coat Johnny Mo had brought me. This lump had been around for about a month, stubborn as poverty, and it had turned hard as a marble under the skin. Still, some days, I could poke around enough with a fresh needle to get some pus out, which meant that it might not have to be lanced. Soon, though, I was going to have to hit a hardware store and grab an X-ACTO knife and slice the damn thing open if it wouldn't cooperate.

In a warm sudden rush, I felt pretty good. The opiates had kicked in and were busy ironing out every kinked nerve in my body. It was like every good thing in the world at once: the feeling of a warm robe out of the dryer, a cotton candy pink sunset over the ocean, a blow job, cold water after exercise, Al Kooper's organ in "Like a Rolling Stone," a peaceful solitude that made you feel like you fit into every fractured crevice of a fragmented hateful planet. A first kiss. Something like love, flowering inside you.

Johnny Mo said, "So, you up for some money?"

I was broke. "Sure. Where in the desert are we headed?"

"Twentynine Palms," he said. "Actually, Wonder Valley. To see my dad."

"You have a dad?"

"Everyone has a dad."

"You've never mentioned him," I said.

"I don't remember you mentioning yours."

Feeling good from the pills, I felt a world away from his influence. "My father killed at least one man," I said. I didn't talk about that dead man much, but he still floated to the surface of my consciousness whenever I didn't expect it. I'd gotten resigned that he always would. There'd be strings of months where I'd only get two hours of sleep before I woke up, seeing him dead on a woodpile. I'd be able to forget the scene for a while, and then the whole cycle of nightmares would start again. Sometimes they were of the man he killed. The worse ones were of my mother's suicide.

Johnny Mo looked over. "You shitting me?"

"He killed this guy in front of me when I was thirteen," I said, and told him about the man who came to buy the used car. I didn't tell him my father's side of the story, because I still didn't know if I believed it at that point. My dad said he killed the guy because the guy had made my dad from his days undercover. He killed the guy to protect me and my mother. It could've been true—anything was possible. But I doubted it, and I didn't mention it to Johnny Mo. "He was a state trooper. He got away with it."

"And I thought Mike's dad was bad," Johnny Mo said.

"I would say Mike's dad was pretty awful."

We drove awhile before Johnny Mo said, "How's the ankle?"

It felt, always, like your foot feels after it's been asleep and starts to jangle with needles of pain. At its best, with some painkillers in me like now, it had a relentless throb of hurt. When I wasn't medicated, I could barely walk on the thing. Johnny Mo felt responsible, to a degree, that my ankle had been fucked up on that deal that he set up. It wasn't his fault, but I wasn't above making him feel a trickle of guilt about it if it could get me more OxyContin.

"It hurts like hell," I said. "But what can you do?"

"I am sorry about that," he said.

I didn't want to talk about it if he wasn't going to offer me more pills. "So, why are we seeing your dad? He have money?"

"I was hoping to borrow his truck."

"You don't know anyone in LA with a truck?" I said.

"Not a big truck. Before he couldn't work, he had a water delivery business out in Twentynine Palms. Lot of people on tank water there. So, he's got this big flatbed with a water tank off the back of it. But I only want the flatbed part. I got a deal on some scrap metal."

Johnny Mo worked, when he worked, at Amoeba Records. Or he sold drugs. "What constitutes a deal on scrap metal? How would you even know?"

"There's this abandoned construction site from a casino they were going to build before the recession. I know a security guard who'll let me in so I can take some of the scrap. Scrap metal's worth a fortune."

"That's not a *deal*. That's stealing," I said.

"It's a very good deal. Don't get all semantic on me."

"Stealing copper wire is jail time," I said. "They take that shit very seriously."

"So, we won't steal copper wire."

"Copper's worth the most," I said. "Plus, all of it's stealing. The same crime whether you take steel or aluminum or whatever."

"So we'll take the copper," Johnny Mo said.

I changed the CD to Centro-Matic's *Redo the Stacks*. One of the great things about an opiate high is that good music sounds so incredible. Like it's seeping into your cells on some level it doesn't normally. An invisible goodness, the way radiation is an invisible bad one.

"This is your way to get money?" I said. "Stealing scrap metal?"

"You got any better ideas?"

The rain picked up as we headed out toward the desert, past the sad towns of the Inland Empire. Billboards announced swap meets and chain restaurants off the 10 freeway. Why people would move here was beyond me. To get so close to LA, to the sunsets over the Pacific and the crash of waves, to Hollywood, but stop in these dirtshit towns made no sense.

Stealing scrap metal seemed like a bad plan. There was surely a lot of money to be had in the world, but I didn't have any thoughts on how to get my hands on it. Sober, I could get paid for playing guitar or sitting at a poker table. Using, I wasn't worth much. The band I'd formed twenty-five years before had fired me twice. Once in my mid-thirties and again when I'd relapsed on a reunion tour just over a year ago. I said, "Amber's making a thousand dollars this weekend doing some sex demo."

"She fuck someone for that kind of money?"

"No," I said. "Well, sort of."

"Make up your mind," he said.

"Her girlfriend's teaching a workshop teaching women how to ejaculate."

"Like those gushers in porn?"

I nodded. "She teaches workshops in it."

"So does she fuck?"

"Her girlfriend up in San Francisco," I said. "Sort of ex-girlfriend."

"That doesn't bother you, dude?"

Amber and I had fucked years ago—before me and Olivia, but I had no interest in anyone else at this point. "They don't really fuck. Amber gets fisted in front of all these people."

"Yeah, that's not like fucking at all," Johnny Mo said, laughing.

"The front row at these things, they practically have to wear ponchos. It's like a porno Gallagher show."

"And that shit *really* doesn't bother you?"

"Didn't bother me when she was my girlfriend, it's not going to bother me now," I said.

I thought about Olivia. It amazed me that anyone was able to make love work in this world, the way our greasy, damaged souls clatter together.

Johnny Mo said, "I don't think I could handle my girlfriend sleeping with chicks." He paused. "Unless, you know, I was there."

"She does that, too," I said.

"Well, that's something," Johnny Mo said.

"That it is."

We got off the 10 and started the climb into Morongo Valley on Highway 62. I poked holes around the abscess on my arm and blotted the blood with the tail of my shirt, which had started to look like a gory Rorschach test. Ike Reilly's *Hard Luck Stories* blared from the speakers and I turned it down slightly to talk.

"Your dad live alone?"

Johnny Mo said, "The thing is, my dad doesn't much leave his place. He's gotten fat."

"Too fat to go out?" I asked.

"Actually, yeah," he said. "He's pretty sick. And over five hundred pounds, I'd say."

"Jesus," I said. "And he's alone."

Alone, unable to go out. How could anyone spend day after day like that? And you'd end up dead and no one would know. Like the guy whose apartment Johnny Mo and I cleaned out that one time for the cleaning company he worked for. The guy'd been dead for weeks. He'd been taken to the coroner with no one to claim his body. Nothing could have prepared me for what his body had left behind in that apartment. The smell of decomposing flesh assaulted my memory and I almost threw up thinking about it. Poor bastard. We split the Ambien and Valium we found in the bathroom. His possessions were auctioned off at public storage— the possessions Johnny Mo and I didn't take, anyway.

The dead guy's bathroom had a ton of porn sort of decoupaged on the walls. On the ceilings and even on the floor. Naked women, very 1970s *Penthouse* beaver shots, legs open, pulled and coaxed vaginal lips swollen and flaring for the camera. All of them under the shiny gloss of some lacquer. And every single one of the naked women had the exact same black-and-white picture of Jackie Kennedy's head on it. No matter what position the body was in. No matter whether the picture was black and white or in color. No matter whether the naked body was Asian, black, or white—every single one had a smiling, blown-up, and pixilated head of Jackie Kennedy on it.

"My mom's up in Humboldt," Johnny Mo said. He lit another cigarette and offered me one that I took. "What about yours? She stay with that killer father of yours?"

"My mom died," I told him, trying not to let the details and memories slug me. I cracked the window and watched the smoke swirl out. I tried to think about something else. "Has your dad always been fat?"

"Fat, but not obese. This is new. The last few years, he's let himself go."

Johnny Mo's dad lived in a doublewide in a half-deserted blight of a trailer park outside of Twentynine Palms. Lonely desert shacks with Christmas lights added specks of gloomy color in the gray and foggy air. We turned in to the trailer park.

I don't know what I was expecting when I heard "he's let himself go," but I wasn't ready for what we walked into. The two trailers on either side of his were abandoned. Each of them surrounded by a moat of liquor bottles and beer cans. Crude graffiti lined the outside walls of the trailer—the most noticeable was the giant word BITCH.

Johnny Mo blew on his hands and I saw his breath in the air. He nodded toward the abandoned trailer. "We call that 'the Bitch House.'"

"That makes sense."

Johnny Mo shook his head. "This place is a fucking eyesore."

Less than ten feet from the steps, there was a mattress, soggy from the rain that had turned to snow. In the center was a giant burn hole that went all the way down to the springs and through to the sand beneath it. A lizard zipped out from under it, stopped, did its little push-ups for a few seconds, and darted back out of sight.

I pointed and looked to Johnny Mo.

"Pop smokes in bed. He falls asleep a lot."

A rusted green dumpster overflowed with garbage. Next to it was, I guessed, the truck we were supposed to borrow. It didn't look like it had been moved in a while and it sagged in an ugly, unfit way on a flat rear tire. It sank into the sand and the fractured asphalt.

Johnny Mo walked up the creaky stairs and pounded on the screen door. "Pop!" he yelled.

No answer. He pounded again, waited, and then hammered the door again even louder.

The door swung open and an enormous man stood there. He did look too large to get out of the door and he stood in a pair of shorts and nothing more, his gut hanging like a puckered waterfall of flesh, hanging so far down that all you could see was the bottom tips of his shorts at the tops of his knees.

"Hey kid," he said.

The minute I saw him, I don't know why, I got a terrible feeling and my first thought was that I should go back to rehab. I felt a familiar dread of self-loathing and wondered why I'd let myself get into this again. Here I was, with Johnny Mo, about to do something stupid for money again. And if I was lucky, the best-case scenario was that I'd make a few bucks, be able to get high for a day or two, and then be flattened and wrecked by despair for who knows how long. I felt uneasy, like something was about to go horribly wrong, and all I was doing was sitting around and watching. But then, I'd had these feelings before, these vague worries that everything was about to go terribly off, and nothing had happened. Or, rather, the same life just happened over and over. Heavy wet snowflakes fell over us but didn't stick to the ground.

The fat man said, "Who the fuck is this?" pointing to me with a cigarette jutting out from between his ring and middle fingers.

Johnny Mo introduced me as "a buddy of mine" and introduced the fat man as Al. When Al didn't respond, Johnny Mo said, "We were hoping to borrow the truck for some work." Johnny Mo lit a cigarette.

"Some work? That what you're calling it now?"

"Pop, it's freezing out here."

Al let us in. To the right was a living room. Al took up the whole hallway, so turning left wasn't an option and we went into the living room while Al followed, forced to walk sideways like a hermit crab in his own hallway.

We sat on a ratty couch in a living room crowded with boxes in piles against every wall in the place. A milk crate footstool with a pillow sat in front of a loveseat, facing the television. The walls were covered with pictures of fifties film and TV stars. In a corner was an old Bell & Howell movie projector with a tube amp built in for the sound.

"Cool," I said. "I used to modify these to make guitar amps."

"Used to?" Al said.

I told him I'd had a recording studio and amp repair shop.

"What happened?"

I didn't feel like telling him the truth. "The economy went south," I said. "Lost my business."

"I know about losing shit," Al said. He pointed around the room. "I used to be a big shot in TV."

"An actor?"

Johnny Mo said, "Pop, can we borrow your truck?"

Al looked at him and smiled. "You can have the fucking truck for all the good it'll do you. Fucking two-ton paperweight." He lit a cigarette with the end of his previous one and dropped the old one on the floor, still lit. He said, "Cameraman. Jackie Gleason's personal cameraman. Jackie wouldn't shoot a home fucking movie without me behind the camera." He laughed. "I shot all his porn, too."

"Jackie Gleason porn?" I said, trying to keep the image at bay.

"That man got more pussy than Elvis and Frank Sinatra combined."

"No shit?" I said.

"Danny Thomas, too," he said. "Wouldn't work without me."

I looked around. The walls, sure enough, had what looked to be framed, signed pictures of Gleason, Thomas, Danny Kaye, Sophia Loren, and a bunch of other faded and mostly forgotten stars of the 1950s.

I said, "Danny Thomas did porn, too?"

Al laughed. "No. Danny did his kinky shit behind closed doors. No cameras."

I nodded. In the awkward second, I looked around at the pictures like I was interested.

"I'm going to tell you something disgusting, kid," Al said.

I didn't want to be rude, so I tried to look attentive. "OK."

"You know what Danny Thomas was into?"

Johnny Mo said, "Don't tell this story."

Al ignored him. "Danny Thomas used to hire two whores to come over to his house and have one tie him up under a glass table and take a dump over his head while the other whore jerked him off."

"Really?" I said.

Johnny Mo said, "I don't believe that for a fucking second."

Al laughed and his laugh turned into a battle for air and a painful-sounding phlegmy cough. When he got his breath back, he said, "Believe what you want to believe, but for years after that, every Hollywood whore I knew called shitting on a table or shitting on a guy's chest a Danny Thomas." He laughed again. "Had to come from somewhere. And I knew a lot of whores. A lot of crazy fucks are into that. And every whore called it a Danny Thomas."

Johnny Mo said, "I thought that was a Cleveland Steamer." He took a drag. "Shitting on a guy's chest."

"Maybe now, for you fucking kids," Al said. "But it was a Danny Thomas in LA and Palm Springs in the sixties." He looked at me. "What name have you heard?"

I'd heard of a Cleveland Steamer, but Al seemed invested in this. I said, "I've never heard of it. But maybe it has local names. Like, you know, in Cleveland. Or LA." I felt stupid being asked to take sides in this.

Jonny Mo laughed at me. "Yeah, you've never heard of it. You've got a girlfriend who probably charges three hundred bucks for it."

Al said, "Your girlfriend does it? Ask her, and she tell you it's a Danny Thomas."

"She's not my girlfriend," I said.

Johnny Mo said, "Either way, I'll bet you a hundred bucks she's shit on a guy's chest for money."

I wasn't going to take that bet.

Al motioned to the amplifier. "Take that, why don't you?"

"You sure?" I said.

He swept a fat arm around the trailer. "Take whatever you want. I won't be needing this shit."

I looked down at the cigarette he'd thrown down, still burning on the floor.

Johnny Mo said, "The truck's not working?" He sounded crushed. His plan, slim and fragile as it was, floating away like a marine layer under the noon sun.

Al saw me staring at the lit cigarette. "Don't sweat it, kid. The rug's asbestos. You couldn't burn this shithole down with a flamethrower, welcome as that might be."

Johnny Mo went to the phone booth of a kitchen, a kitchen so small I wondered how Al could possibly get in and out of it. He came out with two beers and handed me one.

Al said, "Get me one while you're being so generous with my liquor."

"You're not supposed to be drinking, Pop."

"Not supposed to be smoking, either, but if I quit smoking, I'd be dead."

I asked how that logic might work.

He pointed to his enormous chest. Sitting on white chest hairs, I saw fallen ashes from his cigarettes. "If I sleep for more than twenty minutes at a time, I go into congestive heart failure."

I took a long drink of beer and lit a cigarette, happy to be somewhere I didn't have to be banished to a porch to smoke, especially with the snow outside. "How do you not sleep for over twenty minutes?"

Al stuck out his hand. Between his ring and middle fingers was an open sore, cracked and bleeding. A cauliflower of scab and blood and pus and pain. "Just stick a Pall Mall there, take a puff, and sleep until it burns my finger."

Al's hand hurt just to look at. I felt myself making a face. "Jesus."

He flopped down in his loveseat and took a drink of his beer. "Yeah. Nice, huh? It's a hell of a life." He sounded more tired than any man I'd ever heard. Every breath was a wheeze.

"The truck's no good?" Johnny Mo said again.

Al looked at him with a distant expression, like he was thinking about something else. "You know I've loved you, right son?"

"What are you talking about, Pop?"

Al looked at me. "We've had our problems, but he was a hell of a good son sometimes."

I didn't know what to say. But it didn't matter. Al took a hit of his cigarette and fell asleep.

Johnny Mo said, "I can't believe that fucking truck's dead."

"What's the plan now?"

Johnny Mo shrugged. We drank Al's beer and watched him jolt awake every ten minutes or so. He'd jump from his seat, make some hideous snort, and shake the cigarette onto the asbestos rug. Every time he woke up and madly shook the cigarette out of his wounded hand, he splayed blood across the floor. The walls down by the baseboard and the floor looked like a crime scene with all the blood spatter. He'd light a fresh cigarette and fall back asleep.

Around 2:00 AM, I was drunk and trying to figure out a way to get another of Johnny Mo's Oxys. An ad came on the late night TV advertizing money for gold.

"That's it," Johnny Mo said.

"You have gold you've been holding out on?"

"I know where to get some." He took a drink of his beer. "Dude, this could be a little ugly, but we'd get some gold. We could pawn it for the morphine."

"How ugly?"

"You read about those guys last year that tried to rob Lincoln's grave?"

I hadn't heard of much of anything in the last year. "You want to rob Lincoln's grave?"

"No, dude. Fuck Lincoln. My grandmother was buried with a shitload of jewelry on. A couple of miles from here."

Buried? "Are you fucking crazy?"

"She's my family," he said. "If it doesn't bother me, why should it bother you?"

I lowered my voice, not wanting Al to hear me. "You want to rob a grave?"

"My grandmother's grave. Not some stranger's."

"Listen to yourself," I said.

"Dude, she's been dead since I was a kid. She's probably a skeleton by now."

"They have all sorts of chemicals that stop a body from decomposing naturally," I said.

"So, we'll buy some K-Y or something to slide the rings off, if she's still like a person." He paused. "With fingers and skin and shit."

I looked over at Al, who was a snoring wheeze next to us.

Johnny Mo said, "She's in this little plot out in the desert. No one would see us. We could be in and out with gold to pawn. I really don't see the problem."

"You don't?" I said. "You don't see the problem?"

He shook his head, looking a little tired. "I hear you. It's an extreme move. But it's money and I don't know how the hell else we're going to get it."

I looked at him hard and thought about it. She was dead. Who would we be hurting, exactly? "Give me two of your OxyContin and I'll go with you."

"Dude, I only have a few left. We get this money, we'll have plenty for both of us."

"So, give me two now."

"You're just out of rehab. You don't need much."

"A hundred and sixty milligrams isn't much," I said. "You want me to go with you, that's the price."

"You have to do more than go with me, you have to help."

"I'll dig," I said. "In the casket, you're on your own."

"For two Oxys, you're digging a lot," he said and handed me two blue pills. "Maybe all the fucking digging."

I pocketed one of the OxyContin and, in a hurry, chewed the other one. I took several deep breaths, trying to will the drug to seep more quickly into my system, but I knew it'd be ten minutes or more until I felt better.

It had, at least, stopped raining, stopped snowing. I hoped the ground wouldn't be too hard. I'd done some work in Wonder Valley once, digging a new hole for a two-thousand-gallon water tank, and it hadn't been so bad. But then it was dry and it was summer. The heat was too much, but the ground came up easily in barely resistant shovelfuls of decomposed granite, which most of the high desert soil was made of. Now, though, with all this rain and then snow, I had no idea what the ground might be like.

It didn't look like anybody had been buried here in a while—the kind of place you might visit in an old town that showed off graves and one-room schoolhouses like they deserved to be called attractions. Like going to see Lizzy Borden's grave or something. In my hometown, they used to take us on school trips to the town witch Hanna Cranna's grave. She was famous, best as I could remember, for cursing some woman's pie making ability. A pretty

lame witch. Later, some great Connecticut band we played with
named itself after her.

The clouds had parted, and the light from the moon made
the desert look luminous. There was light but little color, like a
black-and-white movie. The fence around the graveyard was old
and broken in several places.

Johnny Mo carried a spade shovel and a flashlight that was
dimmed by low batteries. I had the other shovel. We'd gotten
both from his father's garage. Mine was a square-edged one,
and we followed his weak beam of light and I listened to our
boots crunch softly in the dirt. We'd grabbed work gloves and I
put mine on, getting ready to dig when we found what we were
looking for. He stopped.

"This is easier in the day."

"We're not robbing a grave in daylight," I said.

"I didn't say we were *doing* it in the day. I just said it's easier
to find in the day."

"You better get the right one," I said.

"Don't worry. They're marked. We won't disturb any strangers'
graves."

I didn't really care about that. His grandmother, after all, was
as much a stranger to me as anyone else buried here. I just wanted
to make sure the person we dug up was the one he was sure had
gold on her when they put her down there.

The sand and snow shined in the moonlight. Wind rustled
through sagebrush and smoke trees on the perimeter of the
graveyard. I followed Johnny Mo and his jerky faint light as
he paused and looked at the beaten grave markers. Some were
chipped, a couple cracked from age and low-grade earthquakes
that had peppered the desert over the years. We looked for what
seemed like a long time, but probably wasn't. I was scared of being
caught, so seconds lingered longer in fear-stretched time.

He stopped again, looking down. "This is it."

The pill was starting to work on me and I already dreaded the fact that they wouldn't be working like this in a few days. Stay clean for a couple weeks and you might get three or four days of good highs. After that, life was back to just trying not to be sick every day. For now, though, I had the muted calm of not giving a shit about anything or anyone. My head was gracefully quiet for the first time in a long time, and I started digging a few feet to the left of the gravestone. Johnny Mo started on the right. The ground wasn't too bad. Not nearly as hard as I had feared.

"How much morphine are we getting?" I asked.

He shoveled. Shrugged. "Depends on how much gold. What price we can get. A lot of variables."

I dug deeper. My muscles ached with the labor, but it was labor with a payoff and I felt the sweat on my body grow cold in the night air. Every once in a while, I paused to see if I could hear anything other than us disturbing the world at this hour. I looked at my watch. 5:00 AM. We had less than an hour until the sun started swelling from behind the mountains out toward Amboy. People in the desert got up early.

"We need to get this done," I said.

"Really?" Johnny Mo said. "I thought we could linger. Take our time robbing a grave." He stood straight, looked up at me. "Stop stating the obvious. You think I'm stupid?"

I laughed. "You're not stupid. You're a lot of things, but not stupid."

"What the fuck does that mean? I'm a lot of things?"

"Dude. Look at us."

He seemed to think about it for a second. He lit a cigarette and handed it to me and then lit another for himself. "Fair enough."

We kept digging, not taking a break for the cigarettes, so the smoke filled my nose as it curled up and I breathed hard around the smoke. I hit something hard. It had a warm *thuck* to it, the sound of the shovel hitting wood.

"I think I hit the coffin," I said.

In a moment, he'd hit it on his side. The soil deeper down was packed harder than the sand on the surface, more like dusty clay that came out in fist-sized chunks. We dug faster than I thought either of us was capable of. In under ten minutes, we had most of the dirt off the top of the coffin.

Johnny Mo helped me dig down to the handles on the side. We tried to lift the top. It wouldn't budge. We dug a little deeper to get under the handle, but it was an odd hardware. Not like the clips on a suitcase or a guitar case. I didn't see any way to get into the coffin.

"I think we're fucked," I said. "Maybe they make these with some safety contraption."

"Now why the fuck would they do that? It's not like people try to get out of these."

"I'm just saying."

"Saying *what,* exactly?"

"Maybe they make them so you can't open them. I don't know."

Johnny Mo muttered something about not coming this far and before I could register what was happening, he had already slammed the shovel onto the top of the coffin several times. He got it to chip and splinter a bit, but it didn't seem to give.

He leaped from the ground above and started jumping up and down on the top of the coffin.

"Help me," he said.

The sky to the east warned light was only a half hour away. It seemed as good an idea as any at this point. I joined him.

"Try to stay in the middle," he said. "It's weaker there."

We jumped up and down. At first, it wasn't much different from jumping on a hardwood floor. Maybe twenty jumps in, though, I felt it start to give. We kept on. My bad ankle was a firecracker that went off every time I landed. Even my good foot ached, but it could have been worse. I was glad I'd worn my steel-toe boots into rehab, because they were all I had when I left. The rest of my stuff was scattered like buckshot all over LA County at various friends' places.

My leg broke through the top, and something hard snapped like a twig under my foot. I rolled my bad ankle and I slipped sideways. There was a sharp pain in my upper leg. A chunk of wood as long as a ruler stabbed about an inch into my thigh. My ankle throbbed from whatever I'd broken in the coffin. Splinters ripped my leg and had lodged deep in my skin and muscle above the knee. I needed Johnny Mo's help to get out. After we'd broken a hole, we hacked through the rest of the top with the shovels. Warm blood swelled into my jeans and ran down my leg.

Johnny Mo smashed through most of the wood. Dirt fell inside as he frantically made his way toward where the neck and the fingers should have been.

"Hold the flashlight for me," he said.

I aimed the beam of light to where I'd broken through the top. My blood dropped and seeped onto the splintered wood of the coffin, and for a moment I got scared about being caught but quickly realized my DNA wasn't in any system. Fear had me thinking crazy. The only things we could have left behind that were in the system were fingerprints, and we were safe there with the gloves.

Underneath where I'd fallen into the coffin was the hipbone I'd shattered into several pieces. I shook my head. Why this made it seem worse, I don't know.

Johnny Mo said, "Could you please hold that light where I'm fucking looking?"

I moved it up by the skull. There didn't seem to be any flesh left on his grandmother's body and I was relieved. Clothes still clung to some of the bones. They looked red under the flashlight, but they could have been some other color in full light and I hoped not to find out.

"Yes!" Johnny Mo said.

Down in the coffin, he'd snapped off a locket that sat near the ribcage. He turned and, kneeling, started on the fingers. More bones broke and he collapsed facedown and then pushed himself up. He worked one hand's finger bones, then the other's. He jumped out of the grave.

"Four pieces," he said, smiling. "Not bad."

"You sure they're gold?" I said, thinking that she might have been one of those old women who wore crap-ass costume jewelry and bragged about how much it was worth. My family was positively clogged with people clinging to shit they swore was worth keeping that was junk.

"She had money," he said. "I'm as sure as I can be right now. You want to put it back?"

"No."

"Then why ask me if it's real now?"

He had a point. "Because it occurred to me now."

"Just 'cause shit occurs to you, doesn't mean you have to say it. Stop being so negative, man."

I nodded. "Let's get moving."

"We have to fill this in."

"The sun's coming up, dude."

He looked at me like I was a stupid kid. "We are about to pawn a shitload of old jewelry not more than twenty miles from here. I'd like to be out of this town when people see this." He pointed to the hole in the ground.

I started shoveling the dirt and sand back into the hole. My bad ankle screamed with pain. My thigh was sticky with blood, which had started to get cold on my jeans. I'd need to get a look at it once we made it back to the car.

We filled the grave back up, but with the coffin open, more dirt went inside of it so there was still an indentation in the ground when we were done. It looked like a sinkhole.

"It'll have to do," Johnny Mo said.

We didn't know this long day and night in the desert would send us both back to rehab. Not right away, but the night in the graveyard led to a turning point in a string of turning points that sent us back to trying to get clean, hoping it was our last time.

That morning, though, we'd sell the gold at Rocky's Pawn Shop in Yucca Valley for a stunning eight hundred dollars, which got us enough morphine for a while. A hundred and twenty pills, thirty-milligrams—the time-release kind, but you could get around the time release and get a good dose from them. We'd go to the Highway 62 Diner where, even though I was starving, I would only drink a Diet Coke because I didn't want to screw up the high from the last OxyContin and the two morphine I'd taken.

Johnny Mo said, "What kind of addict are you? Drinking fucking Diet Coke."

This was a running joke with us. Every junkie drank and ate tons of sugar. An ex-girlfriend of mine drank nothing but Tab so I ended up on diet sodas. I smiled. "Laugh, motherfucker, but I have the best teeth of any addict we know."

"Pathetic," he said smiling. "I don't even know you, man." He took a bite of his egg and mumbled around his food. "You're dead to me."

I felt so aligned with the world, like all the molecules had lined up in their infinite potential patterns to let me feel good, even though it couldn't last. But still, in that moment, things were peaceful, and peace was one of the rarest visitors my head ever received and I wanted to savor it. Johnny Mo ate while I took wood chunks and thick splinters out of my thigh with a pair of needle-nose pliers and the waitress winced at me from behind

the counter. I figured I'd take a shower or bath later and soak the
slivers out and try to avoid an infection.

After we left the diner, we rushed back to LA, forgetting that
we left our stuff, meager as it may have been, at Al's. We'd been
in such a hurry to get to the pawnshop, and then the dealer,
and then as far away from that grave as possible that we weren't
thinking right.

We spent the week in an opium fog that managed to be both
delightful and regret filled. We were afraid of the desert cops and
didn't have the time or the guts to go out to Al's to pick up our
stuff until a week later, after New Year's.

When we reached Al's, it was morning, coming up toward a
sunny noon. It'd stayed cold all week. Some people's Christmas
lights had been left up and on and shined dull in the daylight.
The snow still stuck to the ground and glistened on the ocotillo
and smoke trees and cholla. We went in and I knew the smell
from that dead guy's apartment we'd cleaned. It's not something
you ever forget. Al was in the back bedroom, sitting up in his
bed with what was left of his head leaning back against the wall.
I'd never seen a gun suicide before. Nothing prepared me for
what I saw. What I might have expected—parts of his head and
hair and brain and bone splattered behind and above him—was
horrifyingly there. But what I hadn't expected was the image that
stayed with me for months and I guessed would stay for years
after that morning. His left eye was moved across his head, settled
where his left ear should have been. Like it was looking at us
as we entered the doorway, and then stayed looking toward the
door when I was looking at him straight on. His right eye stared
vacantly forward. His jaw was gone, his throat spread open so
that the bone of his spinal cord was exposed.

"Jesus," Johnny Mo said. "Fuck."

I didn't know what to say. It was like all the words at my disposal, all the words that had clanged around in my head and fallen out of my mouth all the years I'd been alive were worthless and hollow and I might as well spit up sand as talk for all the good it could do.

Johnny Mo walked out of the bedroom. He was on the phone, probably calling the cops or an ambulance or whatever. His voice came into my brain sounding like it was under water. The television was still on, and it reminded me of all the car accidents I'd ever had and how it always surprised me, after the accident, in the quiet of the wreckage, how the radio was always still playing.

On the floor, I looked at all the crisscross patterns of burning cigarettes Al had dropped over the years. Cigarettes that woke him up, over and over and over, when all he wanted, needed, probably, was some sleep he knew he would never get again.

But that was a week down the road. At dawn with our fresh and dreadful gold, before things would turn so ugly they'd scar whatever good had come of the morning and the day still looked swollen with promise, we left the graveyard and started back toward Johnny Mo's car.

The sun burned faint sepia yellow as it came over the mountains. We walked back with our tools, Johnny Mo getting farther and farther ahead as I dragged my bloody and damaged right leg behind me, wincing and sweating and seeing my breath as the weak cold light swelled slowly into the morning air.

THE INDIFFERENCE OF HEAVEN

(1979)

My father killed the man in front of me when I was thirteen. At the time, I thought the man was a stranger to my father. They got into an argument over the price of a parts car my dad was selling. The man had a wife who said he'd answered an ad in the paper and had gone to look at a used car, but he'd taken the address and the paper with him so no one had any idea where he went. The cops would end up checking every ad in the paper for a used car, but they had no reason to suspect one person over another. My father was a state trooper. He said he'd never seen the man. He may have called, my father told them, but no one fitting his description had ever been to our house to look at the car.

There are whole stretches—before and after the murder—where I don't remember much of my childhood. Big sections as lost as a drunken blackout. And while for years I tried to blame my addiction on my father, I'd already been in a daily drug and alcohol haze for at least a year by the time my father killed the guy. I'd first gotten drunk when I was seven one Sunday morning after my parents had thrown a party the night before. This was when my mother still seemed like other kids' mothers and when my father wasn't around as much as he would be a few years later.

My parents always slept late the morning after a party. My father never opened a window. In the summer, the AC rumbled 24/7. In the winter, you could walk around in shorts the heat was cranked so high. Our house was colder in the summer than in the winter. And years of cigarette smoke gave the air a stale stink that seeped into everything. A teacher sent me home with notes that my clothes smelled like smoke. The white curtains had turned a sick nicotine yellow the color of parchment paper.

The morning after the party, I was down in the basement. Unfinished drinks sat on every surface, glistening the colors of exotic jewels in the morning light from the windows. Even before tasting them, I was in love with how they looked. I drank something red first because I liked red candy and red drinks like Hi-C. I wasn't in love with the taste but I kept it down. I didn't want to put something that had been in some stranger's mouth into mine, so I smoked one of my mother's half-smoked cigarettes stubbed out in an overflowing ashtray. The smear of her red lipstick tasted and felt waxy. I drank the remains of three cans of Ballantine and a bottle of Miller that was nearly full.

It wasn't long before the floor felt like it was swaying and I closed my eyes and felt myself smile and my head felt better than it ever had. It was like I'd been holding my breath my whole life and I'd finally relaxed. I fell asleep on the orange shag carpet that reeked of years of cat piss and cigarette smoke, as happy as I'd ever been.

After that, I'd get drunk and pass out as often as I could to stay away from the chaos in the house. My father would come home drunk and walls would rattle and my mother would lock herself in their bedroom and my father would beat the shit out of the doors and walls and drywall dust would float in the air. Then he'd grab a beer and sit watching TV and not say another word the rest of the night. When he was angry, it was best to avoid him. I avoided him when he wasn't, too, because I didn't want to be the one who made him explode. Even staying away didn't always work. My mother knew I could never sleep. Before my father was home every night, she'd sit in my room and stay with me, or she'd let me stay up and watch *The Tonight Show* with her in the living room. He'd get home some nights at two or three in the morning, or sometimes with dim early morning light coming through the picture window. I'd hear the deadbolt click and I'd feel cold and afraid and he'd look at me awake and scream at my mother and ask her what the hell was wrong with her and what the hell was wrong with me and why couldn't she just for one goddamn minute leave me alone and have me learn to deal with it and who in the world has a *kid* with fucking insomnia.

Not long after my twelfth birthday, I'd started swiping my mother's pills from her bedroom. By this time she slept in the bedroom alone and barely spoke, and my father worked a swing shift that lined up with my school schedule so that he was always around, always drunk, and always angry. One morning before school, I swiped three pills out of the five prescription bottles she had. I had no idea what they were. It was the first time I ever took a pill, so I waited around to see what it did. Early on, I got lucky—the first two were tranquilizers and made me feel like I was walking on marshmallows. With these, I could finally sleep through a night. I ended up stealing so many that my mother ran out near the end of the month and, after not having said a word for maybe a week, started screaming at my father while I hid in my room.

One day before the school bus came, I took a Quaalude. By the time I made it to school, I had real trouble walking. I couldn't do a straight line and I kept smashing into lockers—first on one side of the hall, and then stumbling to the other side and dropping down, my legs collapsing underneath me. It was right after Christmas break, and the freshly waxed floors gleamed and smelled like lemons. When a couple of friends helped me to a chair in first-period social studies, they dropped me and I cracked my head on the tiled floor. I woke up in the ER with five stitches behind my right ear. They'd shaved most of the hair on the right side—shaved about two inches above the ear all the way to the back.

When my father came to pick me up after his shift, it was five hours later and I was asleep in the waiting room of the ER. The first time I slipped off, a nurse woke me up and told me I couldn't sleep because I'd had a concussion and sleep was dangerous. She gave me coffee. After a while, though, the ER filled up and my head ached and I was still in a Quaalude fog and I fell asleep.

My father woke me up by grabbing my hair and jerking my head toward my chest. I tried to move, but he held my head down, pulling hard on the hair I had left on top of my head.

"Let me see what the fuck you did."

I was still groggy. "I fell."

My father yanked my head up so I was looking into his eyes. I had trouble focusing—his nose seemed to become two noses and then merge and then separate again.

"Yeah," he said. "You fell." He looked up and shook his head. "Christ."

My father pulled me up roughly by the collar of my ESSO jacket and said, "C'mon, numbnuts."

He let me go and walked out of the ER and I struggled to keep up, my legs still unsteady. When we got to the car, he pushed me up against the passenger door.

"I don't have enough fucking troubles, Bud?"

He didn't say a word to me on the way home until we pulled into the driveway. When I leaned forward to undo my seatbelt, he slapped me on the back of the head and it felt like the sutures might burst.

I touched the back of my head and winced. My hand felt slick and came back smeared with blood when I looked at it.

"Enjoy your haircut, dipshit."

I was still having trouble thinking straight. "What?" I wiped blood onto my jeans.

"Bud—if you touch that fucking hair. If you go to the barber or try to even it out? I'll make what's on your head now look like a paper cut, are we clear?"

I nodded, which made me almost throw up.

By the time my father killed the man, I'd been getting high and getting drunk every day I could—which was usually pretty easy since my mother was on so many meds that she could never keep track of what she'd taken. I took her pills, hid from my father, and played my mother's guitar with my bedroom door locked.

I'd always had trouble sleeping and now even when I could sleep, I'd wake up seeing the dead man leaning bloody against the stump. Or I'd wake up afraid my father was going to kill me, and I'd have to sneak out of the house. Sometimes when I couldn't sleep, I'd go out to where we'd been chopping wood and listen to the radio signals come from the wires on the fence, looking back at the pale lights from my mother's bedroom and the blue flickers from the TV my father watched in the living room. I'd smoke my father's cigarettes and wait until I was tired enough to go in and pass out from whichever one of my mother's pills I'd managed to get away with.

When I joined the marching band, because that was the only way they'd let me play guitar in the school jazz band, my father told me that girls were in marching band and boys belonged on the football team. "What's next?" he said. "You going to be a fucking cheerleader?"

Once I knew what pissed him off, I gave him more to hate about me. I grew my hair. I pierced my ears. When he'd get home from work and see me, he'd shake his head and mutter "Jesus H. Christ" and walk out of whatever room I happened to be in. If I was in a doorway, he'd shove me out of his way when he walked by. I stayed away from doorways. I stayed away from him.

The week after my father killed the man, there were stories every day in the *Bridgeport Post* and on all the local channels about the man who'd gone missing. The search started late because since his car was missing, too, his wife couldn't file a missing person report for seventy-two hours because there was no proof anything bad had happened. I was in my mother's room, trying to get her to eat some soup while she sat up in bed. Her thirteen-inch black and white TV was on with the sound off, but she was staring at me. It was hard to say who'd had more of her meds that day—me or her. She wouldn't eat, so I put the bowl on her night table and strummed the guitar. Then, the next week, she'd be out with my father drinking at some bar and, from the rumors that passed around the school, singing with the band and making out with men who weren't my father. And then she'd be back in bed for a week or more.

My father was in the living room, watching the same channel and I heard the sound coming from his TV and saw the image coming from my mother's. On the news, they were talking about the missing man. I stopped playing.

When I turned back to my mother, she was still staring at me. "Did you hear about that guy?" I asked my mother.

She stared at me with a vacant smile.

On the news, they were interviewing the man's wife, whose voice spilled anger and fear as she accused the police of not taking her early calls seriously.

My father screamed at the television, "He's a fucking adult, lady! Adults have a right to go missing! It's called leaving!"

I wondered who he was putting on the show for.

I heard my father turn off his television.

My mother leaned her head on the pillow, still looking at me, and said, "John Cassavetes."

"The missing guy," I said. "Do you know about him?"

"You look like your father," she said, nodding in and out. "Your father." She smacked her lips, which meant nothing to me then, but I found out years later when I was put on it that it was a side effect of lithium. "Young."

She smacked her lips and I felt disgusted. I had no idea in that moment that I would feel guilt over that disgust for the rest of my life. That such a small moment—a moment that could have simply passed instead—would become a fixed image I'd replay whenever I wasn't feeling quite bad enough about myself.

I tried to ask her again about the guy on the news, but nothing was reaching her.

"Like a young John Cassavetes," she said. She reached over and touched my cheek and I backed away out of reach. "Your father, young."

My father had come down the hall and was leaning on the doorjamb. He laughed. "He looks like John Cassavetes' fucking daughter."

My mother, who rarely fought when she was sedated and rarely stopped fighting when she was full of energy, rolled her head on her pillow and looked at me and said, "Bud has . . ." She rolled her tongue over her lips again and my stomach rolled. I wondered which of my parents I was more like and I was frightened no matter what the answer was, though I loved her and I didn't love him—plus, when she was in a good mood, she could be a lot of fun. But I hoped somehow I wasn't much like either of them. She closed her eyes. "Bud . . . has . . . very delicate features." She opened her eyes and smiled at me, and I would try to remember for years if that was the last time she ever looked into my eyes and smiled, or only the last time I remembered it happening. And if the last time she looked at me with love was the same time I was disgusted by her and praying that I had as little of her blood in my veins as possible.

In December, two months after my father killed the man, I came home from school and my mother was gone. My father told me that she'd left. That she'd gone to California.

"California?" I said. "How?"

"However the fuck people get to California, Bud." He looked like he might hit me. "Do you think she flapped her fucking arms and flew there?"

"When's she coming back?"

My father looked up at me. His eyes were red and swollen. He walked into the kitchen and grabbed two beers and handed me one. He had to know I'd been stealing his beer, but it was the first time he'd ever given me one.

"She's not, Bud."

We sat in the living room and neither of us talked. The alarm clock my father kept by the couch he slept on ticked quietly, time feeling like a soft, relentless metronome. The baseboard heaters popped and pinged. I finished my beer and went back to what had been my mother's room.

My father and I were within sight of WADC's radio tower the morning my father killed that man. The tower was close to our house. So close it was the only AM radio station you could get for miles.

Sometimes when I was alone in the woods, I'd hear the radio show voices coming from the barbed wire on the old fence at the back property line. Unseen ghosts of language quietly talking as I sat and listened for hours. I'd sit on tree stumps and listen to the adult voices on talk radio fill the air around me with their authority and blame that I couldn't make heads or tails of.

My father and I had been chopping wood and loading a cord of it into his beat-up old red GMC truck when the man came to look at the car. We'd had the truck radio on, the doors open, listening as the Baltimore Orioles played game four of the World Series against the Pittsburgh Pirates.

The man and my father were talking about the car. It was a 1973 Mercury Cougar that my father had taken in trade for building a bathroom for a friend of his. My father wanted two hundred dollars for the car. The man offered seventy-five.

Somehow, and with staggering speed, this became something to fight over and then a reason to kill, and my father, who was still holding the axe we were using to split the firewood, hit the man on the side of the head with the dull end of the axe.

I looked down at the man my father had killed. I didn't know much about the world. But I could tell right away the man was dead. He fell at what looked like an impossible angle—his legs bending opposite to the way they're supposed to and making a wet crunching sound before he collapsed on his back onto the woodpile. His head was smashed. A cruel divot behind the left ear. On that side, his head looked like an apple with a bite taken out of it. The rest of him, though, looked good enough to sell you something on TV. His eyes weren't wide open and scared like in the movies I'd seen, but kind of lazily looking off into the distance.

After my mother was gone, my father stunned me by treating me like he didn't hate me. Or at least like he didn't care what I did one way or the other. He didn't give me a lot of rules—he let me get wasted pretty much whenever I wanted. In some ways, we were more like fucked-up roommates than a father and a son, but the house became a place I didn't try to get away from at every opportunity.

He bought me my first real guitar—a used 1969 Telecaster that would become the only instrument I never pawned or sold for drugs.

The biggest problem that year was my first psychotic episode. It happened in the middle of the summer after I'd been up for five days, taking acid with my friend Jack. My father worked longer hours and never seemed to care that I slept at Jack's for days until I needed to finally change clothes or take more of his beer.

Jack and I met because he played drums in the school jazz band and we ended up jamming on Rolling Stones and Johnny Thunders songs every day after school and then all day long in the sweltering heat of his garage once school let out. We had a series of kids who could barely play bass for a while, but the two of us had learned to play music with one brain by the time we got our driver's licenses.

And then it became hideously evident that we may have had one brain when we played music, but we had very different brains when we stayed up for days on blotter acid and the amphetamines his mother took for weight loss. I had no idea what I'd done until Jack told me some of it, the worst being me running away from his house only to call him three hours later screaming incomprehensively and crying on a payphone in the parking lot of a Burger King ten miles away. He was listening on the other end of the line while the cops put me in a cruiser and he heard me yelling the whole time. All I remembered about the call was that I thought I was calmly asking Jack to help me and wondering why the fuck he couldn't understand anything I was saying.

"Dude," he told me later. "I mean, you weren't using words."

I'd lost my ID and I couldn't tell anyone who I was. Jack was still deep into the acid and said he had no idea what to do.

My father didn't even know I was missing until I was able to let the doctor know who I was. Once I could answer questions, I didn't tell anyone in the hospital that I'd been drinking and using for years. As far as they knew, I had "tried" pot and, this one time, LSD.

The doctor who came into my room diagnosed me with rapid-cycling bipolar and psychotic episodes. He told me I'd have to be medicated and that I'd have to avoid recreational drugs. He tried to hammer it home that all drugs were bad, and that I could never take any kind of hallucinogenic again, or my brain could get stuck where it had been. Near the end of the doctor's lecture, my father came into the room, looking at me with more concern than I'd ever seen.

The doctor told him the diagnosis.

My father looked at me and back to the doctor. "That's all, though?" he said. "The bipolar?"

"This is a serious diagnosis, Mr. Barrett," the doctor said.

I started to get scared. How serious?

My father nodded. "No, I realize that." He asked the doctor if he could speak to him in private. I had no idea what they said to each other.

I spent four or five blurry days filled with IV diazepam and got sent home. They gave me a script for some tranquilizer I'd run through five days after it was filled and some other pills that were supposed to keep me on an even keel, but they made my head heavy as a medicine ball and made me feel labored and slow, like the blood in my veins was thick as maple syrup. I stopped taking them within a week. And that was pretty much that.

My father stood over the dead man and shook his head. He kicked the man's legs, yelling "you stupid fucking asshole" after the first kick, and then "stupid fuck!" with every kick after that. A couple of times, his boot hit the ground and wet leaves and dirt flew onto the man's jeans. My father stopped and stood still for a second. I hadn't realized I'd been holding my breath until I let it out, thinking he was done, but he kicked the dead man on the left arm, which hung by his side. On the seventh or eighth kick, the man's arm flopped over his chest and my father kicked his head and the man collapsed to the right. His head slammed with a wet *thuck* into a freshly cut tree stump. I thought about running away, but I couldn't move.

The man's neck bent terribly to the side, his cheek parallel to his shoulder, his head hanging loose, looking like it was attached to his body by nothing more than the skin. Like a bird someone had killed with his bare hands. My throat swelled and burned with puke that I managed to force down.

My father stopped, staring at the man. I thought he might kill me. I had no idea what this man had done to make my father explode this way. I froze like a rabbit, hoping nothing would hurt me if I didn't call attention to myself. My heart jackhammered. Radio sounds kept coming from the truck, but I couldn't make out the words because it sounded like jet engines were roaring in my ears.

My father went around to the driver's side and grabbed his bottle of Rebel Yell from where it always sat under the seat and started drinking it like it was iced tea on a summer day. He stayed on that side of the truck, repeating "fuck" every few seconds until he stopped and let out a deep breath. All my life, I'd seen my father's minimal emotional range swing from rage to terrible disappointment with only a quiet, seething resentment breaking the horror of his extremes. I sat there, trying not to let him see that with every explosive heartbeat my body shook uncontrollably.

Blood dripped from the left side of the man's head and landed and swelled on his flannel shirt.

"Pop," I said, my voice strangled and shaky.

He didn't hear me. Or he ignored me, taking another drink.

I forced myself to speak louder, still hearing the fear in my voice. "Hey, Pop?"

My father yelled, "What?"

I pointed to the man. "His head. It's bleeding."

He looked at me like I was an idiot. "No fucking shit, Bud!"

"No," I said. "Not where you hit him. On the side you kicked." My father didn't answer. I said, "I think he's alive."

He shook his head and stunned me with how quiet he'd become.

"Mom says dead people can't bleed."

He took a couple of deep, frustrated breaths. "Your mother has . . . Your mother doesn't understand everything, all right, son?" My father walked over to where I was. His rage had passed.

Which didn't mean it couldn't come back. Everything could seem calm and then he'd be on you like an attack dog.

I didn't want to make him mad, but the man's head still dripped blood like a faucet with one of those leaks so slow you never get around to fixing it. I counted eight drops from the man's head. The sun had slipped behind cold aluminum gray clouds, and it was like someone had turned down a dimmer switch on the world.

My father bent down and looked at the man. "He's not bleeding. It's the way his head's bent."

I looked up at him, confused.

He spat onto the leaves. "Dead people don't pump blood. What looks like bleeding is just gravity, Bud."

My father sounded exhausted, the anger totally gone. He'd kicked his rage out on the dead man. Where the blood had dripped from the man's head looked slick as motor oil under the gray sky and dark enough that I couldn't see the pattern in the flannel anymore.

When I was seventeen, my father started running a poker game at our house. Usually six to eight people played—mostly cops or ex-cop friends of my dad's who'd been run off the force for something shady and corrupt and now ran security for low-rent Bridgeport guys the Mob used, like Nick Anthony. You called Nick Anthony just that, both names. Call him Nick and he'd give you a look that said he knew people who'd sink you in the Long Island Sound—people who not only knew how to weigh you down correctly but knew to knife and slice you with enough holes in enough places that your body's gasses wouldn't turn you into a floater, which happened when amateurs tried to sink a kill. But my father'd told me that while Nick Anthony did *know* those people, he wasn't made. He only ran numbers out of a bar, and he couldn't get any Bridgeport family to put a hit on anyone. Even the Bridgeport families had to ask the five families in New York.

Nick Anthony's kid Kenny was kind of a legend around my school. He was the first running back in the history of the conference to rush for a thousand yards three years in a row, which seemed to impress people like my father who gave a shit about sports. Kenny's other claims to fame were that he drove a Trans Am and brought a hooker to the prom. He was as dumb as a rock, and everyone at school—even some of the idiot teachers—seemed either in awe of him or afraid of him.

I asked my dad if I could play in the weekly game.

"You don't have the money or the balls," he said. "And you don't know the game."

He may have been right about the money and the balls, but I had a plan that would show him I could have both. As far as the game went, I'd been reading his poker books and magazines and watching him and his buddies play. None of them except for my father and Nick Anthony knew any more than I'd learned just from watching and reading. I'd also read about card counting in Twenty-one games. Lately, when I was bored, I'd started dealing out a deck one card at a time, face up. Since my mother had been gone—and with her the endless supply of every sedative and benzo she'd had—I'd been going two or three nights at a stretch without sleep, full of energy and going crazy with nothing to do and nowhere to go. I tried to sleep, but I wouldn't take the brain meds. I'd drink cough syrup to try to get drowsy, but my brain wouldn't slow down. It sounded like I was in a crowded diner, with all this noise and chatter in my head. The best thing to do was to keep my thoughts occupied. When I could, I'd play guitar but, much as I liked it, much as it gave me some peace, I couldn't do it for six to eight hours every night while I waited for the sun and an excuse to have somewhere to be.

For a couple of weeks, I'd deal one deck and test myself: after I flipped fifty-one cards, I'd see if I could call what the last one would be. At first I was right about half the time. I waited until I'd gotten to the point where I knew the last card ten consecutive times, three nights in a row, before I asked my father if I could play. Sometimes, it could take me hours. I'd nail the last card seven times in a row, then miss. I'd deal another five or seven or eight decks and get them right and then mess up again. When I could get to ten in a row three nights running, I figured I was ready.

"What if we start playing?" I said. "What if you show me some stuff?"

"What are you going to use for money?"

I took out my deck. "I'll deal the first fifty-one, face up. Then I'll tell you the last card."

"You want to play poker and you're trying to show me fucking card tricks, Bud? These are men at the table."

"It's not a trick," I said. "I can count the deck."

My father looked impressed. I never forgot that look. I didn't get it often enough to get used to it, but it was there a lot from then on when we played cards.

"Watch," I said, and I'd dealt out only five cards before he stopped me, reshuffled the deck, and told me he'd deal.

The cards came about one a second, and I relaxed and told myself I'd done this more than a hundred times. I forced myself to breathe and concentrate, and when my father dealt the fifty-first card—a three of clubs—he stopped and said, "OK, hotshot. What am I holding?"

I wasn't nervous. It felt incredible to know something I wasn't supposed to be able to know. To do something other people couldn't do. But I already knew I could do that. What felt so powerful was that now my father knew it, too. "Ten of diamonds."

My father dropped the ten of diamonds face up. "Shit, Bud."

I smiled.

"That's not a trick?"

"We can do it as many times as you want."

My father lit a cigarette. "Once more," he said.

I started to gather up the cards.

"No," he said. He grabbed a fresh deck of Bicycle cards, cut the seal and asked if I was ready.

"Sure."

He held up the new deck. "It's not that I don't trust you."

"Yeah, it is," I said.

"I need to know if you can really do this."

I'd never felt better, without being totally wasted, in my life. "I just did it."

"With your own cards."

My father shuffled the deck and I went to the fridge and grabbed a beer and asked him if he wanted one.

"Yeah," he said and looked at me with a dark smirk. "So, now you ask me if I want one of my own beers because you can do some card tricks?" I didn't understand why he sounded angry. He said, "Now we're pals? You're not my son anymore?"

And I wanted to say I'd never felt more like his son than I had when he looked at me as he flipped the ten of diamonds, but it was clear that no matter how much we might be talking, we didn't ever seem to be communicating.

"Deal the cards," I said and handed him a beer.

"Well, look who's been taking ball-growing pills behind my back." I was about to smile when he said, "But then, what fucking pill don't you take behind my back?"

"Do you want to bet me a hundred bucks I can do this?" I said.

"You have a hundred bucks, Bud?"

"I will if you take this bet."

He laughed. "Yeah. That's right, I forgot. I *am* a fucking idiot. I give you my money if you win. If I win, you say you're sorry."

He dealt the cards. "Just do it, genius. We'll talk money *if* you can do it."

I did it five times in a row and my father said, "This is really interesting."

We sat the rest of the night drinking and playing Heads-Up Texas Hold 'Em, which nobody played back then in Bridgeport except in the illegal games because you could have more players at the table than with any other game. All the communal cards meant more asses in the seats, which meant more money to the game. My father and I played freezeout with one hundred each in chips and I had him beaten at three or four crucial moments but I started to play conservatively—the opposite of the way you should play head to head.

I folded on a hand that I thought could take him—he was all-in and I had what would have been an easy hand to fold with a full table, but was actually a decent Heads-Up hand. I knew I should have called him. But if I had and he won, he would have taken the chip lead and I was more concerned with being ahead than I was willing to risk being behind to win.

"You just fucked up," my father said when I folded.

I nodded. "I had you, didn't I?"

"It doesn't matter if you had me or didn't. There's no way you could have known that. And there's no way you'll *ever* beat a real player if you're afraid to lose. Where you fucked up is that you're chickenshit."

I sighed. "OK, all right."

"No, listen to me. You think this is a small thing, but it's not. You want to play with men, you better learn this or you will have your ass handed to you too many times and you'll end up living some safe miserable life with a retirement plan. You want that?"

"I'm going to be a musician," I said.

"Right. The Rock Star plan." He laughed and took a swig of beer and the neck foamed and volcanoed when he set it on the table. "Well, there you go. You don't want to live safe. You better learn to live smart, right?"

"Right."

"Well, you *are* smart, Bud. You know that, right?"

I felt like I might cry. I couldn't trust myself to talk and I cleared my throat and nodded.

"OK. You're smart. But that doesn't mean you're not stupid. So pay attention. Any shithead can bet with chips. Can bet *any fucking hand* in a limit game. If all I can come into you for is fifty bucks when you're holding a thousand . . . fuck, you'll call me every time. I push you all-in and your asshole puckers . . . I just beat you no matter what fucking cards I'm holding. Don't ever get beaten because you're chickenshit. That's not how a man loses. You understand?"

"I do."

My father looked at me like he was trying to figure out what to do with me. Like I had a use that he didn't know I had—which was, I suppose, exactly what the look meant.

"I'll stake you a hundred next Friday. That's it. Show me you can play well off that and we'll talk."

I thanked him, even though most of his sleazy friends bought in with at least five hundred and dropped or won as much as three grand a night in that game. They tended to lose it back to each other over time and it probably evened out enough, with my father and Nick Anthony the only ones with net gains over the course of months. My father even dumped some nights, I'd noticed, probably to keep them coming back.

When Friday came, though, I had a plan. I knew Nick Anthony a little from watching him play on Fridays and from knowing his kid Kenny and his dumb-as-a-rock, hooker-to-the-prom life, and I figured Nick Anthony was probably arrogant and dim enough to underestimate me. He was a bully. I could play that against him. If you can't spot the mark at the table, you're the mark. I went with Nick Anthony.

Sure enough, when my father said I had a chair at the table, Nick Anthony started in on me. "Fuck, Hank. Your fucking kid?" He lit a Swisher Sweet that stank and made me want him to suffer even more than I already had wanted it.

"He's got money."

Nick Anthony laughed and looked at me. "Fucking pecker-wood has money?" He looked at my father, still laughing. "He's holding my money is what he is." He shrugged. "Fine. Let's play."

I said to him, "I have a hundred dollars that says you can deal me any deck you want face up and I'll call the last card." I put my hands in my pockets to hide the tremors. I avoided looking at my father, and hoped this was how a man won or lost.

Nick Anthony snorted. He looked around the room at the corrupt and ethically gray cops and then his gaze settled on me. "Fuck your hundred. I'll only take the bet if it's for everything you're holding."

"It is everything."

"I thought you wanted to play poker." He sat down, opened a new deck and nodded to a chair across from him. "Fuck if I care that you don't want that seat to even get warm."

I sat down, sat on my hands and hid my deep breaths as much as I could.

He said, "Put my money on the table, kid."

I hated him. "Put mine."

My father and his friends laughed.

Some guy named Bill turned to my father. "A hundred says Bud's history."

My father said, "Just because my kid's stupid doesn't mean I am."

It rattled me for a second. But maybe he wanted to see Nick Anthony's face. Maybe he knew Nick Anthony might think he was being set up if he took Bill's bet. My father still had a game to play tonight whether I did or not, and he didn't need Nick Anthony to know anything about what he was thinking. And that's what I told myself.

Nick Anthony dealt.

I called the right card.

Everybody else sounded thrilled and stunned. Everybody was laughing except for me and Nick Anthony.

I left the money on the table. "We can do this again."

He looked like he wanted to hurt me. I felt safe with who was in the room. Plus, it wasn't a heated game. These guys joked and got wasted all night. Only Nick Anthony taunted much and everybody pretty much let him blather week after week. My father's friends, no matter what else they happened to be, were men who had dealt with pressure more important than money.

I said, "Really. We can do this again. *I* can do it again."

Nick Anthony stared for a couple seconds more. He laughed. "OK, kid. Faggot magicians know card tricks. Let's see if you know cards." I took my money.

The night played out perfectly for me. As the hours went by, I gained confidence and I *felt* it. I'd found something, along with getting high and playing guitar, that I was good at. But this was the first thing I could do that gave me a sense of power. That put grown men on their heels and made them, I could see, respect me. And when men respect your ability to take their money, they fear you. And I loved the feeling of controlling every man at that table—including, maybe most of all, my father.

But I didn't want to beat my father. I'd made him respect me—respect me for something more worthy of true respect than my ability to keep, out of nothing but fear, the secret about the murder.

I wanted Nick Anthony Heads-Up. And I wanted guitar and drug money. My father and his friends dropped one at a time, and then Nick Anthony took two of them out when he pushed them all-in with a check-raise that I'd learned never to fall for weeks before I ever got to play at the table. He frequently check-raised from a position of strength. He taunted more when he had a hand, which could go either way as a tell. Nobody taunted without a reason—but some did it with a hand, some did it when they held rags. I'd get a lot better over the years spotting tells, but no one at that table was good enough to have individual tells except for my father and Nick Anthony. Everyone else did the normal shit you could read about: they stared into your eyes when they bluffed, looked away when they had the nuts, and leaned back when they thought they had you beat.

Nick Anthony had me at a two-to-one chip lead, which was an advantage in Heads-Up, but you could turn that around in one hand much more often when there were only two players. Of course, you could get busted a lot quicker, too. And, as my father showed me—and no matter how much you read it, you had to feel it to learn it—the only way to win Heads-Up was to risk losing. Play conservatively all night and you might get to the final two. I would learn real players—guys who played for a living, guys who weren't glamorous and who fed kids and paid mortgages, guys who ultimately were too good and kept me from ever thinking I had the temperament for that level—they knew how to wait. Winners played maybe one out of ten—sometimes one out of twenty—hands. But when they played them, they played them right. Some pros were aggressive as hell when they finally played a hand and beat you with an ice gut, not with the cards in their hand. Others played slow and steady all night long. People could argue it was a legit strategy when the chairs were full. Play Heads-Up conservatively and all you did was guarantee you'd lose more slowly.

I wanted to hurt Nick Anthony. Break him in front of, if not his friends, everyone in the room. I had no idea if anyone really liked Nick Anthony. My father made no secret of thinking he was a small-time loser whose money was "as green as anyone's."

We went back and forth on enough hands that everyone got tired of sitting around and only the two of us and my father were left.

I'd done a good job, though, of avoiding two tempting mistakes.

First, I didn't count money on the table as mine yet. It wasn't my drug money. Or my guitar money. Or my make Nick Anthony run home with his tail between his legs money. The only way it would *be* that was if I didn't think ahead of myself and see it that way.

Second, I hadn't let Nick Anthony's taunting and his general nature as an asshole take me out of my game.

I'd taken three straight hands—totally outplaying him on two and fucking up but getting lucky on the river on the third. I held a three-to-one chip lead. I'd been drinking, but slowly and not too much. All night I'd felt a growing sense that I was the smartest person at that table, with the possible exception of my father. It had started to seem that I could think rings around Nick Anthony.

He went all-in on the next hand, won, and doubled up on a coin-flip call. I wasn't shaken. I had a 45 percent chance to win the hand. I hadn't made a bad call.

We traded blinds for a while and I forced him to fold on a few hands, and I was back up to a two-to-one chip lead.

The next hand I got dealt pocket tens and flopped the set. A lot of people open with pairs, thinking they're holding something good, no matter how low their pair is, not knowing that the odds of flipping the set are only 12 percent. In Heads-Up, though, being dealt the tens was a strong hand. Nick Anthony and I bet into each other. My ten was top card in a rainbow flop. Nick Anthony went all-in.

There was no way he could have been holding anything close to what I had. No matched suits in the flop, so the most he could be holding was a low pair, or a desperate hope for a straight or flush. He wasn't bragging, which also meant that he wasn't sure he had me. I called and turned over my tens and Nick Anthony winced and said, "Motherfucker."

He turned his cards. I beat everything but his hope for a flush. Only two hearts could beat me. I held one from the deck and there were two in his hand and one on the board. Four down from the thirteen in the deck. At most he had nine outs left, but he'd have to catch two in a row.

And then he did.

Instead of taking him out of the game and having all that money, now he had a two-to-one chip lead and I immediately, at the worst possible time, went on tilt. My game was ruined. I played two hands wrong where I *knew* I should have called. Nick Anthony started taunting me.

"Looks like you're freezing up when it matters, kid."

"Fuck off, *Nick*." I'd ignored him all night and it had frustrated him and now I'd lost my focus and I knew it, but I couldn't get it back. "You got lucky on your flush. You should be on your way home the way you played that hand."

"But I'm not home, kid."

"There's no way you could beat me without luck, asshole."

Nick Anthony looked like he wanted to kill me.

My father said, "Bud. Cool off."

Nick Anthony smiled and lit another Swisher Sweet. "No, he doesn't need to cool off. He's done. Deal."

I couldn't have beaten the worst chump at the table by that point. I went all-in when I still had a few blinds left before I had to, no matter what the hand. Nick Anthony called and I turned an unsuited six and nine.

Nick Anthony laughed and showed a pair of kings.

"Cowboys, punk!"

A king came on the flop and I was drawing dead. I got up from the table to get a beer. My father put a hand to my chest.

"Shake the man's hand, Bud."

I looked at him. He was serious.

Nick Anthony was already cashing out his chips into the two thousand dollars I should have had. I hated myself for letting him rattle me.

I turned and shook his hand.

Nick Anthony said, "What the fuck were you thinking with a six-nine? Kenny told me about you and your trip to the hospital. You got crazy in your blood, kid." He pointed at my father. "Your mother, his mother . . . Kid never had a chance."

I moved toward Nick Anthony, who started toward me. My father rushed between us, a hand on each of our chests. I stepped back.

Nick Anthony said to my father, "Get your fucking hand off me, Barrett."

My father said, "Just calm down, OK? Everything's cool here."

Nick Anthony punched my father on the jaw. My father didn't seem to feel it, and in a blur my father head-butted him and blood exploded from a cut above Nick Anthony's eye. My father slammed him into a wall, then grabbed Nick Anthony's head and brought it to his knee as his knee was coming up. Nick Anthony's head snapped back off my father's knee. My father rammed him up against the wall again with his forearm pushed hard against his throat. Nick Anthony struggled to breathe.

My father said, "Who's crazy, shithead? Even my fucking kid knows you never throw a punch at a man unless you're willing to kill him." My father pushed even harder into Nick Anthony's throat and his breathing sounded thin and desperate. "Because how the fuck do you know that man isn't willing to kill you?"

Nick Anthony had the purest mix of fear and hatred on his face I'd ever seen. Though I'm sure I'd had that look for my father, too, I just couldn't see it.

My father said, "You have no fucking idea what *this man* is capable of, asshole. Do you?"

Nick Anthony shook his head.

"Then it was a really bad fucking idea to take a swing at me." My father let him go, and Nick Anthony crumpled to the floor. My father grabbed his money and shoved it in his jacket pockets.

"Get the door, Bud."

I did, and he picked up Nick Anthony and pushed him down onto our front lawn and told him he didn't want to ever see him again.

A minute later, my father and I were on the couch and I heard Nick Anthony's Lincoln spit gravel out of our driveway.

My father calmly said, "You had him, Bud. You lost because you couldn't control your temper."

"I didn't threaten to kill the fat fuck. Who lost his fucking temper?"

"If I'd lost my temper, Nick Anthony would be dead." He took a drink of his beer. "You lost your money. I didn't lose shit. What happened tonight was that Nick Anthony owned you. I owned Nick Anthony."

But I knew that Nick Anthony had done something to us both—that there was a weaker spot in my father than I'd ever seen. The fact that he was willing to kill or threaten to kill Nick Anthony or anyone else was not news to me. But now I knew there was something in him, as much as in me, that hurt about my mother—and whatever the fuck it was about his own mother. Something that constituted weakness to himself since he'd always called it weakness in me. Something that made me know that Nick Anthony didn't own either of us. But he knew what did.

———

And the dead man's mouth was open, and his metal fillings were picking up the World Series radio signal, just like the radio in the truck. My father paced. He lit a Marlboro and the smoke merged with the smell of wet leaves and the smell of damp soil and the smell of freshly split wood. My father paced some more and turned off the radio in the truck, and then stared down along with me at the man he'd killed. The broadcast was still coming from the man's open mouth and we heard that the Pirates had lost and were now down in the series three games to one, which made it all the more surprising when they pulled it off and won the series in seven games, becoming, at that point, only the third team ever to come back and win after being down 3-1 in the World Series.

But at the time, no one thought they'd come back, and my father and I stared at the man my father had killed, his open mouth broadcasting the Pirates' highly improbable odds of victory.

My father crouched down next to me and turned my shoulders away from the man.

"Bud."

I kept looking at the blood dripping.

My father stunned me by gently cradling my face in his calloused hands and turning my head away from the dead man until my father had me facing the other direction.

"Bud. Look at me."

I looked up.

"Don't look at him anymore."

"Are you sure he's dead?"

He quietly said, "Yes, Bud. I'm sure."

"What are you going to do?"

"You need to listen to me. What you saw—" He stood up and lit a cigarette. I wanted one, but I was afraid to ask. "Bud. Do you know what I did before I was a trooper?"

My body wouldn't stop shaking. Fear swelled inside me and I focused on trying not to cry in front of my father.

My father said, "Before I was a trooper, I was undercover. Do you know what that means?"

I'd heard the word. But did I know what it meant? I'd seen *Mod Squad* episodes where Linc and Pete went undercover—that was the extent of my understanding, but I wanted to get away from my father and away from the dead man, so I nodded and said as little as possible and let my father say whatever he felt he needed to say. My head felt like it had the day I cracked it open on the school floor and my father's voice was making me sick, knowing that every word he said was another moment I had to stay where I was.

My father's words droned at me with my head aching, and I had trouble making out everything he said because of the pain behind my eyes and because the radio broadcast kept on reporting that baseball game that had just been played in another city, even though someone had just died where I was and I remember being surprised somehow that the world didn't stop. Nothing stopped. Nothing except that one man.

My father told me that he had to kill that man. That he didn't want to, but he had no choice. He knew him when he was undercover, and the man had made my father as a cop. My father said that the man was a criminal who was going to kill us if my father didn't kill him first, as a cop, to keep me and my mother safe.

He told me that if I ever talked about it, that man's friends would come for me and my mother.

"Bud, you have to swear you won't talk."

I nodded.

"Swear, Bud. If you ever tell anyone this, it would be the same as if you'd killed your mother yourself. Do you understand?"

I shuddered. "I swear."

I spent the next four years afraid of my father and of every man I didn't know, thinking, *That could be one of his friends.*

Coming to kill me. Every man at the mall and every man on the street loomed as a deadly threat. I didn't tell anyone. Not my mother, as much as I wanted to, and not anyone even when I left my father's house after she'd killed herself. I didn't say a word about that man to anyone until I was almost ten years older and 1,500 miles away.

When I was eighteen, we found out my mother had killed herself.

My father and I sat drinking in the living room.

I don't know if I'd ever seen my father in worse shape. He could barely walk.

"Maybe you should slow down," I said.

"Maybe you don't know shit about the world. OK, Bud?"

We sat there for a minute and I couldn't help it. I started to shake, and then cry.

"Grow up, Bud. Will you please?"

I tried to stop, tensing my shoulders to stop them from moving. "She's gone."

"She's *been* gone, Bud."

"She's dead, Pop. Doesn't she matter to you?"

"I'm going to give you a life lesson, Bud. Everyone who matters to you? You want to know what life boils down to? They bury you or you bury them."

My father was making me sick. I looked at him and shook my head. I went to my room and took three of the Valium I was supposed to save and only take one when I had an anxiety attack. Or if I felt a manic episode building, they could sometimes help slow me down enough to make me sleep and avoid it coming. But right then, I was just taking them to try to get as numb as possible. I waited until I'd stopped crying. Stopped shaking. I wiped my face and went back to the living room.

I said, "When the hell did she come back to Connecticut?"

My father started to the kitchen. He yelled, "What am I, Bud? The fucking Buddha? I don't know when the fuck she got back, OK?"

"But. She comes back *here* and jumps off a fucking bridge? They have bridges in California. This has to mean something."

My father said, "People like everything to mean something. Some shit doesn't mean anything."

I looked at him and couldn't talk.

He said, "People are idiots. Saying everything happens for a reason." He laughed. "Everything *happens*. Period. End of fucking sentence."

I didn't want to hear his angry drunken theories on life. I hated him at that moment. I was trying to figure out something about her, and he was talking about himself. I looked at the floor and shook my head. "But why would she do this?"

He stumbled over and unsteadily sat on the couch. He sounded calmer. "Bud, your mother was very sick."

"She wasn't always sick," I said, feeling anger, maybe the first swell of blaming my father for her suicide. "And why the fuck didn't you take care of her?"

My father sat up, leaning toward me. "Did it ever occur to you that I tried?"

"Yeah," I said. "And you did a great job, Pop." I got up to take more pills—enough so I could just pass out.

I hadn't even made it to the hallway when I felt his first punch to the back of my head. When I fell at my father's feet, he kicked me in the ribs and I heard and felt them give, and the image of the dead man flashed on me and I wondered if I was about to die. My father kicked me one last time and called me an ungrateful shit.

He beat me badly enough to break my nose and crack two ribs. My right front incisor wobbled under my tongue and blood spilled from my mouth.

My father turned and slammed the door and I heard his pickup truck pull out of the driveway.

I called Jack to drive me to the ER. By then he and I were already in a band that, once Tony and Mickey joined, would eventually morph into the Popular Mechanics. When Jack got to the house, he helped me pack everything I needed to take. I couldn't carry my guitars or amps or much of anything else with my ribs hurting so badly. Jack made several trips back and forth while I leaned against the wall, bent over.

Jack said, "We need to get you to a hospital. We can come back for the rest."

I looked at my blood on the floor. "I'm not coming back."

Jack filled two Hefty bags with my clothes. He grabbed the prescriptions I needed, and he took me to the St. Jude's emergency room.

The admitting nurse looked up when I gave my name.

"Are you Sarah's son?"

I had trouble talking, trouble breathing without it feeling like knives were in my ribs. I nodded.

She looked at me with worry—a look I was already getting used to from women, even if I didn't yet understand what it meant. Didn't understand it was a look that said, *This poor boy is not going to make it in this world without help.* She said, "I'm so sorry about your mother."

Through the stabbing pain I thanked her, and I wondered how some fucking nurse I didn't know could comfort me more than my own father.

In the ER, the doctor asked what happened and I told him I'd been jumped by a bunch of kids. He set my nose, icing it and giving me a local and then using both hands to straighten it as the cartilage sounded like someone was chewing ice inside my whole skull. He wrapped my ribs and gave me a script for ninety Percocets. We filled it at the hospital pharmacy. I took five right away and gave Jack ten as a thank you and we stopped at Louie T's, a mob bar we played at regularly. We got to drink underage whether we were on that night or not. I wasn't even halfway through my first beer when the Percs blossomed throughout my system, and I thought that if I had known how good this could feel, I would have let my father beat the shit out of me anytime he damn well pleased if I'd gotten painkillers after. But he'd never have another chance.

I was up all night on Jack's couch. Within a couple of months, the Popular Mechanics formed and we moved to Florida because Mickey had an uncle who was a booker for East Coast bands and who said he would let us live and practice in a warehouse he owned. I vowed never to see my father again. I was crazy. My mother was crazy. And he probably drove her away, too. I spent years blocking him from my mind, except when I wanted to resent and blame him for what happened to my mother.

I took more painkillers and more Valium and couldn't get to sleep and thought about my mother. She was gone. But she'd been gone for years and I just hadn't known it. I've tried over the years to remember the last time I saw my mother. The last thing I said to her. The last thing she said to me. It could have been *I love you*. It could just as easily have been *Wipe your feet, Bud*. It could have been some slurred nonsense, the way she'd become that last year. The last time I saw her might have been one of those days when she sat in the kitchen chain-smoking and not saying a word from when she woke up until she passed out. It could have been one of the good days when we'd talk for hours. For years I tried to convince myself it could have been one of our Fridays, when she'd take me to the Sam Goody and buy me five 45s or one album. But those days were already over long before she was gone, so I knew it had to be one of the slow, quiet tranquilizer days, though *I love you* was still something she said up until she was gone. I'll never know the last thing she said to me. After a while, what I wished she'd said stopped mattering. No matter how much I tried to remember the last time I saw her, that moment was lost forever. What her lost good-bye left in its wake, though, was an uneasy fear, anytime I've been with someone I loved, that no matter whether it was a beautiful moment, a shitty one, or the calm uneventful boredom of the in-between where most moments live, I might be seeing them for the last time.

I have no idea where my father took the car that belonged to the man he killed, but he drove it away with work gloves on after he'd gotten rid of the body. I have no idea where he took the body, either, and it was never found, as far as I know. Other cops believed my father's story, and no one ever asked my father about that man again. The last I saw of the man he killed was when my father threw him in the back of his GMC pickup and drove out of our driveway and I stood there watching until the truck was a rusted red dot in the distance.

There were nights I'd snap awake, shaking and sweating and mugged by fear, still seeing the man's face and hearing the static and voices from the radio coming out of his mouth, horrified by the blood that kept coming.

Over the years, the nightmare would morph to where it wasn't always the face of the man my father killed but instead the faces of other people I'd seen dead over the next thirty-odd years. Sometimes it was Johnny Mo's father, Al. Sometimes it was Flip. Sometimes other people. No matter how they actually died, they'd be there on the woodpile, their mouths open, with not even death able to end the useless words that spill out of us or stop the bleeding from wounds that never heal.

BROKEN

(1986)

Everything was fine until the band hit Winston-Salem. We were about halfway through the swing up to a gig in Boston, where we'd then turn around and hit the towns we hadn't played on the way up. But Winston-Salem put a snag in the whole deal.

We were playing this club called The Spotlight and the crowd was good. The place even had a marquee with our name in lights above the other bands:

TONIGHT: FROM FL. THE POPULAR MECHANICS

Some local paper had made us a "must see" and described our band as the bastard child of Hank Williams and the Stooges. It was a pretty fair description. We were, at least for the first couple of records, loud, fast, fuzzy, and, on our good nights, a pretty great cowpunk band.

We were supposed to sound-check not long after we pulled into town around seven o'clock. As we loaded our gear in, I saw the bartender. She looked like a tattooed Clara Bow in a black latex dress and knee-high go-go boots, and I walked straight into a table staring at her. She noticed, smiled, and went about wiping down the bar and rinsing glasses.

After we set up and got ready for the sound check, I went over to the bar to get a couple beers and a closer look at the bartender. The tattoo on her left arm, up by the shoulder, was a red-headed Vargas girl.

"What can I get you?" she said in voice that sounded like cigarettes and whiskey.

I asked for two Bass Ales.

She laughed. "You're in redneck central, cutie. How about a couple PBRs?"

When she called me "cutie" my heart quivered. "Sounds great."

She turned around and I watched her muscular ass and thick, cut legs as she bent over to get me my beers. The latex dress rolled slightly up at her thighs, and while I wondered what it would be like to touch her skin, she stood and straightened her dress.

I said, "Isn't it hot in that dress?"

She put the beers in front of me and smiled. "It's always hot in my dress." She popped open a beer of her own and stuck out her hand, which was covered in silver rings. "Simone. Let me know if there's anything you need, OK?"

A couple of hours later, with one of the opening bands playing and the other two bartenders covering for her, I was making out with Simone in the back corner of the walk-in cooler where they kept all the bottles and kegs of beer.

"Go down on me," she said.

I started to lift her dress and she stopped me.

"Just so you know, I have alopecia," she said.

I wondered if it was some venereal disease, but I didn't know how to ask that without killing the mood. I kept kissing her.

She pulled away. "It's just that it weirds some guys out."

I felt like it would be stupid to ask what it was, but I asked anyway.

"I don't have hair," she said. And then she took off her Clara Bow wig. I hadn't looked that closely, but her eyebrows were penciled on, too.

"You look beautiful," I said.

"You're sure?" she said, and for the first time she seemed vulnerable.

I kissed her forehead, then her temple, and I ran my lips softly across her head until she leaned on my shoulder and I licked behind her ear and heard the most beautiful moan I'd ever heard. I couldn't imagine her doubting how stunning she was. What kind of fucked up planet was this if even people who looked like Simone were insecure? What hope did the rest of us have? "Really," I said. "You're the most beautiful woman I've ever seen."

She kissed me gently on my nose, then on each eyelid. She pushed me down onto my knees. She didn't wear underwear. The cold cement floor had puddles of water covered in sawdust and she sat on a wooden chair in the corner with her legs spread and her latex dress up around her waist. She smelled like clean sweat and hospital gloves. I had my arms wrapped under her legs and my hands on her ass. She had the first pierced clit I'd ever seen and I found myself hypnotized, running my tongue from one end of the barbell piercing to the other while I felt and heard it click rhythmically on my lower incisors.

"Not that this pace isn't nice," she said, "but I'm at work, remember."

I sped up, sucking on her clit, feeling the stainless steel balls hard in between her soft flesh. She'd grabbed a shelf with her left hand and the back of my head with her right. She bucked against my mouth, pressing hard against me as she pulled me by my hair, which felt like she might tear it out. I'd never felt so good with anyone. When she came, she screamed loud enough I worried someone outside could hear.

After she caught her breath, she said, "*You* are drinking for free tonight, mister."

I kissed her inner thigh. Her skin was warm. My knees were cold and wet, the water having soaked through the patches on my jeans. I felt like I could spend a long time kissing anywhere on her body she asked me to. I left my head in her lap and felt the hypnotic rumble of the freezer's motor vibrating the chair and Simone's legs. "I thought I was drinking free anyway."

She leaned down and kissed me hard. "Well, I'll just have to think of some other way to thank you." She stood and shimmied her hips back and forth and rolled her dress back down. "Back to the salt mines," she said.

My face was wet and grew cool and I waited in the walk-in cooler until my hard-on went down. I thought about jerking off but got nervous someone would walk in. I took a bottle of Rolling Rock off one of the shelves and drank it, listening to the din of the opening band.

By the time we took the stage, we were all pretty drunk. At that point in our history, the Popular Mechanics were just about as well known for drinking as for our music. By the time the band fired me, a decade later, the joke in the press was that I'd achieved the impossible by being fired by the Popular Mechanics for being too wasted. On a good night like that one—drunk enough to have fun but not so drunk that we'd fall down—it felt like we were one of the better bands around. The crowd slammed in the pit— which is what it was called when it was a natural, spontaneous thing with men and women dancing and banging around. Before it became the ubiquitous macho pile of stupidity that mutated into the "mosh" pit. A few kids rushed the stage only to jump into the crowd. Usually I paid close attention to them, as they were apt to fuck up your pedals or rip the cord out of your amp, but I spent most of our set that night looking up to the bar and watching Simone. Every once in a while, I'd catch her eye and she'd blow me a kiss and send the bar-back kid over to me with another couple of beers.

Near the end of our set, Tony, our bass player who split lead singing duties with me, fell down drunk and dropped his Fender Jazz onto the stage, creating an eruption of feedback from his amp. Mickey, who played guitar along with me, helped him up. We got through two more songs, one of our own and then an up-tempo, sloppy but fun cover of Dylan's "Absolutely Sweet Marie," and then we were done.

The crowd had us back up for two encores. It would have been three, but after the second one Tony passed out under a table in the greenroom. I put him facedown so he'd be able to breathe in case he puked.

After I broke my gear down and loaded it into the van, I asked Mickey and our drummer, Jack, to take the rest of the stuff out so that I could have as much time as possible with Simone.

She said, "Look, I was trying to figure out some coy way to ask you where you were staying and then see if you wanted to come to my place instead. But I figured, what the hell?" She took a drink. "Come back to my place?"

We had to hit the road. I couldn't believe this. I'd never felt anyone's touch be such an electric charge—never met a woman that sexy and forward, which made me weak with desire—and now I had to leave.

"I wish I could," I said.

She looked like she didn't believe me. "You can just say no."

"I don't think I could say no to you," I said. I explained we had to drive to Roanoke where we'd booked one room at some shitbag motel. It was only a hundred or so miles, which normally meant we could stay in whatever town we played and hit the road in the morning, but we had some in-studio live college radio spot we had to be in for around noon the next day, so the plan was to drive on and stay the night in Roanoke.

Most nights, I wouldn't care one way or the other. I actually liked being in the van late at night, having Tony drive to the next town while I drank beer or dozed in the back. Most nights, however, I didn't meet someone like Simone.

"You sure you can't stay the night?"

I thought about asking the guys to play the radio station as a three piece. If they'd do it, I could just hitchhike to the show later in the day. "You don't know how much I'd like to," I said. I looked for the band. "Let me see if I can."

Maybe I'd beg the guys to stay in Winston-Salem. If we got up early, we could still make the radio station. I found Mickey and Jack talking to some woman at the merch table. Tony was still passed out in the greenroom. I told them what was going on.

Jack said, "We already booked the room, dude. Plus, we're doing the radio spot."

"There's got to be a way," I said.

"It's just some fucking chick. Get over yourself." The woman he and Mickey had been talking to told him to fuck off and walked away.

"Nice," Jack said. "You see what just happened there? Thanks."

"What did I do?" I said.

"You scared her off."

"I didn't call her 'some fucking chick.'"

Mickey lit a cigarette. "C'mon. We need to hit the road."

About half an hour later, the guys waited in the van while I made out with Simone in the parking lot. It was cold, down into the 40s, and she'd put her wig back on. She felt incredible and I knew I could spend a lot of time just looking at her eyes or lying naked and trying to remember every freckle or mark on her perfect skin.

Finally, Tony hit the horn and Mickey leaned out the passenger side window and said, "Let's go, Romeo."

I kissed her again and she slipped me a piece of paper with her number and what she said was a gram of coke in some folded magazine paper.

"I had some more at home I was hoping to do with you, but this guy just slipped me this at the bar." She smiled. "For the road."

Coke wasn't really my drug of choice, but it beat being straight and I could stretch my heroin a little longer, maybe. I thanked her and kissed her again. Tony hit the horn several times in a row.

When the van pulled out of the parking lot, she was still standing there, lighting a cigarette and waving good-bye. I thought about just getting out. The band was great, but I found myself thinking maybe this was one of those moments in life where you roll the dice. Maybe this was as close to love at first sight as I would ever get. Maybe my only chance for happiness in this world was standing waving good-bye in a cold parking lot in a town I'd only just visited and might not see again for a long time.

Why we'd let Tony drive as drunk as he was would've been a valid question in any normal situation. But a band on the road, by definition, isn't a normal situation, and Tony was the one who always drove. He was more fucked up than usual, but Jack didn't have a license, mine was suspended, and Mickey couldn't drive anything more complex than an Autopia car. Plus, we were all drunk and it was, for better or worse, Tony's job.

We weren't ten minutes away from the club when I saw the cop's lights in the side-view mirror and heard the siren. I was in the backseat, drinking a beer.

"Fuck," Tony said. "Lose the open containers."

I had, in addition to the open beer, around ten bags of heroin left in my guitar case, but I couldn't worry about that right then.

The immediate concern was the open beer and the gram of coke I had in my jeans. I quickly unfolded the paper, dumped it into my beer, and swallowed the whole can as fast as I could. The first gulp went down pretty easily, but by the second, the coke was already numbing my mouth and throat and I may have spilled nearly as much as I swallowed. I did, however, empty the can and I'd stuffed it deep under the seat by the time the cop rapped on the driver's side window.

Tony had that studied drunk-trying-not-to-sound-drunk casualness. "What's the problem officer?"

The cop asked for the standard license and registration and headed back to his cruiser, telling us to stay put. The cocaine dropped like a calming depth charge into my guts. It felt great, despite my fear. Like I could cut out my own appendix if I wanted to.

Jack was next to me. "You had blow, asshole?"

I tried to answer him but my throat wasn't really working. The coke numbed and froze my vocal cords and I started to panic a little when I realized I couldn't tell if I was swallowing or not.

"You're such an asshole," Jack said.

My chest felt damp. I looked down and saw drool. I felt my lips but only my fingers could feel—the rest might as well have been a doorknob. I wondered if I'd still be able to breathe a minute later.

Tony dropped his license and registration when the cop handed them back, and before I could realize what was happening, the cop had him walking the straight line and trying to touch his nose with his eyes closed.

A minute later, the cop had Tony in the back of his cruiser.

I still couldn't talk, but Jack had gotten out of the van and was talking with the cop. They walked back to the van together.

Mickey turned to me and said, "Bud, would you say something?"

I could barely croak out a noise from my throat.

"What is wrong with you?"

The cop and Jack made it up to the van. I wanted to hate the cop, but he seemed like he was being pretty nice about the whole thing.

"OK," he said. "Any of you rock stars sober enough to get this van back to town?"

I tried not to make eye contact and hoped I wasn't still drooling.

Jack said, "We don't have anywhere to stay. We're supposed to be in Roanoke in the morning."

"Feel free to head to Roanoke." The cop gestured to the cruiser. "But your buddy there's got a room courtesy of the county. I'm sure we could fit the rest of you."

Mickey said, "I can drive."

We had no idea what to do or where to go, so we drove back to the bar and the guys slept in the van all night while I stayed awake and paced the parking lot and chain-smoked in the cold air. The coke had finally mellowed enough so that I could talk and feel myself swallow. But there was no one to talk to with the guys asleep and there was no way I could sleep. Around five in the morning, I found a payphone at a gas station about a mile down the road and called the number Simone had given me.

A woman who didn't sound anything like Simone answered. "Yeah?"

I asked for Simone.

The woman said, "What kind of fuckhead calls someone at five in the morning?"

I started to explain, but she'd hung up.

I bought a cup of watery, burned-tasting coffee and another pack of smokes at the gas station and walked back to the van. The sun was coming up, starting to warm the day, but it was still cold enough to see my breath as I walked down the highway. My eyes felt hot, my jaw ached from clenching it all night against the coke, and my throat was stripped raw from all the cigarettes.

At noon, the guys were still sleeping in the van and I was shaking in the cold when Simone pulled up in a Toyota pickup. At first I didn't recognize her, because she was wearing a Twiggy-style blond wig instead of the Clara Bow look from the night before. She parked two spaces away from the van, and I waved. She shook her head, smiling, and got out of the truck.

"Hey there, you," she said. "What happened?"

"You said you wished I could stay," I said.

She lit a cigarette. And even though I'd probably had two packs overnight, I lit another. She said, "What about Roanoke?"

"Not as important as you," I said, smiling.

She seemed to tire of the flirting. "Seriously."

I told her about Tony getting a DUI and us turning around.

"I tried to call you," I said, "but I think I woke someone up."

"Feather."

"Is that a person?"

"She owns the house I live in."

"She sounded pretty angry," I said.

"She's always angry, whether you wake her up or not."

"Good to know."

Simone said, "And you slept in the parking lot all night?"

"They slept." I gestured toward the van. "I drank that gram of coke when the cop showed up."

"You drank it?"

I nodded.

"What a waste."

"It felt kind of cool, actually," I said. "Except for the cop. And being worried I'd stop breathing. And being up all night. And it being kind of cold."

"Yeah, except for that." She had a bunch of keys hooked through her low-slung jeans with a carabiner run through a belt loop. She pulled the clip off and started toward the door. "Let's get you inside. You must be freezing."

I followed her to the door. Just before she was about to open it, she turned around and kissed me.

"Welcome back."

"Happy?" I said.

"I'd say this falls into the pleasant-surprise category," she said and opened the door.

My jaw was actually chattering. I couldn't stop it. Simone gave me two shots of whiskey and made me a cup of tea. I crashed on the couch in the greenroom. She brought in a space heater and took a couple of coats from the lost-and-found box and put them over me as blankets. One of the coats smelled liked an old lady's perfume. The couch was moist and reeked of mildew and stale beer. She tucked the better smelling coat under my chin.

"Better?" she said.

I nodded.

She sat on the arm of the couch. "So how long are you in town, stranger?"

I had no idea. "Until we can get Tony out of jail, I guess."

Simone said she was going to get the bar set up for opening. I thought that I should get off the couch and call the police station and then Danny at our record company and try to figure out what to do about Tony, but I drifted off to sleep instead.

Around 4:00 PM, I stumbled out of the greenroom, feeling edgy and toxic from being up all night on the coke and cigarettes. The rest of the guys sat at the bar, along with what looked like some daytime barflies. Simone tended bar alongside a guy named Tim. Neil Young & Crazy Horse's "Everybody Knows This Is Nowhere" came out of the speakers.

Jack said, "You get a good nap there?"

"Ease up," I said. "I was up all fucking night."

"Because you were hoarding your blow," Jack said. Mickey nodded.

"I wasn't hoarding the blow." I wasn't sure if this was true or not. I probably would have shared it with the guys. My heroin was mine, but I didn't like coke enough to hoard it. "I just didn't want the cop to find it on me. I had to do something."

That seemed to satisfy them enough to stop scolding me.

Mickey said, "We need two hundred and eighty bucks to get Tony out."

I doubted we had anywhere near that, even if we pooled all our money. And if we did use all we had for Tony, we wouldn't have gas money to get out of town. I shook my head. "What did Danny say?" If he was rolling in money, he was keeping it a good secret.

Jack said, "He's fucking pissed. He's already cancelled the next two gigs." He took a sip of his beer. "Didn't sound like he was darting off to Western Union."

Simone handed me a beer from behind the bar. "If you guys need to raise some money, you could play here and we could pass the hat."

"Don't you have other bands coming in?"

She said, "Tonight's some local band, so it's booked. But tomorrow and Tuesday are just the jukebox, and Wednesday is karaoke."

We looked at each other. There seemed to be a group shrug that suggested we didn't have a better way to make the money.

Jack said, "I'm hoping we're out of this shithole tomorrow."

I was split on that one. We needed to get back on the road and make some money. We needed Tony out of jail. But I could think of worse ways to spend the next couple of days than in this particular shithole. "Well, if we're here tomorrow," I said, "thanks."

"I got your back," she said.

She went down to the other side of the bar to talk to some of the locals and the guys started in on me, mimicking her. Jack sing-songed, "I got your back."

I told him to give me a break.

"Winston-Salem's treating you OK, man."

The door opened and the faint winter daylight came into the bar for a second. A barefoot woman, wearing sweatpants and a 1970s-style halter top came toward the bar. She was clearly drunk and very angry about something. And we found out, pretty quickly, she was angry at Tim. She pointed at him while she addressed us at the bar, "You want to know what this motherfucker's into?"

We didn't say anything.

"Go home, Tammy." Tim didn't sound angry. Or embarrassed. He seemed calm, like this might have happened before.

Tammy had a beer gut with deep, dark stretch marks that looked like earthworms in her skin. Blurry tats blotted her stomach. "You want to know what a sick fuck he is?" she yelled, still pointing at Tim. She pulled her sagging breasts out of the halter top, stepped up by the stools, and started spraying breast milk onto the bar.

"Jesus," Jack said. Mickey and I looked at each other and winced, trying to hide our laughter.

Tammy said, "That's what this fucker's into. I don't even have a kid anymore. They took my kid away five years ago, and this fucking pervert, he keeps me like this." More breast milk sprayed and dripped onto the wood.

Simone shook her head.

Tim said, "Go home. You're only embarrassing yourself."

Tammy put her top back over her breasts and the moisture darkened the halter. She cried. "You fucking bastard."

Tim told her to go home again. She looked at him for a moment. Then she lit a cigarette and walked back out the door. Nobody spoke for a minute, and I heard Tammy rev her engine and tear out of the parking lot to the sound of spinning tires and gravel being tossed.

"Where the fuck are we?" Mickey said. "What is with this town?"

At eight o'clock, Simone got off and asked me if I wanted to stay with her.

"I'd love to," I said.

"What about us?" Jack said. "We need a place to crash."

"My roommate is kind of nuts."

"We're kind of desperate," Jack said.

Simone seemed to be thinking. "Let's take the space heater. If she throws a fit about you guys in the living room, you can stay in the garage."

Mickey said, "The garage? It's freezing out."

"There's no heat in the house, either," Simone said.

She explained that her roommate, Feather, had the only room in the house with heat and that she slept there with her Harley and her teenage girlfriend, who they were hiding from the girl's father and the cops.

"Her father?" I said.

"Allegedly he abuses her, according to Feather at least. And the cops keep coming by to look for the kid and she hides in the crawl space under the house until they leave." Simone put out her cigarette. "I'm warning you guys. The house is kind of nuts."

What qualified as a house that was nuts after the day at that bar? When we walked out, Jack carrying the space heater, I saw that no one had wiped down the bar and Tammy's breast milk had dried to a faded cloudy film on top of the worn wood.

The guys were settled and drunk on the couch, huddled by the heater. I'd brought my guitar and amp into Simone's room, which was cold enough for us to see our breath until her space heater made the corner of the room warm enough for us to take off our coats. I took out my Telecaster, unscrewed the pickguard, and took out two bags of heroin.

"Do you want some?" I said.

"Coke?"

I shook my head. "Heroin."

"I've never had it," she said. "You sure you have enough?"

There was never enough, really. But this was pretty early and I wasn't even using every day at that point, until that tour. Still, I would have preferred to save it all for myself. Especially since we were stuck in Winston-Salem for who knew how long and I might not have enough to get home. "Of course."

Simone pulled a box out from under the bed. "I have a bunch of this shit, if you want some."

I looked in the box. There were about fifty bottles of liquid oral analgesic, stuff for toothaches that was 20 percent benzocaine.

"Where'd you get all this?"

Simone lit a cigarette. "Feather's ex ripped off some pharmaceutical truck making a delivery. She thought she could get Percocet or something, but all she got was ten boxes of this shit." She opened a bottle and downed the whole thing.

I held the bottle up to the light. It was a pale orange and it burned a bit going down my throat and into my stomach. The burning increased on the bottom of my tongue, the taste buds shouting fiery screams for a moment. Warmth and numbness spread through my chest and stomach, like a milder version of swallowing the cocaine.

"Like it?" she asked.

I nodded.

"Have as much as you want. There's a shitload more in the garage."

I thanked her and drank three more bottles. I snorted two decent-sized lines of heroin and laid out a smaller one for Simone. Since it was her first time, it was plenty. A few minutes later, I lit a cigarette and puked in her garbage can—a sign that I'd done enough to feel really good. I put out the cigarette and had a sip of beer to rinse my mouth. I began to peacefully nod and Simone said she needed a nap and flopped back on the bed and fell asleep with me holding her.

A couple of hours later, I was working on fixing some of the solder joints in my amp. The room was so quiet, the only noises were Simone's deep breathing and the *pffft* my soldering iron made every time I cleaned it on the damp sponge. I felt good, floating on the heroin. Felt warm and calm with my head quiet.

She sat up, looking sleepy and beautiful and asked me what I was doing.

"Fixing my amp."

"You good with electronics?"

"Pretty good," I said.

She opened a drawer by her bedside and came out with a vibrator. "This is my favorite vibrator in the world and it stopped working." She handed it to me.

I held her vibrator. I'd already gone down on her, but somehow this seemed like an even more intimate moment. "Sorry it broke," I said. "I don't know much about them, though. I mostly know amps."

"If you could fix it, I would make it so worth your while." She smiled as she lit a cigarette and blew smoke toward the ceiling. "Do you think you can fix it?"

I said, "I can die trying."

It was a loose wire. Easy enough to fix. I handed it back to Simone and she held the end against my lips.

"Taste it," she said. "It's only been on me."

I licked the end.

"Open your mouth," she said.

She shoved it deeper into my mouth, sliding it in and out, smiling at me the whole time. I closed my eyes and felt the hard plastic against my lips and front teeth. When I opened my eyes, she pulled it out and licked it herself, holding it like a Popsicle.

I saw a red scar crisscrossed with thinner, milder stitch-scars across her wrist. Perpendicular to the scar was a tattoo with some word I couldn't read.

"What's your tattoo say?"

Simone stopped licking. She stopped smiling. She lowered the vibrator to her side and looked away. "You mean did I try to kill myself?"

I did, I suppose, mean that, along with the question I did ask. But her tone suggested it wasn't a topic to explore.

She said, "That tattoo says 'The Clash.' My favorite band."

I didn't know what to say. I'd overstepped the bounds of our intimacy. "Great band," I said.

She nodded. "You want to fuck?"

I said yes, then briefly wondered if I'd ever said no to that question in my life. I'd weaseled out of a few *Do you want to make love to me?* situations, but not any *Do you want to fuck?* ones.

Simone said, "I'm going to trust you with something, OK?"

I'd been in love before. Fallen hard and lost all common sense in the swirl and storm of emotion that left nothing but a confusion of desire without words. Not this quickly, though. I'd never been so swept up in the momentum of a person.

"OK," I said. "Of course."

Simone told me her favorite was to get fucked in the ass from behind while she masturbated herself, by hand or by vibrator. "I hope that doesn't weird you out."

"I don't think you could weird me out," I said. "You're the most amazing woman I've ever met."

She tossed the vibrator on the bed. She took off her top. I saw silver barbells through her nipples and realized I hadn't seen her naked yet, even after our time in the walk-in cooler. She opened her button-fly jeans and left them in a pile on the floor and crawled up on the bed. Out of the nightstand drawer, she grabbed a small tub of Elbow Grease and turned to me.

"Strip, and get in bed" she said.

I stripped, jolted with desire from her tone, and crawled up on the bed. My cock was hard and she started stroking it with the Elbow Grease. I groaned.

While still holding my cock, she said, "Don't get too excited. We're going to need this for a while."

Simone got on her knees on the bed and started to spread the lubricant over her asshole with one hand while she balanced on the other one.

She grabbed the back of my hair and pulled me to her ass. I licked her asshole and stroked her wet clit, which was stunningly hard.

"When I say stop, stop," she said. "I don't want to come yet."

I kissed and licked her ass and asshole for about fifteen minutes until she said to stop.

"OK," she said. "I want you inside me. Now go really slowly. And when you're in me, don't fuck me. Just stay in my ass and do as I say."

My face was wet from my tongue and lips mixed with the lube, and I felt dizzy with pleasure. "Whatever you say."

"You always say the right thing."

She put her head down on the pillow. She turned her head so that I could see the left side of her face and see her smile.

"Now," she said, "just follow me."

She reached back and put the tip of my cock against her asshole.

"Now, stay there until I say."

She removed her hand and picked up her vibrator. I heard the whir of its motor start and then the rattling of the vibrator against her clit piercing.

"Now," she said. "Slowly."

I had my hands on either side of her ass, where her hips joined her waist. Her waist was tight and hard and her ass was soft. The space heater was a few feet away on our left, and my left hand and her skin were both much hotter on that side than the right. I slowly entered her and felt a slight resistance and stopped. Then I felt her relax and she pushed her ass backward until I was fully inside her and her ass was firm against my thighs.

She gasped and said "fuck" in a deep throaty voice. "Perfect," she said. "Don't move."

Simone tightened and released her asshole around my cock. It felt like a fuck and a blow job at the same time. I kept my hands gently on her hips, following her body, careful to not push or pull. She turned the vibrator up and started groaning with every thrust of her ass. When she started coming, her asshole shuddered a deep spasm around the base of my cock—contractions, growing tight and then loose as she pushed back hard against me. Her back curved like she was throwing up. She seemed to come several times, though I didn't feel as if I had much to do with it. Still, I was thrilled to be allowed so close to so much unhinged pleasure.

When we finally flopped on our backs, Simone was breathing hard. After a while, her breath started to slow.

"I did," she said.

"What?"

"Try to kill myself."

I didn't know what to say. The moment seemed to call for honesty, so I told her about my mother's suicide.

She said, "How old were you?"

"Seventeen," I said. "Last year of high school." I lit a cigarette. It had been three years, which surprised me. Somehow it seemed so close and so long ago at once. Time folded and expanded around it.

She stroked my chest. "I'm sorry. You don't have to talk about it."

I'd never really told anyone the whole story—about my mother, at least. I didn't tell her much about my dad, other than that I didn't speak to him.

"I was on holiday break, and I got word that she'd jumped off a bridge. Right after Christmas. She washed up on Mother's Day."

Neither of us talked for a while, and I listened to the whir of the space heater and to Simone ticking her cigarette against the ashtray.

"Kinda fucked up Christmas and Mother's Day," I said.

"She probably wasn't thinking about that."

"No," I said and took a drag of her cigarette and handed it back. I wanted some more of the heroin, but I didn't see a casual way out of this conversation. Plus, I needed to make it last, as I had no idea how long we'd be in town. Not that I was in any hurry to leave at this point.

Simone said, "Do you ever think about it?"

"About my mother?"

"About killing yourself."

I did. Not all the time, but often enough to scare myself. Fifteen years later, after the band fired me, I'd intentionally overdose and only survive because a friend came by my apartment unexpectedly. I kissed Simone on the shoulder. "Sometimes," I said. "But not right now."

The space heater burned my side and droned in the quiet of the room. Simone held her scarred wrist up to my face and I saw her tat that read THE CLASH.

She said, "They're something I love. I figured I might think twice next time if there was something I loved there."

I kissed her scar.

We were in bed, making out, with side two of the third Velvet Underground album on repeat. I'd lost count of how many times the arm had reached the end of the record and the needle made a scratching sound, then the arm recoiled and started the record over again.

It sounded like the front door slammed, followed by a woman screaming in the living room, "Who the fuck are you?"

Simone said, "Shit, that's Feather."

A sound, like a plate smashed against the other side of Simone's wall.

I heard Mickey say, "We were invited."

"I invite people into my fucking house! Did I invite you and just fucking forget? Is that what you're saying, asshole?"

I got into my pants as fast as I could. Simone wrapped a towel around her and we went out to the living room.

Jack and Mickey were backed up into a corner, and a woman who looked like Joey Ramone stood a few feet away from them, holding a golf club. I took a step toward Mickey and she swung the club at me, hitting me in the arm. It hurt like hell. I dropped to the couch that Mickey had been sleeping on.

Feather held the club like a baseball bat and readied for another swing at me. I dove to the floor just in time. The club smashed through a lamp on a table by the couch. She was clearly high. Her eyes were nearly all pupil and she staggered after every swing. At the door, across the room, I saw a teenage girl, maybe fifteen, in a cheerleading skirt and letterman jacket.

Simone grabbed Feather and took her a few feet away. I started to breathe easier when she was out of striking distance. Simone spoke with the calm reasoning tone reserved for dangerously insane people. "Feather. These are my friends."

"They're not my fucking friends. I want them out of here!"

Simone shook her head. She turned and mouthed "sorry" to me, and then she asked Feather if they could talk in the kitchen.

I brought the guys into Simone's bedroom.

Jack turned to me. "What the fuck was that about?"

"I guess she didn't know we were here."

Jack said, "We? Who the fuck is 'we'? You were in a bedroom getting laid. We're the one's getting screamed at by the ugliest chick on the planet."

Mickey nodded.

I said, "You're getting screamed at? I just got hit with a golf club, man."

"OK," Jack said. "Fair enough."

The three of us lit cigarettes and waited for the storm to pass in the house. The Velvet Underground still spun on the turntable.

Finally, Mickey said to me, "Did your girlfriend shave her head in, like, the last two hours?"

I told him she was bald.

"I could have sworn she had hair at the bar. Was I that fucked up?"

I was too tired to explain, so I just told him it was a wig and left it at that.

The voices outside the bedroom came closer and sounded calm, so we risked checking it out. The teenage girl still stood by the front door, looking terrified and feral, leaning into the corner of the room. Feather and Simone sat on the couch.

Feather made a kissing noise like she was calling a cat and snapped her fingers a few times. The cheerleader crossed the room and sat on her lap. "How's my baby?" Feather said, running her fingers through the girl's hair. "No need to be scared," she said. "Daddy's here."

The guys and I exchanged looks. Jack closed his eyes and shook his head, looking as if he hoped when he opened his eyes he might be miraculously Somewhere Else.

The next day, we went to the police station and tried to see Tony. They wouldn't let us see him and again told us that two hundred and eighty dollars would get him out.

We spent most of the day at the bar and then played that night with a coffee can tip jar in front of us. Simone introduced us, told the small crowd of regulars why we needed the money, and we started playing. The first set, I played guitar and Mickey sang and covered Tony's bass parts. We didn't sound bad, but it wasn't our crowd. The night before, the place was filled with college kids who loved us. The normal crowd, however, wasn't in love with what we did and the tip jar barely had any money in it at the end of the night.

Some clown with a mullet shouted, "Play some fucking Skynyrd," as we finished the set. He was the first person I'd heard shout "Freebird" without kitschy irony in years. In the greenroom, we decided that the next night we'd try every classic rock song and country standard we knew. Maybe that would make us enough money to get out of town. We counted twenty-two dollars in the tip jar, and I thanked a god I didn't believe in that at least we could drink for free or else we'd be in debt within half an hour.

When we arrived at Simone's house after two in the morning, we were greeted by three police cruisers and their flashing lights in the driveway. They wouldn't let us in the house. They seemed to be there for Feather's girlfriend. Her father was with most of the cops, yelling in the driveway. Feather stood on the porch, screaming at the father, while a cop tried to calm her down. She wore bike leathers and smoked, blowing the smoke above her and away from the cop.

I knew they were here to find the underage girl, but I worried that if they went inside they'd stumble over all the drugs in Simone's room. If Feather was on the porch, that meant the cops, at least some of them, were probably in the house searching rooms for the cheerleader. I was almost out of the heroin—Simone and I had been doing more of it than I anticipated, but I'd hid what was left in my backpack. I'd hid it just because I didn't know Feather and didn't trust her after her crazy outburst, but now with the cops here I felt good that I'd tucked it away. Simone had some blow in her night table. Mickey and Jack had been smoking pot in the living room, and I didn't know if they'd left it in the house or not.

I said to Jack, "You didn't leave any drugs out, did you?"

Jack shrugged.

Mickey said, "This is fucked. We can't get into anymore trouble in this town."

The four of us leaned on the front fender of Simone's truck. The engine was still hot from the drive and made pinging noises as it cooled. Mickey tossed his cigarette down and said, "Someone has to deal with this shit."

He started toward the house and one of the cops stopped him. I couldn't hear what they said, but Mickey nodded a lot, held up his hands like he was giving ground and then he and the cop shook hands and Mickey started up toward the porch where Feather and the cop were still arguing.

The father yelled, "My daughter is in that house! Let her go!"

Feather gave him the finger. "Fuck off, you fucking rapist."

I was drained, starting to get a little dopesick. I needed to get in that house. Simone slipped her hand into the back pocket of my jeans.

"Sorry," she said.

"Not your fault."

Jack said, "Is this whole town crazy? Or just wherever *we* go?"

Up on the porch, Mickey and the cop were talking now. Feather sat down on the steps and stared with hate at the father who was still being herded in the driveway by three cops. Mickey and the cop kept talking, calm and friendly. It lasted another couple of minutes, and then the cop walked toward the driveway and huddled with the others.

Mickey came over to us at the truck and said, "OK, let's go in."

I said, "What did you say?"

"Told them I lived here and asked them if they had a warrant. They said they didn't need one for a kidnapping, but I told them there was no girl here."

"And they believed you?" Simone said, quietly.

"They seemed to," he said. "They're like anyone. They want their job to go as easy as possible." He shrugged. "Cooler heads prevailed. Lazier ones, too."

Mickey became Feather's favorite person after he rescued her from the cops. Inside, the cheerleader, whose name was Sally, climbed out of the crawl space under the pantry in the kitchen, still dressed in her high school cheerleader outfit, now covered with dirt and clumps of spiderwebs from her hiding place.

Feather said, "You guys get high?"

Mickey said of course, and the four of them started a meth bender that, from the sound of things, went on all night long while Simone and I went back to her room.

There was less heroin than I thought, and we did all that I had left, which for me was only a maintenance dose. This wasn't good, since I'd been doing so much I was bound to get dopesick pretty bad. But I couldn't think about that then—I was in a good mood and in Simone's bed with the first Violent Femmes album playing in the background.

I thought about telling Simone I loved her. I wondered if that was even possible. What had it been, three days? But it was possible, wasn't it? The world was so enormous, so complex. People could know each other for years and never love each other. Why couldn't someone you just met seem like someone you've known for years? I didn't know what to say, so I kissed her. We made out for a couple of minutes. She looked at me with a frightening vulnerability and said, "Do you really think I'm beautiful?"

"I've never met anyone more beautiful than you."

She didn't cry, but her eyes started to well with tears. Not quite enough to fall down her cheeks. "You're the only person who's ever made me feel beautiful."

I ran my hand over her arm, feeling the cool skin. I kissed her over each eye, where her eyebrows would have been if she had them. Then, gently, I kissed each closed eye. How could I leave? I dropped my head in her lap while she stroked my hair.

Later, she tied me to her bed, spread-eagled and blindfolded.

"Trust me?" she said.

I said yes.

I heard her leave the room. I worried for a moment that one of the guys or Feather would come in. After a minute, I relaxed and felt the blindfold sitting tight and comfortable, pressing my eyes into darkness. I tried to see, but I could only get a shard of blurry light from the corner of one eye. My cock was hard. The restraints felt wonderful as I pulled against them.

I heard the door open and close. Quiet, barefoot footsteps on the hardwood floor came toward the bed. Simone grabbed my cock and then gently stroked it. As she slowly reached the tip, I arched my back, trying to stay in contact with her hand, and she laughed as she pulled out of reach.

"Now, this won't hurt. But trust me and don't move too much, OK?"

I nodded.

I heard the sound of some electric motor starting up. It sounded like her vibrator, but stronger. Louder. Then I felt cold metal flat against my pelvic bone and I realized she was shaving me with an electric razor. She ran it across my balls and I flinched a bit.

"Don't worry," she said. "Just breathe."

When she shaved around the cock, she'd hold it away from the razor to gain access to whatever area she worked on. I felt the space heater intensely on the right side of my body, cold air on the left side. The space heater oscillated, and every time it passed my cock I felt a rush of warm breeze.

I heard the *whoosh* of a shaving cream can and then it felt cold as she spread cream over my cock and balls. I shivered. Simone laughed.

"Almost there," she said.

I tensed at first when she ran the razor over my skin. But soon I fell into a hypnotic trust unlike anything I'd ever felt before. The blade ran down the sides of the base of my cock. Over my balls and inner thighs. Across the skin above my cock. After every couple of razor strokes, I heard her tap the razor against the side of a bowl that sounded like it had water in it. A couple of times, she toweled me off and inspected her work and then used a little more shaving cream and ran the blade over a small area of skin. When the breeze from the heater crossed my cock, I felt the air like I hadn't before. The skin was more attuned, more sensitive to everything—touch, heat, motion.

She toweled me off one last time with a dry washcloth.

The next thing I felt was her lubed hand stroking my cock for a minute or two. She'd bring me to the verge of coming and then stop.

Then she fucked me, reverse cowgirl at first before she ended up lying with her back on my chest, grinding her hips up and down as she stroked herself. I felt her fingers, whenever she rubbed herself, at the bottom of my cock. I came and she kept rubbing her clit. When my cock slipped out of her, she used it to rub against her clit until she came.

My wrists hurt from her weight causing me to pull at the restraints. I had cramps in my hips. She collapsed on me for a while, then she rolled over and kissed me.

She untied me and took the blindfold off. I blinked, adjusting to the candlelight in the room. My wrists tingled as the circulation returned to normal.

I looked down at my shaved cock and balls. Simone bent down and kissed my cock a couple of times softly. She came up and ran her fingers over and then between my lips. I sucked them until she pulled them out and kissed me, my lips tasting like her pussy and my come.

"Thank you," I said.

"Was that OK?" she said. "What I did?"

I didn't know exactly what she was asking. Was it OK that she shaved me and fucked me? Or that the act of shaving me made me, in some small way, more like her? More like what I had told her was part of her beauty? Either way, the answer was yes and I told her so.

The next day, I was starting to feel the effects of running out of heroin. The flulike symptoms had started and I was hours away from a misery that would last at least a few days unless I did something. I'd only been dopesick a few times—and it was nothing compared to what would come over the years. Even then, though, I knew withdrawals were ugly.

I drank ten of the small bottles of dental analgesic, and that helped for a while. But by midafternoon, I was starting to get cramps. There was no way I'd be able to play at the bar.

Simone had gone out for coffee. When she got back, I was shivering at the end of the bed. "What's wrong?"

I told her.

"You have a habit?"

"I've been good about never doing it too often before this tour," I said. "Never more than two days in a row." Which wasn't entirely true, and I felt bad immediately about lying to her. I told her I needed to get some dope.

"I have no idea where I can get you heroin."

"I need a script for something, then."

She rubbed my back. It felt good, as good as anything could feel at that moment. "I don't know any doctors who'd write one."

The only way to get opiates at an emergency room was to have a real injury. You could scam a GP or pain doctor with some phantom back pain if you were thirty-five and wore a suit, but for people who looked like me, you needed to be broken or bleeding.

"I need a big favor," I said.

Simone kissed my cheek. "Jesus, you're sweating."

"It's going to get worse," I said. "Please. If I ask you to do something difficult, will you do it?"

"What?"

I dropped to my knees and crawled over to my amplifier. "I'm going to put my pinky under this amp and I need you to sit, quickly and really hard, on it."

"What the fuck are you talking about?"

"I need you to break my finger."

"That's crazy."

"I need some pain pills," I said. "I promise, I'll use them just to keep from getting sick. But I can't be like this on tour. If the guys see me this bad, it could fuck up everything."

I looked at her with pleading eyes.

She lit a cigarette. "I can't do this."

"Please?" I said. "Please do this and drive me to the ER. I need this."

"I can't hurt you, Bud."

"Trust me," I said. "You'd be helping."

She smoked and looked away for a minute. Then she ground the butt into the ashtray sitting on the bed.

"This has to be fast," she said.

I lifted the amp off the floor and slipped my right pinky under the corner of it. If I broke the right pinky, I could still play guitar. Any other finger and I was fucked, but this one I could work around.

"OK," I said.

Simone shook her head a few times. She paced from one side of her small room to the other. I closed my eyes, waiting for the pain.

I was just about to say please again when I felt an electric shock on the big knuckle of the pinky. It sounded like a stick popping and cracking under a boot in the woods. The pain went all the way up my arm. I instinctively pulled away while she was still on the amp and tore the skin off the back and top of my finger as I did. The amp clunked on the floor when I got my finger out from under it. The fingernail ripped halfway out and dripped blood. I screamed and curled up in the fetal position. After I'd screamed the first time, I caught my breath and screamed some more.

"I'm so sorry," Simone said. "Oh, god."

Sharp pain throbbed all the way through my arm, exploding into more pain in the hand. I'd fucked up the finger more than I'd wanted to. At least it looked that way, skin stripped down to the bone, over the second and third knuckles. And it seemed broken at the big knuckle, already swelling to twice its normal size.

At the ER, after a three-hour wait, we got in to see a doctor. A doctor who didn't seem to care very much and who, after a quick look at the finger, cleaned it up and put it in a splint. He seemed like he was going to leave it at that and I started to get desperate.

"Can you give me something for the pain?" I said.

Simone looked away. I couldn't tell if it was from embarrassment or if she was angry at me in some way.

The doctor said it should be fine in a few days.

"I'm a musician," I said. "I'm on tour. I need to play tonight." I thought for a minute and lied, "I'm on the road for another month. If it hurts at all in the next thirty days, I'm in real trouble."

He nodded and scribbled on his script pad and handed it over. I didn't look at it while he was there, fearful that by appearing desperate, he might snatch it out of my hand.

Out in the parking lot, I finally checked the script.

"Fuck," I said.

"What?" Simone said.

"It's for Tylenol 3. With codeine."

"Isn't codeine good?"

"Not break your finger good," I said. But it was something, even if it was only for sixty shit pills. Only good for a few days if I wanted to get high, but they could last longer if I used them to avoid getting sick.

It wasn't until Simone pulled in to the parking lot at the pharmacy that I realized I had another major problem: I had four rumpled singles and some change in my pocket.

"I'm really sorry," I said. "But I'm broke."

She looked over at me for a second. She closed her eyes and shook her head. In a clipped voice she said, "Give me the script."

Simone slammed the car door and went into the pharmacy.

This started the pattern of the next twenty-five years of my life. Depending on women to save me, take care of me, heal what was broken and make me feel, however briefly, worthy of love. But in less than one week's time, I'd already become a creature so needy I was starting to wear thin. Starting to tax the compassion of the woman rescuing me, which would become a pattern in my life, too.

I lit a cigarette and waited for Simone. I shivered in the car. The sky turned the color of aluminum and it looked like there might be a storm. The air felt heavy and wet, and I wondered if it was cold enough that we might see snow.

Simone got in the car and tossed the bag with the pills on my lap.

I chewed two and waited for some relief.

"Do you want some?" I said.

"Don't worry about me," she said. "You *need* them."

"Did I do something wrong?" I said.

"You made me break your fucking hand," she said.

"Finger."

"Oh, finger. That's totally different." She cracked her window and blew angry smoke in front of her that got sucked out of the car. "Sorry to overstate. It was only a finger."

"What's the problem here?" I said. I still felt sick. The codeine hadn't kicked in, and I felt icy painful cramps everywhere. My mouth filled with saliva and I worked hard to hold the puke down as long as I could.

Simone looked at me, then back to the road. "You really don't see the problem?"

"No," I said quietly.

"With what you made me do?"

"I didn't make you do anything."

"You begged me," she said. "And I fucking *cared* about you, so yes you fucking did make me do it."

I took some more breaths and it seemed like I might not throw up. I looked down at my splinted finger, wet with bloodied gauze. I held it up. "I'm the one who got hurt here."

"No," she said. "You're the one with the broken finger." She tossed her cigarette out the window. "You're not the one who got hurt."

Back at the house, I found out that Feather had driven Mickey to the Western Union, where our record label had wired us the money to get Tony out of jail. When Simone and I got out of her truck, Tony was there, looking pretty dazed and angry, and the band's van was already packed. The guys stood around, seeming to expect me and Simone to have a long, drawn-out farewell. But from the way she moved and the hurt look in her eyes, it seemed that we'd already parted in some fundamental way.

Jack went into the house and got my amp, since I couldn't carry it. I followed, grabbed my guitar case and backpack with my one good hand, and came out on the front porch where she was waiting, smoking a cigarette and not meeting my eyes.

I wanted to say I was sorry I'd done it. Sorry I'd hurt her in some way I still didn't fully understand. I wanted to say I loved her, and I wasn't sure it would have been a lie. But I knew, truth or not, the chance to say it was in the past.

There seemed to be some small forgiveness, though, when I put my guitar case and bag down and she put her arms around my neck. I had my hands around her waist, holding her firmly with my left hand and as gingerly as possible with my broken right one. She wore the same Clara Bow wig she'd worn the night we met and I tried to study her face, to remember it, knowing even in the moment that no matter what else life had in store for me, I wasn't going to meet anyone else quite like her.

The van was running and the guys waited. And if Simone didn't seem filled with love and destroyed to see me go, she didn't seem mad anymore, either. There was something enormously kind and sad about the way she kissed me and then broke our embrace and stepped back.

Before I turned to go back to the van, she said, "Please, Bud. Take care of yourself."

INTERSTATE

(2003)

In Salt Lake City, you could still sell your blood. Most states, when the AIDS crisis hit hard and fast in the 1980s, they stopped buying blood. It made sense. People who sell their blood—that's the blood you don't want, pretty much. So when Flip and I found out from the kid at the All-Niter Motel that we could pick up a few bucks in the morning selling blood, we stopped rationing and budgeting and we drained our pockets to keep the party going.

The kid's name was Norman, and he was next door with his girlfriend, Trudy, who was pregnant. They were Mormons, from what I gathered. Or at least they were from Mormon parents, because they talked about how stupid and oppressive Mormon families were, and they were maybe eighteen and dressed all Summer of Love. They talked hippie shit and used words like "copasetic." If the Dead still had been around, these two would've been following them and trading crap bead necklaces for veggie burritos, thinking everything was right with the world.

But in the motel room, they buzzed like 60-cycle hum and listened to the jumpy lameass crap of Dave Matthews or John Mayer or Jack Johnson or one of those edgeless guys. Music that'd been Zambonied. All the roughness and the dings replaced with consumer-friendly sheen.

"You guys want an attitude adjustment?" Norman said. This was hippie talk for *Do you want to get stoned?*

Flip said, "What the fuck are you talking about, kid?"

The kid had puppy dog eyes, sloppy with trust. He said, "We've got some bud and some E, some speed, next door, man. We heard you guys opening cans, and we were thinking about some bartering."

Barter. More hippie talk. Burning Man talk.

"We?" said Flip.

"Me and my girlfriend," Norman said.

"Bring your drugs," Flip said, looking at me. I shrugged. I could've used some speed or some E if I was going to stay up drinking all night. Flip said, "Let's party."

The kid smiled. He said "copasetic" and went back to his room.

Flip was from Florida, and I was leaving Florida. I'd only gone back there to be with my ex-girlfriend Jess while her mother died, but Jess and I died before the mother did, and Jess kicked me out. So, Flip and I were driving a car from Florida to Los Angeles. It was supposed to be just me driving for this transit company that paid me three hundred up front and three hundred when I delivered. An eBay car: a 1974 Dodge Dart. The guy must have paid as much to transport it as he did buying the damn thing.

I was a line cook with Flip in Sarasota, and he'd had a connection for some cash, so he caught the ride. I knew very little about Flip before the drive—we worked staggered shifts as grill cooks at this tourist shitfest called Cha-Cha's Bar and Grille in Sarasota on Turtle Bay. I only saw Flip after my shifts. I'd be covered in grease and beaten down by the world, and we'd have drinks at the bar. If I'd known more about him, maybe I wouldn't have gotten involved, but there was time and money invested at that point. Pot committed, as they say in poker.

The deal? Flip and I were picking up a drug package in Salt Lake. A package from some chemist, some anti-government militia nut job named Clay. I didn't know if Clay was his first or last name. Or even his real name. But early the next morning, we would pick up a package. We'd drive the package to Long Beach, California, where we'd meet some guy named Ron who worked at FedEx, loading toxic and explosive shit on their high-security flights. We'd give the package to Ron, and he would check it out and give us a boatload of cash.

"How much?" I asked Flip, when he told me about his connections.

"Big money," he said. "That's all I know."

"What's in the package?"

He shrugged. "Meth?"

"You sure?"

"Nope," he said.

A finger of doubt poked me lightly, lifting my insides the way they lifted at the first drop of a roller coaster. "Can be dangerous," I said. "Meth people, I mean."

"So can falling in the shower," Flip said. "Lot of dangers in this world."

"What if it's not meth?" I said.

"Then it's not meth," Flip said. "People who need to know what's in their package don't tend to make as much money." He lit a cigarette and cracked the window. We weren't supposed to be smoking in the car, but we figured we could just say the guy who sold it lied about being a nonsmoker. "Or live as long."

We were due in Long Beach late the next night. Then, I might go to Vegas, where I knew some people who'd let me crash at their place while I looked for work. I had a buddy who dealt Twenty-one at Binions and said he might be able to get me some work there or else in Jean, twenty miles down the I-15. Or I could play cards, which I was good enough to do, and had done. Maybe I'd go back to Florida, to my shit job and shit life. But probably not. What I'd left there, I didn't need. Some clothes in a month-to-month room and an ex-girlfriend who could effortlessly catalog my numerous flaws but had only a dim recollection of any good qualities she used to see in me. My cat, Lumpy, had died a while back. Nothing left to miss.

Either way, I had to get my shit together. I was thirty-seven, a few years removed from my music career, and staring down too many years ahead of me like the ones behind me. I needed cash to get started. Which was why Flip was in the car and in my life.

Norman's pregnant girlfriend, Trudy, snorted lines of their meth in our hotel room. Norman talked Flip's ear off about some jam band shit on the boom box they'd brought in. It wasn't Phish, but it could have been. Noodles and noodles of aimless guitar wavered and loitered out of the speakers. I would have died for some Jason and the Scorchers then. Some Tex & the Horseheads. Thelonius Monster. Something that didn't suck.

"What'd you do to your hand?" Trudy said to me.

My right hand had two freshly broken fingers and some small crushed bones—the first break ever on my ring finger and the second on the pinky. The pinky had always ached, but at least it'd reminded me of Simone. Not my best moments with Simone, but still. The new break would forever remind me of the shit my life had become. A guy I owed some money to crushed it with a brick on the lid of a dumpster two days before we left Sarasota. Another reason not to go back. I had my right pinky and ring finger duct-taped together. I hoped to get them looked at when I got somewhere and stayed put for a while. I wondered if my hand would ever heal properly to let me play guitar like I used to. After Winston-Salem, I could still play with a pick, but I'd never fingerpicked the same again. The right hand was too messed up, and now it would be worse than ever. Still, it could have been my fretting hand, and that would have ended any and all guitar playing. So, it could have been worse.

"An accident," I said. I looked at the tortured hand and got depressed I didn't play much anymore. I got more depressed for the reasons I wasn't playing: my old band was still touring and selling records, while my life stagnated. I had nobody to blame but myself, and this hit me all at once, like an air-conditioned bar you walk into on a hundred-degree day.

"Well, yeah," she said. "I figured *that*." She smiled at me. "You're cute."

I looked over at Norman, who was talking motorcycles now with Flip.

"Thanks," I said.

"Don't I know you?" she said.

Norman and then Flip looked over at me. I'd still get that sometimes. Less often, it seemed, every year. One of the regulars at the bar in Sarasota told me I looked like the guitar player from the Popular Mechanics. I was half-flattered to be remembered and half-horrified at where I was. I told him I wasn't, and he replied, "Well of course you aren't. Like he'd be *here* cooking for me!" I laughed and wanted to grab him by the back of his head and smash his teeth out on the fucking bar.

Norman said, "You're that dude from that band." He stared at me for a moment. "I saw you guys on TV."

Normally, I just tried to deny it. But people liked to give drugs to guys in bands. Sometimes you could use it, even if you were no longer in the band. "I haven't been with them for a while. Kind of between projects," I said.

"You play music?" Flip said.

"Like I said, it's been a while."

Norman said, "I thought I saw your band . . . I'm sorry, dude, I forget your band's name."

I told him.

"I thought I saw you guys on TV just a while ago."

"They're still playing," I said.

Trudy said, "Doing your own thing?"

I shrugged. "Yeah." *I'm doing my own thing.* Pathetic. I lit a cigarette, having trouble with my lighter and my fucked-up hand. I winced and shook the hand.

Trudy pushed the mirror to me.

I did a line. I didn't like meth, but what the hell? Anything that would stop them from talking about the band. I drank half of my Mickey's Big Mouth in one gulp that strained my throat.

Trudy took the mirror back and snorted another line. She leaned back her head like she was looking at the ceiling and snorted her speed snot into her throat then wiped the back of her hand all over her face. Scabs all over her arms. Picker's disease. Typical meth-head. I wondered if I should be contributing to this cycle. Her kid would be fucked in more ways than I could count. She was a mess. And she was only a kid herself. Soon I'd be picking up a package from this Clay somebody or somebody Clay. A package that lead to shit, to lives like Trudy's.

It was none of my business. But my conscience butterflied all over the place and it landed, briefly, on Trudy. I thought about my mother. Wondered what she might have done or not done before I was born.

I said, "You sure you should be doing that?"

She looked at me, her face blank as drywall.

"With a kid on the way and all," I said.

Flip shot me a dirty look. I took a hit of pot from a joint Norman passed to me. Skunky. Kind of wet and resin-y. I felt the pulse of anxiety behind my eyes and took another hit before handing it over to Trudy.

Trudy said, "I won't be pregnant much longer."

She looked huge. Easily third trimester. "Abortion?" I said.

"No," she said like I was an idiot. "I won't be pregnant much longer."

Norman said, "She's due in a month, dude."

I finished my beer. "Gotcha," I said.

Norman was jacked on the meth. His attention flittered on to me. He said, "Dude, like in a month, like, we've got this plan, right?" He snorted another line and lit a cigarette, wiping his nose repeatedly on the back of his hand while he sniffed. He clicked his Zippo open and closed about twenty times quickly until I thought I might punch him for that alone. He said, "Like, we're going to these friends in NoCal, right, and we're, like, having a ceremony."

"Ceremonies are ace," Flip said.

Norman nodded.

I looked at Flip and wondered if he was being nice to the kid for the meth, or if he believed what he said. I was trying to stay straight enough to think about this Clay we were supposed to meet with. And to keep tabs on Flip. The kid droned in back of me. He was a hornet's nest, a transistor radio between stations. I wanted to shut the fucker off.

I shook my head. It was like my brain'd been laminated. The pot was strong and it mule-kicked my head. I needed to focus. I made a mental list of things to do, early the next morning:

1. Pick up the package
2. Sell blood for gas and beer money
3. Drive the fifteen or so hours to Long Beach and drop off the package with FedEx Ron
4. Get some sleep, somewhere

After that, I would drop off the car in LA, and then I was free to do whatever I wanted. To start my new life. Clean as new chrome.

I saw myself dealing cards in Jean. The desert sun announcing another beautiful morning though my closed blinds. A life better than this one. It was—I had to remind myself—possible.

Meanwhile, Norman talked like a fucking filibuster. Like a skip in a CD.

Most of it I didn't catch, and then he said, "Right, man, and after that, we all eat the placenta."

"What?" I said.

"Part of the ceremony. And I'd understand if you don't understand, 'cause that's part of why me and Trudy are heading north to NoCal, 'cause, like, nobody understands."

"You eat placenta?" I said.

Norman said, "It's part of the ceremony."

"What's placenta?" Flip took a drink of the Mickey's Big Mouth. "Some Mexican shit?"

"It's my union with the baby," Trudy said.

Flip blinked. "What?"

"It's a Native American ritual," Norman said.

"I don't follow," Flip said.

"A *ritual*," Norman said.

I hated it when people repeated themselves and thought that this made things more clear. "I don't think it is a ritual," I said. "I think you've been sold a pile of shit."

Flip said, "What the fuck is placenta?"

I said, "It's the gooey shit that comes with the baby."

Flip laughed.

The two kids looked at him, confused.

Flip was still laughing. "Fuck you," to me. He looked at the kids. "You're serious?"

I said, "That's what it is."

"But that's disgusting," Flip said.

I said, "That's what I'm telling you, man."

"No," Norman said. "It's the ritual."

I wondered how fucked up these kids' home lives had to be to make getting pregnant at eighteen, snorting meth, and eating placenta seem like a road you wanted to go down. But then, I was no poster child for what to do with your life.

"It's my union with the baby," Trudy said again.

Flip blinked, methed and cartoony. He'd gone Tex Avery and Chuck Jones on me, and I half expected to see his eyes jump out of his head and snap back to the sound of an aooga horn. "You eat the baby goo?" he said.

"It's full of protein," Norman said.

"So's cheese," Flip said. "Eat some fucking cheese if you want protein."

Norman said, "What's your guys' problem?"

I wanted to leave. Though I didn't know why I was so edgy, other than I was angry at myself and depressed at seeing people younger than me do the shit that led to where I was. I knew what happened when you took the wrong forks in a lot of roads. They might not have known how off-course they were.

Flip handed me the joint. "We need to mellow."

Norman nodded. "Time for an attitude adjustment, dude."

I tried to smile. "Sorry. I'm a little tense."

"You want some E?" Trudy said.

"That might help," I said.

"Give me six of your beers," she said.

I had fourteen left. Flip drank less than me. I could've used the E, but it could keep me up all night, especially with the line of meth, and then I'd have to slow my drinking.

"Four," I said.

"For four, I want you to make out with me," Trudy said.

I looked at her. At Norman.

Trudy said, "It's cool. We're not into that jealousy trip."

I was not into pregnant women. We all have our things. With me it was a woman's ass, or a well-muscled leg. Garters. Glasses.

I was a fucking sucker for the slutty librarian look. I thought of all the bookish, pierced, and pervy Florence Nightingales in fishnets and tall boots who'd rescued me over the years. But I'd never jerked off thinking about a pregnant woman. Or a teenager. Let alone a pregnant teenager who was young enough to be my daughter, if I'd been as sloppy and dumb as she was when I was her and Norman's age.

But it was two extra beers and some E.

"Deal," I told her.

It was 4:00 AM. There was the promise of a hot day, and the sun was in its starting gates behind the mountains. Flip was out in the parking lot, pacing. I saw his shadow cross the window of the motel room every few minutes. Norman strummed in an awkward rhythm on a plinky acoustic guitar and sang "Wonderful Tonight" in a warbly voice, rough and choppy as whitecap waves to Trudy, who was making out with me. She had a beautiful tongue, with a massive metal stud in the middle that slid on my lips and clunked on the backs of my teeth as she worked herself in and out of my mouth. Kind of a greedy kisser. She took my lips and tongue deep in hers and sucked hard. I felt and tasted blood, to the point of a really nice pain, in the compression between her lips.

She ran her hands over her huge stomach. Then down between her legs.

"I need to come," she said.

I was horrified I was supposed to do something more, but she started rubbing herself feverishly and I was enormously relieved.

"Being pregnant makes me so horny," she said in a shy voice, with a smile that reminded me how incredibly young she was. I didn't want to upset her moment, but the situation was throwing me out of my buzz. A jolt of self-loathing hit like thunder in my head. She kissed me some more and sucked hard on my tongue while she bucked on the bed, coming repeatedly for about a minute. I watched her hand moving in fast circles, her picker's scabs a blur of activity. Trudy screamed "Fucking YES!" three times. It dominated the sound in the room, even with Norman abusing his guitar. She flopped back on the bed.

"I need to pee," she said.

Norman laughed. "You always need to pee, girl."

Trudy waddled to the bathroom and left the door open as she sat. "I'm *pregnant*, Norman."

Norman looked at me. "She's *always* had to pee lots."

I walked outside to see if I could clear my head and if I could find Flip.

There was no sign of Flip. I walked east, toward the temple that ruled people's lives in that odd town. I had a beer in my pocket and I was careful not to make a show of it, since Salt Lake was a place where they would actually put you in a cell for drinking in public.

The E had me wide awake, but kind of fuzzy. Everything was out of focus and my broken fingers didn't hurt at all. The E tablet was thicker than usual, and I thought I might have taken ketamine by mistake. Which was cool by me, since ketamine was a painkiller in addition to being a hallucinogen and tranquilizer. I started shaking my hand in the air, trying to feel the pain of my broken fingers. I couldn't. I touched my numb, messed-up hand. The hand I used to make a living with. The hand reduced to a swollen clot of fingers. The hand that if I hadn't fucked up might still be playing guitar, not stuck in Salt Lake doing the shit I was doing.

I pounded my broken hand against my thigh to see if I could make it hurt, but I couldn't. I'd done real damage to this hand. The worse it got, the harder it would be to play guitar again, and I found myself filled with anger at what I'd let happen.

I took the beer out of my pocket and drank it in two big gulps. I held the green bottle up to the streetlight and looked at the world through the green for a second.

I put my right hand out in front of me and chopped down on it with the beer bottle. I heard a dull *thuck*, felt my arm jerk down from the pressure of the impact, but no pain. I swung again. And then again. It made a wet sound. A fish on a chopping board. I tried it three more times, but I couldn't break the bottle or make my hand hurt much, so I tossed the bottle toward a pile of dirt in an abandoned lot and kept walking.

The ecstasy had kicked in and my brain relaxed. I felt so light it was like I could feel the gravity of the air, the weight of everything around me, even the dust landing on the world. I stuck my hands out. Closed my eyes. Opened them. Spun around. Still no pain, no matter what I did to the hand. The world, for a very brief moment, seemed impossibly beautiful. I thought about the day ahead of me, and the money, and the new life, and everything seemed good.

I turned around and headed back to the motel. A semi blew by me and kicked up wind and chilly dirt from the side of the road.

I got back around six in the morning. I didn't have our room key and I knocked on our door. No sound came from inside. I went next door and tried the kid's room but there wasn't anyone there, either. The car Flip and I'd driven from Florida was still in the lot. Early morning light flashed off the glass, making it hard to see into our room, and it took my eyes a minute to adjust before I saw a couple of legs between the bed and the bathroom.

I knocked harder. Some guy from a couple of rooms away screamed at me to shut the fuck up and I finally kicked near the lock, thinking it would take more power than I had, but it tore and splintered the doorjamb on the first try.

Flip was face down, OD'd, on an orange carpet blotted with dark stains. I said his name more times than I could count and rolled him onto his back. Next to his body was a slimy, thick pool of white, foul-smelling foam that had trailed from his mouth.

I turned away and threw up, leaning on a table, and once I caught my breath I went to feel for a pulse but gave up when I realized that the table and Flip were the same temperature.

The kids had stolen all of our drugs and beer. All of our cigarettes. I'd left my clothes—and a meager supply of Xanax—in my bag in the car. I'd felt like an asshole when I did it, but I felt like a genius now.

The keys to the Dart were in Flip's pockets. I got out of that room as fast as I could.

In the car I tried to think. We'd paid for the room in cash. No names. Clay only knew Flip. The kids stole our drugs, so they wouldn't mention that part of the night even if they bragged about meeting That Guy from That Band. Plus, they would be dead soon enough if they pulled that shit too many times.

I drove as slowly and calmly as I could on my way to the blood bank. My right hand hurt too much to steer. It was brutally swollen around the duct tape on my fingers. My watch looked like a tight rubber band on my wrist. From the forearm down, everything was a bluish purple.

I still couldn't feel a thing, other than the swelling putting pressure on the tape. I started to get scared. I didn't have any beer or pain meds or money, and I kept smelling the room and seeing Flip on that carpet that I couldn't get out of my head. Of everything in that room, why the carpet?

At eight in the morning, there was a short line to donate. Obvious junkies. One guy so dopesick, I let him ahead of me in line. My hand ached and throbbed. I couldn't believe what I'd done.

When it was my turn, I had to write with my left hand and awkwardly filled out some papers that asked if I'd done IV drugs or if I'd been tested for HEP C, and I filled it out with the right answers, whether they were the true ones or not. My nurse or phlebotomist or whatever was a guy named Jerry, and he seemed pretty nice. I squeezed a Nerf pill that said PFIZER on it. Jerry tied my arm off, and I looked at my swollen vein and wished he would shoot something good in it, rather than take blood out.

"How are you doing today?" Jerry said.

I looked away and hoped Jerry was good at his job. Sometimes you'd get a butcher who took fifteen minutes to get a nice vein. "Pretty good." I wanted to puke.

"Late night?" Jerry said. He undid the latex tie. The room smelled of early morning cleanliness. Disinfectants and rubbing alcohol and latex gloves and powder. Jerry smiled kindly. "Or early morning?"

I smiled back at him and he gave me a weary look that said he'd seen worse than me in that chair. I rolled my head back and felt the pulsing of my body for a moment before he said, "Would you like me to wrap your hand in something cleaner?" Jerry touched the duct tape. "And maybe something . . . more appropriate?"

I got thirty bucks. Jerry gave me some Advil, like they'd do anything, but still it was nice. I pulled into the Sinclair station. Deep stings of pain shot through my hand, like something sharp was tumbling inside me and trying to get out in a hurry. A stampede under the skin. Festival seating.

The sun started to heat the morning. I wondered where Norman and Trudy were, and how far they'd get before they fucked with someone a lot tougher than me or Flip.

Two weeks later, I was staying at our old road manager Nick's house in Eagle Rock. Nick might have been the only old friend willing to take me in. His wife had left and he seemed to want the company—no matter how messed up and broke it was. I slept on his couch in the front room, which was also the storage area for his art-frame poster business of a bunch of bands from the

1980s and 1990s. He even had four of ours, and I looked at four younger, clearly loaded versions of myself—three from concert posters and one from our first record on Matador. The dull eyes made me want to punch the pictures of me—holding guitars I'd long since sold for dope money. A pictorial timeline of me as a loser. The last poster—Nick had three of the same shot—was from the cover of my first solo album. It was a weak record. Me on acoustic, recorded in one day. Really lo-fi demos of a drug addict. But I'd needed the money. The poster was a close-up of my face with my hair going all directions and my eyes dominated by the irises and pinned pupils.

From one poster to the next, I looked about the same except for the length of my hair, the progressively thinner junkie body, and a couple of forearm tats that showed up in the more recent posters. Typical Richard Hell meets Keith Richards with hair that was last combed when Reagan was president. I hadn't combed my hair since the tour where I met Simone. I wondered for a moment about trying to find her. With the Internet, it was possible. It was possible, too, that she'd forgotten or gotten over me and didn't want to see some lunatic who'd begged her to break his hand so he could get a buzz. It was probable that she'd have a heart attack when she found out I was still alive.

At Nick's place, in exchange for meth, I'd traded some of my old clothes to a woman who owned a vintage store in Silverlake. Nick had told her I was in the Popular Mechanics and she wanted to have my clothes for her shop, saying she could sell them on eBay for a ton, so long as I signed a certificate of authenticity next to the clothing while she took a picture.

After she left, Nick said, "Fucking crazy, dude. Getting drugs for dirty fucking laundry."

My plan was to sell the meth and get some dope money. If I tried to sell any opiates, I'd just do all of them. Meth was one of the few things I didn't do much of—I didn't even like it. So, there'd still be some left over to make some money.

A week later, I was doing too much of the meth since it was all I had, and I hadn't slept, and this Russian criminal named Sergei from Long Beach didn't have any money and wanted to pay me with a nine millimeter.

When Sergei offered the gun, I told him to forget it—take his meth and go. I didn't front drugs, but when a guy tells you he has a gun, you just play it as cool as possible and try to keep the situation calm.

He said, "You must have gun."

"I don't like guns."

He said, "Guns just like people, except guns have no legs."

I had no fucking idea what that could mean. "That's cool. I'm just not a gun guy, OK?"

He said, "Then, with interested, I get you back next time, Bud Barrett, rock star, yes?"

The sharp-dressed black guy next to him said, "With interest, motherfucker."

Sergei said, "What?"

"With inter*est*," the other guy said.

"People know what Sergei says," he said. "Fuck you, piece of shit thesaurus in nice suit, you."

I never thought I'd hear from the Russian again, but since he looked like a mountain of 'roid muscle and scar tissue and tried to pay for drugs with guns, I figured it was stupid to press the issue. I took the gun and said sure. We shook hands. "Get me back when you can."

Most of what I remember after that was doing the rest of the meth and being up three or four days and drinking Nick's beer and then gobbling his Ambien and Xanax in an attempt to calm myself down from the meth. I don't remember much after that, but Nick told me—when he visited me in the psych ward a day later—that I'd taken every poster of me I could find and brought them out to his backyard and emptied Sergei's nine millimeter into all three posters of my face.

Nick said, "Dude, you were laughing and shooting your face over and over and you scared the living shit out of everyone. I had to call the cops."

I was pretty sedated by this point. "What are you talking about?"

Nick leaned in close. "Bud, I got the gun away and had a friend get rid of it. You'll avoid a weapons charge."

I actually felt pretty good and the bad news wasn't registering.

Nick said, "You ran away after you tossed the gun."

"Gun?"

"They found you on the sidewalk with meth and some pills." Nick looked around. "You're fucked on a possession charge."

Once they let me out of the hospital, they were going to transfer me to County, but Nick put up my bail and told me on the way home that he was taking my Telecaster and my Tweed Deluxe as collateral. I was still pretty fucked up and could only nod.

My lawyer, Ms. Green, was on my side of the table wearing a suit and looking as hot as Helen Mirren. If things were different— hell, if *I* were different—I would have asked her out. I wore one of Nick's suits that hung on my rail-thin body and I looked ridiculous. Ms. Green and the assistant DA talked back and forth and I really couldn't follow much of it, but I figured they'd come to some agreement and I'd walk out like I had every time before. But while I didn't catch their legalese, it was becoming pretty clear that she wasn't like the lawyers the record companies had always sent in situations like this. She never mentioned music. She never mentioned any redeeming qualities I had. All I could follow was that she was saying I should have another chance.

The two of them walked out and I saw them in the hall. After thirty seconds, both nodded, and my lawyer came back in.

Before sitting down she said, "Their offer is six months in county jail or six months in a drug rehab facility."

I nodded. I still felt sick from not sleeping for days and then being pumped full of liquid diazepam in the psych ward. "OK," I said. "What's the best deal we can get?"

"I just saved your ass with the judge and the DA," she said. "That *is* the deal."

Every other lawyer had gotten me got knocked down to a sentence of community service. And community service was playing music for free.

I said, "You're joking."

She stood looking at me while I sat exhausted. "I *fought* for this." She shook her head. "I don't think you understand the gravity of your situation, Mr. Barrett."

I said, "I can't go to jail."

"Then you're going to rehab."

I'd been to plenty of rehabs, but only before tours when the bookers or the record company needed me clean enough to function. I'd *been* in rehabs—I'd just never stayed in them. Never a full month, let alone six. "There's no way I can make it that long in rehab."

She sighed. "Then you can find out if you can do that long in jail."

I shook my head and picked rehab and hoped I could make six months without fucking up. I did the math. I'd be able to get loaded in just over one hundred and eighty days if I could make it.

A "YES" TO FIVE QUESTIONS MAY BE A WARNING.

A "YES" TO TEN OR MORE QUESTIONS MEANS THAT DRUGS HAVE ALMOST CERTAINLY BECOME A PROBLEM OR ARE BECOMING A SERIOUS PROBLEM.

1. Do you ever use alone? *YES*
2. Have you ever substituted one drug for another, thinking that one particular drug was the problem? *YES*
3. Have you ever manipulated or lied to a doctor to obtain prescription drugs? *YES*
4. Have you ever stolen drugs or stolen to obtain drugs? *YES*
5. Do you regularly use a drug when you wake up or when you go to bed? *YES*
6. Have you ever taken one drug to overcome the effects of another? *YES*
7. Do you avoid people or places that do not approve of you using drugs? *YES*
8. Have you ever used a drug without knowing what it was or what it would do to you? *YES*
9. Has your job or school performance ever suffered from the effects of your drug use? *YES*
10. Have you ever been arrested as a result of using drugs? *YES*
11. Have you ever lied about what or how much you use? *YES*
12. Do you put the purchase of drugs ahead of your financial responsibilities? *YES*
13. Have you ever tried to stop or control your using? *YES*
14. Have you ever been in a jail, hospital, or drug rehabilitation center because of your using? *YES*
15. Does using interfere with your sleeping or eating? *YES*
16. Does the thought of running out of drugs terrify you? *YES*
17. Do you feel it is impossible for you to live without drugs? *YES*
18. Do you ever question your own sanity? *YES*
19. Is your drug use making life at home unhappy? *YES*
20. Have you ever thought you couldn't fit in or have a good time without drugs? *YES*
21. Have you ever felt defensive, guilty, or ashamed about your using? *YES*
22. Do you think a lot about drugs? *YES*
23. Have you had irrational or indefinable fears? *YES*
24. Has using affected your sexual relationships? *YES*
25. Have you ever taken drugs you didn't prefer? *YES*
26. Have you ever used drugs because of emotional pain or stress? *YES*
27. Have you ever overdosed on any drugs? *YES*

Do you continue to use despite negative consequences? *YES*

AMENDS

(Summer 2005)

Step Eight: "We made a list of all persons we had harmed, and became willing to make amends to them all."

Step Nine: "We made direct amends to such people wherever possible, except when to do so would injure them or others."

I had to go see my father.

At least I didn't have to do it alone. Olivia was going to be with me. We'd been together for about a year. I'd violated a rehab consensus by starting a relationship during my first year of being clean. All the old-timers, my counselor, and my sponsor had told me that I shouldn't hook up with anyone until I had at least a year, but I wasn't much for groupthink or for rules. Still, I had to admit that my way of doing things hadn't gotten me anywhere in life except into a series of dead ends where every bottom seemed to lead to an even lower bottom, so I tried to at least listen to other people's opinions. People who knew how to live without drugs.

But love didn't work on some schedule. And if I'd met Olivia when I was only six months clean, at least I'd met her when I *was* clean, and I didn't want to wait the extra six months to see if she'd still be around when I had my year chip.

I'd seen her every morning where I had coffee before going to my morning meeting. A perverted June Cleaver, with librarian glasses, conservative vintage dress with fishnets and cowboy boots, and a ring on every other finger, including a tattoo of a ring on her left thumb that for some reason made me weak with desire. She looked healthy, which was more than I could say for me, even six months clean. I was still the 145-pound junkie version of John Cassavetes—or his daughter. Her eyes were a freakishly perfect mahogany with no other specks, streaks, or interruptions of any other colors. Eyes that beautiful would have looked fake if they weren't so alive with an intelligence that seemed to suggest she knew what you were going to say and she'd already decided she wasn't interested. She had a smile like one of those three-way light switches: there was a general smile she gave often, with close-pressed lips and mischievous eyes as though she had a secret, and then a bigger smile that showed her full lips and white upper teeth. When she really cut loose with a laugh, she looked up and you could see the roof of her mouth, and I dreamed of what it would take to make her so happy that I could see that laugh. Whenever she walked into the room, I stared at her ass and hoped she wouldn't catch me and think I was a creep.

On our first date, at some place in Long Beach that still allowed outdoor smoking, she wore Levi's men's button-fly jeans, rolled down at the waist to stay up, with streaks and hand slurs of paint over her thighs, and a wifebeater that showed her small breasts and nipples. Her hair that had seemed pretty tame and combed when I'd last seen her the week before looked like she'd ridden in a convertible on the way over. I hadn't noticed the highlights the week before. The dominant color was burnt orange, but it had streaks all through it—the colors that kids use to accent fires in crayons—and it was going in wild directions like every strand of hair was trying to run away from its neighbor. I had a feeling she'd slept in and hadn't combed her hair, and I got a shock of desire for wanting to see that hair on the pillow next to me as soon as possible.

She admitted to being a fan of the Popular Mechanics and laughed when she told the story of seeing us on *Saturday Night Live* when we played in drag on our second song. I knew about that—it'd been in magazines and I'd read about it on the Internet—but of the two of us, she was the only one who remembered it.

She told me she wanted us to know everything we could know before we'd decide on a second date.

"I already want a second date," I said. "Besides, that's a lot to ask of a first date."

"Listen," she said. "I'm not some rock star's girlfriend."

"I'm not some rock star," I said.

She laughed.

"What?"

"Knock it off with the false humble shit," Olivia said. "You were a rock star and no doubt you dated runway models or heroin-chic actresses or whatever." She paused. "You don't know anything about me."

"I know you're smart and you're creative." Olivia looked healthy, but not athletic—like the kind of woman who'd had an eating disorder in college and who'd learned not to make herself sick over it anymore—but there was still no way she was going to get *fat*. I took a drag of my cigarette and decided to risk it. "And you're beautiful."

She smiled her in-between smile that showed her upper teeth. She seemed, somehow, to have more teeth than other people in the most beautiful way possible—each one white and perfect. I worried about mine that looked like my father's: yellowed and aching worse than ever with no real pain meds and with gums as soft as bruised apples. They'd needed work for ages, but I hadn't been to a dentist in seventeen years. The last time I'd gone was on tour in Amsterdam, where the dentist could give Dilaudid and I went four times before the band's week-long engagement was up.

Things were going well until the early warning sign that her father had been some big time sculptor and an addict she loved and who'd spent the greater part of her life disappointing her in increasingly painful ways. When she'd turned sixteen, he ruined her party by passing out in front of kids and parents, and the next day she tried, for the first time, giving him an ultimatum—telling him she wanted to see him more than anything, but she refused to see him again if he was loaded.

She never saw him again. She found out a few years later that he'd died of liver disease in some Arizona hospital.

I had no idea what to say to that. *Yeah. Fuck-ups like me and your dad can really do some damage, can't we?*

I don't know if it was because I trusted her right away or because I was desperate for a second date, or both, but I told her about my mother and my father and that I was scared beyond words that I couldn't stay clean for the rest of my life. How I blamed my father for driving my mother away. She told me how she'd spent years blaming herself for her father.

"So, we're made for each other," I said. "Where are you going to meet someone as fucked up in a similar way?"

"Sadly, just about anywhere."

Later, we were making out on her bed—she told me she used the one bedroom as her painting studio, so the bed was in the living room—and she ground herself against my outer thigh and whispered in my ear, "I want you to go down on me." She bit my lip and spoke lock-jawed with her teeth digging into my flesh.

She kissed more intensely than most people fucked. I had no idea how I was going to stop this.

Olivia slid her hand under my belt, but as soon as her fingers grazed my cock, she pulled her hand out.

"Do you have a pierced cock?" she said.

"Um . . . yeah," I said. "Sorry."

"Sorry?" She looked at me like I was nuts. "Let me see it."

What I didn't plan on telling her, but for some reason still did tell her: I hadn't been with anyone in ages. Dope had killed my desire for sex—and I was such a fucking mess I had no time to worry about it. And here I was, six months and change clean, with a woman who was the most attractive woman I'd ever met, and I was on the best brain stabilizers and antidepressants I'd ever been on but I had no idea if I could get or keep my cock hard. I wanted nothing more than to impress and please Olivia Richards, and I was scared shitless that I wouldn't be able to do what I wanted more than anything in that moment.

I asked her if we could just hold each other, and when she was cool enough to say sure, I pushed the envelope by warning her that I probably wouldn't be able to sleep, but if I did, I might wake up screaming.

But I didn't wake up, screaming or not. I slept through the night in her arms.

As the sun started to brighten the room, she told me that if we were going to be together, it was over if I ever chose drugs over her.

A year later, after things had been going better than in any other relationship in my life, after I realized that no matter what my meds may have threatened to do, my desire for Olivia overrode it and we'd been having the best sex of my life (and to hear her tell it, her life), after I realized I was knocked silly by love in a way I was positive I never would be again, I asked Olivia if she wanted to get married. It was the same day we'd left Long Beach to drive cross-country to see my father.

She looked over at me. "You're serious?"

"I think I am," I said.

"You *think* you are?" she said. "A little more conviction might make your proposal more attractive." She smiled and sarcastically said, "You romantic fucking schemer, you."

"I hadn't thought about it until now," I said. Which was true. It wasn't my thing, and she'd said she thought marriage was a sexist tradition unless you were going to have kids, and even then it wasn't necessary. Plus, this trip was so I could talk to my father for the first time in over ten years. I'd been nervous, edgy, and distracted the whole week leading up to the trip. But now, with Vegas quivering in the heat waves on the horizon, I thought, *Ask her.* Olivia was the first person I'd ever wanted to spend my life with. After a year together, the only thing I'd even questioned about her was her taste in loving someone like me.

I said, "I love you. I've never loved anyone the way I love you." I cracked my window and lit a cigarette. I looked into her smiling eyes. She wore a thigh-high cotton vintage summer dress and had her black cowboy boots up on the dashboard. "You want to get married in Vegas?"

"Not really," she said. She'd said she didn't believe in the institution, sure, but I thought maybe that was for everyone else, and not me.

"Why not?"

"I could give you a few reasons," she said.

I must have looked hurt.

She said, "If it means a lot to you, I'll do it." She wore these big sunglasses that always made her look European to me and she pushed them up onto her head and took Ike Reilly's *Salesmen and Racists* out and put in his *Sparkle in the Finish.* We'd been rotating those two CDs over and over since we'd left town.

"That's not exactly a huge yes."

"Huge or not, don't fuck the sale when you've got the customer on the hook," she said and smiled the smile that never ceased being the most beautiful smile I'd ever seen. Every time was like the first time I'd seen it, and it made my stomach jump and my skin explode into an excited chill and I hoped that I could make her smile forever.

When we hit Vegas, there was a heat wave fierce enough to render the car's AC all but useless and traffic bad enough to seem like maybe the city'd been ordered to evacuate.

Olivia said, "You know, if we get married, you have insurance from my union contract."

I looked at her, my brakes on in the traffic. "That seems like a hell of a reason."

She shrugged. "You know, Bud, that's by far the best reason I can think of." She took a sip of her Diet Coke. "You live-fast-and-die-young types don't plan well."

"I planned on dying before thirty," I said.

"Yeah, um. That's not planning well." She rubbed my leg. "I worry about you, baby." She looked over at me. "You don't eat right. You never sleep. I need you to be around. Do you understand me?"

"Ah," I said. "I'll sleep when I'm dead."

"That used to be cute, Bud." She paused. "But maybe it's time for you to take better care of yourself. People count on you. I know you don't like to hear it, but it's true."

I *did* need insurance. My right hand was a cluster of scar tissue and unconnected ligaments and pain. All I could take for it, safely, was ibuprofen. My playing wasn't close to what it had been at my best. And doctors told me the only way to even partially fix it was a surgery we couldn't afford, even with Olivia's university salary. It *did* seem like a good reason, but somehow I couldn't help acting hurt, even though I knew I was being childish.

I said, "Well, I thought, you know." I tossed my cigarette out the window that I'd rolled all the way down. "I thought love would be a pretty good reason."

She laughed a friendly laugh. "Be real, Bud. You need a state and some shithead judge to know that I love you?"

"No." Even though I'd just finished one, I lit another cigarette. My last vice in a life of vices and I'd promised to quit when we got home from the trip. When I'd first cleaned up, I had no idea who I was without drugs. For almost six months, I was afraid to talk to any strangers. Ordering coffee made my hands shake in fear. I was afraid to call for a pizza. Well, I was still afraid to call for a pizza. Every minute, I felt like an intrusion in everyone's life. I spent terrified days and months with no idea what life could possibly be. I felt like a mannequin who looked like me but who had to be clean and didn't act like me at all. After a year and a half, it was only starting to get anything close to familiar.

Olivia said, "Well, you're stuck with me for life, judge or no judge. Why, other than for insurance, would we need to get married?"

"We don't *need* to."

"Stop pouting," she said. "I love you. Period. Until you hear otherwise, you need to remember that." She crossed one boot over the other.

We tried to check in at five hotels before some desk clerk told us the town was so filled with conventions, there was no way we'd get a room anywhere except at the Rio, since they were having some labor issues and had rooms because the staff were picketing.

We pulled up to the Rio. I stopped the car, blocked by a bunch of workers holding "unfair labor" signs and looking slugged by the heat and whatever miserable mistreatment they'd been suffering at the hands of the greedy fucks who ran their hotel. Olivia started reading the signs aloud. She stopped after we got the gist that the hotel was making obscene amounts of money and treating people who actually worked for a living like shit—which we didn't really need to read the signs to know.

Olivia said, "Let's get the fuck out of this town."

"You don't want to get married?" I said.

"I don't want to cross any picket lines to get married," she said.

"Bad mojo," I said.

"I don't want a scab wedding," she said and put her sunglasses on as I pulled back into the scrum of traffic on the strip.

We ended up getting married in Salt Lake City. We were the only two people getting married at the Justice of the Peace's office. In Salt Lake City, it was way too easy to get married, but that worked out fine for us. If you were fourteen or younger, you needed the permission of one parent. What kind of fucked-up state was this? A guy who Olivia and I were pretty certain was the janitor took pictures while this old Mormon woman married us. Our only request was that she leave god out of it, but she snuck it in and asked, "Do you, Bud, in front of god and these witnesses promise to cherish Olivia?"

I paused while I looked at Olivia, who started to laugh. I laughed, too, which seemed to piss off the old Mormon woman, and I said yes, I would cherish Olivia.

The whole thing was quicker than an oil change and afterward we drove around looking for a place to eat, and I was struck blind with a happiness I'd never expected in my life.

She pointed to a Waffle House. "How about this charming establishment?"

Olivia made fun of the fact that I actually like Waffle Houses and pretty much any crappy breakfast joint from my years on the road. Having breakfast at three in the morning seemed as normal to me as waking up hundreds of miles away from where you were the day before and having the post office suspend your mail service pretty much year round. I was only just starting to get a sense of the way people with houses and jobs and lawnmowers and shit lived.

I smiled. "Don't bust on Waffle House. They kept me alive for years."

Olivia was reclining back in the passenger seat, as far back as it could go. She leaned her head forward past the center console and I touched her hair, which was hot from the sun.

"Bud, if I'm with you, I don't give a shit. The Waffle House is the best place on Earth."

I pulled in to the parking lot. "Listen to you," I said. "Getting soft on me."

She took my right hand and kissed it before she sat up. "Tell anyone and I'll kill you." She looked closely at my hand. Olivia was the first person who'd ever loved my hands. She called them, especially the more damaged right one, "delicately ruined"—just, she said, like the rest of me. She'd once said that she worried about me all the time because the world hit me full in the face every day. Because I came home with literal cuts and bruises.

"You're like a stray cat, Bud." She kissed my eyebrow and my skin shivered. "What are we going to do with you?" She slammed the door and half skipped and half walked ahead of me to the restaurant. I watched her ass and wondered how life had gotten so good.

We ordered our breakfast, Olivia joking that she'd have the "Manager's Fat-Ass Special," which only got a confused look from our server, a kid with a pierced lip and blue hair who looked like his only goal in life was to get the fuck out of Salt Lake City. I liked him and felt sorry for him all at once, remembering the same desperate need to flee a hometown, though at least the band had made it seem like I had a plan. But I guessed he didn't have a mother who offed herself or a father who killed someone in front of him, so maybe I was ahead on points. Becoming a rock star didn't really amount to a plan, but try telling things like that to an eighteen-year-old. That the Mechanics ever made it beyond a local bar scene owed as much to luck as the fact that we were good. But still—we'd gotten out.

While we waited for our food, I went outside to have a smoke. Life was good but the trickle of dread over seeing my father wouldn't let up. I paced the parking lot and smoked and then stopped and really looked around for the first time. Across the street from the Waffle House, maybe half a mile up the road, was an abandoned motel. I made out the rusted sign that was so faded the letters were hard to read: ALL-NITER MOTEL.

I was within walking distance of where Flip had OD'd.

I didn't know why I hadn't thought about the connection. About Salt Lake. But maybe it was because Olivia and I were just blowing through town and we'd gotten married and the day had a momentum all its own that I'd been swept up in. Plus, shitty as it may sound, I didn't think about Flip much. I mentioned him at meetings when I shared sometimes but, really, him dying was, other than the times in dreams when he talked out of the mouth of the man my father killed, only one of many images that clung ugly to me from that night—from those last few months before I got busted and had to go to rehab.

I lit a new cigarette with the end of the last one. I felt sick. I winced at the memory of making out with a pregnant meth-head for drugs. At smashing my hand out of self-hatred. At the fucking moronic ways my hand had become "delicately ruined." And at the memory of seeing Flip, with that rancid-smelling foam from his mouth.

I'd have to explain it to Olivia later, but I went into the Waffle House and told her we had to get on the road. Right then. At first she started to ask what the fuck was wrong with me, but there must have been enough in my eyes to tell her this was something truly important. I left a twenty on the table, and the kid with the blue hair looked confused as he brought our food just as we headed out the door.

I got on Interstate 80 and headed east, speeding and trying to get as far away as I could from Salt Lake. Olivia didn't ask any questions right off, but about fifteen miles out of the city, she said, "Look, whatever this is I'm here if you want to talk about it."

I loved her for not pushing and about an hour later, when we needed to gas up and grab some coffee, we sat at a picnic table outside some small convenience store and drank rancid truck-stop coffee and I told her.

She knew some of the story—I'd told her a lot of who I had been before we met. But she didn't know all the details of this one, and I worried she'd like me less the more she knew, but she just held my hand and told me she loved me and that who I had been had no bearing on who I was now.

I was having trouble breathing—unable to get a deep breath. I tried to keep the anxiety attack at bay, but once one started there was no way to stop it. I smelled the death from Flip's mouth—it wasn't like a memory, it was like it was happening over and over every moment while we sat at the table. My shrink had said it was part of the PTSD. Usually it was about my mom, but sometimes it got triggered by other shit.

Olivia held my hand and told me to breathe and asked me if I needed one of the Xanax I was allowed to take when I had the attacks. She carried them. I still didn't trust myself with the whole script, fearing it would be too easy to chew them like Tic Tacs. I used to take thirty of them a day to stretch an opium high. It seemed absurd to take one. But one of them actually did help with an anxiety attack.

I felt like I was going to die, even though I knew I wasn't, and I told her yes, I needed a pill. She gave me one and we sat there until I started breathing deeper and slower. She took the keys and we got back on the road.

Two days later, I was driving, and we had Jay Bennett and Edward Burch's *The Palace at 4am* on, and I hit the Repeat button three times in a row when "Drinking on Your Dime" came on. A perfect pop song. Great lyrics, astounding use of instruments and arrangement.

I'd been chain-smoking all day. Biting my nails. Barely answering Olivia when she tried to start a conversation. After several minutes of not talking, with the blur of green trees surrounding us on the highway, she said, "You might want to go easy on those fingers."

I'd bitten and torn them even more than usual and enough that I was wiping blood onto my jeans. I nodded and kept biting my nails. "Just making them more ruined for you, baby." I forced a smile.

Olivia said, "You want to let me know what's going on?"

"Just nervous about seeing my father."

"He can't do anything to you," she said.

I nodded.

"You're an adult. There's nothing left he can do."

I took a deep breath. "I don't want to see him, and I wish I didn't have to ever talk to the bastard again."

She looked away, staring out the window with a look I knew as calm anger.

"What?" I said.

Her voice was small and quiet. "You can really be a selfish prick, sometimes."

"What did I do?"

She took one of my cigarettes and lit it. She cracked the window and looked straight ahead.

I said, "You want to tell me what exactly makes me such a prick?"

"Did you ever, just once in your pouting on this whole trip, realize you're lucky to have a father to talk to?"

I didn't say anything. I'd learned early on that the only way to talk about her father was if she brought it up calmly. Not when she brought him up with any kind of anger. She wasn't looking for a conversation then—she was looking for a target, a fight.

She said, "Can't you even consider how it might affect me to hear how fucking hard it is for you to talk to your father?" She threw the cigarette out the window. "Fuck you."

Olivia heated up like a microwave and *fuck you* was her way of ending a fight. It always left me sick, desperate to fix things and have her love me again, even if she'd told me more than I could recall that *fuck you* meant nothing more than what it said and *I don't love you* didn't live on the same planet. I let it go.

She changed the music to one of her Joan Jett mixes and didn't say anything. When we'd met and she'd first played Joan Jett around me I'd asked her if that was one of her guilty pleasures, and she'd said one of the first of many things that changed the way I thought and saw the world: "I don't believe in that. I have pleasures. I don't feel guilty for pleasure."

Whenever we fought, I went straight to an enormous fear that she'd leave me. It wasn't logical, but it was there. The minute she raised her voice I had to stop myself from begging her not to leave me.

I tried to remember that a normal person would think this was a fight—not the end of the marriage. Olivia thought my fucked-up brain was also a special brain in some ways. But still, I always felt like I came up short. That I was never good enough. Especially when I pissed her off.

After fifteen or twenty minutes, she said, "I know you're nervous, Bud. But you're destroying your nails."

I bit another nail. Six of the ten fingers were in pain and blood pooled around their cuticles. She smiled. I smiled back. "You know, I've been chewing my nails for so long, I've probably consumed more than my body weight in fingernails."

She made a face. "You swallow the shit you bite?"

"Yeah."

"That's disgusting," she said.

"Am I supposed to spit out bloody chunks of skin and nail? Is that less disgusting?"

"And you go down on me with that mouth?"

"I do."

She laughed. "Well. It seems to have worked out so far."

A day away from my father's town, we stopped at some big gas station that had the new issue of *Rolling Stone*. Some pretty-boy and pretty-girl actors were on the cover—stars of some new zombie or vampire or werewolf flick, or whatever the fuck dead/undead thing was sexy that year. There was an interview with the new lineup of the Popular Mechanics—the three original guys and some new guitar player. A couple of years ago, loaded and depressed, I don't think I could have looked. But now, even if I was dreading seeing my father, I was curious to see what the band was up to.

When I paid at the counter, Olivia laughed at me.

"What?"

"You carry your money like a fucking kid, Bud." She pushed me in the shoulder. "All balled up in your front pocket."

We walked out to the parking lot. "How am I supposed to carry it?"

"You're supposed to carry it just like you do," she said. "You're adorable." She smiled. "I love you, baby."

"Did your other boyfriends use wallets or something?"

"Bud, anyone over eighteen uses a wallet," she said. "But, they're not you."

A few hours later, at our hotel, I realized that maybe I'd made a mistake in buying the magazine. I read the piece while Olivia was in the shower. The general thrust of the article was that the Popular Mechanics had finally regained their momentum and surpassed their early popularity that was halted when I was kicked out of the band.

We'd gone from being a loud cowpunk band to a lo-fi kind of alt-country band before there really was anything called lo-fi. For us, it was just the way we sounded. Then, there was that last album with me, where I tried to do something really different from what we'd done before. After I was fired, they dumped any "experimental" sounds and went back to being a straight alt-country band. To be fair, a great one. The gist of the article seemed to be that they'd finally released a record that would forever put *The Suicide Variations* (and, by extension, me) to rest. They were playing some of the biggest clubs they'd ever played, the reviews for the new album were great, and they seemed to have finally equaled and possibly even surpassed their past.

Not that their past, and me, didn't come up. On Internet fan groups and websites, people had long and dull flame wars about which version of the band was better—my tenure, it seemed, was known as "the Bud years." My solo stuff was considered to be more of the indie, lo-fi stuff the band had left behind.

The article was mostly about all their new work, but there was stuff about me, about the early records many fans still liked the best, and about the album that ended our relationship.

Bassist/songwriter/vocalist Tony Carlosi, when asked about *The Suicide Variations*, says, "Bud was listening to a bunch of . . . god knows what. Tom Waits and Lee Hazlewood and radio static. He wouldn't sleep for days, and he was on downers. Not speed. Taking . . . well, a lot of shit that should have made him sleep. Should have made an army sleep. He tracked and overdubbed and remixed songs that were done. He was in the studio twenty hours at a time, and by the time that record was released, the rest of us didn't even recognize it." Carlosi takes a sip of his coffee. "It was Bud's attempt to be a genius, and there was some amazing work on it. But we were a rock and roll band, and there was no way you could take a record like that on the road."

There wasn't a lot of that record I could recall recording, and I had a hard time listening to it without thinking with gauzy recollection of how bad and sick I'd felt. I remembered retracking a whole song when the band and the record company thought it was done. I recut an entirely new version of the song "Maintenance Dose" so that it sounded like a 1930s field recording, then merged it with the original version so the two sort of battled between dissonance and melody. The original was our shot at a hit on the record—what had been a radio-friendly mix. The label had tapped it to be the single, the one we'd already decided we'd play on *Late Night*, and I made it sound like it was playing on an AM radio while driving through the mountains. It cost us seven thousand dollars in studio time for me to change what could have been in video rotation into an interesting but indulgent song that had no chance of being on radio or TV. Not that we got a lot of radio play to begin with. Plus, no matter what, until that record, it didn't seem to matter what we did—we still ended up with the lo-fi tag. Our previous record on an independent label, we cut for six thousand dollars. Our first on Elektra had a seventy-thousand-dollar budget. We still sounded like us. Tony once joked that we could make any budget sound like six thousand dollars. I read the rest of what they had to say about my last days in the band.

Drummer Jack Lester is far less generous or diplomatic in his assessment of *The Suicide Variations*. "It's a piece of pretentious crap, and I wish they'd take it off our discography and call it what it was: a Bud Barrett solo record. A pretentious turd solo record. It's taken us years to get our audience to trust us again. And it's pretty obvious it's an addict's record," he says, referring to Barrett's well-known substance abuse issues that contributed to his release from the band.

Carlosi holds to his slightly different take. "Bud wrote a lot of these beautiful songs. Really, some of his best. Then he buried them in noise and dissonance. It was hard to watch. I've never seen someone so easily create something truly beautiful, and I've never seen someone who at the same time couldn't seem to avoid destroying whatever beauty he created," he says. "In the music and in the band."

The article then closed with everyone doing fine and looking forward to playing their new record and a bunch of the back catalog on tour, but clearly nothing off *The Suicide Variations*. I looked around the hotel. Even with some of the harsh comments, I missed the guys. Especially Tony.

Olivia came out of the shower, looked at me and said, "What's wrong?"

"Nothing," I said. "Just nervous." I held up the magazine. "And I probably shouldn't have read this."

She looked at it for a minute, then tossed it to the ground.

"How about I take your mind off it?"

I felt sorry for myself. "I'm not sure."

"I'll make it worth your while," she said. "You ever fuck a married woman?"

"Not one I was married to," I said and smiled.

I fucked Olivia from behind, which was one of our favorite positions. I loved seeing her tattoo of the infinity symbol between her shoulder blades. Late at night, when I couldn't sleep, I traced the outlines of that tattoo with my lips and dreamed that we'd be together for as long as both of us lived. I'd gotten the same tattoo on my left forearm to cover up the damage I'd done to my veins over the years.

I grabbed her hipbones and pulled her roughly against me so that her ass would feel sore the next day, the way she loved, and I pulled her hair back hard so I could see her smile while I fucked her. After pulling hard enough that her spine bent back like a parenthesis and she yelled *Yes!* I forced her head down onto the bed and told her to tell me that she loved me, and it sounded beautiful between her clipped breaths.

She rolled on her back and I went down on her, kissing her thighs and then licking her pussy until she grabbed my hair hard and pulled me to her clit. When it seemed like she was about to come, she bounced off the bed and got her vibrator from her luggage and told me to stick my tongue out as hard and long as it would go.

She said, "I'm going to fuck your tongue with my ass," and lowered herself over my face, her asshole surrounding my tongue while she began running her vibrator over her clit. As she rose up and down on her knees, she kept hitting my forehead with the vibrator and I'd feel it rumble against my skin and bones, and she apologized a few times until I finally said an ecstatic, breathless "I don't care" and quickly put my tongue back up her ass until she came.

Later, her head was cradled on my chest, and my right arm slowly stroked her shoulder. I kissed her head. My arm was starting to fall asleep, but I didn't want to change positions. Didn't want to ruin this moment, with this incredible woman falling asleep happily on my chest. I didn't want to ruin a single moment with her, but I worried, even then, that I would fuck up. Destroy something beautiful.

I didn't believe in any gods. I had trouble with the whole *higher power* aspect of NA. But I knew there was more to the universe than just me. Like Einstein said, you'd have to be a fool to live in this world and not know there's a greater force than yourself.

Love, at least, had to be a higher power. So, maybe I was praying to love when I prayed, *Please, please, please let me be with her forever. Please don't let me fuck this up. Please.*

I held her long after my arm had gone tingly and fallen asleep.

I gave Olivia directions to my father's house, the house I'd grown up in but hadn't seen since I'd left home at eighteen. I hadn't spoken to my father in over a decade. I tried to place how long it had been, but with the drugs and the lost years and the fuzzy memories, I could only guess at somewhere between twelve and fifteen years. Through some weird long-term memory, though, I knew which turns to take as we drove down Route 25 past what used to be the town diner and what used to be the mom-and-pop supermarket but were now strip malls with Starbucks and Denny's and a variety of other generic suburban clusters that seemed the same everywhere you went these days.

My old street looked pretty much the same, though. Raised ranches, single- and double-story suburban houses built in the 1960s and plopped down on half-acre lots with woods so that every family who had the means to escape the crime and decay and urban poverty of Bridgeport and instead raise their family in a town with decent public schools could have somewhere to go. The houses looked close to the way they'd looked when I left. Some had new paint jobs. Some had vinyl siding. Newer cars lined the driveways. This had once been the middle-class section of town, but now it was the older working-class section, while the cattle farms and grassy wetlands on the other side of town had been turned into McMansions and had left this side of town filled with what realtors now called "midcentury charm."

The front yard of my father's house looked so neglected, you'd think he'd made it his life's mission to fuck up his neighbors' property values. The grass was patchy and uncut. Our old dogwood trees stood skeletal by the property line. A blue spruce that used to be pruned so you could sit under it in the summer shade had lost all of its needles and now was just a huge, glum triangle of dead limbs.

All of the trees in the yard had a two-inch-thick ring around the trunks about five feet off the ground. My mother and I had slathered them with some amber-colored goop back in 1973, the year the gypsy moths had been at their worst and were killing all the trees. The amber stuff was thick as Vaseline and sticky as pine tar, and the idea was that the bugs that were killing all the trees would get caught in the sticky stripe as they climbed up the bark. It took me and my mother a couple of weeks to paint those stripes around the trees with some of my dad's cheaper paintbrushes, but that didn't stop him from yelling at us for fucking with his tools.

Still, it was one of the better memories I had of my mom. Working day after day to save the trees. And it had worked. But now, it'd been nineteen years since she'd killed herself in the Connecticut River and nineteen years since I'd seen this house or my father, and something, whether it was the gypsy moths or not, had finished these trees off. But my dad seemingly couldn't be bothered to cut them down.

I felt Olivia watching me while I stared out at the yard and tried not to think too much about my mother. When a good memory about her, like this one, came into my mind, I used to try to hold on to it and maybe think of other good moments. But after years and years of it happening, I knew now that one good memory didn't lead to more good memories. It would always be swallowed in an undertow of a series of terrible memories— images of her death that never seemed to fade or diminish in time. Stubborn, tenacious snapshots of how she looked when she washed up way downriver, three months after she jumped into the seven-degree water.

The strange thing was, and I'd recently told my drug counselor about this in rehab, my mental pictures of my mother when she was alive faded and got harder and harder to keep in my head. The images of her dead and bloated, though, I saw all the time, and they stayed fresh and crisp. Even images I *didn't* see, technically, like when she made impact on the frozen river. Images of her trapped under the surface—me imagining her alive and under ice, even though I knew that was impossible from what I'd read.

So it wasn't so much memories, but more that those images kept happening, over and over and over.

Olivia pulled into my dad's driveway. "You OK?" she said.

I shrugged. "I'll be OK." I touched her hand on the gearshift. "Have to get this done." I lifted her hand and kissed each knuckle near the tips of her fingers, which were cool and wet from her holding an iced coffee while she drove. I said, "Thank you for coming."

"Of course," she said.

I didn't say anything.

"Want a blow job before you go inside?"

Olivia was cute in her belief that a blow job could cure most things. But then, if anyone's blowjobs could solve the majority of the world's problems, they would be hers.

"Maybe if I have trouble sleeping after, OK?"

She kissed me. "Deal." She looked at me. "I love you more than I have ever loved anyone, Bud."

"You love me more now that the state of Utah is cool with it, right?"

"I love you more for what your tongue does to my ass. Fuck Utah, baby." She kissed me. "Seriously, baby. Don't forget, ever, how much I love you, OK?"

"Never," I said. "Thank you."

She rubbed the back of her hand on my cheek a couple of times. I felt cold drops of water where her hand had been when she took it away. "Remember," she said. "This is for you. You aren't asking him for anything. Do what you need to do for yourself."

I nodded.

She said, "You can do this."

"I haven't said a word to him in so long," I said. My hands shook. I didn't know if I was still afraid of him, afraid of seeing him without being high, or just afraid.

"This is about today," she said. "Not about the last twenty years."

"Well, it *is* about the last twenty years," I said.

"You know what I mean," she said gently.

"I do," I said. "But you know what I mean, too, right?"

She said she did. She tried a smile meant to support me. A smile with love and hope, but not without fear. She was in love with a train wreck—she knew that much.

I said, "I have no idea if he's going to be violent."

"If he's violent, you leave," she said. "You call me. You're an adult—he can't do anything to you."

I wondered about that.

She looked at my father's house and nodded. "And you'll call me whenever you want me to come back?"

I thought about my father inside. He knew I was coming. All I'd told him was that I needed to talk with him, and all he'd told me was that he wouldn't talk about my mother. Which was OK. I was here to make my amends to him, to say my piece, and to move on. I wasn't here to ask him about my mother. I would have loved to know more about her, but I'd given up on finding out anything about her from him a long time before.

I said, "I'll call."

"If you call me in five minutes, I'll be right back here, OK?"

"This will probably take a little longer," I said.

"Call *whenever* you want me here is what I'm saying," she said and kissed my cheek. "Understood?"

"Understood."

I walked up to my father's porch and lit a cigarette and smoked it there, watching Olivia pull away and drive back toward the bed-and-breakfast we were staying in, about ten miles down the road. When my cigarette was done, I flicked it off the porch into the overgrown grass. I thought about knocking on his door. I lit another cigarette and sat down on the front step, looking out at the road.

On my third cigarette, I'd counted how many ex-neighbors' houses I could name several times, drawing a blank only on a green house on the hill where they didn't have kids. I was still trying to get the courage to knock on my father's door when I heard his front door swing open and slam against the inside wall.

I turned around and looked up at my father, who looked worse than I ever imagined he would. The tyrant of my childhood no longer looked like he'd ever been capable of threatening another man, woman, or even child. He was skinny enough to drop with just an arm punch. His head had brown spots the size and general shape of kidney beans where he was bald on top, and he had weak, stringy white hair hanging from the sides of his head. He reminded me of some community theater version of Scrooge.

I sat on the step, stunned that he couldn't even scare me while standing over me.

He said, "What's your fucking problem? Sitting out here for ten fucking minutes without knocking on my door."

I stood up. "I was gathering my thoughts."

"You're a fucking drama queen like that mother of yours," he said. "You call a man and tell him you have something to say to him, you don't sit all chickenshit on his porch."

I took a drag of my cigarette and thought about punching him. Hurting him. Fuck Step Nine. Fuck NA. None of those people knew him.

I said, "She's the one thing you said you wouldn't talk about, and here you are saying shit about her before I'm even in your house?"

"I suppose 'How've you been, Dad? Great to see you!' wasn't realistic." He shook his head and turned into his house, leading the way for me to follow him inside.

"Maybe dads who get 'Great to see you!' acted a little differently than you did," I said. "Ever think of that?"

He laughed a sad, weary kind of laugh, took two Rolling Rocks out of the fridge and put one on the table in front of an empty seat. He opened his and sat down.

My father lit a cigarette and looked up at me. His skin looked both too gray and too yellow to be human skin. He said, "OK. I'm not the father you wanted. I pretty much guessed that from us not talking the last twenty years."

"It's nineteen."

"Big fucking difference! Whatever the fuck it's been. It's *been,* OK? And now you're here for some fucking reason that must be important, since you have to talk to the worst father who ever lived, so what the fuck is it?"

I stared at the beer he'd put on the table. I wanted it. We were alone. I could do what I had to do—talk to him, do my Step Nine—but maybe have a little help and who would know? But I hadn't come this far, stayed clean this long, to blow it now.

I sat down and pushed the beer away.

He said, "Not a classy enough brand, rock star?"

I took a deep breath and let it out slowly. "That's what I'm here to talk with you about."

"That you think I should drink something better than Rolling Rock?"

I'd forgotten my father could be funny. I hadn't allowed myself to remember any good qualities he might have had. All I remembered was the violence and that I blamed him for my mother leaving. And, by extension, I blamed him for her suicide, even if I knew suicide was more complex than any easy cause and effect.

"This is hard," I said. I felt and then saw my hands shaking. I put them in my pockets. I tried to regulate my breathing, but it felt like I was starting to have an anxiety attack. I needed a Xanax but all my prescriptions were with Olivia.

My father finished his beer. "You sure you don't want this?"

I nodded and just sat there.

My father got up and went into the living room and sat on the couch. I followed him in, sitting on an old Morris chair my mother used to read to me from. The house was still so full of little

pieces of her, of my life here, of everything that had happened. I
kept trying to breathe steadily and repeated the Serenity Prayer to
myself a few times in my head.

"So," my father said. "What's the big news that means we're
talking again?" He put his feet up on the coffee table. I saw clumps
of cigarette filter used as cotton for filtering dope, plus a couple of
needles—the orange-capped ones diabetics use. But the fat candle
and the spoon with the black stains on the bottom from using it
to cook gave away to anyone who saw the room that my father
wasn't a diabetic.

I gestured to the table. "What are you on?"

"This better not be some fucking drug lecture," he said. "Who
called you?"

"Nobody called me."

"Was it Jessica? Because I don't want any fucking help, and I
don't need any fucking help." He took a long drink of his beer.
"And where does she get off calling my junkie fucking son to
lecture me, anyway?"

"Calm down, Dad," I said, and I realized I hadn't said the
word *dad* in so long I really couldn't place the last talk we'd had,
or what that talk was about. "I don't even know who Jessica is."

"She didn't call you?"

"It's pretty fucking hard for someone I don't know to call me."

He got up and grabbed himself another beer and asked me
again if I wanted one. I said no, and he came back and dropped
onto the couch.

On the table, along with the needles and tossed cotton and
everything else was an opened old cigar box with three bottles of
pills inside it. A small bottle of water sat next to the box, probably
for cooking the pills, rather than for drinking.

I couldn't believe that my father was a junkie. I knew him as a
guy who sometimes smoked pot at the parties he and my mother
threw. But back then he was a weightlifter, too, a boxer and an

athlete. Something had to explain how he'd become this old man in front of me—it was like he'd aged thirty-five years in nineteen.

He lit a cigarette and I did the same. We looked at each other for a moment. I wondered if I'd look like that in twenty years if I kept using and stayed alive. I wondered, too, why I'd spent so much of my life so afraid of what was in front of me.

"So, if Jessica didn't call you to get me to mend my ways, to what do I owe this unexpected honor?"

I looked down at my red Chuck Taylors, feeling stupid, like a sober man in his late thirties should maybe wear something else. I looked into my father's sick eyes. I still felt hatred for him. And now I felt anger that he had fucking dope in his house. Beer, I'd been ready for. But the whole day was starting to feel like some supreme cosmic test.

I said, "I don't know how much you know about my history with drugs and alcohol."

He laughed. "You're joking, right?"

"No," I said, trying to control my temper. "I'm not joking about much of anything here." I felt itchy and dangerous. I wanted, badly, to steal that cigar box off the table and use whatever I could, but then I tried to get centered on better trains of thought—my sponsor telling me to repeat the Serenity Prayer, for instance, or just focusing on Olivia and how, if I wasn't clean, I wouldn't be with her.

My father leaned back into his ratty couch. I needed to say what I had to say before he started cooking those pills. Otherwise, I'd either join him or beat the shit out of him and take them all.

My father said, "OK, Mr. Serious. What do you want?" He pointed at me while holding a bottle of Rolling Rock, and green light danced on the far wall while the afternoon sunlight shone through the bottle.

"I've been clean now for eighteen months," I said. "And there is some stuff I have to tell you about me, about what I've done."

There. I'd started it, and the relief drained from my tense body. For better or worse, I was going to be able to do this.

My father laughed so hard, I thought he might do a spit-take. "You're Step Nine-ing me? *That's* what all this is about?"

I wanted to tell him to shut the fuck up with his laughter, but then it hit me. "You know Step Nine?"

"I know every fucking one of those horseshit steps."

I looked at him for a moment, not knowing what to say. "You have anything I can drink here? A soda or something?"

"Have a fucking beer," my father said. "That shit isn't going to work."

I got up and filled a crud-crusted glass with tap water that was less clear than it should've been. The house was falling apart, inside and out. "I've been clean for a year and a half." I wanted some understanding. Some recognition that what I was fighting for was worthy of respect. "I can't have a beer."

"A year isn't shit," my father said. "I had almost ten years once."

He was only in his mid-fifties and he looked like he could die at any moment. "When did you have ten years?"

He shrugged. "Doesn't fucking matter. Not going back to those judgmental fucks. This is who I am." He lit a cigarette and pointed at me. "And it's who you are, too."

"Not what I need to hear right now."

"Whether you think you need to hear it or not, it's the truth. You need the truth. You're a fucking addict and it's all you'll ever be."

I thought about what my sponsor'd told me. What Olivia told me. I was here to say my piece and move on. "Look," I said. "There's some shit I have to say. For me. If you've done this, you know what I'm going through." If my father ever cleaned up, it was probably after I'd left the house. He'd never apologized to me for anything. Not for killing that man. He made his excuse, whether it was true or not, but he never seemed sorry. Never apologized for driving my mother away. Anger burned inside me. "When were you clean?"

"What the fuck does that matter now?"

"I need to know," I said.

"*You* may need to talk about your past, but I'm not here to talk about mine."

"You owe me this."

"I owe you shit," my father said and threw his empty bottle against the mantelpiece. It bounced off the wall and smashed when it hit the bricks around the fireplace. In the fireplace was a phone book only slightly burned and blackened at the corners of the pages.

"Just answer me," I said.

He looked down. "I answer this question and you'll stop grilling me?"

"Sure," I lied. I'd decided I was going to ask him everything I ever wanted to know. I'd never see this bastard again. For all I knew then, it was my last chance to make some sense of my life, and I was going to try to get some information.

"It was when you were a kid. A little kid."

Which meant it was before my mother left. Which also meant I was too young to have gotten a Step Nine from him, and I was pissed that he was off the hook on this one. "So, it wasn't after you killed that guy?"

"Why do you want to bring up shit that's in the past?"

"Because it fucking matters to me, Dad!" I scared myself by yelling. I felt small. A child out of control. Ready to cry if I wasn't careful.

"Tell you what," he said. "You give me your sponsor-approved Step Nine, and then we can talk about anything except your mother." He paused, looking weary. "But I told you all there was to tell about what you saw that day."

"You told me shit," I said. "You tell a kid people are out to kill him? Fuck you."

"Look. Say what you came here to say. After you say what you need to, we never have to see each other again, OK?"

I took a sip of his tap water, which tasted vaguely of rust and chemicals. I thought of everything I had to say that I'd rehearsed in my head for weeks. A bunch of my Step Nines were filled with apologies from me—about what I did wrong, about what I stole, about what a terrible person I was. But with my father, I'd originally had no idea what to say. When I'd gone over it with my sponsor, he'd told me that an amends is not always an apology. It's a person announcing their change. It's a recognition of emotions, resentments, and feelings.

"I've hated you my whole life," I said. "And I'm sorry for that." I wasn't really sorry I'd hated him, not *sorry* in the sense of my responsibility, but sorry that it had dictated so many of my feelings and actions. "And I spent a lot of years hiding from my emotions. I blamed you for Mom leaving. I blamed you for her suicide."

He yelled, "That had nothing to do with me, you judgmental little prick!"

I held my hands up. "I'm not saying I was right. I'm saying what I felt, and then I'll leave it, OK?"

He nodded, looking at me with a resentment and hatred and anger I recognized from before I even knew words.

I said, "I'm living a different life. It's important for me to move on. I can't live the life I'm trying to live and hate you. So, I wanted to let you know, I don't hate you."

"That's pretty fucking big of you to forgive me."

"I didn't say I forgave you for anything."

"You have nothing to forgive me for," he said. "You have no idea about *anything* about my life."

"I'm not saying I do," I said. "All I'm saying is that I'm trying to make a new life. A clean slate. And I need to move on from my feelings about us. I don't expect you to change. I'm not *asking* you to change. I just needed to say what I needed to say." I paused. "You said you understood the steps. So, please understand what I'm trying to do."

My father nodded. He seemed to have calmed down a little. He leaned forward and dumped two forty-milligram OxyContin into the spoon and carefully dripped a little of the water onto them. He put the spoon down on the table, which was wood and filled with years of crisscross cigarette burns and oval burn marks where hot spoons had been placed on it. I'd seen tables like it for twenty years. I'd owned tables like it.

He said, "I don't need to hear this shit. I don't need *your* feelings in *my* life, understand?"

"I understand," I said. "But thanks for hearing me out."

He lit the candle and he was about to cook the pills over it. "You want some of this?"

"What did I just tell you I was here for?"

"Well, I'm getting high," he said. "You can join me or judge me."

"I'm not here to do either," I said.

"Very adult of you," he said, while he held the spoon over the flame. It smelled delicious—the powdery chemicals dissolving.

I said, "I have to leave."

"You don't want to hear what I have to say about that day?" He looked needy—shaky. I didn't know if it was because he needed to confess something, or because he needed the drugs.

I was reasonably sure he was talking about the dead man. But maybe if I humored him telling me his excuses, I could get something about my mother out of him. "I want to hear it," I said. "I don't mean leave for good. I need to leave the room. This is a little hard."

He laughed. "You sure you don't want to get high?"

"Of course I do," I said. "I just can't anymore."

My father got serious, nodded and looked at me with something that seemed like compassion. "Give me a few minutes. Go smoke on the porch. I'll join you in a minute, OK?"

I thought for just a second about joining him and got scared and knew I had to leave the room. "Thanks."

The screen door bounced a couple of times after I closed it. I could still smell the drugs cooking from the porch, but I lit a smoke and closed my eyes tightly and tried to remember why I was staying clean. I called Olivia.

Without saying hi, she answered, "Do you need me to pick you up?"

"Not yet," I said.

"How's it going?" She sounded tense.

"My father's shooting dope in his living room," I said. "I'm out on the porch."

"What?" she said. "I'm coming over."

"No," I said. "He promised me he was going to tell me some things."

"You can't be around someone shooting dope."

"Actually, he's shooting Oxys," I said.

"Totally different," she said, a little angry sounding. "Baby, I'm coming over."

"Really," I said. "I'm OK. I'm smoking on the porch." I paused. "Not inside shooting his drugs. And he offered."

"That was very nice of him," she said.

"I'll give you a call in a bit," I said. "I just wanted to let you know I was all right."

She said, "This sounds pretty fucking far away from all right."

I was about to try to reassure her some more, but she hung up.

I waited for my father to let me know when to come back in the house, but I didn't hear anything other than the drone of some crime TV channel he'd put on. A neighbor rode a lawnmower and the sweet smell of freshly cut grass drifted in the air. It'd been about fifteen minutes and I was starting to worry that he might have OD'd. I was just about to go in and check on him when I heard his boots scuffing on the wood floor. The screen door opened and bounced a few times before slamming again. He sat next to me.

"Feel better?" I said.

"You know how I feel."

I stared straight ahead. "I do."

"What I said in there," my father said. "That you won't make it." He lit a cigarette. "I hope you do."

"But you don't think I will?"

He looked at me. "Does it matter what I think?"

This man was my blood. He must have held me once, when I was small. He must have loved my mother. There *had* to have been at least some of those moments that other people talk about when they talk about family. "I don't know," I said.

"That thing you saw," he said. "With that guy."

He seemed to be struggling getting whatever he had to say out, but I wasn't going to help him.

"That *thing*?" I said. I wanted to hear him call it what it was. A murder. I wanted to hear his story was bullshit.

My father looked at me. His pupils were fine points. He looked like he might cry. There wasn't a thing on earth I'd do to help him. I wanted to see that he hurt, even if I knew from plenty of experience that he wouldn't be shooting up if he felt good about himself and his life.

He said, "Look, you like dope. You know what it does, right?"

"I do."

"It shuts you down," he said. "And all this." He gestured around to his house falling apart and to himself falling apart faster than the house. "You know." He paused. "Not wanting to feel."

"I'm supposed to feel sorry for you because you killed a guy?"

We each stared straight ahead, not looking at each other. The street I'd grown up on, the street I'd ridden my bike on when I was a kid, the street that filled with the smells of burning leaves every fall and was full of families and life now seemed to be a street that harbored either withered husks of people like my dad in shut-up houses or else people with little kids. Every once in a while, you'd see one of them push a stroller past his house. Nobody waved at us.

"There's a lot about what happened that I could have . . . well, I could have handled better." He took a drag off his cigarette. "Differently. I didn't know any right way to tell you. I still wouldn't know what to say to a kid, really."

My father seemed to really be having trouble talking about it. My brain admitted a sliver of possibility that he might have told me the truth from the start. There was no statute of limitations, though. If he'd been lying all those years, he'd need to protect himself forever.

My phone vibrated. Olivia. I put it back in my pocket without answering.

"Who's that?" my dad said.

"My wife."

"Wife?"

"We just got married, driving cross-country."

"She an addict, too?"

"No," I said. "She's amazing."

And now it seemed like my father and I were actually talking to each other. Like he was my father. Like I was his son. "She why you're trying to stay clean?"

"Not at first," I said. I told him how we met. "But now, when I feel like slipping, yeah, sometimes she's the reason. *A* reason, anyway. She's what keeps me thinking it might be worth it to stay clean."

"You're in love?"

"I'm *married,* Pop," I said. "What the fuck kind of question is that?" I couldn't imagine anything feeling bigger, more important than what I felt with Olivia.

"Then maybe I was wrong earlier. About it being who you are."

It felt like we were talking around so many things at once—maybe he was talking around the borders of my mother. Yet it also felt like we were finally talking, so I wanted to let him go where he wanted to go. If I brought up my mother, it might shut him down.

I said, "She feels like my last chance. Music, career, all that shit. None of it mattered enough to keep me clean."

"Another person can't keep you clean," he said. "That's a hell of a lot of pressure on her."

"I'm not saying she's going to keep me clean. Just that she's one of the best reasons to keep myself clean."

"I hear you," he said. He paused a long time. "Good luck with that, Bud. Seriously."

My father hadn't called me by my name, especially phrased with love, in so long that my throat went tight at the sound of it.

"I told you the truth about that guy," he said. "About when I worked undercover."

I had no idea if I believed him. I made a mental note to check later, but then I realized that if he had been undercover, I might not be able to check.

My father said, "After you showed up, your mother thought it was too dangerous. Thought I could get killed, which, yeah, I could have, so I transferred and we were going to have another kid."

I said, "Mom told me she couldn't have kids after me."

He shrugged. "True, in a way. She couldn't have kids after the miscarriage after you." He coughed. "That's when she started getting really crazy."

"Don't call her that."

"Look, it's all over now." He looked at me hard and cruel. "Let's be honest. After she lost the kid, she stopped talking. Spent whole days in bed. That's when it started."

It was, of course, her insanity, which led to her suicide. Neither of us talked for a moment.

My father said, "When I was undercover, I did some bad shit. You have to. You live around criminals. It's a dangerous life, like your mother said."

"So you transferred," I said, trying to get him back on track.

He nodded. "State Trooper, which was pretty safe. You were growing up. Your mother was sick, and she and I were drifting apart." He stopped, and it looked like he was thinking about her. "Anyway, that guy who came for the car *was* dangerous. A dealer I'd run with when I was in Narcotics. He made me. I saw him spot my badge on the dash."

My phone vibrated again. I didn't even look. She was probably on her way over.

My father said, "I thought about you. About your mother. These were dangerous people."

"You had me thinking I could be killed," I said. "Every fucking day. You realize that?"

He sounded angry. "You *could* have been. *You* realize *that?* You want a kid to keep his mouth shut, you scare the shit out of him." He drank about half his beer at once and laughed. "I learned something from my old man."

I'd spent most of my life convinced my father was an unthinking savage. If all this was true, though, maybe I'd never really known him. I'd seen him fucked up and angry, but it never occurred to me that there might have been a different person who existed before the one I knew. And I'd lost our whole lives. But he still could have been lying, telling me what I needed to hear to make me think what he wanted me to think, and I would never know the truth about anything.

He went in the house and came back with another beer. Neither of us talked and the lawnmower next door ground deeply into a lower gear as the neighbor hit an incline in his yard.

He said, "After that, I got into dope again pretty deep. And then, nothing mattered." He laughed sadly. "I'd killed a man—a man I *had* to kill, but it's still not something you want on your head. My wife was crazy. My kid wouldn't even look at me." He took a drink of his beer. "So, I started spending every day as fucked up as possible."

I smoked. Wished I could drink. That I could take some of his Oxys. I wished I had my Xanax even though I wasn't sure I'd be taking it for the right reason. "Did Mom know?" I said. "About that guy?"

He nodded.

I paused. "Did she say anything about me?"

"Look, Bud. She was gone. She was gone before she left. It wasn't about you. It wasn't even about me."

"So, she just left?" I said. "Things happen for no reason in this world of yours?"

"Things happen because people are sick," he said. "Among other things."

"Did she leave because you killed that guy?"

"Now you're asking questions that don't have answers."

I saw Olivia's car coming down the road. I stood up.

"Tell me," I said. "Tell me what she said."

My father shook his head. "I can't help you with that, Bud." He looked up and squinted from the sun. "I really can't." He let out a deep breath. "Look. If I had something to tell you that made sense, I'd give you that much."

Olivia pulled into the driveway. She took the turn hard and it looked like she'd been gunning it all the way over. Which I guess I should have expected when I told her I was at a house where people were shooting up opiates.

"That your wife?" he said.

"Yup."

"She's heard your horror stories about me?"

"She has," I said. "What I knew until today, anyway."

My father stood. He was shorter than me. Weak. An old weak man. "Is she going to hear your new stories about me?"

I looked over at Olivia. She hadn't gotten out of the car. "Are they true?" I said.

"Why would I lie?"

I thought about that joke: *How can you tell a junkie's lying? His lips are moving.* "Why wouldn't you?"

He laughed—the first real laugh of the day. "I've lost everything. What the fuck do I have to gain by lying to you about this?"

I tried to think. "To change my opinion about you?"

"So what if I did?" he said. "My life's over. I'm not looking for redemption. Maybe you and I could have had some father–son relationship, but we didn't. So, that's over. I don't expect it's going to start now." He paused. "I am who I am. I don't give a fuck what anyone thinks about me anymore. I got tired of trying to change, and I got tired of apologies."

I heard Olivia idling the car in the driveway. Beck's *Odelay* was on and coming from her rolled-down window. I wondered if she would walk up, or if she was watching to make sure everything was OK.

I waved at her.

She made the "OK" sign. I nodded.

"She's worried about you," my father said.

"Yup."

"Worried about you and your scary, violent dad."

I felt bad. If he was telling the truth, what he did was terrible, but it was what he had claimed from the first—he'd killed a dangerous man to keep us safe. And it explained, even if it didn't excuse, the years of alcohol and violence in the house after that.

He said, "Is she special? Really fucking special?"

"More than you could ever know," I said.

"No," he said. "I know that feeling."

I wanted so badly to ask if he meant my mother. He *had* to. But what if the answer was no?

He said, "I'm in no place to give advice. But do everything you can to keep her, Bud, OK?"

"That's my plan."

We stood there for a moment. Neither of us seemed to know what to say. I heard the continuing idle and the music coming from Olivia's car. The crime show was still on my father's TV and some talking head was angry about some criminal not being punished enough. Olivia looked at me, and I could tell she didn't know what to do next.

My father said, in a very small voice, "Could I meet her?"

My idea for the way the day would go had been that I'd call Olivia to come rescue me as soon as my father started yelling at me, whether that was two minutes inside his door or an hour later. But this—us standing there with so many wasted, broken years behind us and who knew what in front of us—this was off script.

"If you want, sure," I said.

"You think she'd want to meet me?" my father asked. He said it like an eighth-grade kid asking if you think a girl likes him. All insecurity and like it's the most important thing in the world.

"C'mon," I said and I walked him toward our car.

When I got close, Olivia got out. She'd changed at our hotel and wore a pair of men's jeans low on her hips and one of my snap-button cowboy shirts. She looked stunning. I didn't know if I was being paranoid or not, but she seemed to be checking my eyes to see if I was loaded. Even if she was checking, I couldn't have blamed her.

My father looked frightened—as frightened as I'd felt only a short while ago on his porch, too scared to knock on his door. I wasn't sure how I felt now. Nothing seemed certain. All this hatred I'd carried for years had been replaced by a riptide of confusion. But the fear of my father that I'd felt my whole life was gone for good. He was an old junkie, falling apart and scared to meet the daughter-in-law he'd just found out he had.

"Olivia," I said, "this is my father, Hank."

He put out his hand and she looked confused, but she took it and said, "Pleased to meet you."

My father said, "I'd say welcome to the family, but it's not much of a family." He smiled, but the joke fell flat. He cleared his throat. "Congratulations. On the wedding."

"Thanks," she said.

We all stood in the gravel driveway where I used to sit and cut my arms with my father's razor blades while the summer sun set and my parents argued in the house and the woodpile sat a couple hundred feet away. There was too much history in such a small place. Images came at me without me being able to brace for their arrival.

No one seemed to know what to say or do.

My throat felt tight. I said, "Let me walk you back in, Dad."

Like he needed my help walking back to his door. But something needed to be said to break up this group of three people who had no idea how to leave the moment.

He said good-bye to Olivia, nodded to her. She said it was good to meet him and she waited by the car while I walked him back to the porch.

On his porch, we each lit a cigarette and looked at each other. My father's weak, sad eyes stared into mine. "Good luck, OK, Bud?"

"I'm doing what I can."

"I'd offer to help, but there's nothing I can do to make your life better."

We stood there. Strangers. I didn't love him, at least not in any way I could recognize. But I couldn't hate him anymore. Not the way I had for years. Ever since I could remember, what had connected me to him was my hate. And now that was gone, or it had at least lost its center and I'd spun away from the orbit of anger that had held me for so long.

My father held out his hand. I thought for a moment about hugging him but figured he hadn't offered, and I wasn't sure if I wanted to do it because I'd always wanted to hug *a* father—not necessarily *my* father. This could be my last chance, but instead I shook his hand, which was less calloused than I'd guessed it would've been. Than I'd remembered.

He said, "Thanks for coming. I'm glad you did."

"Me, too," I said, though I wasn't sure *glad* was the right word.

We stood there for another moment, again seeming stumped about what to do next.

"I'm sorry," I said.

"For what?"

"I'm not sure," I said. "For a lot of things."

He smiled. "Well, me too, then."

And then:

I would climb back into my car with my beautiful wife and my chance for a life with connection and beauty.

He would walk back into the house I knew so well, and he would shoot up some OxyContin and he would feel peaceful for a few minutes, maybe a couple of hours, and then he'd be back alone and pushing forever against his world of regret and self-loathing and loneliness.

I knew exactly where he was headed. I had no idea where I was going.

FINISHED BUSINESS

(2009)

Things didn't start off that badly. We did a couple weeks of practice in LA to get ready for the short reunion tour designed to support the release of a Popular Mechanics anthology. I never expected the call, but Tony asked if I wanted to do a short tour of the West Coast, and I felt like I couldn't say no. This was a chance to, if not get back what I had, at least have it end on better terms.

At first, some things were a little rusty, but mostly it felt like we'd never stopped playing at all. When a band clicks, when four people swing as one and can anticipate what everyone else is going to do without even thinking about it, it's like you're levitating. There's nothing in the world quite like playing with a good band.

We recorded two new songs for the career retrospective CD. We did one of my new songs and one of Tony's. He'd been the main songwriter in the years since I'd been gone, and there was some debate at the start of the tour practices about which songs we'd be playing on the road. It was weird—these were guys I'd known all my life, but they were strangers after the last nine years in some ways. Tony was getting divorced. The other guys had girlfriends or wives I didn't know. Mickey even had kids. It made sense—we'd all grown up after all—but I had no idea, other than what I read or what Tony'd told me in our sporadic contact, what they'd been doing all these years.

I didn't really feel I had the right to call any of the shots, so I figured whatever Tony and the guys decided, in terms of the set list, would be fine. Most of the early material for the band we were supposedly reuniting was written by me. Most of the material for the second version of the band—which I wasn't in— was written by Tony. Some by the guitar player who replaced me, Eddie. Everyone agreed we weren't doing any of Eddie's material. Beyond that, though, Jack seemed to assume I wanted to fight for my old songs. I didn't really feel it was my place to dictate anything and I'd hoped he would pick up on that, but he hadn't. It was incredibly uncomfortable to be afraid at every turn that I would offend someone. To not speak my mind in a band I used to run. But here I was, feeling like the reprimanded child, let back in the playpen—but with orders not to be myself or get out of line. That may not have been the way the guys looked at it, but it was the way I felt.

After we'd run through a bunch of the early songs, Mickey said, "So are we just going to be some fucking oldies act?"

Jack put his sticks down. Tony's bass amp hummed. It seemed like the question was posed to me. I said, "We can do whatever you guys like. I'll get up to speed on the other stuff."

That seemed to break the tension. It wasn't going to be the Bud Barrett show, and we all seemed happy enough with that development. I learned the songs they picked from what Mickey and Jack started calling the "Tony era" (or, "the new shit"), and we would play about ten songs from what I supposed had been my era, though no one called it that. Jack did, however, call it "the old shit."

The only problem that came up with the proposed set list was that it contained a song of mine that I didn't want to do, called "The Problem with Drugs."

We were going over the set list and the covers we might want to do, when I said, "Is it cool if we don't do 'The Problem with Drugs'?" It was my song, so I figured it might be all right if I asked to take it out. I hadn't played it at any of my shows since I'd gotten clean. I hated the me who wrote it, and I didn't want to live in that guy's head for three loud minutes of self-loathing a night. Asking to take out one of Tony's or the rare song of Mickey's we did might have seemed rude, but this was mine. I figured I was safe from offending anybody. I knew I might get an argument, though, because it was the most popular song from my time in the band. It had once taken status as the encore song that audiences would sing along with.

Jack said, "That's the only one of your songs that's still in every set."

I said, "I'm just not that comfortable with it." It was a good song, one of my best and by far my best known, but it romanticized getting loaded and included a chorus that ended, *The problem with drugs is that they always run out.* Crowds cheered at that line, always. It was a song to play in my twenties, not in my forties.

I tried to explain all this to the guys. I said, "It just seems like a really irresponsible song."

"Since when is rock and roll supposed to be *responsible?*" Mickey said.

I laughed. "Fair point." I popped the fifth and seventh fret harmonics and tuned my guitar while we sat around. "But I just don't feel good doing it."

Jack said, "I *do* feel good doing it. Fans like it."

Jack and I had known each other forever, longer than anyone in the band, and we'd gone from being friends to two guys with not much to say. I played the only card I had left. "I haven't requested anything else. I'm playing everything people've suggested, and I haven't tried to push anything of mine you guys wouldn't want." I hadn't, and everyone had to have noticed this, asked for a single song off *The Suicide Variations*.

Jack said, "So you're more important than two thousand fans a night?" He spit tobacco juice into a coffee cup, and I remembered a show in Boston where I was fucked up and we'd played terribly. It was dark backstage at the Rat and I accidentally drank from Jack's spit cup and puked all over a wall covered with posters and band stickers and Sharpie graffiti. The next time we played the Rat, close to a year later, my dried vomit was still caked on top of the posters on the wall.

Mickey was calm and trying to make everyone happy. Nine years apart and in some ways nothing was different. "We've got a full set. We don't need it in there."

I wanted to hug him.

Jack said, "People are going to want to hear it."

Tony said, "People are going to want to hear a lot of stuff. And they'll hear most of it."

Jack stood and walked toward the bathroom, throwing his sticks at his drum kit. One of the sticks hit his ride cymbal— the other flew over the toms toward Mickey, who sidestepped it. Jack yelled back, "This is a stupid decision. But fuck it. I'm not going to beg the fucker to play a song he wrote." He slammed the bathroom door.

The three of us sat without talking as the ride cymbal rang out and faded away after a while.

Tension flares aside, after about ten days playing together, I was amazed at how good we sounded. A band, when it works, flows as naturally as a river. I'd played with other people. So had the other guys. Probably we had all played with people better at their instruments than any of us—none of us were great musicians except for Jack. But somehow, when we played together, the years melted away and everything, at least musically, felt like home. Mickey and I played guitar together like one player, and Jack swung like few rock drummers ever did. Not many people could play like him. Charlie Watts. Linda Pitmon. He could drive his kick foot like Bonham or Ken Coomer when he needed to, and he had as distinctive a style on his toms as Ringo Starr did. He was the reason we had a swing. We all played together the way the gears of a clock seamlessly interact. There isn't another feeling like it.

But Jack and I hadn't been friends for a long time. We'd had some good times early in the band, but a couple of albums in, our relationship became a cold mutual respect, replaced by his open and public hostility toward me once I'd left.

But we could coexist for music this good. He was being professional, mostly. We were being as civil to each other as we'd been since the late 1980s. I found myself, in the second week of playing, both overjoyed that I had this back in my life, and incredibly regretful that I'd ever let it go.

The only thing giving me much trouble was my right hand. I'd had one surgery on it after I cleaned up. But they hadn't been able to make it what it once was, and now it swelled and ached if I used it too much. Playing several days in a row in rehearsal had it thick and throbbing. When I did solo tours, it wasn't so hard. My newer music was quieter and had a lot more space, in general. Easier on the hand. Playing Popular Mechanics' songs was a lot more physically demanding. Still, I was back in the band.

Even with all the stress, I was reminded we'd been brothers once. When you're a band, no matter how much you fight—and we had fought a hell of a lot in the old days—it's still you against the world. At one point or another, everyone in the band had punched everyone else. Even me and Tony, who were true friends—always—we'd had massive blowups. But, back then, we never talked shit about each other to the press, and if anyone outside ever said or did anything to threaten the band, they were the enemy.

Fans like to think bandmates are all friends. You start as friends—most bands do. But you live in a cage on wheels every day between two hundred and three hundred days a year. People start to hate the sound of other people's voices, the way they eat, you name it. Tension grows in exponential ways, like a virus that keeps splitting and reproducing. Rivalries fester. And usually, since you tend to get together when you're in your teens or early twenties, you have no idea how to talk any of it through. If you start to make any money at all, you're no longer just four friends—you're business partners. Which is where songwriting royalties come in. If you write the songs, you get more money. The people who don't write the songs get less money, and they tend to resent it. And the people who do write the songs think, *Fuck you, you think it's so easy, you write a good song and you'll get more money, asshole.*

And if there are two or more writers, one of them gets pissed when the other one wrote the song the record company asks you to play on *Letterman* or on *Conan* and shit like that. Somewhere down the line, that leads to resentments that clot the heart of a band. Bands are made to break up. It's in their DNA. If I had stayed in the Popular Mechanics, they might not exist anymore. But since I'd left, it became sort of a new band. And now we were back, if not to the original roles then to the original sound. And it felt pretty great, at least until the music stopped and we had to talk to each other again.

We'd been there and gone to war over all that years ago. Hopefully we'd reached a kind of peace. Plus, there were only two new songs on the compilation CD, so there wasn't much to fight about. We'd recorded those quickly—two songs in three days in the studio. Tony's was a great tune called "Green" and mine was a Popular Mechanics' version of the title song off my latest solo album, a song called "Death of the Party" about when my life went to shit. So, we were set. Any money we'd make on the tour we'd get from venue guarantees and merch sales. Split four ways, after management and crew and expenses. Not much left, it seemed, to argue about.

The trouble started the first day on the road, when the new issue of *SPIN* hit the stands. We all knew there was going to be an article about the tour. But you never know how these things are going to turn out when you're being interviewed by the writer.

The tour manager, a guy named Joe everyone else knew well, but who I'd just met the week before, had been talking about the *SPIN* piece when we gathered to leave LA for our first show at 5th & B in San Diego. I don't know where he got them, but he passed out a bunch of copies on the tour bus as we made our way south in a clog of traffic on the 405. I tucked myself into the lower bunk down by the back wheels—the worst bunk in a tour bus, which I'd picked on purpose, trying to be considerate and to show I knew I was the low guy on the totem pole.

Which might have started us off on a good note if the *SPIN* article hadn't been such a disaster. The writer didn't have much at all to say about the Popular Mechanics and our reunion tour. I'd been promised, repeatedly, it would be about the band. Instead, it was mostly about me, and mostly about things I would've rather not seen printed in a magazine.

"The Death of the Party"

Bud Barrett estimates he's played more than a thousand shows in the last twenty years, but he's nervous about the recently announced Popular Mechanics reunion mini-tour. "You always get a little nervous going onstage," he says, sitting in his home studio in the garage of his Long Beach bungalow. "But when you have a tour lined up with the band that fired you a long time ago for your bad habits . . . well, there's a lot to be nervous about."

Those "bad habits" Barrett talks about are hardly a secret to fans of the Popular Mechanics. As he's quick to point out, while he may have played a thousand shows, his once and future bandmates have played probably twice as many. After leaving the critically acclaimed band following more than a decade together (there is still some dispute about the facts surrounding Barrett's departure—Barrett says he was fired, while co-songwriter Tony Carlosi claims it was a "mutual decision"), Barrett disappeared deeper into his drug-fueled self-destruction. One he didn't climb out of until 2004, when he entered rehab. "Not the first time," Barrett says with a tired smile. "But the one that seems to have stuck."

When asked why that rehab worked when others hadn't, Barrett shrugs. "Hard to say. After a while, you can't live that life anymore." He pauses, walks out to the back patio, and lights a cigarette. "My last fucking vice," he says, laughing. "Apparently I need at least one." Barrett continues, "A lot of the rehabs weren't really to get me clean. They were the record company detoxing me for three weeks so I could perform on tour. I don't blame them. I was an asset they'd invested in, and they wanted a return," he says. "But it's hard, when you're loaded, to not be cynical of their motives. I was dollar signs to a record company and they figured they needed me for the band." He laughs quietly. "As it turned out, their career kept going without me. I wasn't helping them any by the end, and they didn't need me."

Carlosi says, "I feel bad that I was a part of all that. We should have taken six months off and really tried to get Bud help. But it's hard. We're touring behind what everyone always thinks is a career-making album, so nobody—not managers, record companies and, yeah, even the band—wants to mess with that. Still . . . we should have stopped. Bud was losing his mind."

Fans might argue with Barrett's statement that the band didn't need him. While the Popular Mechanics have released a series of solid, well-received records in Barrett's absence, and they continue to draw well in medium-sized theater venues, many fans have long hoped for the return of the man who wrote much of their strongest and most eclectic material. After nearly a decade apart, however, it seemed impossible. The odds of reading that Barrett had rejoined the band seemed a lot lower than the odds of reading his obituary.

However, Barrett's surprising sobriety and his voluminous output during the past few years have put him back on fans' radar. Since 2004, he has produced two CDs with his band and side project, Red Asphalt (an inside joke since it was, very briefly, the original name of the Popular Mechanics in 1985), and four solo CDs, the most recent of which, *The Death of the Party*, has drawn the best reviews of his career and seems a lock to end up on many of this year's Top Ten lists. Barrett's solo CD was released within a week of *Looking Back*, a Popular Mechanics' retrospective of their early indie-label years plus various B-sides and demos. "Total coincidence," Barrett says.

And now the Popular Mechanics, despite their comfortable niche in alt-country circles, have asked Barrett back into the fold. While some fans speculate in on-line forums that this signals a reunion of the band, Carlosi points out, "We've decided to reform the original band in support of this anthology of recordings from that era. There really haven't been any long-term talks about this going on beyond this tour."

Drummer Jack Lester says, "I'm looking at this tour, quite frankly, as a way to make some money. I have kids in school.

I'm an adult. It isn't in any long-range plans of mine to be in a band with Bud again."

The long-running feud between Barrett and Lester is hardly news. "I tend to think everyone hates me," Barrett says. "It's an insecurity of mine. But Jack really does hate me. So it's nice, in a way, that he says it out loud so I don't feel crazy when I think he hates me. But, it's cool. For years I wished Jack would like me the way he did when we started. But we were kids. I was nineteen. We're all over 40 now, and I can't worry about what Jack thinks of me, so long as he respects me, which I think he does. He respects the music, at any rate."

Guitarist Mickey Wiles, when asked about the band tension, responds, "Nobody has to be having sleepovers. We're adults. The egos go away when we have a job to do, and none of us is interested in doing anything bad to the name of this band."

Barrett, while clearly trying to stay on the high road during most of the interview, in the end can't seem to resist saying this about Lester: "As a musician, Jack is living proof that drum machines can never replace human beings. As a human being, Jack makes me think it makes total sense that someone tried to invent a machine that could replace drummers."

CHICAGO READER music critic Ron Clark writes, "With Barrett, the Popular Mechanics were an eclectic, unpredictable band who were always interesting, even when they didn't hit the mark. The lack of production—lo-fi before it had a name—gave their recordings the same frayed charm of their best live shows. Live, they could be the best band you ever saw—or the worst."

"Not true," Barrett says. "The Replacements were better than us. And they were probably the only band that could be worse than us!" He laughs. "They had *range*." The comparison to the Mats is hardly new. In the early 1990s, after their drunken ragged cowpunk years, it wouldn't have been totally unfair to write the Popular Mechanics off as a band—albeit a good band with catchy songs—that was trying too hard, perhaps, to pick up the drunken torch The Replacements had dropped (including famously playing their second song on SNL in drag in what many saw as a tribute to Westerberg & Company's changing into each other's clothes for their second song during their own mid-1980s appearance on the show). By mid-decade, though, love them or hate them, the Popular Mechanics had gelled into an original outfit. Their increasingly erratic live performances promised you would catch a great show or a disaster, and either way people had something to talk about the next day. Which is exactly what happened as the band played into the age of Internet chat groups. As Carlosi puts it, "We kind of got more famous for the wrong shit than we did for the music."

After Barrett's departure, the Popular Mechanics became a strong band that reverted more to their alt-country roots—one of the best in the genre. They were a very dependable and professional live band, but not very exciting. In fact, they wouldn't again release anything as interesting—or as self indulgent—as *The Suicide Variations*.

TSV, as the album is known to fans, is easily the most polarizing record in the band's discography. An equal number of fans seem to claim it as either their favorite or their least-favorite record. Barrett actually sides with the naysayers. "I don't think it's very good, really," he says. "It could have been. But . . . I was trying to make a masterpiece, which is the wrong fucking thing to do in a rock band." He puts out his cigarette. "I was trying way too hard, and I'd stopped listening to anyone. I'm a little embarrassed by that record. But, hey, I'm embarrassed about a lot of shit from that decade. And half of this one!"

It's also the only record entirely missing from the second-generation Mechanics' live set list. The strongest indictment of the polarizing album has always come from band member Lester: "It's Bud's record," he says. "And it sucks."

When asked about what made him finally quit the hard life that he'd become famous for in indie-music circles, Barrett says, "It's not that interesting. There's a danger in talking about addiction. It doesn't make you special or cool." He pauses. "There's nothing romantic about it. People die when they should have lived. People live when by rights they should be dead." He laughs again. "It's a hell of a life."

And a remarkably different life from the one Barrett leads now. Today, he runs a recording studio in Long Beach and produces his own releases. He volunteers as a music teacher at inner-city schools, and he's settled into a life he says he's "stunned" by with its new domesticity. He met his wife, Southern CA visual artist Olivia Richards, five years ago. "I'd just been diagnosed as bi-polar with manic episodes. News to me. I thought everyone stayed up for a week or two doing their thing and then felt like killing themselves for a month. I'd gotten out of rehab for the last time, and at that point, after 40 years of these kinds of ups and downs, I figured I'd covered the range of what life might have in store for me. Falling in love wasn't something I could see happening anymore. And then Olivia and I got together." He smiles. "Who doesn't like a story with a happy ending?"

Who indeed? And if this is the last go around for the original lineup (nobody's saying one way or the other), Barrett will have another story with a happy ending.

The Popular Mechanics are back together, at least for this tour. Nobody saw it coming, but the band and their fans are eager to hear these songs again.

"Something happens when the four us of play together," Carlosi says. "Something special."

I read the article on the bus as we crawled our way toward San Diego. I could see all the guys reading it, too. I'd never tell anyone, but I loved reading about myself. I didn't like talking about myself much. Didn't like being interviewed. But, if I was honest—and the only person I'd be this honest with was Olivia—I'd admit that I loved reading praise about my work and loved it when people treated my career as if it were important. And maybe it was—as much as any indie-band career can be important. This wasn't The Beatles we were talking about, after all. But it was enormously gratifying that people cared about what we'd done twenty years ago and what I did in my garage these days. Gratifying that it had some meaning beyond myself.

When I rolled out of my bunk, Mickey looked up from the magazine. Tony and Jack sat at the little breakfast-nook table. Everyone looked at me like I'd done something wrong. Traffic had opened up, and the bus was now moving at normal freeway speeds. It's a strange sensation. On a tour bus, you get something like sea legs—you have to lean toward the front of the bus in order to stand straight up.

"Well, lookie here," Jack said. "It's our savior."

I said, "I had no idea she was going to write that."

The tour manager, Joe, sat on the couch looking down at his phone and acting like he was doing something.

I said, "I never said I was your savior. I went out of my way to say you guys didn't need me."

Jack said, "You got that right."

Mickey didn't sound mad, but he said, "Bud, you have to know the angle they're going to take on this."

I looked over to Tony for support. Once, he was my best friend in the world. "Seriously," I said. "I had no idea she'd write all that. I was told it was going to be about the band. Not about me."

Nobody said anything, and I felt the rumble of the wheels under my feet. I waited for someone to say, *Hey, it's not your fault. We know how the press is.* But nothing was coming. Just the three guys in the band looking at me, and the tour manager and the rest of the crew I'd just met looking down at the floor.

I shook my head and went to the back of the bus, where there was a couch away from everyone else. I had my Gibson LG-O there and sat down and started playing the guitar, hoping this storm would pass soon enough. I tried to fingerpick, but my fingers wouldn't work and hurt like hell, so I used a pick and strummed mindlessly, using the beat of the wheels on the freeway as rhythm.

The first seven or eight years we were together, we traveled by van. Just the band and, near the end, one guy who'd do quadruple duty as a driver, roadie, guitar tech, and guy who'd run the merch table. The last year or two I was with the Popular Mechanics, we'd signed to Electra, and we had a bus—a bus like the one we were on now—and real guitar techs and sound people, and a tour manager who sold the merch and kept everything running smoothly. But at that point, I was a full-blown drug addict and the guys weren't talking to me much anymore. And, while I know we had a tour bus on that last tour in the 1990s, I couldn't remember much about it. I was so fucked up, I had no idea what cities we were in and no clue what was going on in the band, and I didn't really care much.

This time around, I felt every ripple of tension and judgment. Maybe I even felt judgments that weren't there. I sat in the back of the bus and strummed my guitar. Everyone else seemed clumped up front against me. Maybe twenty minutes later, Tony came

to the back of the bus and closed the curtain behind him. The
curtain didn't block sound, but it gave us some privacy.

"Hey," he said.

"Dude, I'm really sorry about that article."

"Not your fault," he said. He stood above me with a beer in
his hand. "Cool if I have a drink?"

It was nice of him to ask, but I'd long ago gotten used to
people drinking in front of me. People are weird around addicts
and alcoholics. They think that your not drinking is some sort of
statement on their lifestyle. Hell, if I could have had a drink, I would
have. If I could do heroin without it ruining my life, I'd still be doing
it. But what I could and couldn't do had no bearing on anyone else.

"Of course," I said.

"Just wanted to check."

"Thanks," I said, grateful for the first kind gesture since we'd
hit the road. "But don't sweat it, OK?"

Tony sat on the couch next to me. "Sorry for what Jack said."

"I guess I expected it," I said.

"The article?"

"No," I said. "Just that this is a strange situation."

"That it is."

"You really want me here?" I said.

"What do you mean?" he said. "I asked you, didn't I?"

"Seems to be causing a lot of tension." I wanted a cigarette, but
the bus driver said it was a nonsmoking bus and I'd have to wait
until we stopped somewhere. Since there was a bathroom on the
bus, I had no idea when we'd be stopping. "Things seemed cool
at practice. Even in the studio." I thought about Jack. "Mostly,
anyway."

Tony said, "You have to understand. Nothing's different for
them, except that no one's paying them much attention." He took
a sip. "That article just shoved it in their faces."

"That's not my fault."

"But it *is* a fact."

"I never said I was a fucking savior," I said.

Tony nodded. "I know."

I took a deep breath and let it out. "I specifically asked her if it was going to be about the band."

"I'm not pissed at you."

"Really?"

"You didn't write that shit. But you've got to realize, we've been out here doing this for years, and now the whole piece is about you."

I said, "It's not like I've been in some amusement park the last ten years."

"I hear you." Tony took a long drink of his beer and now I wanted one for myself, which blew a breeze of fear through me.

I nodded. "Well, at least it's a short tour. There won't be any more major magazines hitting the racks before we're done." I smiled.

Tony smiled back.

I said, "I'd be happy—more than happy—to not do any of the press for this tour. You guys want to do the radio shit, I'm fine with that."

He shrugged. "Hell, they'll just ask us about you whether you're there or not."

Neither of us said anything for a moment. The bus rumbled over the freeway.

I said, "Are we cool?"

"We're cool." He finished his beer and grabbed another from the mini-fridge. He laughed quietly. "If I was going to kill you, I would have done it years ago. We've been though way too much not to be cool by now, right?"

He got up and held out his hand. I shook it, felt a tinge of pain in my bad hand, and said, "Right."

I called Olivia between sound check and the show. I paced and smoked out back while we talked. The smell of the ocean hung in the San Diego air, and the sun bounced orange and pink off fluffy clouds that looked like cotton candy.

Olivia said, "How's my favorite rock star?"

"Your favorite rock star's OK. A little nervous."

"You'll be great."

"Hope so," I said. "Did you see the new issue of *SPIN*?

"I don't know if you've noticed, Bud, but I'm not in college. I haven't seen an issue of *SPIN* in fifteen years."

I told her about the article.

"Ouch," she said. "Is everything OK?"

I told her we'd see. She said she'd read some article in the *Times* about housing loans and credit scandals.

"The economy's going to hell," she said. "The stock market keeps getting worse."

I took a drag of my cigarette. "It's a good thing we don't have stocks, then."

She laughed. "We have stocks."

"We do?" Olivia handled the money. Whenever I got a check, I gave it to her. Whenever I wanted to buy something, I asked her if we had enough. Any more information than that, and I'd get so stressed about going broke, I'd feel an anxiety attack coming on and start to have trouble breathing.

"Of course we have stocks," she said. "It's part of my work retirement plan."

"We have a retirement plan?" This time I was half kidding, although I didn't know we had one until Olivia had just said so. "So are we in trouble? If the stock market's going to collapse?"

"Jesus, Bud. Five minutes ago you didn't know we had stocks, and now you're worried about their value?" It sounded like she was listening to Mingus in the bedroom. "We're fine. It would only be a problem if we were going to cash out in the next year."

"And we're not doing that?"

"We're not doing that," she said. "Everything's fine. Just have fun and play guitar, OK? Enjoy life, mister."

"I'll try," I said. Tony and Mickey came out to the loading zone to get me to go in for our dinner buyout. I told Olivia I had to go.

"Love you bigger than big things," she said.

This was an old joke of ours. It had started years before, in the car, while we were listening to the Stones' version of "Not Fade Away" with the line in the song, "My love's bigger than a Cadillac." One of us, I don't remember who started it, said, "I love you bigger than a Cadillac." And for the rest of the drive, we'd go back and forth: *I love you bigger than the Empire State Building. I love you bigger than the ocean. I love you bigger than the moon. I love you bigger than the sun.* And when we'd run out of big things, it became what it was now.

I said, "Love you bigger than big things," and hung up.

Tony and Mickey looked at me.

"What?" I said.

Mickey made a kissing noise and singsonged, "I wuv you bigger than big things."

The friendly abuse felt good. One of the guys again. At least until the next article came out.

The first shows went as well as any of us could have dreamed they would. We played sold-out theaters, and the fans crackled with energy. When the crowd gives you that push of energy, you get more power than you knew you had. San Diego was about as perfect as the first show of a tour could be. We played some of the old stuff, some of the newer numbers of Tony's, and we got called out for three encores. For the final encore, we had no idea what to play. In our time, we'd been nearly as famous for our live sets full of covers as for our originals. Tony called out "Roadrunner?"

Jonathan Richman & the Modern Lovers. The first song we'd ever played in front of a crowd, at some rich kid's birthday party on a lake, more than twenty years before. We hadn't practiced it at all, but it came off. The fact that it's a two-chord song made it easier to do than it might have been otherwise, but still, you feel invincible when that happens.

The next shows went almost as well, but my hand started to give me real trouble. I played the fourth or fifth show of the tour with my pinky and ring fingers taped together with medical tape I got at a drugstore. The next night, I had to tape the middle finger to the other two. If they weren't taped together, the fingers moved too much and the pain exploded into my arm. Shooting pains that would jolt up the arm and flash lights behind my eyes. My playing was starting to suffer enough that Mickey asked if I was OK after the show that night. I told him the hand was bad and showed it to him.

"You can't use the fingers?"

"Just the thumb and index finger," I said.

"Dude, you have to get that checked out."

In San Francisco, we had a day off before our show at the Fillmore and I went to the emergency room. I sat in pain, feeling sorry for myself that while everyone else was out at Amoeba Records or eating good food, I waited and watched as people with bigger problems than me went first. An old homeless woman across from me had an enormous open wound on her foot that fifteen or twenty flies kept landing on. She was asleep, but her rotting foot smelled like rancid meat and twitched every once in a while and the flies would take off then come back again.

I gave the guy next to me five bucks to come get me if they called my name, and I went out front to have a smoke and call Olivia.

She asked what was up and I told her I was at the hospital getting my hand checked.

"The hospital? How bad is it?"

Along with the pain, it was getting weaker every day. I couldn't hold a cigarette without pain, so I'd shoved it between the middle and ring fingers so it couldn't fall out. "It's not so good. But we'll see what they say."

"Should you cancel the show?"

"I can't do that."

"You can if you can't play," she said.

I let out an irritable sigh. "I'm playing," I said. "What are you doing tonight?"

"I was going to have a glass of wine and jerk off thinking about my favorite rock star two or three times."

"Two or three times?"

"Keep talking and it might be four," she said. "Your voice makes me wet, Bud."

"I miss you, baby."

She said, "Wish you were here, sweetie."

I thought about a night with Olivia, instead of a night waiting at the ER. "That makes two of us."

The guy inside the ER waved to me. I told Olivia I had to go, that they were ready to see me.

"Call me later and let me know what they say?" she said.

"I will."

"I wish you were home, Bud," she said. "I miss you."

"Miss you," I said. "Love you. And lust you."

She told me she loved me and told me again to call her later.

Inside, I showed the doctor my hand and explained that I was a guitar player on the road. She put me through a range of motion tests. She pushed on the fingers and the wrist, judging the pain, which had grown substantial.

"You're going to have to get this looked at by a specialist," she said.

I said I would when I got home.

She started writing a script. She seemed to be in a hurry to get rid of me. But maybe that was just the nature of her job. The more the day went on, the more the waiting room seemed to swell with poverty and despair and disease.

She handed me a script for a hundred and twenty ten-milligram Vicodin. I read it a couple of times. The doctor seemed ready to leave. I was stunned. For years I'd tried to scam ER doctors out of scripts, and they never wrote you anything. Now, when I wasn't looking for them, here they were.

I said, "How many of these can I take a day?" And right away, I felt like a lying addict when I added, "I don't want to overdo it."

"If the pain stays this bad, no more than ten a day."

And she left.

Ten a day? She was a quack. One ten-milligram Vicodin was cut with three hundred and twenty-five milligrams of Tylenol, which was poison. Ten pills a day would be more than three thousand milligrams of that shit in what was left of my liver. There used to be days when I'd eat thirty or forty of them, but I was an addict, not a doctor. Half of me was amazed she still had her license and half of me wondered where she'd been ten years ago.

There was no way I'd take ten a day. I'd just try a couple like a responsible person. I'd been clean five years. Maybe I could be normal, take the stuff as it was directed. And it wasn't like I went out trying to score drugs. I was in serious pain, and I needed to be better by the next night. There was no way I wanted to play poorly at the Fillmore.

I got a text from Olivia.

Hey baby. Wish I was there to kiss that gorgeous messed up hand of yours. I'd give it a kiss that would make all the other kisses in the world hang their heads in shame.

By the end of the day off, I'd taken well over ten of the Vicodin, and it felt physically incredible and emotionally dreadful. All the physical tension, all the worry and nervousness just disappeared. I knew I'd fucked up, but I didn't have to play that night, and no one needed to know that I was high. But here I was again. A fuck-up. Why couldn't I ever just do the right thing?

My phone rang and I saw it was Olivia. I thought about answering, but she might be able to tell I was fucked up. I let it go to voicemail and realized in that second, I'd just started lying to her and I wondered from experience if I'd be able to stop. I thought seriously about taking the rest of the pills and killing myself.

I was high for the Fillmore show and the guys could tell. No one talked to me in the greenroom after the show. I was stretched out on the couch, my hand still hurting, probably the only part of my body not feeling the opiates. Some writer wanted to do an interview, and I asked out of it, saying I was really tired. Mickey, Tony, and Jack went to get some food with the writer and I was alone. On the table, next to the classic Fillmore spread with the chocolate-dipped strawberries, was a bucket of high-end microbrews on ice. Also in the bucket was the six-pack of nonalcoholic beer I'd had Joe put in our rider.

I closed the door to the greenroom and swallowed ten Vicodin and then drank three of the microbrews in five minutes. I was passed out on the couch when Joe came in and told me the bus was getting ready to head to Portland.

Sometime late the next morning, we were in Portland, where we were playing the Wonder Ballroom. We loaded in around noon, and I found the greenroom and closed the door so I could be alone and get some sleep.

Someone knocked.

"Go the fuck away," I said.

"Dude, it's Tony." He paused and I closed my eyes. I was halfway through the pills and I wasn't even feeling high anymore.

I'd heard this happened. No matter how long you were clean, after you relapsed, eventually you couldn't even get high anymore. It evens you out, like a maintenance dose. But there's no more euphoria. Just dread and regret.

He knocked again. "Open the door."

I got up and unlocked the door and flopped back down on the couch.

Tony closed the door behind him and locked it. He sat in the chair facing me. He had his hands together and he stared at the floor. "We're putting it on the band website today that tonight, Eugene, and LA are going to be our farewell shows with you."

"What?"

"Don't act surprised," Tony said. "And don't make me explain why, when we both know." He looked at me. "I'm sorry. I thought this could work. I wanted this to work."

"I'm taking pills for my hand," I said.

"I don't know why I thought you'd changed."

"I've been clean five years," I said. "I *have* changed." Though I knew that didn't feel true, anymore.

He said, "I argued for you to come back."

I knew I'd fucked up. And maybe five years of fighting this thing in me should be wiped out by a couple of bad days. Maybe I'd just run out of second chances. But what about everything I'd done right? "Most of the shows have been strong, Tony. I fucked up last night. No one else has ever played a shit show in this band?"

"You played fucked up at the Fillmore," he said with anger.

"Yeah. I'm the first person who's *ever* played the Fillmore high." I looked at him. "*You've* played it high."

"When I was a fucking kid."

"So now I'm a child?"

"You pick the most important venue we play as the night you can barely stand up straight or talk into your mic. Jack and

Mickey are looking at me like they want to fucking kill you. And I'm standing there feeling like an idiot wondering why I fought for this. And now this shit's on YouTube so everyone can see how damn pathetic we looked." He paused. "I have to think about the future of this band. I have too much at stake to blow nights at the Fillmore."

YouTube? Fuck. Someone would tell Olivia. I didn't know what to say. "I'm sorry."

"You know better. Fuck you, you're sorry."

I turned around and punched the bathroom door. As soon as I'd done it, smashing a hole through the cheap hollow outside half of the door, I realized I'd both fucked up my bad hand even more *and* I'd just broken property at another club, which wasn't going to help the band any, either. I pulled my bloodied hand out of the broken door and saw pieces of eighth-inch wood veneer driven and slivered into the cuts on skin that was already swollen and felt stretched tight.

I turned to face Tony. "Fine! I'm the asshole. I'm the fuck-up. I'm the reason anything bad has ever happened to anyone who's ever played in this fucking band. You happy? Get it out of your fucking system." I tried not to care, at least not what anyone here thought. I opened a beer in front of him and drank it. "I've been bending over backwards to make you guys feel comfortable, but maybe that fucking article was right. Maybe people gave a shit about this tour because I was back in the band. You want the truth? Maybe you're not as good without me."

"We've really struggled all these years having a guitar player who actually stays conscious for shows," he said in a sad, calm voice.

I was exhausted. I tossed my empty beer bottle in the trash and opened another. Tony didn't look that mad, really. He looked disappointed, and that hurt more.

I nodded and sighed slowly. I was too old and too tired and had done this too many times to make a case for myself. I had more years behind me than ahead of me and I'd never been this tired in my life. "Do you want me to just leave now?"

"We've got three shows left."

"If you guys don't want me, do them as a three-piece," I said. "Or call your conscious guitar player you like so much."

"That wasn't fair of me." He paused for a very long time. I heard people outside the greenroom moving equipment around. Someone checking mics. "We *are* better with you," he said. "And I want you to play the shows." He rubbed his face with his head down for a second. He looked up at me. "Just be clean enough to do them right, OK? For me?"

I thought about Olivia. About going home. I'd only had a few days on the pills. I wouldn't even get dopesick if I quit now. We'd been talking about trying to have a kid, and she was making noise about needing to decide before she got too old. Maybe I should just go home and straighten out. "I don't want to be around if no one wants me."

"I *just said* I wanted you to do these shows, OK?"

The way he said it made me realize he was alone. Mickey and Jack weren't in the room. They weren't here firing me, while still trying to talk me into staying around until the end. "Who wants me out of the band?"

He took a drink. "If you need to know, well . . . Mickey seemed on the fence and I didn't want you out. I *did* want to come in here and kick your ass for what you did at the Fillmore, and then move on."

I was calmer now. I realized I was in a room with my only real friend left on this tour. "Thanks," I said. "But it's pretty awkward playing with two guys who want me gone. Who hate me."

"They don't hate you."

"No?"

"Well, Mickey doesn't hate you." He laughed, cutting the tension a little. "He's just older. He doesn't need any drama in his life."

I could smile. "And I'm drama?"

"You've had your moments."

I looked away. "Fair enough."

At least Mickey didn't hate me. A small victory. Jack really hadn't been able to stand me since 1989, so it's not like I lost him on this tour. I said, "I really appreciate you coming here. Being honest. And I am sorry I let you down. But why don't I just split?"

"We've booked these shows with you. We didn't sell tickets to a thousand people a night to see a three-piece," Tony said. "So, one: you owe me this. Two: I'm trying to help you, Bud. You leave the tour now, everyone's going to know you're using. It'll be all over forums and YouTube comments and all that shit. If we put on the website that your hand is too bad for you to tour full-time, and we wish you could stay but you just can't, and if you play the last shows well, you can just have a graceful exit."

I felt like I'd let the world down. Worse, I'd become the same piece of shit I always was, after they trusted me not to do all this again. "And Mickey and Jack are OK with me playing the shows?"

"I'm here representing everyone," he said.

He'd probably had to lobby to get me this much from the guys. I doubted Mickey or Jack really gave two shits about whether anyone knew I was using again or not. And I couldn't blame them.

Tony hugged me. I hugged him back with my left arm, my right hand dangling in pain.

"I'm really sorry," I said.

He was still holding on to me when he said, "Don't be sorry. Just get yourself together, OK? And play these last shows right."

I had probably felt this bad before, but I couldn't remember feeling much worse. My stomach ached and I was afraid I'd start crying like a kid. "OK," I said.

He let go and patted me on the shoulder twice. "I'm really sorry, Bud," he said and left me alone in the greenroom. I thought about locking myself in the bathroom and overdosing. Olivia'd said we were done if I started using again. But worse, she said the one thing she would never forgive me for was killing myself. And I hated and resented her in that moment—ready to die, set up with a plan, and then stopped by love dressed as guilt or guilt dressed as love.

I held it together enough to play a good show in Portland. After that, we played the WOW (for Woodsmen of the World) in Eugene and, knowing that this was coming to an end, I did my best to play a great show and pulled it off. Three encores, with us playing a bunch of the covers we'd played over the years. In a way, covers were more fun than your own tunes. It's just you playing for fun—like when it started in a garage when you were kids. Our last encore was all covers—loud, cowpunk versions of the Louvin Brothers' "The Great Atomic Power" and Woody Guthrie's "Do, Re, Mi," with me and Tony hitting tight, ragged harmonies on both. Then we did a pretty straight take on Richard Hell's "The Kid with the Replaceable Head." All of these were spontaneous, shouted out to each other. We hadn't rehearsed any of them. When the crowd wanted more, I started the riff to the Replacement's "Color Me Impressed." I don't think we'd played it since 1987 or so, but it all fell together.

Jack hadn't spoken to me since San Francisco, but Mickey said "good show" and Tony thanked me twice. At least I didn't blow the whole tour, even if I was counting down to what I guessed would be the last times I'd ever get to play with the best band I'd ever had.

I called Olivia because I had to. If I kept avoiding it, she'd know something was wrong. If I called her, I could at least try to lie, even if every lie tightened a vise of self-loathing on me.

"I've been worried," she said.

I told her not to worry.

She asked about the hand, and I told her LA would be my last show. A final Saturday night at the Wiltern—which wasn't the Fillmore, but it was almost as good.

"Are you OK?"

"My hand hurts." I paused, then lied, "Otherwise, I'm fine."

"It sounded like you were loving the tour."

I lit a cigarette. "There were no guarantees," I said. "I knew it might just be this short tour. And that's all it's going to be."

"You don't sound right."

"I'm fine," I said. "Just in pain. A little sad. I'll be OK."

"I can't wait to see you Saturday," she said.

I'd forgotten that. LA. She'd be coming to the show. She'd never seen me with the Popular Mechanics—except on TV and YouTube. At the start of the tour, I'd been thrilled she'd see me. Now it scared me.

"I should get going," I said.

There was a pause. Joe, the tour manager, was still settling up and packing the merch. The diesel engine of the bus hummed and the fumes filled the air, along with the smell of my cigarette.

I said, "I love you."

"Big?" she said.

"Bigger than big things," I said, and pushed the End button on my phone. I went onto the bus and crawled into my bunk and pulled the curtain closed.

Fans posted on our website, responding to the news that the LA show would be the last show ever with me, and they seemed largely pissed that the whole tour hadn't been announced as a "farewell" tour. I didn't see how it mattered that much. Six months before, no one thought we'd ever play together again. Now they were mad we'd only played a few weeks, and by the time we announced our last show, it had been sold out for a month. There was talk, briefly, of adding a matinee show on the day of our final Saturday night appearance. Jack was the only one who voted yes—not because he wanted to play any more than was necessary with me, but because a sold-out matinee would have meant another eight to ten grand for the band.

Olivia met me at the Wiltern about an hour before the opening band went on. I showed her around the greenroom.

"Fancy," she said.

"You missed the years of bars with greenrooms filled with band stickers and penises drawn on them with Sharpies," I said.

"Really?"

"Every fucking club in the country," I said. "And Europe. The only difference is the band stickers are sometimes in different languages."

"Still with the penises?" she said.

"All over the world. Penises are very popular."

"Some of my best friends have penises," she said.

I stretched out on the couch and she lay down next to me and kissed me.

"Missed you," she said.

"Missed you." I felt awful about it, but I wished she wasn't there. I wanted to get high. Get drunk. Something. I wished I had killed myself in that bathroom.

Eventually, people started wandering into the greenroom. A hometown show is always the worst, greenroom-wise. Everyone's wife or girlfriend or boyfriend and family and friends are there. Even fucking kids. The greenroom is supposed to be private, a few good friends at most. A place to clear your head. To get ready for a show.

We were due onstage at ten o'clock. By nine, the fucking room was clogged with people I didn't know.

I whispered to Olivia, "I need to be alone for a while before we go on."

"OK."

"You cool up here alone?"

"I'm not exactly alone," she said.

I got up. She stood with me, and I worried for a second that she hadn't understood I wanted to be alone. We left the greenroom, and she said, "I'm going down to the bar. How do you stand rooms that like before a show?"

I thought about the Fillmore, alone on a couch full of Vicodin and beer. The frightening privacy. "It's not always like that."

After Olivia went toward the bar, I snuck back up to the opening band's empty greenroom and grabbed four beers and put them in every pocket I could find in my leather jacket. I went out back behind the Wiltern, and I smoked four or five cigarettes and drank the beers, looking up at a foggy sky, a nighttime marine layer that smelled like salt and reminded me of home.

If the last show wasn't the best show we'd ever played, it was up there. About midway through, I started to feel really emotional, thinking, after every song, *That's the last time I'll ever play that song.* It became a somewhat sad countdown as the set list dwindled. Every once in a while, I looked up to where Olivia stood, off to the side of the stage with our guitar tech. She danced, blew kisses, and seemed to be having fun. When we finished the set proper, before the encores, we headed offstage, and the crowd was as loud as any I'd ever heard.

Again, they wouldn't let us get away with the two encores we had listed, but that was to be expected for our last show. We did all the covers we'd done the last couple of nights, and added a couple of Stones' tunes, "Torn and Frayed" and "Rocks Off," and finally two old Warren Zevon tunes that Tony and I had first played in the early 1980s, "Gorilla, You're a Desperado" and "Lawyers, Guns and Money."

We left the stage for what seemed like it would be the last time. I was drenched in sweat. The security guard opened the back door for me, and I lit a cigarette.

Tony came out. "Got a couple more in you?"

"If you can figure out what we know that we haven't played."

"I want to do 'The Problem with Drugs'."

What did it matter? "Sure."

The first encore, and usually the second, is a formality. People expect it, and so do the bands. The light guy knows it's happening. Everybody does. It's built into the set. It's only when you get called out for a third that you know the night is special. This was our last night, so why not four?

I was at the mic. "This is a song I haven't played for a hundred years," I said.

Tony said, "We've played it a little more recently."

The crowd seemed to get what that meant. People started screaming for "The Trouble With Drugs."

I said, "Thanks for coming out." I turned to Tony, and then to Mickey and Jack, but ended up looking back at Tony. "I want to thank these guys for letting me come out and do this again for a while." The crowd cheered.

I started the song, a simple D-to-G pattern, and it was only when I stepped back up to the mic that I realized I'd forgotten the opening words. I stopped, and the band sputtered to a halt after me, laughing. Even Jack didn't seem pissed.

I said, "I told you, it's been a while." I wiped sweat from my stinging eyes. "What's the first line?"

A woman in front screamed, "I woke with the chills and I stole your pills."

"Right, I said. "OK, let's try it again."

As it turned out, after the first line, I really didn't need to sing it. At least half the room was singing it. We just played, and the crowd carried the lyrics to a song I'd written in a motel in the late 1980s. Bizarre. At least, if this had to be the last time we played, it wasn't going to get any better than that moment.

Olivia had to get up in the morning to teach, so she only stayed about twenty minutes after the show, which was a relief.

"That was amazing," she said, as I walked her to her car. My car was back at Tony's house where I'd left it at the start of the tour. "Really," she said. "You were incredible up there."

I smiled. "I used to be."

She kissed me. "You were fabulous. I'm not listening to that."

She waved as she pulled away from the pay lot. I waved and walked back to the Wiltern.

I walked through the bar, shaking hands with my good hand. Some huge guy, maybe in his mid-twenties, came up to me and handed me five eighty-milligram OxyContin. He screamed in my ear, "I heard about your hand, man, and I wanted to help out."

I brought him past security and backstage. The greenroom was still filled with people, so I brought him to one of the band bathrooms.

The kid seemed to be nodding out on his feet. Pupils tiny as the end of a sharpened pencil. I couldn't believe I'd spent years like that. I wondered if I should take the pills. It was the end of the tour. I was almost out of the Vicodin. I could lower my dosages, not get sick, and get back on track. But it was only five pills—and I didn't know any dealers in LA anymore. "How much do you want?" I said.

The kid rocked back and forth on unsteady legs. He slurred when he spoke. "I usually get eighty bucks a pill." He paused, and in the pause, I thought about doing the right thing and handing the pills back. I didn't need to spend four hundred bucks for something that might make me high for a day if I was lucky.

The kid dumped five more pills in my hand. "Dude, you're the Popular Mechanics."

Was he giving me the pills? Or giving me a break on the price? I said, "What do I owe you?"

The kid smiled and said with the most undeserved tone of awe I'd ever heard, "There's no way I'm charging you." He paused, and I wondered later if a sentence had ever been spoken that held such a different meaning to the two people talking as his next one did. "You're Bud Barrett," the kid said. He said it in a tone that meant, *You're a rock star, you're a genius, I wish I lived your life.* But all I heard was the dread of confirmation: You are Bud Barrett. *And you ruin everything you touch.*

I snorted one of the OxyContin in the bathroom after the kid left. It felt good enough that I snorted half of another. I went outside and had a cigarette and puked by a dumpster, which meant I was pretty high. I could pretty much always gauge how much I could take before OD'ing by when I started puking after having a smoke. I sat down. It felt amazing—like a sunrise inside my body. Even full of regret and hating myself, I tried to relax and enjoy this while I could.

I grabbed my Tele, left the rest of my gear with the guitar tech—I'd get it later—and caught a ride to my car. I blew Jack off, thanked Mickey, and hugged Tony and told him I loved him.

"You have to take care of yourself," he said.

"I'm fine," I said.

"I've seen you 'fine' before."

I looked at him. Why argue? Especially when he was right. I nodded and thanked him again, then caught a ride from a friend back to my car and drove home.

When I walked through the front door, Olivia said, "Hey, sexy rock star."

"I thought you'd be in bed."

"I'm about to turn in," she said. "But I wanted to see you."

I put my guitar down and kissed her. "Thanks."

"You OK?" she said.

"I'm OK. A little sad," I said. I held up my hand. "And in pain."

"Well, I love you, if that helps."

"That helps," I said.

And I said I loved her, too, and I think I meant it—meant it as much as I'd meant anything in my life.

In three months, I'd be kicked out of that house, that life, and Olivia would tell me with tears in her eyes that she loved me way too much to watch me kill myself.

But for that moment, I went into the bathroom and locked the door. I was shaking while I turned on the faucet as loud as it could get, and I crushed and snorted a finger-length line of OxyContin, hoping it would numb me enough so that I could stand myself when I opened that door to tell Olivia again that I loved her.

THE FOUR QUEENS

(Spring 2010)

I had a buzzing suspicion that something wasn't right about the guy Johnny Mo was setting us up with. I was carrying $1,100 for a pot deal that Johnny'd set up with this guy, Mike, who used to deal at the Frontier, but who got bounced for being the inside man on some Blackjack scam. To hear Johnny Mo tell it, word got around quick enough that this Mike was dirty and he couldn't pick up a dealing job anywhere in town, even at the most rat-ass casinos. We were supposed to meet him in an hour, at a room at the Four Queens, where he'd been living off some sports book score he made a few months before.

Johnny Mo said the guy was desperate for the money.

Johnny Mo said we'd get high-grade weed that we'd be able to move plenty fast in LA, and that the quality and the amount were in our favor because we had the fast cash this guy needed.

"He's an addict and he's desperate," Johnny Mo said.

Johnny Mo said these things like they were all pluses, which they could have been. A desperate addict is often willing to go for the short money with a long money product. But, looked at in the glass-half-empty way I had of seeing things, these could all have been negatives as well. Desperate people don't make predictable decisions. Addicts will fuck you. Not to be trusted, even if the deal sounded sweet. But Johnny Mo and I needed the money almost as bad as Mike. We were just willing to do a little more legwork for it.

I'd chewed two diazepam twenty minutes earlier, and my tongue was still running over the chalky residue couched in my molars as the calm started to settle on me like a dimmed light in a movie theater. I would have taken more than twenty milligrams, but I needed to be a perfect balance between calm and sharp to pull this off, as I was the one holding the money and I was the one who could say no, no matter what Johnny Mo or Mike had to say about it.

This was my money. I'd turned three hundred into two grand at a limit table at the Palms, and when my chips fell below fourteen hundred, I walked away with enough for the deal Johnny Mo had going. He'd begged me to pull out when I hit $1,500, but I got dealt pocket kings and bumped it back up a few hundred before the cards stopped coming. Too many weekend players and low-grade amateurs at the table to bluff, so I had to walk when luck ran cold. At a table with real players, you can play rags and win. At a table with losers, you need the cards. Plus, I'd been taking way too many painkillers, and they fucked with my focus. If I was going to play serious cards again, I needed to get, if not clean, at least cleaner.

Me and Johnny Mo were walking by the Neon Museum, which really isn't a museum but a bunch of cool old neon signs on Freemont.

"How well do you know this Mike?" I said.

"Who knows anybody?" he said.

"What the fuck are you?" I said. "The Buddha? Answer my question."

He lit a cigarette, happy to be in Vegas, where smoking was not only still allowed, it was celebrated and encouraged. "All I'm saying is, who knows what the fuck can happen in any given situation? Mike seems cool from what I know."

Tourists meandered all around us, making us zigzag through their lack of purpose. They were pudgy. Mostly white. Doughy-looking, buffet-stuffed, and soft. They looked like a parade of manicotti. They couldn't have looked more American than if they were dressing up as fat-ass Americans for Halloween.

"You're not helping me," I said.

"Hey, you asked me a question. I know him fine, but we've never had money on the table. Shit changes with money on the table."

"What's with you?" I said. "You trying to scare me?"

"What?"

"I ask you about the man we're doing business with, you're supposed to tell me he's fucking aces."

"I'm supposed to lie to you?"

"Hell, yes. Instead of giving me this philosophical horseshit about the unknowability of the fucking universe."

"OK," Johnny Mo said. "The guy's great. The man needs money—we have money. It's perfect. Nothing could go wrong. Supply and fucking demand. The stars are aligned, and your motherfucking biorhythms are perfect."

I glared at him.

He said, "Happy now?"

"I am not happy," I said. "Not close to happy at all." I thought about pulling out of the deal. But Johnny Mo said he knew some rich guy in Silverlake who would give us twenty-five hundred. Easy money. Almost doubling up for just taking a drive.

Johnny Mo said, "The only thing you got to watch is he's kinda scattered and jittery." He lit a new cigarette with the end of his last. "Like something happened to him. Like a stroke or some shit."

"How old is this guy?" I said.

"What do you mean?" he said.

"Don't you have to be old to have a stroke?"

"Roof stroke," Johnny Mo said.

"Do you know any of what you're talking about?" I said. "Is there any such thing as a roof stroke?"

"He was a roofer, and something happened to his head. Heat stroke or he fell or something. He doesn't seem to like talking about it."

"Well, sure," I said. "But he's not dangerous?"

"He fucked up his vocal cords, so he kinda mumbles his words. Quiet. Kind of a belch, kind of a whisper, but speedy. Rushed. Try to hear him the first time, though, 'cause it pisses him off to repeat himself. He gets all stressed and frustrated and his eyes bulge out of his head all freaky."

I stopped walking. "Seriously," I said. "Listen to what you're telling me."

"What?" Johnny Mo said.

I said, "What if this guy has a gun or something?"

"You don't have a gun?" he said, looking back and not stopping.

I followed him. "You *do?*"

He shook his head. "You're lucky you're good with cards, man. You got no sense in the world."

"So he's got a gun?" I said.

"I hope he does," Johnny Mo said. "I would not respect the motherfucker who would sell a hefty bag full of weed unarmed. That is not someone I'd want to be in business with."

Johnny Mo was wrong. I do have sense, but I'm not a violent guy, and I made the mistake of thinking that since I didn't carry a gun, neither would whoever I was hanging with. I should have known better, that in certain rooms—maybe most of them by that point in my life—I was in the minority.

I am, however, good with cards, like Johnny Mo said. Mostly because I know the odds and I can read people pretty well. Unlike most of life, except for the fact that bad luck will fuck you no matter how well you've played, you can rig the odds in your favor. Poker, when it's played right, is a perfect game. It's about knowing yourself and playing your opponent, not the cards. But nothing's perfect, ever, so when it's not played right, which is most of the time, you play the cards' odds *and* the opponent. And you keep a close eye on yourself and what you do in certain situations. If you brag when you bluff, chances are other people do it, too. Stare someone down when you're holding shit? So do most people. Everyone but the best pros will look away when they're holding the nuts. Clowns who talk all fucking night finally shut up when they get dealt anything special. We aren't that different, much as we try to think otherwise. Pay attention to your own habits and tendencies, and you'll be stunned how often they show up in other people.

You play someone who doesn't know how to play and they'll almost always come in with medium to high pairs. The odds of catching the third card to make a set? Twelve percent. A sucker bet, most of the time. And if you know they're trying for a set, you move in on them, because they're too dumb to dump the rags they're holding.

My style is aggressive. Better suited to no-limit. Someone sitting across from you at a table might feel pretty good with a middle pair if the most you could bet into him was, say, fifty bucks. It takes no guts to risk losing fifty bucks. That middle pair would start to look a lot shakier—and so would the person holding it—if you pushed their last thousand dollars in the world onto the table. Read the guy who can't afford to lose, focus on him, and he can't beat you unless the cards drop from heaven into his lap. But you have to know he could get those cards, dumb as he might play the game, and that you have to always be ready to lose everything you have. Or else you're him. That stiff who's afraid to lose, the one you're looking for at every table.

The big problem is it's tough to bluff a stooge out of a hand they should toss. And with poker on ESPN II every other night, the card rooms are swollen with weekend idiots who think they can win a bundle. It's fucked up the game. A stooge'll stay in a hand long after common sense should have slapped them on the head and told them to fold. Playing with amateurs, you always need some luck, because they simply don't play right, which is what I was thinking as we headed over to see this Mike guy.

The Four Queens is a dump. Not a glorious dump with a noteworthy history of meaningful poker tournaments, like Binions. Not really a historic dump like The Golden Gate. Not even a particularly memorable dump like the El Cortez, where the elevators never worked and the carpet reeked like urinal cakes and watered-down drinks that dated back to when those poor bastards who built the Hoover Dam came out here every Friday and blew through their checks before heading back to their Tent City housing and building the Eighth Wonder of the World every Monday morning.

People gamble differently at places like the Four Queens. There's a hopefulness to the out-of-towners on the strip, even if it's a naive, stupid hope. But downtown, the gamblers pretty much expect to lose. Even if they're ahead they know they'll blow it. Winning is temporary, while losing is a force as constant as gravity.

The Four Queens is so pedestrian in its squalor, so unremarkable in its everyday gray cardboard dreams, so run-of-the-mill in its filth and debris, that it makes your emotions swing like a pendulum from hatred to pity and back for every last one of us.

We walked through the casino to the elevators. There was a beefy security guard barely paying attention to anyone, wearing one of those generic SECURITY shirts you see at concerts. He looked the other direction, but I said, "We're just going up to see a friend."

He looked at me. "I don't give a fuck where you're going."

When the elevator doors closed, Johnny Mo said to me, "What are you talking to the security guard for?"

"They're not supposed to let anyone up to the rooms," I said. "I was making up a story."

Johnny Mo said, "You don't *say* anything. You walk around like you're supposed to be there, and you can go anywhere. Dumbass."

He was right, but I'd never been able to fake belonging or to act like I was supposed to be anywhere, really. My whole life pretty much felt like a party I wasn't invited to.

"So, if everything goes cool with this Mike, the rich guy in Silverlake is a sure thing to buy it off us?"

"*When* it goes cool with Mike," Johnny Mo said.

I just looked at him.

He said, "Mac in Silverlake's totally cool. A little crazy. When you meet him. Don't eat anything out of this bastard's shelves. Out of his pantries."

"What?"

"He puts acid in his food, in case people try to steal from him."

"Who steals food?"

"No one, if they know what's good for them. That's what I'm telling you."

I said, "Isn't this buddy of yours a millionaire?"

"I wouldn't say we were buddies," Johnny Mo said.

"But he's a millionaire?"

"Pretty much, yeah," Johnny Mo said, thinking for a moment. "At least."

"Who's he inviting over that steals food out of his pantry is what I'm saying."

Johnny Mo shrugged. "I'm just telling you, the man puts LSD in his food."

"What if he wants the food?"

"Then he takes the acid. Mac's always fucked up on something. He doesn't give a fuck."

A maid got on at one floor and off at the next.

"What about the fridge?" I said when the elevator door closed. "Is the shit in his fridge spiked, too?"

"Just don't take the man's food."

"I'm not taking his food," I said. "I'm just curious if he does it to shit in the fridge, too."

Johnny Mo looked at me and shook his head. The elevator door opened and we walked the rancid hallway toward Mike's room.

Johnny Mo knocked on the door.

"I don't take people's food," I said.

"I never said you did."

"Then why bring it up?"

"As a warning, motherfucker."

This guy Mike didn't look right was the first thing I thought as he let us into his dank room. His head seemed too big for his body. A giant, human-sized bobblehead doll. His eyes were a frightening cartoon, wide open and bulging out of his head, the result, as I'd seen before, of a thyroid problem that made what looked like half the eyeball sit outside the skin. And he was six-five, so the giant head with its bulging eyes drooped over you like a tall sunflower. It gave him a look of shocked anger, no matter what came out of his mouth. Like Johnny Mo said, he talked in a sort of jerky belched mumble. What was left of his voice was quiet, yet deep.

The first thing Mike said, before Johnny Mo finished the introductions, leaving me with my handshake frozen awkwardly unanswered in midair, was, "You guys have a bolt cutter?"

I pulled my hand back and tried not to look into Mike's intense, raging eyes. The carpet was a slurry brown and pumpkin orange, with crisscrosses of charcoal black cigarette burns patterned all over it by the foot of the bed.

I figured this was Johnny Mo's play. He knew this guy. I stayed back.

Johnny Mo said, "Bolt cutter?"

"I need a bolt cutter," Mike said. Every word was an ugly labor for him. He pushed down air hard and then expelled it with his words. A clenched face before every syllable on its escape from his tortured body. "You guys have a bolt cutter?"

"We're here to do some business," Johnny Mo said.

Mike blinked a lot like he had dust in his eyes or bad contacts. His eyes seemed to telescope in and out of their sockets.

I said, "Where's the pot, man?"

Mike looked at me for a second, then looked back to Johnny Mo. "I need a bolt cutter. My fucking dad, the fucking drunk. He's locked me out."

Johnny Mo glanced at me, then back to the giant bouncing head looming over us. He said to Mike, "Look, we're here to do a deal. We're here to do some business and be on our way. We can't help you with your dad."

"The pot is in that drunk fuck's house. We don't get in the house, there's no deal."

I shook my head. "We can't break a window?"

"What?" Mike said.

I said, "Why bolt cutters, man? Why can't we just break in a window?"

"He'd hear us."

I looked at Johnny Mo, thinking, *Why wouldn't this guy hear us busting through a bolted door?* but whatever.

Johnny Mo said, "There's no other way to get this done, Mike?"

"That fucker. He locks me out of his fucking house and I'm his fucking son. The guy's so drunk. He's a fucking zombie, man. I mean, like, when I see zombie movies, it's like I'm watching documentaries."

"So, we need bolt cutters?" I said, trying to get Mike back on the subject of us getting our pot and me making my money. We needed to get on the road to LA and meet Johnny Mo's rich acid-head guy and get this done with.

Mike said, "Like we're the zombies, you know, eating our own brains and shit and it's not a movie—well it is a *movie* movie, but like a documentary movie, you know what I'm saying?"

"You need bolt cutters?" I said.

"What?" Mike said.

"You need bolt cutters," I said. I tried hard to sound like I was calm, but this was starting to piss me off. Why had I let my life come to this? To rely on people like this was to *be* people like this. I needed to straighten out and get my life back together. I said, "To get into your dad's house? You need bolt cutters."

"Oh, wow. You have some bolt cutters? That would be great. 'Cause yeah I need some."

Johnny Mo shook his head. "Fuck this," he said and started toward the door.

I followed him.

Mike said, "All the pot's at my dad's place. We just need to break in. He's so drunk, he'll never wake up."

"So let me break a window," I said.

"I thought you said you had bolt cutters."

Johnny Mo rolled his eyes. "Fuck," he said. He took a deep breath and let it out slowly. "Let's get this shit done."

Mike said, "I got to hit the head." He went into the bathroom. The fan started to whir in there and he turned on the water. It was easy to tell he was doing some drug.

I whispered to Johnny Mo, "This guy used to deal cards at the Frontier?"

Johnny Mo nodded. "Before his stroke, yeah. Not like he is now."

We took Johnny Mo's crap-ass powder blue '89 Toyota Celica to the father's house, which wasn't a house at all, but a fleabag motel off of Carson in the Naked City section of town, where Stu Ungar, maybe the greatest poker player who ever lived, died in the Oasis Motel, drug-wrecked and homeless only a year after winning the World Series of Poker for the third time in one of the greatest comebacks ever seen. A week before the tournament, he'd been homeless, strung out on crack. And then he ended up winning the tournament, nearly twenty years after winning his first two. I thought about someone as gifted and great as Ungar dying here alone, and I got pulled by a riptide of sadness. But we had a job to do, so I tried to wipe away the bad thoughts.

The father's building was from the 1950s, and, sure enough, he'd run a chain from inside the apartment to the outside. I'd never seen anything like it. There was a half-inch hole in the door, and then one in the wall under the doorbell, and the chain ran through them both to what Mike told us was a high-end padlock on the other side.

"I'm thinking the landlord is not happy about this particular behavior," Johnny Mo said.

"What?" Mike said.

Johnny Mo pointed to the chain. "Not your best tenant—the man who goes and does this kind of thing."

"Some people wipe shit on the walls," Mike said.

"I'm not saying it couldn't be worse," Johnny Mo said.

I looked for other ways into the place. It was an old motel. Single floor. The same kind of structure that sprang up all over America after Eisenhower veined the country with highways and interstates filled with vacationing families taking to the road from their freshly minted suburbs for two horrifying weeks out of the year.

Next to the padlocked door was a picture window, eight panes over eight in a military blue trim cut in so sloppily the glass was smeared with an inch of paint. Behind the window was a drape the color of burlap. Blue-gray light flickered from the TV.

Mike said, "Like I lived with some tweakers for a while and man, they shit on everything."

"Maybe they were zombies," I said.

Mike said, "I don't understand what you say when you talk."

Johnny Mo lifted the chain and let it drop quietly. "Why doesn't he just lock the door?"

"The lock's broken," Mike said.

Johnny Mo said, "Your average person, it might have occurred to them to have replaced the lock." Johnny Mo seemed amused by all of this. Didn't seem to be putting off any vibe that giant, weird Mike was a danger, and this soothed me.

"You guys have any speed?" Mike said.

There was no way I'd give this kid any of my drugs. I hated speed, but I made a mental checklist: Maybe five diazepam left. Two OxyContin. A couple of Vicodin. And eleven hundred dollars thick and dangerous in my pocket, making me nervous to do this deal and be comfortably broke again. We could get mugged outside that skanky room and have nothing to show for the stupid night.

"I'm tapped," I said.

"Speed?" Johnny Mo said.

"I'm kinda crashing, and I can't crash 'cause, like, I need some fucking money for this guy who I need to pay back. That's why I'm selling to you at such a fucking good deal man, because this guy will fuck me up if I don't get him the money tonight."

Johnny Mo looked at me. Danger ratcheted in his eyes. "This guy know where you live?"

"Since I moved here, yeah," Mike said. "He didn't used to know where I live but, yeah, now he does know where I live. Not like where I used to live—he didn't know that."

"OK. I got it," Johnny Mo said.

"And he's a fucking monster, man. You have any speed?"

"Nothing," Johnny Mo said. Which was probably true.

Mike started pulling his hair out to the sides of his head. "Oh, fuck, oh fuck oh fuck," Mike said. "I'm feeling kind of jangly." He closed his eyes tightly, then opened them wide again, all freaky, bulging big as golf balls out of each socket.

"Let's get in this apartment, now," I said.

"Man I'm so fucking jangly," Mike said. "And that fucking zombie in there, man, locking me out of my own fucking house."

People would hear us being this loud. Apartments like this were full of paranoia and restraining orders and twitchy, nervous people who couldn't be trusted to be rational. "I can give you a Valium," I said.

"That's not speed," Mike said.

"It could take some of the edge off that jangle." I looked at him. His eyes wouldn't stay still. Totally strung out. Coming down off speed, your brain's like a skipping CD. Living with a drunk father who padlocked him out of the house. The poor bastard. If I hadn't been afraid of him and annoyed, there might have been more space in my head and heart to care about him.

"That's not speed, man, that's not what I'm asking for. Oh, fuck, my head hurts."

I shook my head.

Johnny Mo lit a cigarette and turned to the street. Cars slunk by. The light at the closest intersection went a full cycle, green to yellow to red. Menthol-laden smoke hovered in the air. A car pulled into the parking lot and lights swept across the three of us standing outside the padlocked room.

Johnny Mo's car was three parking spots away. I thought if Mike knew exactly where the pot was, we could just go with smashing the window, go in and race out. Me and Johnny Mo could keep an eye on the drunken dad, and we could dash out of there and do the deal down the road somewhere.

I told Mike and Johnny Mo my plan, such as it was.

"What are you going to take the window out with?" Johnny Mo said.

"I don't care," I said. "My fucking hand if I have to. This needs to get done."

"We can walk away," Johnny Mo said to me. "End this crazy night right now. Fuck this stupid deal."

Mike yelled, "I need this fucking money, fuckers. There's no way this can't happen."

Mike made some high-pitched screeching noise that sounded like a fan belt when it's about to snap. If this was going to get done, it had to be then. And I was worried about what Mike might try if we backed out.

I asked Johnny Mo if he had anything in the car we could use to break the window.

Johnny Mo tossed his cigarette and walked across the lot. I heard the trunk pop open on his car while I looked at Mike.

Mike said, "Bolt cutters would have been a good idea."

Johnny Mo came over holding a peach pearloid bowling ball that shined under the porch light and said, "Will you shut the fuck up about your fucking bolt cutters?"

Mike pushed Johnny Mo in the chest and he fell to the ground, the bowling ball clunking hard on the asphalt. All I could think of was that Johnny Mo was carrying a gun, and so was this lunatic Mike. I jumped between them.

I said, "Mike, you need to calm down so you can get your money. We need to get this done, now." I tried to make eye contact but he stared across the parking lot. "Do you know *exactly* where that fucking pot is?"

Mike said, "It's in the closet."

Johnny Mo got up. "Do not ever touch me again, motherfucker."

"All I said was we needed bolt cutters."

"You said it like a thousand times," Johnny Mo said. "You could see where that might get a little redundant? Where that might get a little fucking old?"

Johnny Mo was right, but I said, "Will you please be quiet? Let's get in this apartment." I took the bowling ball from Johnny Mo. "Mike, you're sure you can get that pot in a hurry?"

"Yeah." Mike turned toward the door and gave it the finger like it was a person. "My fucking drunk father does this all the fucking time."

"You know, you might want to buy your own bolt cutters if this happens a lot," Johnny Mo said.

"People have them when I ask."

I stood back from the window. I wound back with the bowling ball and knocked myself a little off balance, but I recovered and smashed it through the window. I'd meant to hold on to it, so I could smash it all around the window casing, but the ball fell from my right hand that'd never been right after all the damage, and I heard it thud on the carpet inside. I only took out two of the windowpanes, leaving an opening a little bigger than a sheet of paper. There was a drunken grumble from inside—Mike's dad, I guessed. Blue-white light flickered from the TV, and I heard *The Tonight Show*'s theme music.

I hadn't thought through my plan for getting in. I thought I could reach in the window and open the door, but the whole chain and padlock madness didn't allow for it.

Johnny Mo said to Mike, "You are *sure* you know where the pot is? We can get in and out in a hurry?"

"Yeah," Mike said. "We just have to be careful with my dad."

I looked around the parking lot. Nothing seemed to have changed, but the longer we stayed, the more dangerous it was. I wondered why I got into this. At best, Johnny Mo and I were going to make a profit of about seven hundred each, which was hardly the kind of money to change your life. Not "fuck you money" as my father would've said. I might as well get a straight job if I wasn't going to do better than this. Job to job was no way to go, especially if these were the jobs. But I needed to get some OxyContin money just to stay healthy at that point. If I skipped a day, by the end of the day, my whole body ached and my skin hurt. I needed to get off it, but it wasn't a cold-turkey drug. I'd tried that and nearly killed myself doing it a few times. You had to scale it down by halves every few days if you wanted to do it without suffering terribly. I couldn't play music for money, the shape I was in. And if I was going to get my card game back together, I needed focus and endurance. Neither of which I had. If I could get somewhat straight by the next month, I had a chance at the satellite Omaha Tournament at the Bicycle Club in Torrance.

I reached in the broken window and yanked hard on the burlap curtain, cutting my arm on one of my angry upswings, giving the curtain three violent tugs till it let go. I wrapped it around my right hand—even fucked-up forever, it was stronger than my left. Plus, it was my dominant hand and I still used it out of habit, even if I shouldn't have. I started punching every windowpane out, one by one until I'd taken out three rows of four panes.

Johnny Mo went in first and pulled Mike through after him. I went in last, swinging one leg over the other like I was hopping a fence.

I unwrapped the now bloody curtain from my hand. The glass that cut me was still stuck in my forearm, jutting out in a glinty triangle the shape of a slice of pizza. I took it out and maybe it was the endorphins or fear, but I didn't feel any pain at all.

Mike said, "Keep an eye on my fucking drunk father."

Johnny Mo nodded. I stood by the broken window, looking out and trying to see if anyone had noticed the noise.

Mike stood in the middle of the room. "Man, I'm so fucking jangly."

Johnny Mo whispered, "Get yourself to the closet, man."

Mike turned in circles. He blocked the TV and threw shadows across the room with every turn. "Oh man, oh man, oh man," he said.

"Where is the closet, fucker?" Johnny Mo said.

Mike didn't answer. There were several loud knocks on the other side of the wall. A woman's voice yelled, "I'm calling the police."

Johnny Mo ran through the house. Mike still spun in front of the TV. The woman next door kept knocking.

Johnny Mo said, "I found it, man."

"Let's get going," I said. I tried to get Mike's attention, but he kept spinning. Finally, he spun away from me and stood over his father, amazingly still asleep through all of the noise and motion.

Mike said, "You drunken fuck." He punched the father in the face. "You drunken fucking zombie." He punched the father again. The woman pounded on the wall. The father made a groaning noise. Mike punched him again. More pounding came from the wall.

Johnny Mo came from the back room carrying a Hefty bag and looked at Mike standing over his father. "What the fuck are you doing?"

"Mike!" I shouted. "Let's go."

The father opened his eyes. He said, "Shut up, Mexicans."

None of us were Mexican. Johnny Mo headed toward the door and I turned and we realized at the same time we couldn't walk out the door—we had to go out the way we came in.

Johnny Mo turned toward the room. "Mike, you want your money, you leave now."

That got his attention and he walked toward us. I heard a small *pop*. I remembered the first time I heard a .22 go off. I couldn't believe it was a gun. I expected guns to sound like backfires, like huge explosions. But a .22 is quieter than a champagne cork. Mike grimaced. He stumbled toward me and needed my help to make it through the window, and I thought for a moment about leaving him there with his father. But something in me made me grab him and push him out. I heard two more pops. What the first one did, I had no idea, but the second one hit my ankle as I swung out the window. I fell to the parking lot and smelled motor oil.

Johnny Mo already had the car swinging around, and Mike and I struggled our way over. Mike moved sluggishly. My right foot dragged behind me like it wasn't attached anymore.

Mike's father came to the window and shouted, "Fucking Mexicans!"

Mike got in the back and I limped into the passenger seat and we pulled out of the parking lot.

"What the fuck did you start hitting him for?" I shouted at Mike. He didn't answer.

I looked back. Mike had turned as white as ceiling paint. "Oh shit, man."

"Is he dead?" Johnny Mo said.

I looked for a while. His breathing was labored. Blood spread from his groin. He moaned gently, like someone who just woke up—not like someone who'd been shot.

"Nope," I said. "But he needs a hospital."

"We'll have to drop him off at the ER."

"Can you do that?" I said.

"Yeah, I don't want to break any fucking rules," Johnny Mo said. Mike groaned some more.

Mike was still alive when we dumped him on the sidewalk in front of the emergency room at the Sunrise Medical Center.

Johnny Mo did most of the lifting, as Mike wasn't helping us at all, and I was pretty much on one foot. I took the cash out of my pocket and put it in his left pocket, the side that had less blood.

"You giving him all of it?" Johnny Mo said.

"That's the deal," I said, wincing. "He might make it."

"He might not. Let's keep the fucking money."

"We fuck him and he lives, we could be in trouble."

"Yeah, we don't want trouble," Johnny Mo said.

I looked at Mike and doubted he'd live. If he did, he'd never find us. I grabbed the roll of bills, the corners on one side red from the blood spreading all over his shirt and pants.

Johnny Mo looked at the entrance. No one had come out, but they could any second. "Move."

I got back to the car, a slur of blood behind me from my dragged foot. Johnny Mo sped us out of the driveway, blaring the horn so that, hopefully, someone would come out and find Mike.

When we were five miles south of town on the I-15, Johnny Mo pulled into a gas station. He filled the tank and took the Hefty bag of pot from the backseat and put it in the trunk. It still reeked. I looked at my ankle and the pain throbbed as every beat of my heart pumped blood out of my foot—a metronome of agony. I hoped we didn't get pulled over driving to LA. Between the pot and my leg, we'd go to jail before we even had a chance to bullshit our way out of it.

My right Chuck Taylor was soggy with blood that'd pooled out onto the carpet. It was sticky, and it squished when I lifted the foot with my hand and put it back down on the floorboard. I tried to wiggle my toes, but they didn't work. Johnny Mo said, "Can I get you anything, man?"

Caffeine can help block pain. Not much, but I was desperate for any help. "A big Diet Coke. A big bag of ice."

I sat in the car. Johnny Mo left the keys in, and, from a road-mix CD I'd made, Howlin' Wolf's "All Night Boogie" rocked from the speakers. Bugs revolved and darted around the buzzing parking lot light above me. My foot throbbed. I was pretty sure, feeling around with my finger, that the bullet bounced off my anklebone and wasn't still in there, which was good news. But my fingers ran over the greasy hole and came up slathered in blood, and I had a couple of little splinters in my slick finger. Splinters from my own bone. I shook my head. Even with the money we didn't give Mike, it'd probably cost more than I made from the deal to get it fixed. I thought about taking one of the two OxyContin I had left, but I didn't want to waste them on pain. While Johnny Mo was in the store, the Ike Reilly Assassination's "It's All Right to Die" came on.

Johnny Mo came back. He handed me a liter of Diet Coke and passed over a party-sized bag of ice cubes that I gently placed on my foot.

"You OK?" he said.

"I need a pipe," I said. They sold pipes at gas stations in Vegas. I felt a brief caress of luck for the first time in a while. If we'd done this in another state, we'd need a smoke shop or a head shop.

"What?"

"Go back in, buy a pipe, and fill me a big bowl of that weed."

"You going to be all right?" he said.

"Not so good," I said. "I need to be really high. Do it."

"You need a hospital?"

I thought about it. We'd have too much explaining to do in Vegas. "Maybe when we get back to LA. For now, buy me a pipe, get it packed, and give it to me."

I squeezed my eyes shut until everything was black. I kept them closed and pushed my fingers on my eyelids until I saw stars and shapes behind my closed eyes. I heard Johnny Mo come out of the store. I kept my eyes closed. I heard him pop the trunk and close it soon after. He got in the car. I opened my eyes and he handed me a green pipe with the new tag still hanging off it. He handed me a lighter. I took a long hit of the pot and tried to focus on Ike Reilly's voice. Anything to get me out of that moment. I felt dizzy and my eyes were tearing up. I didn't like pot much, but I was using it purely as medicine then. I took another hit and closed my eyes.

"Is the pot any good?"

Lights danced in the darkness of my closed eyes—like a negative of the bugs darting around the gas station lights. "It's not good enough," I said. "I can still feel."

He shook his head. "What was that fucker thinking? Hitting the old man. We were out of there." He lit a cigarette. "Out the motherfucking door, you know?"

I didn't say anything. I was lightheaded and I let my head lean back. Pain still pulsed in my foot. I opened my eyes and saw stars and almost puked. I looked for cops and, not seeing any, I closed my eyes and took another hit of the pot. My plan was to open my eyes, and if I saw one of anything, keep taking hits until everything was at least double vision.

Ten minutes later, we were headed west and south, climbing out of town. Once, not so long ago even, you could drive out of Vegas at night, and you'd climb the hill on the 15 in your two-lane traffic, and the city behind you would gleam and quiver for miles in your rearview like some UFO had landed. But these days, with new casino towns everywhere, with Primm and everything else clotting the 15, it never got dark enough for Las Vegas to be that glowing, shrinking, humming mass behind you. There were lights everywhere, and Las Vegas never really disappeared anymore, it just blended into the next town you left behind on your way back to Los Angeles.

DIVERTERS

(Summer 2010)

The day had started out with me shitting blood. A little later, I was shivering in Doc's passenger seat under the warm July California sun, asking Doc about the blood while we were on the way to Tustin to see this friend of his who was supposed to help us get some morphine.

Doc and I called each other friends, but we both knew without saying that we were drug buddies. That if I didn't have the five hundred bucks in my pocket that would pry this hospice care friend of his from her ethics long enough to give us some terminal cancer patient's painkillers, Doc would be in this car alone, or with some other human ATM. He had the connection, I had the money, and this made us, however temporarily, partners in the world.

I was worried the blood could be an ulcer, maybe something more serious. Lately, I hadn't been able to get much more than Vicodin for my habit, and it had been corroding away at my stomach, a million tiny pickaxes mining the walls of my guts, so I figured I'd caused an ulcer, caused myself to rip and bleed and leak slowly away from the inside out. But, too, my mind slid easily to thoughts of cancer and that I could have been dying—at least dying faster or in a different way than from addiction. I'd asked my friend, Amber, and she figured it was nothing. So I asked Doc, "Is blood out of your ass always bad news?"

"It's never good news," he said.

"I didn't ask if it was ever good."

"It's not ever good," he said.

I took a deep breath. I had the start of what would be full-blown dopesickness in a few hours. The metallic taste at the back of my mouth, the chills. Soon, there'd be sweats. Then puke and diarrhea and my body making a tortured fist of itself. I needed exactly what we were going to get. While, of course, realizing that it was what we were going to get that caused this in the first place. Every day, the same cycle of desperate need met with desperate opposition and sickness. I couldn't tell my todays from my tomorrows anymore than you can tell the sea from the horizon in a marine layer fog. It all just blurs together. "But is it always bad?"

"Not always," he said. "But it's never good, so disavow yourself of that silliness right now."

I looked at him.

He said, "This is your ass and your blood, I'm guessing?"

Sometimes things are simple. Doc was called Doc because he used to be a doctor. Maybe he still was—I wasn't sure, but I knew he wasn't allowed to practice medicine anymore, at least not in California. He wrote some bad scripts, and he ended up losing his license. Or it may only have been suspended. But if anyone official was checking up on him, he wasn't living too cleanly. He'd been able to hook me up until recently with a pretty steady flow of Vicodin, but that only kept me going and didn't really make me high anymore. Without it, I was sick—a shivering, noxious presence to all who had the bad luck or bad sense to enter the debris field I'd made of my life. With it I could function, more or less—get to another day of clawing through the hours, wishing the next day would be better, but not seeing any reason it would be. I looked out the window at the towns under the 22 freeway. We'd left Long Beach maybe twenty minutes before, and now we were passing the suburban sprawl of northern Orange County, flashing by under an army of tall palms, blown by the offshore winds. It was a beautiful place, even from the freeway. Rooftops of homes glided under us to the right—to the left, a series of car dealerships in Garden Grove, and just east of them, out of sight from the freeway, a series of Vietnamese Pho joints and body-piercing parlors in strip malls.

I met Doc when he was still able to get OxyContin, eighty milligrams for a while and then forties. Oxy was a dream for a newly-off-the-wagon user like me—a time-released chemical equivalent of heroin, without the sloppy, desperate need to fix with needles. But, as they always do, the drugs stopped working and then, worse, Doc's source dried up, and the mirage of beauty and ease that Oxys gave, they took away with them.

Right now, though, Doc had talked about an old friend he used to work with who could hook us up with some morphine and maybe more in Tustin and was I in? I heard morphine and said yes and committed my last five hundred bucks from a poker win a few nights before. Normally I needed a lot more info, but most of Doc's friends, even the addicts, were very white collar. They were all liars and cheats, but generally not as dangerous as street dope fiends. Plus, we were talking about morphine. The risk–reward was too good and I jumped without a second thought, quick as a seismograph at ground zero.

Doc said, "You and Amber been, you know, doing anything?"

"What?"

"From what I hear, strippers like to strap one on now and again."

"She's a dominatrix."

"Oh, well," Doc said. "I stand corrected."

"Fuck you, dude. Lawyers use strap-ons, too."

"Do not tell someone who has worked in the ER that ass play is limited to sex workers. Trust me. I fucking *know* ass play knows no boundaries."

"Then why even ask?"

"Nevertheless, strippers—" He turned to me. "*And* dominatrixes have been known to strap one on every now and again."

Amber did, in fact, like to strap one on now and again. But she hadn't been my girlfriend in almost eight years. It had caused some blood, but only a little, and, well, a hell of a long time ago. Not for days like it had been happening. "Dude, that's a stereotype," I said.

"I'm your doctor."

"You're not my doctor."

"Well, I'm *a* doctor," he said.

"Are you?"

"Nevertheless," he said. "I have been an internist. I have a certain amount of experience with insertables. I've seen an astounding amount of things up guy's assholes. And women's assholes. You can tell me. Plus, I need to know the facts to know if this blood is an issue."

"OK, fine," I said. "Amber fucked me with a strap-on ages ago. Happy?"

"Don't get so defensive, man. I'm your doctor."

I let it slip that time.

Doc said, "When was the last time?"

"For the blood?"

"No," he said, smiling. "When you let your pervert girlfriend sodomize you."

I looked at him and he smiled and laughed. He said, "You need to lighten up." He was driving and not looking at the road much as he hunted for his smokes in the backseat. I gripped the door handle and had visions of car wrecks and blood. Being a passenger scared the shit out of me—if I had any, I always took a few Valium before getting in any car. He said, "Everybody loves something up their ass during sex."

"Really?"

"It can sure as hell seem that way when you work the ER."

"I can't talk to you at all, man."

"C'mon," he said. "I'm trying to help. Are you shitting blood? Or is there blood *in* your stool?"

"What's the difference?"

"Color?"

"What?" I said.

"It's an issue. What color is the blood?"

"Red," I said. "Blood colored."

Doc nodded. He put in a CD—Jonathan Richman & the Modern Lovers' *Rockin' and Romance.* He cracked the window and lit an American Spirit. He offered me one. Doc had quit for years and only recently started again since his divorce. I took one.

Doc said. "Red isn't the only color blood can be. Especially on the inside."

"So is red good?" I said.

"Nothing is good," Doc said. "No blood in your shit, that's good. That's our goal. Our vision. An America with no blood in their shit. That's the ticket I'm running on. The no-blood-in-your-ass ticket."

"Red is less bad?" I said.

"That is true," he said. "Red is much less bad. If the blood in your stool is a greasy-looking dark red, almost black, *that* is a major and immediate concern."

"And this?"

He shrugged. "Probably nothing. How many Vicodin a day are you taking?"

I was, until a week before, taking about thirty—but I was stealing, when I could, from Doc's stash, when he had a stash, so I went with a low estimate. Our supply had run out five days ago and I'd halved my intake from twenty to ten to five to only three the day before. My eyes felt like sandpaper, and the suffocating heat in my head made every pump of my heart an oil-derrick throb of pain all over my body. Like every nerve ending burned with Fourth of July sparklers. "Ten to twenty if I can. Less, lately."

"That's probably it right there," he said. He ticked an ash. "How is Olivia?"

"We don't seem to be talking," I said. "She won't talk until I'm back in rehab."

"Ah," Doc said. "True love."

Jonathan was singing about his jeans and how they were a-fraying as I looked out the window at the blur of objects racing by.

I knew I couldn't continue on the way I was going. My short-range plan involved the morphine and, after that, a meeting with this guy, Leroy Marcus, about some pot he wanted me to sell. The morphine was supposed to be my last for a while—the plan was to use it and slowly wean myself off, using Vicodins when I had to, to try to detox as painlessly as possible and start clean. Go back to meetings. Be humble and start over. I'd done it before. I could do it again. And, maybe, if I could ever get clean, try to make Olivia think about taking me back.

But at that point, I'd tried to quit various opiates—whether it was by myself or in rehabs—somewhere between thirty and fifty times in my life. Which meant thirty to fifty intentional detoxes. And that didn't even count the dopesickness from simply running out. Withdrawals made you sorry for ever being born—which sometimes seemed the point of the whole thing. The self-loathing burning hot enough to make the sorrows you suffered from withdrawal seem something like justice for the liar and cheat you'd allowed yourself to become. The twisted core of wrongness at your center everywhere you went was something that made suffering seem valid and just, in some way.

"I can't drop all five hundred on the morphine," I said.

"You have to."

I said, "I can't. I need at least a couple hundred for tonight."

Doc said, "You got a game?"

I shook my head. "You know Leroy Marcus?"

"That 'roid rage guy?"

Leroy had a justifiable reputation as a guy you didn't want to fuck with. He'd been a boxer and had ended up recently with an ultimate fighting obsession. Leroy liked violence—seemed to like getting hurt as much as he liked hurting people, which made dealing with him an uneasy proposition at best. Someone who's not afraid of getting hurt, someone who actually welcomes the pain and raw savagery of the fight, is not someone you want to face off with. Like my dad told me when I was a kid, you never throw a punch unless you're willing to kill the guy—because he might be willing to kill you. Leroy probably got the same lesson somewhere along the line. But he threw punches, and I don't.

"That's him," I said.

"What the fuck have you got going with that beast?" Doc said.

"A pot deal," I said. "I need at least two hundred to sell some medical quality shit he has."

"You smoking pot?"

I shook my head. "Pot's dollar signs to me. I'm trying to make some money."

"Pot's legal now, dude."

"Not legal," I said.

"More or less. Any fuck off the street can get a script for it. How you going to make money?"

"Getting a couple hundred's worth off him and selling for double to this nut in Silverlake I know. Quick cash. No risk."

"You can't trust Leroy. There's plenty of risk just walking through his door."

That was true enough. "I need money," I said.

Doc smoked the end of his cigarette and rubbed it out on the outside of his door—the side of his car was streaked with the ends of his butts. He'd pinch out the tobacco and let the filters pile up at his feet.

"We're scoring morphine—a real fucking drug—in Tustin," he said.

"Are we?" I said.

"We are."

I felt the sickness overcoming me. "We better be."

"My point is," Doc said, "we'll get enough to make some money off that, if you want."

I had tried over the years to make money with heroin, with Dilaudid, with OxyContin, and a variety of other opiates. All I ever did was end up doing them all, either fast or slowly. With them, I never could seem to go from *intent to deal* to ever actually dealing.

Doc said, "What if we spend your whole five hundred bucks on the painkillers?"

"Then I'll do them."

He looked hard at me.

I said, "I'll do half of them."

"Right," he said. "But what if you let me tuck a couple hundred aside and deal that."

"For both of us?"

"Of course for both of us, man," he said. "Who you going to trust to make a buck? Me, or Leroy Marcus?"

Neither of you, I thought. *Leroy's a brutal beast of a businessman, and you're a dope fiend.* But, given the choice, I answered honestly. "I'd rather be in business with you."

Doc merged off the 22 onto the 55 southbound, where it splits going to Riverside one way and Orange County the other. We were headed toward Tustin, just a few miles away. We seemed to have reached some tacit agreement about the extra two hundred and the profit on the deal.

"So, tell me about your connection," I said.

"She's a hospice worker with a terminal case."

"And?"

"She's a diverter. She's helping us out."

Diverter is the medical term, and the narc term, for a medical professional who diverts pain meds from the people who need them. The language of distance and euphemism. They're thieves, and people like me and Doc pay them to steal from people in pain. I tried not to have any more illusions about what I did. I used to be able to lie about it—to others, to myself. But after years of clean time, it was hard to see yourself as anything but a hideous failure. My next drug possession case would put me at what's known as the SAP pits, SAP being short for Substance Abuse Program.

"How terminal?" I asked him.

"What?"

"How terminal a case?"

"There aren't degrees of terminal," Doc said. "Trust me, I'm a doctor."

"I mean, how close to dead is this person?" I don't know why it mattered to me, but it did. As if the closer to dead they were, the less I'd be ripping them off, somehow.

"Close enough to be designated terminal and to have 24/7 hospice care," Doc said. "That's usually pretty late in the game."

I nodded.

Doc said, "And it usually means a *lot* of pain meds."

The drug talk, along with my system being weaned off meds the last few days, started to make me feel cravings that hurt. But they were cravings with hope—that tingle when you're close to the drugs, in both time and distance. "Any chance for Dilaudid?"

Doc shrugged as we reached the two Santa Ana–Tustin exits for Seventeenth Street. The second exit heads south toward Tustin, and we took that one. "Hard to say," Doc said, lighting another cigarette. "Pain management theory these days shies away from Dilaudid. But we should get plenty of morphine."

Back when I still shot up, which I hadn't done this relapse, Dilaudid was like gold. About five to eight times more powerful than morphine. Less went longer.

"Listen," Doc said. "There is something difficult we might have to do."

"Difficult how?"

"It's a relatively new procedure. I haven't asked Sandra if he's on it or not, but this guy may have a permanent morphine vial implanted near the base of his spine."

"Lucky bastard," I said, and I sort of meant it.

"It's the wave of the future," Doc said. "Going to hurt people like you and me. Pills and shit like that are going the way of the horse and carriage."

"I don't follow."

"All drugs are going to be administered using time-released delivery methods," Doc said. "Soon, there won't be any pills to steal."

"You said there'd be morphine at this place, right?"

"Right," Doc said. "But, worst case scenario, you're going to have to cut the vial out of this guy."

"I thought cancer patients had IV drips and patches and stuff."

"They do," Doc said. "But, in addition to that, depending on how far gone he is, he might have this semipermanent vial."

"Why do I have to cut it out?"

"Well, no one's saying for sure it's there."

"*If* it's there, why the fuck am I doing the cutting?"

Doc shrugged. "Because I don't want to."

And that was that—his connection, his call. No matter how desperate I was, I didn't think I could do it. Cut a helpless dying person? Only a monster could do it. And, I told myself over and over, I *can't* be that monster. But I'd already crossed so many ethical lines I said I would never cross in my life. I'd become a man I couldn't recognize more times than I could ever count. "He may not have one of these, right?"

"He may, he may not. But you might want to wish he does—concentrated morphine drip."

"I'm not cutting open some poor fuck who's about to die," I said.

"Well, let's hope it doesn't come to that. I was just warning you about some of the potential difficulties."

I shook my head and looked at the faces of the other people driving out on the freeway. I wondered what they were talking about. What they were thinking they might have to do in the next half hour and how sick they made themselves.

As we got off the freeway, I realized how tense I was, realized I hadn't been taking regular breaths, realized I'd actually been holding my breath. I tried to take in a few deep breaths while Doc swung across four lanes of Seventeenth Street.

"Be careful," I said.

"It's important to blend in," Doc said. "Cops pull over people like you and me when they're doing the speed limit. People drive like maniacs here. So should we, if we want to be left alone." Someone honked and Doc gave them the finger. I turned around and looked at the **WELCOME TO TUSTIN** sign behind us. This other side was for the people just leaving Tustin and it read:

Work Where You Must But Live and Shop in Tustin!

A Vons supermarket slid by on our right. I took nervous breaths and felt my heart beat like a rabbit's heart in my chest. A church with an impossibly high peaked roof stood on our left with an announcement out front:

"WHY DO THEY WANT US DEAD?
What the Bible says About Islam."

Doc said, "Almost there."

I nodded and took several attempts at a deep breath.

He took a left on Mauve—a sign that read NOT A THROUGH STREET greeted us as we headed down to the second to last house on the right. There was a Toyota in the driveway and we pulled up next to it, blocking one of the garage sides. I pointed and said, "What if someone needs to get out?"

Doc shook his head. "No one needs to get out. Look. This is a call I only get a couple times a year—the situation has to be perfect. We are going into this house and we are going to score, OK?"

"OK," I said.

"Like I said, this is rare. The patient is alone, they probably don't have much family. They may have none. My connection has, more or less, the run of the place. It's like an opiate candy store in there, and we are here to clean them out, understand?"

It was starting to sound too good to be true, but it had a momentum that I couldn't pull against. Plus, I needed to get high pretty soon, or I'd be a wreck. I wasn't in a position to argue.

"Give me the money," Doc said.

I reached into my front pocket and took out a wad of rolled, moist bills and gave them to him.

Doc said, "Dude, you carry your money like a ten-year-old boy."

I thought of Olivia. "Sorry," I said.

"You have to stop apologizing for everything, too."

"Uhm . . . Sorry?"

Doc counted out the bills and folded and rearranged them.

"Tell you what. After we make a few bucks here—will you wear a fucking proper billfold if I buy you one?"

"Is that like a wallet?"

He shook his head. "The way you carry money, there's no way anyone's going to take you seriously."

"People take money seriously—they don't seem to care how it's folded."

"You're wrong," Doc said. He lit a cigarette, took one deep drag and then a second. Then he put the cigarette out. He turned to me. "If anyone asks, you are my assistant."

"Who's asking here?"

"Inside. There should only be Sandra, my friend. But *if* someone else is here . . . family, friend, what*ever*, I am a medical professional Sandra called for an opinion and you are my assistant. Got it?"

I nodded, looked down at my torn jeans and Chuck Taylors held together with electrical tape on the right toe, and thought, *Yeah. Medical assistant.*

"Great," Doc said. "Let's do this."

The house looked like the Brady House. Midcentury modern blighted by a 1970s renovation and then left to become a domestic ghost town since. Doc's friend Sandra met us at the front door. She wore blue scrubs, with one of those infantilizing tops that nurses and hospital workers all wear these days. The shirt was littered with Cookie Monsters and Ernies and Berts and some Muppet I didn't recognize that I figured might be Elmo.

"He's asleep," Sandra said before we could say a word, and before I knew it, we were in the house, the quiet suburbia of Tustin a whisper of lawn sprinklers and muffled TVs on the other side of the closed door.

Doc introduced me and we shook hands. Sandra wore her stethoscope draped across her shoulders the way people did on TV these days. I wondered when they stopped wearing them with the earpieces around their neck, the way they did when I was a kid and my Mom was an ER nurse.

The house smelled like the ERs of my childhood—the vague mix of cleaning fluids and urine and medicine and latex and rubbing alcohol. Doc grabbed two lollipops out of Sandra's pocket and gave me one.

"Sandra and I have some business to attend to."

She gestured upstairs. They went up, with Doc telling me to wait for them.

"Is there a bathroom down here?" I asked.

Sandra told me to go into the living room and keep going to the right and back.

Which would have been fine, except the living room was where her patient happened to be. I was alone in a room with a dying stranger. The poor bastard. I walked into the room slowly, afraid to startle the guy. The house opened to the stairwell to the right, where Doc had followed Sandra upstairs to wherever they were now, their talk muffled behind walls and hard to distinguish under the gentle drone of an oxygen machine.

Walking forward, the main floor opened to a kitchen on the left and a huge sunken living room to the right. He was on a hospital-type bed in the middle of the room, facing away from me and toward a big-screen TV that was set to some talking heads, but had the sound muted. The oxygen machine ground on, regularly interrupted by the beeps and peeps of a series of diagnostic indicators that spat out numbers that were meaningless to me.

The man was on his back, his head turned painfully to the side. A tube ran into his mouth. He was motionless, except for a mindless chewing of the tube. His eyes were open, but he didn't seem to register that I was there. His catheter bag seemed dangerously full and I made a note of mentioning that to Sandra when she came back down. It looked like it was going to spill onto the floor.

I walked by, careful not to step on any of the various wires and tubes, on my way to the first-floor bathroom.

I closed the door behind me and searched the medicine cabinet. This, too, was mostly a time capsule from 1972: there was an Alberto VO5 oil treatment, a glass bottle of Listerine, a jar of Brylcreem. There didn't seem to be much of anything worth taking, or anything from this century, aside from a bottle with two Xanax that I emptied on the spot. I took a couple of deep breaths and felt the lollipop that Doc had given me in my pocket. I took it out, realizing it was a fentanyl lollipop.

It was supposed to be cherry, but it was really just some odd, vaguely red flavor. I licked it for about ten seconds before chewing it to pieces, sliding it down my throat, and waiting for whatever relief it might offer. I sat on the closed-lid toilet and read through a series of *New Yorker* cartoons. I closed my eyes and rested the back of my head against the cool tile and waited for the drugs to unclench me. Soon, soon, *soon*, I told myself, breathing. I tried to take deep breaths and before long, I found myself breathing in sync with the oxygen apparatus out in the other room. I opened my eyes. The bathroom was small and dusty. The tub was filled with cobwebs. There was a door that led out to a side yard and, out of habit, I made sure it was locked. I took some more breaths and waited for the drugs to produce some effect. I left the bathroom, hoping that by now Doc and Sandra would have returned to save me from being alone with the dying man.

This guy, mind-numbed and clearly on his way out of this life, probably would have cut a deal with whatever deity he believed in just to get a few more days of life—even a life like mine. That was just fact. But I watched him. So little of him left. Was this how it would end for me? With some stranger in scrubs checking on me every hour? Or overdosed and alone and left behind, with no one who would ever know, like the way I'd left Flip? Slipping away alone. He gnawed on the tube—his mouth the last thing moving, but not saying anything.

Who was he before he ended up in this living room? He'd had a life. He must have laughed and, even though no one was here now, he must have known at worst slivers of happiness and connection at some point. And it was ending here with someone like me a few feet away. I felt like I might throw up.

No matter what it came to—no matter how sick it made me—there was no way I could cut into what was left of this guy and add to whatever pain he would feel until everything ended and the morphine quietly escorted him out of this life and these machines hooked into him went silent.

I could still hear Doc and Sandra upstairs—they seemed to be fucking, or at least in a conversational intimacy that suggested fucking. Loneliness crashed down on me and swelled and filled my body. I hated being left alone in rooms, being alone where I didn't know anyone. Being alone anywhere turned me into a scared child. And this qualified as me by myself, even with the guy on the bed. I took deep breaths and felt a speck of luck that he couldn't move those wet sad eyes of his to focus on me.

On a tray next to the bed were a bunch of boxes that looked like they had pharmacy papers on them. Score. They were fentanyl patches. This box had been opened, but there were several others under both the table and bed. I grabbed five boxes. I tried several times for a sixth, but I would drop them all over when I did that, so I went with five and brought them back to my carrying bag.

The boxes held six patches each. I tore open the boxes, trying to be quiet, as I wasn't sure if this was part of the deal with Sandra or not, and neatly stacked the patches until I had thirty for my bag. I would have taken more—would have taken every single one I could find, but I didn't want to fuck up our connection for the future. I'd love to be able to say I was thinking about the dying guy. Not cutting into him was at least a groundswell of a decent human being surfacing, like it did at times—and often enough to not seem like a miraculous fluke. Though not slicing into a dying man hardly qualified me for sainthood.

I chewed another of the fentanyl lollipops I found. They seemed pretty useless. I wondered if they'd put this guy on any Oxy or anything good, pill-wise, before they had him on the patches and the pops.

In the kitchen, next to the coffee cups, was a cabinet filled with bottles of pills. The usual useless suspects: Advil, Tylenol, gaggles of vitamins and, scattered throughout the cabinet, the snake-oil desperation of shark's fin and whale cartilage and shit like that. I pocketed a bottle with about ten ten-milligram Vicodin and kept scrambling through the cabinet until I found something worthwhile in a near-full jar of eighty-milligram OxyContin. I smiled. I took two of the eighty-milligram tablets, crushing one and allowing the other to slide down my throat and release itself over time.

There was nothing else of value in the cabinet. I swapped the contents of the Advil and the OxyContin bottles and kept the Advil bottle in my pocket.

Back in the living room, I looked closely in the guy's eyes. Nothing registered. He was alive—that's what the machines seemed to be saying—but there didn't seem to be much going on.

I sat on the couch. There was an antique musket over the fireplace. The house looked like old people lived there. Murder mysteries piled up by the end table. This guy, or maybe Sandra, really liked mysteries. There had to be a hundred newer hardcovers in that room alone. There was Luna's *Penthouse* CD case open on the stereo—so, evidence of someone not old, maybe. I suspected the CD was in the machine and I really wanted to hear it, but I didn't want to do anything wrong, so I didn't hit Play.

I listened again for what Doc and Sandra might be doing. If they were fucking, they were being plenty quiet about it. I fingered a stray fentanyl patch in my pocket. I wanted to ask Doc how much longer we'd have to wait. I was starting to get nervous. We'd been there for twenty-five minutes, and I had no idea if this guy ever had visitors and, if he did, when they might be coming by.

Still, all this was Doc's call. I was just along for the ride. I went back into the bathroom, still feeling vaguely sick. Not dopesick anymore—the OxyContin had trickled some help into my blood and brain—but sick from the familiar nerves of being somewhere I didn't belong. The fear of being caught pressed on me like a vise. The idea of telling Doc there was no way I'd cut into that guy frightened me. I didn't know Doc that well—you rarely do with drug buddies. I had no idea what he was capable of.

I started running the bath. When the water first came out, it was rust brown, and then slowly it started to clear. The fentanyl patches worked better if you were warm. I put one on my right arm and one each on my right and left thigh. I took some deep breaths and made the temperature as hot as I could stand it and slowly lowered myself into the water. I took two more eighty-milligram OxyContin.

Twenty minutes later, I was nodding off. It felt good, a warm waking dream. I was worried that I might be close to overdosing. I puked in the sink—mostly clear bile as I rarely ate anymore. With my diminishing supply, I needed to squeeze every bit out of the drugs, and food fucked that up.

I slid happily down to the floor with my back against the wall. Incredible warmth flowed inside me—it was like my heart was a glowing road flare and my bones were hollowed-out bird bones. Balsa wood. I could have weighed ten pounds, the way I felt. Behind closed eyes fireworks displays fired in slow motion. My head rolled from one side to the other, and it didn't seem connected by anything thicker than dental floss.

Voices came from the living room. Yelling. A man's voice I didn't recognize.

"I said, who the fuck is this?" he screamed.

Sandra said, "He's a doctor I was consulting, Rick."

Rick? Who the hell was Rick?

Rick yelled, "Consulting? Is that what the fuck you were doing? Consulting?"

She started to talk again, but the man named Rick said, "Get the fuck downstairs—do you understand?"

I stood on legs that could barely hold me up and banged into the towel rack and knew instantly the noise was too loud—Rick had to have heard it, even over his yelling. My bag was in there with me, along with twenty-seven patches and the bottle of OxyContin I'd taken, and my clothes. I had a few lollipops. I thought about Doc, but didn't figure I could do him any good. It was one of those situations where my presence could only have added to the trouble. Behind that door: Rick. Doc. Sandra. That dying man, helpless to do anything about the anger that swirled around him.

And what would it do, adding me to that situation? It couldn't make it better.

I got dressed as quietly and as quickly as I could, without drying off. My clothes stuck to me, and I held my arm out to the wall to keep me upright. I double-checked my bag and made sure I had all the drugs.

The guy kicked the door in as I was trying to reach for the other door.

"And who the fuck is this wet fucking junkie?"

I closed my eyes for a minute. I turned.

Rick had a gun. "Back in the fucking room, junkie."

The three fentanyl patches clung wetly to me and itched under my clothing. I looked at the door to the outside and noticed the doorjamb was all but destroyed by termites, and it didn't look like anybody had used the door in a while, and it didn't look like I'd be using it now, either.

I came back into the living room. Rick had Doc and Sandra in front of the TV and told me to get there.

"Dude, you took a bath?" Doc said.

I nodded, not wanting or feeling much need to explain.

Rick pointed with his gun at Doc. "So, you're a doctor?"

Doc nodded.

Rick said, "So am I. And *this*," he said, waving the gun around, "is my hospice connection." He looked hard at Sandra. "Or did someone forget that?"

"I'm sorry, Rick."

"Shut the fuck up!" he yelled.

He wasn't on dope—he paced and chewed his lips and had picker scabs. All speed and meth shit. I can't take speed freaks—they pounce on everything, darty and unpredictable as bats at sunset.

He walked back and forth. "Yeah, I've done fucking seventy-two-hour fucking shifts sewing up idiots like you, you careless fucks. Fucking shitbags. You *buy* this shit from me, you don't take it, is that understood? You better bet that's motherfucking understood."

He rambled on for a while, not even looking at us, just screaming while the oxygen tank and the machines did their jobs.

"You want to know something about our fucking insides?" Rick said. "My first day in ER they tell me to sew this guy up. They needed to get at the liver, and you know what they fucking do to get at a liver? They take the fucking twenty-five feet of your guts and they put them in a silver tray next to you. Upper, lower intestine, all out and throbbing in a bowl—still connected to you but outside your fucking wrecked body—while the doctors fix you idiots. And then, they tell me to put it back together, and you know how we do that? We just motherfucking *dump* the guts back in, all thirty feet, forty, or whatever feet of guts, any old place and sew the fucker up. It takes about five days, and they're all back to where they're supposed to be."

I was still kind of nodding, having real trouble seeing where this guy was headed with all this. In my brain he was reading like those poetry magnets people let their kids put together on fridges. Words not adding up to anything. He seemed careless and floppy with the gun, and I thought about my dad. I thought of that man whose toxic, hopeless blood ran through my veins, and I tried to remember if you rushed guns or knives, and I figured it had to be guns because you'd run away from a knife, for sure.

I heard my father's voice so clearly it sounded like it was in the room and not in my head: *Never punch a man unless you're prepared to kill him, because you have no idea what another man is capable of.*

Rick was in front of the dying man's bed, now pointing the gun back and forth at all three of us like carnie ducks he was getting a bead on. "And you motherfuckers want me to put you back together after you rip me off?"

I still had no idea what he was getting at, but I figured, *I'll try to get this gun and if he kills me, that's cool.* Maybe this was where I'd die. Everything slowed down. My blood felt like roofing tar. All I saw was that gun and Rick's hands holding it and everything else went away. I was going to let this fucker shoot me. And if he did, well, so what.

I jumped into his chest, head down. I slammed him over the side bar of the dying man's bed and started punching his sides. I know I hit Rick, but I also hit the bed rails, and I hit IV tubes, and I punched the dying man's chest and once landed hideously on his ventilator tube. Rick clawed at my back. He had both hands on my back, which meant he didn't have the gun. I smelled piss from the catheter bag that'd spilled on the hardwood floor, and a moment later, Rick and I were rolling in it, the dying man's bed rolling away sideways like a drifting luxury liner, me still punching at Rick's guts, because that's where you hurt a man. Idiots punch heads. I'm not tough, but I know that much. I kneed him in the balls repeatedly until he was making sounds like a whimpering dog and spit bubbled slowly from his mouth. I did it hard enough for my knee and thigh to hurt doing it.

By the time Doc pulled me off of him, I think I was ready to kill the guy. I was willing to let him kill me, but I'd never before felt the savage rush that I was still feeling. I was briefly sickened by the notion that my father, in all his animal brutality, would have been, for once, proud of me. I felt like puking in a corner.

Doc held the gun and Sandra busily tried to reattach all the tubes and wires I had ripped out of her patient, whose machines I now noticed were all going faster and louder than before. I didn't know if the guy was worse off, or if I was just in some adrenaline-fueled space where noises were louder. Rick clutched his balls in a puddle of the dying man's piss. I was drenched from the piss, from the tub, and from sweat, which flowed out of me like my pores had tripled in size. My shirt clung to me.

Doc said, "Sandra, we're going to take what we came for."

She nodded. "What about Rick?"

"We could call the cops," I said. "After we leave."

Sandra shook her head. "If he talks, cops are going to talk to me." She paused and pushed it. "And then they'll talk to you," she said.

We should kill him, I thought. This was not a thread to leave loose. This was the string where if you leave it where it is, but then you happen to snag or pull it later, the whole sweater unravels. My father would have killed him, and he might have been right. But that was him.

I said, "Maybe you don't know us as well as you do. When Rick wakes up, you tell him we're strangers."

Doc looked at me. "He'll come looking for us."

I thought about my father's advice and said what I didn't want to say. "It's that or we kill him. And the biggest idiot cop on the planet would connect the dots to us in one interview with her." It occurred to me that if we killed Rick, we'd have to kill Sandra. I couldn't believe I was even thinking about it. At least I still had enough of who I used to be left to jettison that shit out of my head. Which meant the man I used to be was still in me, no matter how disgusting I'd become. Rick rolled around semiconscious on the floor. Doc kicked him in the thigh. Then he did it again.

"Fucker." Doc shook his head. "Let's get the fuck out of here."

I got my bag. Doc put the gun in his pants and started to get more of the patches and pills from Sandra, who I'm guessed already had the money, or else she was too scared to ask about it.

Either way, I went out the side door I'd tried to use before Rick came in. Doc followed. I walked past the blue and brown recycling and garbage cans and out the side yard gate. The driveway had a newer Lincoln next to Doc's car. Rick's car, I logged, in case I ever saw it again. I stopped, looked left, away from the dead end and toward Seventeenth Street, my hair still wet and the sun warming me as I looked down the street, and I walked toward Doc's car, trying hard to look like what I was: a man getting into the passenger side of a car on a beautiful day.

We got in. Doc took a deep breath and then another and had both hands on the wheel without starting the car. He lit a cigarette. I told him to give me one. He said, "Dude, you were a fucking hero in there."

I didn't look in his eyes. Lawn sprinklers ticked on at the neighbor's house. I lit the cigarette. Doc steered the car and we pulled out of the driveway, away from the Lincoln I hoped to never see again in my life.

Doc said it again. Said, "Dude, you are fucking heroic."

And this time, just to shut him up, just so I'd never have to hear it again, I said, "Yeah."

ST. JUDE'S

(Summer 2011)

My father is dying. I'm six months clean and I'm worried about a trip home, a trip full of "triggers" Ray said on the phone—and he told me I should be hyperaware of the triggers and make as many meetings as I can and call him, no matter what time of day or night if I feel like I'm in trouble. Ray's advice is solid enough—he talked me down last night—but if I'm in trouble I'll probably call someone I really know: Johnny Mo, who has almost the same amount of clean time as me and had the same bottom, more or less, as I did. I don't have to explain anything to him. I might call Olivia. She and Johnny Mo know about losing fathers and missing last chances.

I haven't been clean long enough to deal with much. This happened last time, too. Without drugs, it feels impossible to even know who you are. You've never really known *this* person walking around in your clothes—the one that has to deal with everything. Even six months after cleaning up, I can barely walk into a grocery store and function without a panic attack. A crowded sidewalk makes me want to run away. People's voices sound like a hundred jackhammers. Pigeons take off so loudly

I fear their wings will do damage. Everything's frightening and everything hurts behind my eyes. I haven't slept more than two or three hours a night since I got clean.

It's getting a little better now, but I still had nerves and trouble at the airport and on the flight and all the way in the cab to the hotel across from the hospital.

The hotel makes sense because the doctors said my father could go down quickly. The main reason, though, is that I'm not sure anything on earth could make me sleep in the house where I grew up.

I still blame my father, fairly or not, for my mother's suicide. Still blame myself for it, too, though I know rationally that you can't change the way someone else feels. But hearts don't know anything about rational. Hearts long and they ache and dream and desire and need. If love and wishes and hope could save someone, my life would be unrecognizable to me. But then, so would everybody else's.

But I still wonder, and figure I always will, whether my mother would have killed herself if she had never married my father and never had me. Life can go in infinite directions. How many times in her life did she turn right when left would have offered hope and beauty? How many men—or women for all I know—might have offered her a safety and love she'd instead never know? How many times did she *know* that her life was wrong and yet not leave that life for one that could have been better? And how many of those times did she have those thoughts when I cried or needed or pestered and added to the things that chipped away at whatever keeps a person wanting to stay alive? How much despair did she allow to become normal before it no longer seemed like despair— it just felt like every day, every sunrise stealing hope, one after the last one behind her and the next day and the next day and the next, looking the same forever.

It could be a fact, even if I'm not to blame: she might have been better off if I'd never been born.

Among all the clichés you hear in AA and NA rooms is "feelings aren't facts."

Which is true enough. But facts didn't make my mother jump off that bridge. Feelings did. Feelings lead to actions, and actions become facts.

So, no, her feelings weren't facts.

But the fact is, my mother killed herself, and the fact is I never really got over it.

I haven't told anyone, but I've decided that the next time I use, I'm making that final choice between being one of the living and one of the dead. I don't have another detox and rehab left in me. If I go out again, I'm going to kill myself on dope. I have no idea what's going to happen, and I don't know if I have the will or the strength to keep fighting this brain of mine that I've been fighting so long. And then, the next minute, I think, *You've come this far. If you'd offed yourself whenever you'd wanted to, you would have missed a lot of great times.*

But I have to coax those good thoughts out of hiding. The bad ones never shut up or go away. Like regrettable bad tattoos that are always there, reminding you of mistakes and regrets and stupidity that will be there forever. I've messed up so much that there are other times I think, *If you'd offed yourself, think of all the shit you would have avoided and all the pain you might not have caused. You need any more evidence that you're a fuckup? You haven't tried to be clean enough times to know it's impossible?*

And then, there's maybe still another shot at something close to happiness. What I had with Olivia when I was clean for those years. And it wasn't just five years with Olivia—it was five mostly good years, more or less, with myself. Being clean helped—my meds helped. My life was as close to normal as I figured a brain like mine would ever get. But, of course, I blew that, too, and then the negative thoughts erupted through the broken dam, and there was nothing left to hold them back.

And here I am, clean again, and on better meds than I've ever been on. Some days I feel like life's something worth clinging to and filled with such an unspeakable beauty that I wonder if this is what life is like in most people's brains.

Most of the friends I have left told me that I should seriously consider not making this trip. But it's my father. And there are some things I need to say and hear, before saying and hearing things with him are no longer an option in this world. I've lived a life filled with questions about my mother that will never have answers. That can't happen twice, if I have a say in it.

A doctor called me two days ago. "You'd better be here soon."

I'm broke. I'm living in an empty rehearsal room that doubles as equipment storage at a buddy's practice studio. I fix amps and engineer recordings in trade for rent.

To make the flight from LAX to Kennedy, I borrowed the money from Olivia, only after I assured her it wasn't for drugs.

I called her, and she let out a sigh—a sigh that contained years of dashed expectations behind it. A sigh that I wish I'd never heard in my life. "I can't send you money, Bud." She paused. "You know that."

Of course I knew that. It's the first thing they tell people who love addicts when the partner or friend or family does Al-Anon or any of those programs. Rule Number One: Never send money to an addict. Rule Number Two? Refer to Rule Number One.

"My dad's dying," I said. "I can send you the obituary in a couple of weeks if that would make you trust me more."

"It's not that I don't trust you," she said.

"Sure it is," I said. "I don't blame you."

And there was a long pause. I pictured her, standing in our old kitchen, with the tile job she'd done and the copper ceiling and the custom sink I installed right after we'd moved in and figured we'd never leave.

I said, "You have no reason to trust me. It's OK. I'm not mad or upset." I hoped the lack of desperation and the tone of reason and understanding in my voice would prove to her that I wasn't using the money for drugs. "But he *is* dying, and I need to ask him about my mother while I have the chance." I thought about Olivia and her father. And I said, "I want to settle up with him. And say good-bye, too." I felt lousy, trying to guilt her by playing off her lost desires with her father. But the fact that I was a manipulative man was not news to Olivia—the difference was, I was being manipulative about the death and not about drug money.

She said she'd pay for the ticket. I promised her it was a loan, and she said, "Whatever."

I asked if I could pick it up—I was living less than a half hour away, but it could have been continents since she'd said we couldn't see each other—but she said she'd buy it online under my name, and she'd call me back and let me know the flight and I could check in at LAX. I couldn't blame her for handling it that way, but it still hurt.

For the first year and a half after I started using—after I'd moved out of our house—she said she couldn't and wouldn't see me while I was loaded. I let her know I'd quit when I went into rehab—I had to ask her for some of her insurance paperwork to get in. If I relapsed, she'd be sure I was a truly lost cause and she'd move on for good.

If she could *see* me clean, in person though. If we could sit in a room together. If she could know I could be who I was, there had to be a chance she'd take me back.

"I have to go Bud," she'd said. "I really am sorry about your father."

"I've got six months, 'Liv."

She paused. "That's great to hear, Bud," she said quietly, sounding weary and scared. "Really."

The doctor must have told my father I was coming, because he doesn't seem surprised. Even under the sheets I can tell he's thin beyond belief. The man I spent so much of my life afraid of—until I saw him last time looking like a dying junkie—is now probably half his normal size and down close to a hundred pounds. His skin is the gray of the sky during an autumn drizzle. His eyes are deep in their sockets. The whites of his eyes look like someone took a yellow highlighter pen to them. You don't need to be a doctor. I've seen enough addicts and enough drunks with their yellow eyes of death. His liver's clearly shutting down, flooding all the toxins back into his body. His head shows the lines of his skull under skin frighteningly close to bone.

"Hey kid," he says.

"Hey Pop."

Neither of us seems to know what to say next. The machines he's hooked up to make beeping noises every once in a while. The guy in the other bed seems to be on some device that breathes for him—with the menacing apparatus bellowing in a clear tube to make his chest move along with it. I see it behind the privacy curtain, making a steady churning noise and pumping breath into him as the machine accordions up and down. My father has oxygen tubes up his nose. A catheter bag that someone must have recently emptied and that quickly reminds me of that dying guy in Tustin. Reminds me of jobs I could never do. My father's IV slowly drips and I think *morphine*.

My father rolls his eyes toward the guy on the breathing machine and says, "He can't hear us."

"I wasn't worried about that," I say. Although I was. I have some things I have to say to my father and I thought we'd be in private. But I guess we sort of are, since this guy seems more machine than man at this point.

"Pop," I say. "I came here because I have some things we need to talk about."

"Oh, fuck. This isn't more of your AA crap you're pulling on me, is it?"

I have my own issues with AA and NA. But what I've been doing my whole life clearly hasn't worked and those programs, cliché-riddled as they are and filled with annoying religious people I try to tune out, have probably saved my life at least twice. "No, it's not about AA or NA," I say.

"Thank god for that minor miracle." He looks at me. "How are you doing with that?"

"I've been better." I'm shaking a little from having to tell the truth. But if I'm going to be asking for the truth, I have to offer it. The machinery keeping all these people alive makes its noises. "I started using again on tour a couple of years ago."

"I told you," he says.

"Turns out you were right."

He takes a shallow breath that looks like it hurts. "Well, I'm sorry about that. Didn't want to be right on that one."

"Thanks," I say.

My father gestures me closer to him, like he has a secret. "I'm sorry, but when they sent me here, the hospice workers took away all the pain meds from the house."

He's trying to be kind, in his way, and I've long forgotten how to process *nice* from him. "Thanks for the thought," I say. "But I'm clean."

"Again?"

"Yeah."

"Why?"

It's a good question.

It's the question I asked Johnny Mo on the phone from rehab when I was thinking about whether to die or stay clean. I was haunted by images of all the years: Tearing out that dead guy's tubes and fighting with Rick on top of what was left of his body. Seeing what I'd seen with Al—and Al was his father. My mother in midair, never hitting the water before I woke up. I was having trouble sleeping, trouble living with myself. And he'd been clean a couple of months longer than me.

I'd said, "Why should I be clean? What's the argument for it?"

He paused. I heard him light a cigarette. "Look at where you are. You hate yourself. You're letting down people who love you. You're breaking their hearts. You're ashamed and you feel like absolute shit, physically. You can't even get high anymore, so the best you can hope for is to not be dopesick, right?"

I smiled. "Well, there's that."

"So, what's the argument *for* that, Bud?"

"I'm not making any arguments for it." I paused. I'd been through the drill. I knew the rehab answers to most questions, but not this one: "What if Olivia never takes me back?"

Johnny Mo took a deep breath. "I can bullshit you and say it'll all be fine if you do the right thing from here on in." He took a drag on his cigarette. "But she can't be part of your thinking. Whether she's with you or gone, your choice is yours."

"What if there's no chance?" I said.

"There's only ever *no chance* when you use. You want to control the future? You know the one way to do it—we both know *that* future, right, bro?"

"Why?" my father says again.

Why change? Like Johnny Mo had said, there were no surprises to a life using. Every day was desperation and lies and sickness. I had no energy left. So, *why change?* Why *not* change? Where's a good argument for what I've done to myself?

For now, I try to cling to what happened when I got clean before. Life got better. I met Olivia. I had friends I loved who I'm still too ashamed to call now. But, I *did* have a decent life for the only time in my life.

My father looks at me like he's expecting an answer.

"It seems to be that or die at this point," I say, honestly.

"You might not want to wait around to die," he says, wincing. "Doing it on your own might be a better plan."

I think of my mother killing herself. His wife. Why would he bring that up to me and not expect a response?

"That seems to have its downsides, too." With a little anger in my voice, I add, "It kind of fucks up the people who care about you."

"Sorry I mentioned it," he says. He coughs for a minute and the nurse comes in to adjust his oxygen level.

After the nurse leaves, my father gestures for me to come close again. "Good luck staying clean. Your wife will be happier, at least," he says, without much investment or hope.

"Olivia left me," I say.

He nods, eyes closed. "Of course she did," my father says. "People like us? Either we live with junkies, or alone. Normal people don't get it."

"She gets it," I say, thinking about her father, but I don't want to get into that here.

"Divorced?"

I tell him about her kicking me out but keeping me on her university insurance.

"She loves you," he says with no emotion. Like it's an observation, but not something he can get invested in. But, why should he? He won't be around for the outcome, either way.

That she loves me is not really in doubt. How much love itself matters, in the long run, I don't know. "She does."

"Sorry that didn't work out," my father says.

"Me, too," I say. And again I cling to the hope that Olivia hasn't only stayed married so I can have health care. It won't leave my mind, no matter how much I try to push it away for now, that maybe there's still a chance she'll take me back if I can prove to her that I can be the man I was. But the man I was turned back into the man I was before that. I have no idea if I can make it at life. If I can't trust myself, how can I ask her to trust me?

There's a long pause. My father fights the pain for a minute. His body tightens like a fist then releases, and his breathing gets back to its normal, shallow, steady pace again.

"The pain bad?" I say.

He has trouble breathing after the wave of pain. Then the breaths get more even and he says, "You could never guess, kid."

I feel stupid for asking, because it's obvious that the pain is awful. When I was a kid, I saw my father drop a 351 Windsor engine from a 1968 Cougar onto his chest when a pull-chain broke. He ended up with five broken ribs and a broken collarbone, and he wouldn't let me drive him to the hospital. I tried to tell him to let me drive, and he screamed, "I'm not some fucking invalid. You want to come, get in the fucking passenger seat." Blood flew from his mouth when he yelled. I've seen him reset his own broken nose, which he later showed me how to do, and I've done it three times in my life. It makes you weak in the knees, but the pain isn't as bad as people think. It rarely is.

The pain isn't as bad as the fear of the pain—he taught me that. And he was right. Getting punched? Not nearly as bad as people think. Broken bones? The fear hurts worse. But *this* pain, what he's experiencing now, seems real beyond belief. Stronger than any fear of pain could ever be. Like every pain he fought through in his life joined forces and came back at once.

He falls asleep and I stay next to his bed, watching him sleep, in visible pain even when he's unconscious. After about twenty minutes, I grab a coffee from a machine on the floor—the kind that comes with a hand of cards drawn on the cup. It tastes like coffee-flavored chalk in hot water.

Back in his room, there's a sign that says not to use cell phones. I sit by my father's bed and think about going out and calling Olivia, but I can't make myself do it. I sit, half reading an old copy of *People*.

The room falls into a steady rhythm of beeps and the hiss of oxygen from some unit on the wall. Medical personnel walk by the room. Some visitors cross the door now and then. Every once in a while, some patient hooked into a rolling IV shuffles by on their way somewhere. The place smells of rubbing alcohol and hand cleanser and that vague scent of ill dread that floats in hospital air.

In sleep, there's a tense frown of pain on my father's thin, gray face. I wonder how much time he has left, and I go back and forth between thinking he deserves to leave this world in as much peace as possible and wanting to extend that suffering if it means I can ask him some questions about my life, his life, and what exactly happened with my mother.

The pain wakes my father up. I'm afraid, but I need to at least bring up what I came here for.

I say, "You feeling OK?" My voice is weak and shaky and tight from my nerves.

He laughs, which turns into a long, painful-sounding cough. "Define OK."

I try to smile. "There's some stuff I need to ask you about."

"Can't I just die in peace?"

"I'm not trying to upset you."

"But you are."

I close my eyes and try to stay calm, running the Serenity Prayer through my head a couple of times. I say, "There's nothing you want to set straight? Nothing you want to talk about before it's—" I pause, "too late?"

"I want, like I fucking said, to die in peace," he says. "But apparently it's too late for that."

He coughs and turns his head, pointing to a kidney-shaped container next to the bed. I hold it by his mouth and he spits phlegmy blood into it. I hold it next to him for a second, waiting for more. He waves it away. I put the white container with the slick, black-red clot of blood in it next to his bed.

I say, "Maybe you can die in peace if you and I are on better terms."

He lets out a wet angry laugh and closes his eyes.

This wasn't the start I was hoping for. But I'm here. I made it this far, and whether he wants it or not, there are some things I came here to do.

I pull a chair up close to his bed, careful not to upset all the tubes and wires running through and around the metal side bars. Everything around him seems so fragile, and I'm scared just sitting there. I take a deep breath. I've planned what I want to say, gone over it in my head several times at home in LA, on the plane, and in the rental car coming to the hospital. All these things to say. But none of what I've planned seems to be coming easily.

"Pop, I want to say that I'm sorry I haven't always been the son you wanted. The person I should have been."

He turns his head toward me and I see how weak he is. How even the slightest motion causes him pain. "None of us is who we wanted to be."

True enough. The gap between who I wanted to be, who I *could* have been, and who I have been is a wide one. The gap where sorrow seems to take root and grow.

A nurse walks by the room. I turn to see her pass, then I turn back to my father. "I need to say I'm sorry."

"Fine. You've said it."

The morning light from the window shows dust specks floating in the air, and I'm reminded of how foul with germs hospitals are. I had a friend once who had a bone marrow transplant, and they had her stay at the Motel 6 across the street from the hospital because it was cleaner than the hospital and she had less risk of infection there. I want to ask my father to forgive me, but I also remember what Ray and Johnny Mo and everyone else have told me: that expectations on my part were foolish at best and dangerous at worst. You can't live without hope, but expectations can kill a person.

I lean in close, even though the other patient in the room can't hear and the people outside don't seem to be paying any attention to us. "I need to ask you about that guy," I say. "The guy who came to buy the used car?" I want to say *the guy you killed,* but I don't want anyone to hear us.

"I told you about it," he says. "Everything you need to know."

"I need to know that it was true."

"Of course it was true," he says. "What the fuck point would there be to lie about it?"

"Because your version of the story makes you look better."

"There *is* no other version of the story. Only the one you made up. That I killed some fucking guy for no reason." He looks hard at me. "That's *your* version." He shakes his head. "So, yeah. My version does make me look a little better than the psycho you peg me for."

"But what about Mom?"

"What about her?"

"What was *her* version of it?" She left, in my memory, not long after my father killed that man. The two actions had to be related. "She just left for no reason?"

"Nobody does anything for *no* reason." My father looks away. "Jesus," he says. "It's the fucking past."

"I need to know," I say.

"What do you need to know?" He starts to cough, quietly at first but then it expands again into a deep, wet cough that sounds and looks like it hurts. Blood spittles off his lip and onto his neck. I wipe it away and rub a slimy little clot on my jeans. He gets his breath back and looks angrily back to me. "What the fuck? I'm dying." He closes his eyes. "What exactly do you need to know?"

I say, "I just want to know what happened." I want a cigarette but figure I'll have plenty of time when visiting hours are over.

He's quiet for a long time. I count twenty-seven beeps from one of the machines he's hooked into. The pumping of air from the other guy's breathing apparatus hums steadily in the room.

"What I need," my father finally says, "is my CD player. It's in my bedroom at the house and I need you to bring it to me. Don't touch it. Don't look in it—I'll know if you do. Bring that to me."

I don't say anything. Ray and I had talked about me staying at my father's house and decided the hotel would be much safer. But I might be able to find something related to my mother. Maybe he saved something, anything, that I haven't ever seen. Maybe *some* answer was hidden there.

He says, "Bring me that CD player tonight. You want to talk, we'll talk then."

I want to get into that house, but I want him to feel like I'm doing him a favor. I want him to need me. "We'll talk about what I want to talk about?"

"Do what I ask and I'll talk," he says. He tells me to get the keys from the desk nurse who took his clothes and possessions when he was admitted. I feel queasy looking at him and realizing that he'll never wear those clothes, never use those keys, ever again. He's never leaving this room.

He seems weary, but still filled with the inner power that once made him so frightening, even if a five-year-old could knock him out now. "I need a favor. You need to *talk*," he says, making *talk* sound like something frivolous and beneath a real man.

At my father's house, I find the CD player/radio by his unmade bed. It's old, not ghetto blaster sized but huge by today's standards. I bring it downstairs and put it on the kitchen table. I make some coffee and sit at the table smoking cigarettes until my throat is raw and I have a headache.

I go back up to his bedroom. I sit on his bed, the bed my mother used to sleep in. His sliding closet doors are broken and leaning against the wall, and I see a box with a bunch of papers in the closet. It feels like a violation, but I figure he'll be dead soon and I'll be going through these papers anyway.

Inside the box is a Polaroid of me as a kid, washing his blue Buick Skylark that as a kid I called his "Bluik." I'm in diapers, pointing a garden hose at the car. I don't remember when the picture was taken.

There's a picture of my mother and me at what looks to be Thanksgiving. I stand next to her and she has one arm around me and the other arm is on the table, holding a cigarette. She smoked Marlboro Reds, although you can't tell that from the picture. She's smiling. But she doesn't look happy. She looks like a sad person trying to look happy because she's supposed to look happy in photographs.

Deeper down in the box, I find a manila file marked SARAH SUZANNE BARRETT. My heart feels like it's punching its way out of my chest. My hands shake as I open the file.

All that's inside are a police report and a coroner's report. In the column reserved for manner of death, it reads "suicide."

The next page is a handwritten report that reads as follows:

Husband states they had not spoken in three years and that she had no permanent address. Personal vehicle parked, running, on bridge. Wallet and ID on passenger seat. No note. Search was attempted, but aborted after three hours of checking the surface and banks. Water approximately seven degrees, dive search impossible. Subject had history of mental illness and had been prescribed Thorazine. Husband states she would frequently stop taking medicine.

In another manila envelope, this one much thicker, are the contents from her car, itemized on a police sheet. I take out her wallet, looking at her driver's license. She had a picture of me in her wallet. From sixth grade. Dorky glasses and an unfortunately enormous collar. There's a fake bunch of clouds behind me. I remember the day at school they took those pictures, combing and recombing my hair with a thick black comb that I kept in my back pocket, like the cool kids, even though I was far from one of them. Her social security card is in there. Seven dollars. Nothing special. Nothing that carries any kind of message or solves any mysteries. Just life shit.

I put his papers back together the way I found them, though I don't know why I'm being careful. He won't be back in this house. He won't see that I've gone through his things. But out of habit, out of fear, which is also a habit, I put his things back as close to the way I found them as I can.

I find a box filled with clippings about me and the various bands I've played in. Articles cut from the pages of *SPIN, Rolling Stone, No Depression, Musician*, and the *New York Times* review where they referred to me as "Mr. Barrett" when talking about my songwriting.

My father kept all these, all through the years we didn't talk. Why does it feel like so many people I know surprise me with their good acts, while I seem to let everyone down by fucking everything up—doing the thing that, ultimately, doesn't surprise them at all?

I take the picture of my mother and also take her wallet and I put them in a small suitcase in the closet.

A few minutes later, I take the report on her suicide and put that in the suitcase, and then I find two last items at the back of the closet. They're notes from my mother.

One reads: Went to store. Be back.

The other: Do not read between the lines Do not read between the lines Do not read between the lines . . .

Written maybe a few hundred times in a row in the smallest printing I've ever seen. Nothing but that one sentence multiplied—and no room between any of them.

Scattered around my father's house is the evidence of someone who's been dying for a while. Empty bottles of Percs and OxyContin and torn-open cases of morphine patches. More orange syringe caps than I can count litter the floor, and I'm careful to avoid being spiked. No way to know what my father could have. I'm scared in this house, wondering if I can manage to stay clean if I find any of his drugs. I start to go through the drawer by his bed, and I find a spoon and several unopened syringes, but thankfully no drugs—and a picture of him and my mother at Niagara Falls.

They smile toward the camera, squinting with the sun in their eyes. Horseshoe Falls glows like a blue and white jewel behind them. The blue is the color of Earth from outer space. They look young, impossibly young. The photo must have been taken a few years before I was born, and they have the look of young people who are blissfully unaware that any trouble will ever come their way. That trouble happens, but to other people.

I take that picture, too. I think about my father's drugs: Behind the bed? On the floor? In a drawer somewhere nobody checked? No one would know. It would be understandable. If I just got high today to stop these thoughts. To try to turn my brain off, if only for a while, before I have to go back to the hospital for evening visiting hours.

I think about my mother. Thorazine. In one of my earliest seventy-two-hour observations after a suicide attempt, they had me on it. That plus some other drug, after I had a seizure from detoxing. Thorazine makes you feel like the walking dead. Like all of your thoughts float just beyond your grasp. You shuffle around without energy or animation, looking like one of the machines in Disney's Hall of Presidents. As bad as I've ever felt in my life, that only made it worse. Every single thought I had seemed like the shore when you're stuck in a riptide. No matter how hard you work, you don't get any closer. The day they let me out of the psych ward, I zombied around town with the hospital's ID bracelet still on my wrist. People saw me for what I was—a nutcase who'd been let out—and I saw the fear in their eyes as I struggled to walk, the Thorazine feeling like it added twenty pounds to each foot.

I think, *Mom felt like that. Felt like that for days and weeks and months, when only a few hours is enough to make you wish you were dead. Wish you could just stop everything.* If it doesn't make me forgive her, it makes me understand her a little more.

I leave my father's bedroom and check my e-mail on my phone. Nothing important. Nothing that needs my attention. I do a Google search on myself to see if anyone's written any new articles about me. There are a couple of new reviews of a compilation CD of all my solo work from when I left the band. Most of the reviews have been good, but I don't care enough to actually read the two new ones.

I want to get high.

I should call Ray, but I call Olivia. Lunch here is morning there and she'll be up. Even if she's not, I need to talk.

When she hears my voice, she sounds tired but not without concern.

She says, "How are you?"

"I'm at my dad's," I say. "It's hard."

"Maybe you shouldn't be there."

"Where would I be that wouldn't be hard?" I say, and I immediately feel like self-pity may be the least attractive quality I have, and I wince that I'm showing it to her. There's a dread—I never felt like I had to impress Olivia until now. I felt like I could just be myself, and now I have no idea who that is or whether she—or I—would like what we found if I *could* be myself ever again. "I found a bunch of pictures of my mom," I tell her. I tell her about the suicide report, about the faded images of my parents before I was born, about the pictures of me when I was little.

"I bet you were cute."

"I was fat."

"You always think you're fat," she says.

"Fat little kid with Henry Kissinger glasses."

"I'm sure you were a catch for all the little girls."

As quickly as I felt like a stranger trying to impress her, I forget for an instant that we're not a couple. I forget that I'm the man who let her down. I forget, just for a second, that I made this woman weep in our bedroom while I was dopesick in the bathroom, sick and wishing I could die, thinking I could never feel worse—and then hearing her quietly cry a room away and realizing you can always feel worse. There is always room to bump the worst moment of your life down a few notches, no matter how bad you feel. But so far that one is, if not the worst, one of the finalists. I'd let her down that much. I knew about her father. I wasn't stupid. I didn't do it to hurt her, but I did it to help myself in the short run, all the while knowing it would hurt her forever, and I wonder if there's much of a difference in the end whether I meant to hurt her or not. I knew it would—I just foolishly thought I could keep it a secret.

I've caused her despair that will never totally go away, no matter how long and how well I live from here on in. I worry that I can never change how she feels about me. It causes me physical pain just to think about it. There are things we can never fix. Things we can never make right. And if that's the case, what will I do?

She asks me again how I am.

"I'm in this house and I still have six months clean," I say, working to make it sound light and funny.

"That's great, Bud." Olivia sounds flat—clinical and unemotional. I'm clinging to a hope that it's work for her to sound like this, not easy.

"I'm really trying, 'Liv."

"I know that," she says. "I do."

I say, "I was thinking the other day that, combined, I've spent more than two years of my life in rehab."

"Well, if that's what it takes," she says.

"Two years, doing nothing but rehab," I say. I shake my head, even though I know she can't see me. I think about those stats you read in *Harper's Index,* the kind that say the average person spends three months of their life waiting in traffic and a year on the toilet and all that. "I can't believe I've wasted two years of my life in rehab."

She laughs sadly.

I say, "What?"

"Just that you think the two years in rehab was the waste," she says. "Not the twenty years you spent fucked up."

"You got me there," I say. "I guess I'm looking at it wrong."

"If it takes five years, it's worth it."

And I want to say, *Is it? Will you take me back if I make it five years?* But I know it's not a fair question. I also know the answer might shatter me.

I light a cigarette and push the pile of newspapers back to make space for my instant coffee on the dinner table.

I say, "Is there any chance I could see you when I get back?"

I hear her breathe. "I don't know if that's such a good idea."

It hits me how long it's been since I've been back to our house. Her house. I relapsed over two years ago. There's probably no way she could have just sat around for years. You don't go from being a woman who likes sex four of five times a week to some nun, just like that. Just because I'm out of the picture. Odds are, her life hasn't been on hold.

I say, "Are you seeing someone?"

She doesn't say anything.

I say, "I mean, I'd understand if you were. I wasn't trying to put you on the spot or anything."

"I really don't want to have this conversation," she says.

"Are we ever going to see each other again? Or even really *talk* to each other?"

There is a pause that feels like it might be the longest pause of my life. And I know right away this moment is dreadful enough that I'll never forget it. Other terrible moments will be judged against it. Every day I live, whether I'm dead today or in thirty years, I'll remember this chill and the way every organ feels shoved into my chest and throat like I'm in an elevator that's snapped its cable and is rushing to the bottom. Time slows down, and I hear her walking in what used to be our dining room, and in this house I hear my father's refrigerator cycle on with a rattle and hum.

And even lost with an ache for what I know can't be good news from Olivia, it hits me that my father will never hear that sound again.

"Bud, I will never love anyone the way I love you."

I'm afraid I'll cry before I get a sentence out, but it doesn't matter because I have no idea what to say. My hope soars for a second. She loves me more than anyone else. How can that have more than one outcome?

"Bud?"

I clear my throat. "I'm here."

"I'm so sorry," she says. "I haven't wanted to tell you this, but I've known that I have to sooner or later. You have to promise me you won't . . . take it wrong and do something stupid and hurt yourself."

"What are you saying?"

She doesn't say anything. I get up and pace the kitchen. I go out on the back porch and see the patch of dirt where the grass never grew back from where I used to shoot baskets at the hoop my father mounted on the tall dogwood. Birds make their racket somewhere out in the woods.

She says, "I just can't live my life worried that you won't be there." She pauses. "For me. For—" She's crying quietly. "For a family, Bud."

And even already knowing I'll always remember this moment with dread, I suddenly know it's about to get worse, though I don't immediately see how.

Her voice is muffled, like she's got her hand over the mouthpiece, but I hear her say, clearly and not to me, "Please. Just—please."

There's someone else in the house with her.

"Who the fuck is that?"

She says quietly, "Bud. Give me a minute. I need to go somewhere private, OK?" I hear her go out what must be our back door. Hear the security door slam and bounce open again because I never fixed it even though I meant to, and then I hear her push it closed.

I'm walking in circles, still trying to take a deep breath, but I can't and I'm seeing stars, lights popping like silent firecrackers and it feels like someone punched me in the chest and I realize *this* is a pain that hurts more than the fear of it had. I can't have an anxiety attack. Not now. I rush back into the house and chew my last two Xanax—one I was saving for the hospital and one I was saving for the plane ride home. I try to sit down, but I can't stay still and head back outside. Up the street some kids are playing kickball.

She says, "Bud, you have no idea how much I wish I could be with you."

"I don't have an idea? Clearly you wish it a little fucking less than I do."

There's a pause. "That's not fair."

"Fuck fair," I say. "What are you telling me?"

"Bud."

"No! Exactly *what* are you saying?" I say. "You owe me that much." If anyone other than me and the loud kids is outside, there's no doubt they hear me over the laughter of people young enough to have no idea how bad life can get.

"Please," she says. "You have to understand."

"I don't have to understand shit," I say. Every day of the last six months—which felt like ten years the way the days wouldn't end to give me some quiet peace—I worried she wouldn't take me back, but somehow I always thought she would. I was almost positive I knew how much she loved me, even before she told me that she loved me more than she'd ever loved anyone. I'd made no emotional space for this. "You're giving up on me?"

"I've stayed married to you so you could afford rehab," she says. "I can't *get* married, because I want you to have medical. Don't you dare tell me I gave up on you."

Can't get married? I toss my cigarette and light another one, but I can't come close to taking a draw on it. I feel like I felt when

I first found out about my mother. Like there should be a bigger word than loneliness in this fucking language, but there's not a word in any language that could ever reach this space. No matter what she says, it feels like there's not a person left on Earth who cares about me. "Who is he?"

Every answer feels like it's coming after a five-minute pause, even if it's only seconds. Still, these are seconds I'll remember more than some whole years of my life. "He's a good man," she says. "But he's not you, Bud." It's obvious she's having trouble talking. At least this isn't easy. I feel selfish enough to hope that this is a moment of dread *she'll* never forget. That it leaves a wound that will never heal. All I've ever wanted is for her to be happy, and if this guy's good for her, I know I should be happy, but right now only the idea of her suffering can make me feel the least bit better. I hate myself for thinking it, but it doesn't stop me. This Good Man who will be there to raise Olivia's children.

Out of nowhere I get an image of her fucking whoever this guy is. I don't see him—I see her. Her grabbing his hair while he goes down on her and the clipped-breath, high-pitched way she repeats *oh, yes, oh, yes* when she comes, and I see her sucking his cock when he can't sleep, but of course he probably has no trouble sleeping, since he's the Good Man whose head is no doubt less of a fucking mess than mine, and my eyes ache like someone's shoving their thumbs into them and I feel as hollow and sick as I can ever remember in my life.

She says, "I need you to always know that."

I almost ask who he is again, but I don't really care at all who the hell he is. Whoever he is, he couldn't and never will mean a fucking thing even if I spend the rest of my life hating him—this *Good Man.* I want him hurt. And even in this moment, I know her saying she loves me more than anyone is important enough for her to need to say it. But all that matters is the sickening thought that makes nothing else in the world matter: He's not me.

No matter who she may love more or less, he'll be in that house—our house—and I won't be. She's gone.

"I'm so sorry, Bud. All I ever wanted was to never, never hurt you."

I'm dazed. "Great job there."

"Bud."

My brain is changing back and forth from wanting her to hurt and wanting to change her mind. I'm trying to say the right thing. Trying hard to make her think a life with me is not impossible. "I'm sorry," I say. "That wasn't fair."

"This isn't easy," she says.

"Please tell me that's true."

"Bud, I'm hiding in the fucking driveway so the man I live with won't hear that I'll never love him the way I love you. I'm admitting to you I'll never be with the man I'm in love with." She pauses. "This is the hardest choice I've ever made."

Never be with the man I'm in love with? Never? I wonder when this choice was made. How long has she known this? She lives with this guy. She knew this when I asked her for the plane tickets. I'm fighting anger when I say, "You don't have to make it."

"Yes," she says. "I wish I didn't, but I do."

I stand still and the floor feels like I'm on a boat.

She says, "I need to know you won't—do anything, Bud."

"So *my* actions have repercussions but yours don't have to?"

She's quiet. "Bud, I know you never meant to hurt me. Whether you did or not, you didn't mean to. If you do something now, you'll be hurting me because you want to."

And I want to say, *Fuck you! Live with it.* I try to make my voice calm, even if it's the only part of me that is. "My life is mine to fuck up, 'Liv. More than ever."

"No," she says. "It's not."

I want to kick everything I see, but I don't want her to hear it. I can't talk.

She says, "I don't want to fight with you, baby."

And I want to say, *I don't want to fight with you, either. I want you to take me back.* I say, "I'm sorry. I'm dealing with a lot of stuff here and I needed to hear your voice." I let out a breath. "And this . . . this threw me."

"I know," she says. "And I'm sorry. You have to know this is the hardest thing I've ever done."

"Do I *have* to know that?" I say. "That changes things?"

There's a pause.

She says, "I hope someday you'll feel like it does change things, even if you can't feel that right now."

I don't answer her.

She says, "Are you OK?"

I swell with hope that she cares enough to ask, but I can't stop myself. "No, I'm not fucking OK. Did you just seriously ask me that?"

"I love you."

I can't say anything. I picture her fucking the Good Man. The bastard who will get to spend every day with her. I see her laughing at some restaurant. I see her at some fucking party with his arms around her, and I want him at least to know, for how little it's worth, that she loves me more. I hope that this fact would crush him—even if it's not helping me much.

"Bud, I need to know you're OK in that house."

Before I went into rehab this last time, my plan was to take as many drugs as I could scrounge up, shred my ID so no one would know who I was and they couldn't report it to Olivia, and drive out to Twentynine Palms and OD in one of the thousands of abandoned cabins out there. I got as far as picking the house. At some point I realized that shredding my ID wouldn't matter, since my prints were in the system. I sat in an empty shell of a house for ten hours trying to decide if I wanted to live or die. I never told her any of this. I didn't want her bearing the weight of thinking she was the main reason I did or didn't do it. The next day, I checked into rehab, still having no idea why I made the choice I made.

There are plenty of days, still—even with better meds—when I want to just end it all. It's not every day anymore, but too often the pain and the regret and the shame and my messy, noisy brain make it all seem like too much. Days when I just want it all to stop, days when my options seem reduced to that last bit of control I have: to kill myself. And again I hear her saying that killing myself is the only thing she could never forgive.

I love her too much to leave her with what my mother left me with—even if I *am* thinking it's the last way I really could hurt her and I want to make her suffer, but just as quickly I realize she *is* suffering with this. I don't want to be the person who's thinking the way I'm thinking.

I've made her life a mess. It feels, often, like everyone would be better off without me. But I know she's not lying when she says she loves me. And she's not lying when she says my killing myself is the one thing she could never forgive. And apparently she's not lying when she says that she and I are done.

"Bud, I need to know you're OK."

I want to stay angry, but then it comes to me that this could be the last time we talk for a long time. Maybe forever. I already may have *seen* her for the last time in my life and I had no way of knowing it. I breathe in and out, as deeply as I can. I'm shaking, and I may have an attack no matter what pills I take unless they knock me out. "I'm not getting high," I say. "I'm not killing myself."

Neither of us seems to have anything to say for a minute.

"How's your father?" Olivia says.

Before I can answer that he's almost dead, I hear our door open—and I catch myself that it's not *ours* and it hasn't been for a lot longer than I knew. I hear a man's voice from a distance. The

Good Man. She says, "Bud, I'm sorry, but I'm going to need to get going."

I feel like throwing up. She's almost done even talking to me. "I love you," I say.

"I know that, Bud." She's talking even quieter. "You have to know that I love you more than anyone."

I can't even talk.

She says, "I have to go. Please tell me you know how much I love you."

I could hurt her. I could not answer and make her hang up without hearing what she wants or needs to hear, because her Good Man is probably getting closer, wondering why the fuck she's talked more than two minutes on the phone—which is about all she can stand—and why she's hiding in the backyard while she does it.

It would hurt her. Not as much as me, but enough.

"Please," she says in a desperate-sounding whisper.

I think about hanging up, but I can't. "I know," I say, realizing that I want the last time I hurt her to be somewhere in the past. Not here. Not anymore. "I'll be OK," I say, even though I have no idea how that could ever be true.

Then she's gone.

I go inside and try to keep the thoughts of her with someone else out of my head, but they're relentless and pound steady as an oil derrick. The only other thought I have is to get loaded. I have no idea how to get dope in this town, so I think about getting drunk instead. The slideshow of jealousy and envy for the Good Man won't stop.

At the hospital, I bring my father his CD player. It seems strange to me. He's never much cared for music, but maybe he wants to listen to talk radio or Yankee games or something.

"Hey, Pop," I say, lifting the CD player. I find room on the table next to his bed to put it down. I'm nervous. I feel my hands and my legs twitching and shaking and I sit down to try to hide it.

He asks me to hand him a cup. I do it. The cup has a straw, since he can't bring his head up far enough to take a drink without it. He can't bend his head up enough, so I bend the straw down more so he can drink.

"Thanks," he says, finally.

"Sure."

We don't talk for a while and, again, the hospital sounds fill the quiet. I know I should be thinking about what I came here for, but all I can think is that I may have just talked to Olivia for the last time. What's my father against that? I force myself to keep my head in this room. I'll have a lifetime to think of not being with her.

"I don't like this," he says.

And I don't know what he means. He doesn't like talking to me? Being in the hospital? Or maybe the obvious—dying? I don't say anything.

He says, "You know I've never liked asking for help."

I nod.

"I need you to do something for me," he says. "I need your help."

And I don't know what it is, but I figure I came here for a chance to make things, if not right, as right as they can be between us before he's gone.

"Sure," I say.

He says, "You want me to forgive you for the way things are between us? The way they've been?"

"Yes," I say. "I'd like that. I don't know if I deserve it."

"Who knows what we deserve?" he says. "I wish life could have been different, but it wasn't." It's clear that it hurts him to talk. "And it doesn't make a lot of sense now saying shit to try to make it different." He takes another labored sip. "But I do. I do wish things had been different."

I look down at the tile floor, trying to find some design or pattern in the random streaks in the floor. "Me, too."

"Then do what I ask," he says, his breathing shallow. "Do me this one favor."

I don't know why, after all that's passed between us over the years, but I still want to please him—to make him happy, proud of me. I hated him for years. Thought of him as a savage who, if he didn't ruin my life, he set it way off track. I've blamed him for so much. Then, after I cleaned up and started to see what killing that guy had done to him, I stopped hating him and started hated myself even more than usual for misreading so much of my life. I stopped thinking of him as a monster. I still blamed him for what happened to my mother, but how could that blame really add up to hate? She did what she did. She was an adult. No matter what he was like to her when I was too young to understand something as complicated as love, something as complex as a marriage, he didn't have a gun to her head. She jumped off a bridge four years after she left him. It couldn't all have been his fault.

And even if it was, so what? She's gone. He'll be gone soon. I'll be gone eventually. A friend of mine who's trying to figure out the origin of the universe at Cal Tech told me once that the entirety of human existence would be less than a nanosecond if the universe was a hundred years old. We're nothing, in terms of time. The Hoover Dam has concrete that is still curing around the bodies of the men who fell into it while it was being built. What does it matter? What purpose does it serve for me to blame him for anything?

But now I feel like a little kid, just wanting to make Dad happy. I can't place where this desire is coming from, but maybe it's just hard-wired between fathers and sons.

I say, "What do you need?"

He nods painfully toward the CD player. "Inside the battery compartment are eight vials of morphine and a syringe." He coughs a little and strains to control his breathing and not turn this into one of his brutal coughing fits. "I need you to overdose me."

I look behind me to make sure there's no one at the door. I open the battery compartment and see the morphine. My first thought is to take it and shoot it myself, wondering how long I could make eight vials last. But then my thoughts return to what my father is asking. I close the battery compartment door and put it back on his table.

"I can't," I say.

"You have to," he says. "You're all I have left."

I realize, again, that my father has no friends. How can he have lived almost seventy years on the planet and have no one he can ask but me, a son he's seen once in twenty years? How staggeringly lonely can a life get?

We've looked more or less alike my whole life. I look at him and it feels like some mirror image in a flash-forward. Like I'm getting a peek at how I'll look if I go out on life's terms and not my own.

For years, even in the first years of getting loaded, I was afraid of dying. Later, deep in my addictions, I grew to not really care whether I lived or died. But now my own death doesn't frighten me nearly as much as the deaths of people I love. When I think of losing another friend, another lover, another ex—it feels like my insides are made of ice and ready to shatter at any point. I've been enough places and seen enough to know there are worse things, things I dread more, than dying. I still can't think of anything as empty as dying alone.

I look at what's left of my father and decide, no matter what else might change or remain the same, that I'll never let *this* happen. I'll OD now, or I'll live a life different from his and a different life from mine and if I ever end up dying in a bed like this, the room will have more in it than a son I don't even know. I don't know what I'll choose, not sure I even care right now, but it won't be what I'm looking at.

"I don't know," I say.

The drugs he's on already have him tired and sluggish. The morphine drip has him nodding in and out. And either that, or the fact that he's dying, or some combination of reasons has him talking more than he ever has.

"I wish I'd been a better father," he says. "My father? The doctor?"

I nod. The grandfather I never met and only ever heard was a bastard and that was the end of what I knew.

"He had my mother committed. She tried to escape."

He pauses long enough to make me think he wants me to say something in reply, but he's just getting the strength to talk more so I leave him alone.

He says, "I know the spot she died on the Merritt Parkway." He asks me for an ice chip and I give him one. After a while, he says, "Drove by it my whole life, thinking about her freezing out there in some gown from the nuthouse. Frozen." He looks at me. "Between exits forty-eight and forty-nine, just west of New Haven."

I say, "Why tell me this now?"

"I did my best," he says. "He took my mother away. I hated the man."

I'm looking at the vials of morphine.

My father says, "I'm sorry you've had so much trouble. I didn't want it that way—didn't want you to not have a mother, most of all."

"I know," I say, though I didn't really know it until now. And I still don't know if any of this is true or he's in some morphine nod and just jabbering nonsense. I want to believe this moment is him telling me something that matters.

My father winces. I wonder at first if he's playing it up, but he's not. The pain is real and it's hard to watch. I get scared of dying again and then wonder how selfish I can be, thinking about me. But I want to know what he knows in this moment. What he feels. "How much worse is the pain than withdrawals? Than full-blown dopesickness?"

"Off the fucking charts worse," he says, and I'm amazed he can even speak. He sounds so weak and small.

He's at my mercy. I control what's left of his life and this fills me with an ache. This man, my father, has lost all of his power. He can't even hurt himself anymore, let alone anyone else. He says, "I became a cop because I thought I could stop people like my father."

"I'm sorry," I say, because I have no idea what else to say.

"Nothing I did worked."

I don't know exactly what he's talking about now. He's fading in and out with the drugs.

"What you asked me," I say. "I'll do it."

He closes his eyes and smiles a thin smile. "Thank you."

"But I need some answers first."

My father starts to sit up, but it's too painful for him and he collapses back into his bed. All that's left of the man I remember growing up is the anger in his quiet voice. If words could punch and bully, his still would. He closes his eyes. "I'm asking for some peace here."

"So am I," I say.

"I've tried to tell you I'm sorry." He looks at me angrily. "What the fuck else do you want?"

I look down at him and feel so many emotions at once I can't keep track. My hands shake and my knees wobble. It feels like I might pass out. I'm weak and dizzy, like I just got off one of those rides that pins you against the wall while you spin yourself sick. I said I'd do it, but I'm already wondering if I can possibly kill him.

It feels like a kindness. Like all that's left to show him any speck of love in his life. Then I think that I can't, no matter what, I just can't. Every thought argues with the thought that came before.

"I need some air," I say.

"Please," he says. "Do it."

"I'll be back," I say, but I don't know if I will be or not. I'm afraid I'll run. I take the CD player full of morphine vials with me, walking numbly down the stairs, out of the lobby with its waxed, gleaming floor. I walk to a curb and sit in front of the hospital parking lot, smoking one cigarette after another, lighting the new one with the cherry on the old, drinking harsh lukewarm coffee and turning down cabs that slow and ask if I need a ride.

I sit, watching people come and go, for twenty minutes.

I wonder what's going on in their heads. What their lives are like. Some of them must be dealing with the end of someone in there. Are they all as scared as me? There must be some grace among them. Some wisdom. Some guy I know whose wife died said at a meeting that death isn't the opposite of life, but part of it. It sounds pretty, but I don't see the difference now. Opposite or part of life, it's still the end.

I think about Olivia. That maybe my father felt like this toward my mother once. Maybe she did with him, too, before everything went wrong.

There's a reason most suicides are gun suicides. You want to kill the source of all your trouble—your brain. If you let your brain live, you'll rot out from the inside with cancer, or your heart will finally give in. Hearts break and they shatter and they hurt and they get lovesick and they need and they ache and they die when there's no reason for them to keep working.

I think about calling Olivia again, but what is there to say? I should call so she can tell me again that she loves me more than the guy who gets to spend his life with her? Hearing it twice won't help. I am tempted to ask her to help me here. To talk to me about this—not about Us, but about my father. The biggest reason I can't call her is that somehow I may have become a name and a number that will go to voicemail for the rest of her life.

Anyway, this isn't her decision. This one is as much mine as killing myself is. Choices like this are beyond words. Beyond advice and logic.

I close my eyes and try to breathe my way out of being dizzy. My father is in agony eight floors up, probably wondering if I'll ever come back. More probably thinking that I'm taking his drugs. Assuming, probably, that the last thing I ever did to him was to steal his dope and let him feel the worst pain of his life for longer than he had to.

I've spent my whole life thinking that my father and I were so different, and now all I know is that I don't know anything and that my father wants to die and I'm the last person on Earth who can end his suffering and that maybe this is a time in my life when I need to face things and not run away from them.

In his room, my father tries a smile and asks, "Is there any of my morphine left?"

I put the CD player on his table. "Believe it or not, it's all still there."

He laughs quietly. "I thought I might have seen the last of it."

I sit in the chair next to him. "What happened between you and Mom? Why did she leave?"

He closes his eyes for a while, as if he's thinking, or maybe just trying to find the right words.

He says, "You'll do what I asked? No matter what I tell you?"

The thought of killing my father sickens me. I would never have imagined my life would come to a moment like this. But then, my life has been filled with moments I never would have guessed were coming. Everyone's life is, I suppose. None of us are special.

I try to measure this moment against others. It's one of the worst. Not as awful as listening to Olivia weep while I crawled on the bathroom floor, smeared in piss and shit and puke and knowing I had caused her pain. It's not as bad as my mother's suicide, though that's not really a moment but a series of moments. An ache that never reduced. A dread that still sucker-punches me when I'm least expecting it. Always there, even when it seems gone for a while.

It may not even be the worst moment of this fucking *day*.

But this moment, by itself—this moment where my father has asked me to end his life—this might not be the worst, but it could be the most difficult.

I say to him, "If you tell me the truth, I'll do what you asked."

Machines beep and push air and hiss and clang and hum around us. I'm close to my father's bed, on the side where his catheter bag hangs, his urine an uneasy pale red-yellow. He looks at me with his jaundiced eyes. He's clicked the morphine controller over and over since I've been in the room, even though he knows they shut the fucking thing off, no matter how frantically you push the button. I wonder if he's doing it so openly to remind me of the pain he's in. But he doesn't really need to remind me—just lying on that bed is causing him such agony, I don't know how I could say no to him, even if I still hated him. But now that I know he made his choices in life based on a hatred of his own father who he blamed for the loss of his mother? That we fucked up our lives, both of us, trying to destroy the memory of our fathers and find our mothers?

I remember I once nearly screamed at a rehab therapist who suggested that maybe I hated my father because I thought we were alike.

"Trust me," I told him. "I hate him and I hate myself. But we're nothing alike."

And now this? We've lost so many years of the chance to know each other. I don't really know if I'm like him or not, and I never will know. His life is almost as much of a mystery to me as my mother's life. I cut myself off from him, not the other way around. I lost him as much as I lost her the morning she jumped off the bridge.

Olivia and the phone call keep bullying their way into my brain. I laugh at myself even as I'm thinking it's overdramatic, but I've lost everything. There's no one to blame for any of it. But how many more wrong choices could I possibly have made in one life if I'd been trying?

He looks at the ceiling, then back at me. "I'll tell you the truth."

"Thank you."

He nods. "Thank you. I know this isn't easy." He coughs a small laugh. "Although, I would have loved the chance to put my dad down."

"There were some times I thought I would have, too," I say, trying a smile.

"Was I that bad?" he says.

"Let's talk about Mom."

He shakes his head. "I don't want this to sound wrong." He pauses. "I'm trying to think of a way to phrase it."

"Just say it, OK?" I want a cigarette, badly. I wish I could leave the room, but I've never needed to stay in a room this much, no matter how awful it is. "Don't try to spare my feelings. Just tell me about her. Tell me why she left."

"She left because she was crazy, Bud."

"I found that note of hers you kept," I say. "The *don't read between the lines* one."

"I didn't keep that many. There were worse. After a while, you can't look at that shit anymore."

"I've seen the note. I read the paperwork. I get that she was crazy or sick or whatever." I look at the numbers on the machine behind my father. The only one I know how to read says he's breathing at 70 percent.

I say, "Please. I need more than that."

He says, "I wish I could. Believe me. I tried to come up with plenty of reasons for your mother's behavior over the years. But the bottom line was always the same: she was crazy."

I should have made a list of my questions. Some, though, I'd never forget to ask. "Did I have anything to do with her leaving?"

He gives me that look I've known since I was little that says, *Are you fucking stupid?* It's the first time that look has had an ounce of reassurance in it.

I ask the question I've asked in my head all my life: "I mean, did she leave you—leave us—because she didn't want me?"

My father opens his mouth and moans. He can't talk for twenty seconds because of the pain. His body relaxes a little and he starts breathing better. "It's all over now," my father says. "What does it matter to go over all this? Please. Just give me the morphine."

"What does it matter? Would it have mattered if you could have talked to *your* mother before she got taken away? If you could have known her?"

He nods slowly. He tries hard to swallow and makes an anguished fist out of his face. Finally he says, "The day you were born, she held you and she started crying. I mean weeping. Uncontrollable. And she'd scream every time they took you away for a test or anything. Then, she'd get you back and hold you and keep crying. All week at the hospital. And it didn't stop when we got you home." My father shakes his head. "I tried to ask her why, and all she would say was that every time she looked at you, she realized someday you'd be dead." He closes his eyes.

"That's it?"

"That was the start," he says. "I'd go in your room at night and she'd be crying, staring down at you, saying how someday you'd be dead. That she'd brought you into the world and you'd die because of her. Your death would be her fault."

"What?"

"Your mother was always . . ." He pauses, closes his eyes and lifts his eyebrows like he's struggling to find the right word. "She was different. Strange. She could be a lot of fun. But the year before you were born, she started with the depression. The crying. Days without talking. Weeks not getting out of bed except to mope to the bathroom."

"Didn't you take her to see anyone?"

"Fuck. Who *didn't* I take her to see? They tried drugs. Shit didn't work. When it worked, she stopped taking them," my father says. "Where do you get off asking me that?" He stares hard at me. "She was my fucking *wife*. You don't seem to get that."

I take a deep breath. He's right. "I'm sorry," I say. "I wasn't there."

"She went crazy. Neurologists. Shrinks. They all had some name for it, but the bottom line was she went crazy. Then it just got worse. As soon as you were born, she turned hysterical, saying how you were going to die. And then, she needed to have you around her all the time. That's why I let her take you to the hospital."

"I thought that was because we were poor."

"Well, we weren't rich," he says. "But the hospital was because she'd freak out if she was away from you. She thought you'd die and she wouldn't be there. So she took you everywhere."

My father tells me things got worse. Kept getting worse. The depression got so bad she got fired from the hospital. She was at home, then, not letting me out of her sight and making suicidal threats.

His eyes are closed. His voice sounds more tired. I feel guilty—I should just let him go. But I can't. I'm getting answers that don't seem to mean anything, and I'm still feeling empty.

He says, "When she got dangerous around you, I did the thing I never thought I'd do. Not after my old man." He coughs up a little blood that we both leave on his chin. "I had her committed." He coughs again, but no blood this time. He asks me for an ice chip. I take one from the plastic cup by his bedside table and lean to him and put it on his tongue. The chips are melting and are smaller than when I gave him the first ones. I wipe the blood from his chin with the back of my hand, holding the hospital bed railing with the other hand. He sucks the ice for a minute. "She was getting crazier and I had to be around you more, even after she came home."

I can't say why I know it, but my father isn't lying. "When was this?"

"Right before . . ." My father hesitates. "Right before I had to kill Hastings—that was his name—Tommy Hastings. Worked for the Montessi family." He lifts his IV arm, which has a dark red and black mark on the skin that's spread beyond the boundaries of the gauze wrapped around his wrist. He takes a labored breath. He looks at me. "Did it ever occur to you that you might not want to hear this shit?"

"Never," I say. "Tell me."

"I found her diary. She was going to kill you." My father has tears in his eyes that run down his face when he blinks once hard. "Kill herself after you. She said she couldn't leave you alone in the world. That's when I had her committed for good."

"I thought she left me," I say.

He turns his head toward me and looks in my eyes. "She was going to kill you, Bud. I didn't want to tell a son of mine that his mother was gone because she was going to fucking kill him. What could I have done? Tell me. Believe me, I've thought about

other options over the years. And I haven't found a good one yet."
He closes his eyes and breathes shallow breaths until he can talk
again. "I told you she was sick. Do you remember that?"

I try to remember it, but I don't. I wonder if he's lying to me. I
shake my head. "I remember you told me she went to California."

"California sounded . . ." He pauses and tries to swallow, but
phlegm thickens his voice when he says, "Happy." He closes his
eyes. "California."

The machines behind my father beep and blink. The breathing
apparatus for the guy in the other bed makes a tortured wheeze
every few seconds.

"She wasn't always crazy." His weak sad eyes rest on me for a
second. "She was my wife, Bud."

I feel my eyes starting to tear and I look away. I feel like
throwing up. Everything I thought about my life seems turned
inside out. My father was protecting me? I've spent my life
thinking, if nothing else, that I wasn't anything like this man.
Even when I found out he was an addict, I wouldn't give him
the right to have anywhere near the reasons I used to justify my
choices. I wouldn't give him the right to be damaged or fearful.
To be capable of love—for my mother or, worse, for me. To be
a just another person with a heart full of questions and a mind
filled with even more of them. I had no room in my mind or heart
to ever think that I'd spent years hurting him, and not the other
way around.

The more I find out about my mother, the less she seems to
be the person I wanted, the person I needed her to be, all those
years. I came here for facts. And facts don't explain anything. And
I could have known, or at least tried to know, my father. And now
that's over, too.

This—the not knowing, the endless questions without
answers—this will be with me forever. This won't resolve. This
won't end.

My father coughs. He's tired. In a pain I haven't known and hope I never do. I walked into this room thinking he owed me answers, and that I'd reward him by OD-ing him, like I'd beaten him in some final negotiation. And I did, and I feel shame I haven't felt since my last relapse. And I feel like I may never be the person I could be. And would it matter if I did, with no one who matters around to see it?

I'm having trouble trying to talk, afraid I'll cry. My throat's strangling itself and my eyes start to tear uncontrollably and I try to breathe steadily enough to be able to talk to him.

I close my eyes and feel both of my cheeks get moist and chilled with the AC from the vent above me. I wipe my eyes with the backs of my hands, and my right hand reminds me of all the damage I've done to it by throbbing with pain, and I think again about the morphine and how easy it could make things. I force myself to look back at my father.

He says, "I didn't know how to raise a kid. Undercover—you have to—you live around criminals. It's a dangerous life. And then there was Hastings." He shakes his head at the mention of the man's name. "I can't even tell you what it's like. When I was under, Hastings was my *friend*. I knew his wife. His kids."

"What was wrong with her? What did the doctors say?"

"I'm trying to tell you what it's like to kill a man. You listening to me?"

I'm still thinking about my mother. I say, "I'm sorry."

My father groans, his whole body spasming in pain. "I told you what you asked," he says. "Now you're asking about something that doesn't have answers."

I know enough to know that's true. I've spent so many minutes and hours and days of my life trying to figure out what my mother thought and felt. It never occurred to me that my father wouldn't know, either.

"I'm sorry, son."

The word *son* makes me want to break down and hold him, but I'm afraid—both of the intimacy, and of all the tubes running in and out of him and of his own fragility. Nothing in my life makes sense. Solid ground seems to swim.

The sounds of the room return. Blood rushes to my head and I feel my pulse pounding in my ears.

My father stiffens with pain and relaxes a bit. Then he goes rigid, fighting the pain again. "Shit. Please, Bud," my father says. "Please."

I sit there doing nothing for a moment and he says it again. And then again:

"Please."

I think of Olivia begging me to tell her I understood that she loves me. And now my father's begging me to show love for him.

"OK," I say.

I open the top of the CD player, checking for more needles and see that one of my solo records is in the player. An all-instrumental album I did after the guys fired me the first time. I did it for some French record label, recording it all in less than a week to get drug money. I'm afraid to talk, thinking my voice will break. I hold up the CD. "You have this?"

He looks at me. He's fighting a lot of pain, you can see from his face. He takes as deep a breath as he can. Then another. And then he says, "You're my son."

I open the player's battery compartment. I check the hallway to make sure none of the doctors or nurses are close to the door. I draw as much morphine as I can into the short syringe and look at my dad. He nods.

There were probably times in my life when I dreamed of killing him. I know I wanted him to hurt. And even if I never would have killed him, I wanted my father dead. I made this deal to make him talk, and I figured I'd owe it to him if he kept his end of the bargain. But I never thought I'd kill him because it felt like the closest thing to love as I could offer him.

No one on the floor seems to care what I might be doing in this room. Just in case, I slide the gentle little alligator clip they keep on your index finger to read your vitals from my father's finger to my own so that the numbers don't dip.

I want to say good-bye. That I love him—even though I'm still not sure if everything he said is completely true. It feels true. Either way, though, a person on his way out of this world should hear that someone loves him. I want to say something, but it's hard. My tongue feels like a rock. My father's eyes plead with me to just end his pain.

"I'm sorry," I say.

Shooting into the IV line might take too long, so I find the best vein I can on his left foot, pull back as my father's blood swirls like ink in water, into the morphine, and empty the syringe into his vein. Within seconds, his body relaxes weakly into the bed. I load several more shots. By the third one, the needle starts to fight his shitty vein, so I have to use the IV line. I keep filling and emptying the syringe until three full vials are empty.

He's straining hard to speak. In a thin, tired voice that I have to lean down to hear, he says something I can't make out. I want it to be *Thank you, son* or *I love you,* and maybe there will be nights I can convince myself that he did say one of those two, but the truth will always be like the rest of our relationship, the rest of both of our lives: one of us tried to say something and the other one couldn't hear it.

I start to draw from the other vials, but I see his eyelids fluttering and his breathing getting more and more shallow. My father looks close to gone, but I don't want them to have any chance to save him, so I draw into one more vial and give him a final shot.

I look at the CD. I remember for a moment the apartment on Second Street in Long Beach where I wrote the songs. I'd sold nearly every piece of equipment I owned for drugs. All I had left was my broken 1969 Telecaster. I had to borrow equipment to record this album.

I touch my father's hand, hoping he'll wrap his fingers around mine, but he's gone. I take the monitor clip off my finger.

I need to get out of the room, or else stay here and play dumb. Not knowing which is better, I put the remaining morphine in my pocket with the empties and the syringe. I put the CD in my jacket pocket and leave the player on the table and walk as calmly as I can out of the room. I don't look back at him as I pass the window next to the door.

I walk down the hall, trying not to make eye contact with any of the nurses or orderlies. I wait for the elevator and look for a moment at a group of people in the waiting room, sitting in quiet nervousness, anxious for news about whoever it is they love, somewhere on this floor. A TV no one seems to be watching blares down at them. The elevator is taking too long. I take the stairs to the first floor.

I walk out the hospital's front sliding doors. I hear the doors close behind me. Then open again as someone else enters or leaves behind me. They close once more.

I don't go to my rental car. I light a cigarette and walk toward a garbage can near a bench by the smoking area. I feel the vials in my pocket and think about keeping the full ones. I could stretch them out and get high. But how would starting that over do anything? It'll end the same as it always has, or it'll end worse.

If I did them all, I could kill myself. I feel the smooth glass in my pocket and run a finger over the top and feel the slight give to the rubber tip.

I look up the side of the hospital, trying to find my father's room up on the eighth floor, though I don't know which one it is from the outside. I scan all the rooms on the eighth floor and hope that he went as painlessly as he could have. The reflection of the sun off the windows of St. Jude's stings my eyes and I'm blinded as I look down at the sidewalk and I have to blink several times before I can see again. When my eyes recover enough, I glance back at the hospital. I wonder what floor I was born on. But I don't suppose it matters. I was born here. That much I know. And my mother held me here once, and my mother was crazy and there was probably nothing anyone could have done to change that. And whether it could have been changed or not, it wasn't. The same with my father. The same with every moment of my life up until this one. They could have been different—maybe every single one of them—but they weren't.

I rub my eyes. I know myself well enough to know that I'll beat myself up forever for letting the loss of my mother turn into the loss of my father, too. The past is the past, but that doesn't mean it's ever over. I try to tell myself that shit that the guy said at the meeting: that death isn't the end of life; it's a part of it. That misery isn't the opposite of happiness, but part of it. And it may be true and it may be some form of wisdom, but it feels like empty meaningless horseshit that doesn't make a speck of a difference at this moment.

I feel the vials in my pocket and think about calling Olivia and telling her it's OK. Think about saying, *We did the best we could, right?* in the hope that she might be kind enough to agree. I think about wishing her the best life she can possibly have and making sure I sound like I mean it because I know, at my best, that I do—even if at this moment I'm not at my best, and a dark sliver of me still wants her hurting as much as I am. I can't trust myself to sound happy and supportive, so I decide to wait.

Tonight, I'll be alone in my father's house or alone in my hotel room with the pictures and the papers and all I have that's left of my mother's and my father's lives, and I'll call her then.

I'll need to talk with her and all I can do is hope she'll understand. I'll need to hear her voice. I'll tell her that I killed my father this afternoon and that I did it, no matter how late it was between us, because I loved him, and I'll tell her because no one knows me better and she understands that how things end with people matters. And maybe we'll both say *I love you* again and both mean it as intensely as anything else we'll ever say. And we're both old enough to know that love, by itself, isn't always enough, and I hope I'll let her know, as best as I can, that I understand what she's doing.

I dump the vials—the empty ones and the full ones—into the garbage can. I toss the CD. I feel bad about not knowing some junkie in town because, whether I'm doing the morphine or not, it just feels wrong to throw the full ones out. I walk down the sidewalk and cross on the green even though I have no idea where I'm going, but wanting, for some reason, to be in motion among strangers in this city where I was born.

ACKNOWLEDGMENTS

Many thanks to all my friends whose support and love have helped me through more days than I can possibly count. And who are, luckily for me, too numerous to mention here. You know who you are and I know who you are and I love you.

To everyone at Dzanc who participated in helping this book see the light of day, especially Steve Gillis and Dan Wickett. I can't tell you how much of a pleasure it is to be part of Dzanc.

To Steven Seighman for his wonderful design.

To those who were generous enough to read the numerous "final" versions of this manuscript and offer their comments and help: Craig "Please, forgive me brother, if I'm sounding preachy" Clevenger; Gayle "There are truly an astounding amount of typos" Fornataro; Patrick "Not to correct another drug detail, dude, but…" O'Neil; Billy Pitman, and Zoe Zolbrod. All of you made the book better and supported me more than you know.

Extra thanks to Patrick for reminding me I was a writer and picking up the pieces when I'd all but forgotten how I'd ever written a sentence, let alone a book. And to Gayle, for always being there and being the greatest supporter my work and I have ever had.

To Stacy Bierlein and Leah Tallon at Other Voices Books for everything they've done for me and for this book. Many thanks to Allison Parker for her meticulous eye in copyediting the mess I dumped on her desk—it's much appreciated.

Lastly, great thanks to Gina Frangello, the best friend and the toughest and best editor I have ever worked with. Anything good in this book has her mark all over it and she should share in any credit. Anything that isn't so good, I probably slipped by her when she wasn't looking and is all my fault. Thank you, Gina, for such a great experience. I can't imagine any future collaboration surpassing this one.